Dear Reader,

Welcome to the premiere editions of Harlequin Duets!

This new and exciting series is written by authors you love and published in a great new format. Have you ever finished reading a romance and wished you had another one you could start right away? Well, we have the answer for you. Each and every month there will be two Harlequin Duets books on sale, and each book will contain two complete brand-new novels. (You'll always have your backup read with you!)

Harlequin Duets features the best of romantic comedy. Our opening lineup is an exciting one: stories by Vicki Lewis Thompson, Christie Ridgway, Jacqueline Diamond and Bonnie Tucker. Wonderfully romantic and funny stories about cowboys, bridesmaids, babies and one very unusual hero, a supposed gangster.

Harlequin Duets—double your reading pleasure!

Sincerely,

Malle Vallik

Malle Vallik
Senior Editor

P.S. We'd love to hear what you think about Harlequin Duets! Drop us a line at:

Harlequin Duets
Harlequin Books
225 Duncan Mill R...
Don Mills, Ontari...
M3B 3K9 Canada

D0721080

Kidnapped?

If you are going to distract a gangster, you must take advantage of any opening.

So Melanie tightened her grip on Hal's neck, feeling a delicious thrill at being held so elegantly by a deadly killer who shuddered when she blew in his ear. Then she pressed her lips against his. His mouth was hard and hot.

Before she could make a strategic duck, the man did not have to maneuver far to progress from kissing her mouth to trailing his tongue down her throat.

She had to admire the Iceman's grace. With the litheness of a dancer, he shifted her position so her body arched toward him.

No wonder he had been able to land three wives. He had probably consummated their marriages while still kneeling with a ring in his hand.

But this was not what Melanie had had in mind. She'd planned to give him the slip!

I Got You, Babe

There was no doubt Nick had changed, matured.

Potent virility had replaced his boyish handsomeness. There was only a faint trace of the youthful guilelessness that had so attracted her to him in the first place. Nick had grown into a rugged, virile man. All muscle and radiating heat. The air crackling around him was worldly and experienced, not naive.

His dark brown hair still came below the collar, and even though he had brushed it back off his face, strands fell across his forehead. His eyes, though, hadn't changed at all. They were still the very deepest blue and, against his tanned skin, very intense.

If Diana ever had any doubt before why she had been so caught up in a memory, she had none now. Nick Logan radiated potent male sexuality. She had been caught in his web when she had been sixteen, more deeply entrenched at eighteen, and now at twenty-four, had no desire to escape. She wouldn't doubt that other women had felt the same way and were hanging off him everywhere he went. Like the one hanging off his arm.

The little girl.

Little girl?

Nick's baby? No. *Yes.*

HARLEQUIN DUETS

ISBN 0-373-44068-5

KIDNAPPED?
Copyright © 1999 by Jackie Hyman

I GOT YOU, BABE
Copyright © 1999 by Bonnie Tucker

This edition published by arrangement with Harlequin Books S.A.

® and TM are trademarks of the publisher. Trademarks indicated with
® are registered in the United States Patent and Trademark Office, the
Canadian Trade Marks Office and in other countries.

Printed in U.S.A.

JACQUELINE DIAMOND

Kidnapped?

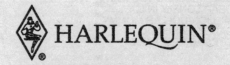

TORONTO • NEW YORK • LONDON
AMSTERDAM • PARIS • SYDNEY • HAMBURG
STOCKHOLM • ATHENS • TOKYO • MILAN • MADRID
PRAGUE • WARSAW • BUDAPEST • AUCKLAND

Dear Reader,

Although I used to be a news reporter like my heroine, I never managed to get swept away to a mysterious island by the most feared hitman in Las Vegas.

However, during a break in the Watergate hearings, I did hide my camera in my knitting bag and sneak onto a private island off Newport Beach, California, where I waylaid H. R. Haldeman, who was trying to take a nap.

As I tried to pull out my camera and got it tangled in my knitting, he said politely, "Sorry, but if I talk to you, I'd have to talk to all the other reporters."

Well, it didn't exactly count as a scoop. But considering that I was several thousand miles from Washington and therefore at a distinct disadvantage compared to Woodward and Bernstein, I think I deserve some credit.

Jacqueline Diamond

Books by Jacqueline Diamond

HARLEQUIN LOVE & LAUGHTER
11—PUNCHLINE
32—SANDRA AND THE SCOUNDREL

HARLEQUIN AMERICAN ROMANCE
642—ONE HUSBAND TOO MANY
645—DEAR LONELY IN L.A....
674—MILLION-DOLLAR MOMMY
687—DADDY WARLOCK
763—LET'S MAKE A BABY

To Oprah, Dave, Jay and Conan, their production staffs, their families and their dogs, in the hope that someone will invite me on their show.

1

HAL "THE ICEMAN" Smothers was given to grand romantic gestures.

So far they had netted him three wives—now of the ex variety—as well as one broken arm and a lawsuit. There was also an interesting scar on his left shoulder where a certain object of his affections had put a bullet through it.

She had been the wrong woman for him. He could see that now.

They had all been the wrong woman. But this time, he would not fail.

Until now, true love had passed him by. But if he had to wrestle Cupid to the ground and blacken both of his eyes, Hal intended to nail the little pest once and for all.

"So," Hal said one morning in September while playing golf with Louie "the Swamp Fox" Palmetto. "If you wanted to take a lady someplace from which she could not easily escape, where would that be?"

Louie, a sharp-toothed man with the worst complexion Hal had ever seen, even on a gangster, was a good man to ask this because he owned his own fleet of airplanes. His planes were renowned worldwide for their ability to fly below radar.

"I dunno," he said, positioning his ball on the tee. "Would this lady be a certain socialite of our mutual acquaintance?"

"Certainly not!" Hal squinted into the sunlight charbroiling Las Vegas. The sun was particularly close because they were standing on top of a twenty-seven-story building. "The socialite that you have mentioned is someone I hold in high regard and would never abduct. However, she *has* asked me to remove a certain obstacle from her path, and I have agreed."

"As a sign of your affection?" hazarded Louie, who knew Hal and his romantic gestures all too well.

"In a manner of speaking." Hal hated to admit to anyone, even the Swamp Fox, the depth of his appreciation for Margarita "Rita" Samovar, the aforementioned socialite.

At thirty-six, Hal wanted a wife and, especially, children, more than he had ever wanted anything, even to be completely accepted as a member of Chester "Grampa" Orion's crime family. And the wife he wanted was Rita.

It was neither her raven-dark hair nor her intermittent British accent that appealed to him. There were two deciding factors.

One, she had a three-year-old son from a former marriage. This proved that Rita was not only fertile but willing to temporarily dislocate her figure, which had not been true of his previous wives.

Hal told his friends that he wanted children because you can't trust anyone the way you can trust family. The truth was, he found kids fascinating and funny, and he could hardly wait to get down on the floor and play with them.

Also in Rita's favor was that she had recently come into several substantial inheritances. Hal did not need her money, as he had managed to amass a large personal fortune in spite of being mostly an honest businessman. However, it meant she should have no need to sue him for an outrageous amount if, by some grave miscarriage of Cupid, they became uncoupled.

The only people who had ever robbed the Iceman and gotten away with it were his three ex-wives. This was beginning to hurt Hal's reputation.

If another woman pulled the same stunt, he might be forced to remove her from the visible world. Therefore, he must choose a wealthy woman who need not risk such a fate.

The Swamp Fox paused in the middle of lining up his swing and eyed Hal dubiously. "Let me see if I understand this. To win Rita's gratitude, you are prepared to kidnap some other dame and stash her away?"

Put that way, it did sound odd. What Rita had actually said about Melanie Mulcahy was, "You want to impress me? Get rid of her."

Hal had been shocked by this. To tell a fellow called the Iceman to get rid of somebody could be interpreted as meaning in the permanent sense. This was not a ladylike request.

On the other hand, Rita was a social butterfly who raised money for Rescue the Whales. She was entitled to a weakness or two.

Besides, according to Rita, this Melanie person was a writer of some sort, press releases or poetry or something, who earned extra income from the whaling industry for disrupting Rescue the Whales charity events. A person like that deserved to be stopped.

"Yes, you understand correctly," he said. "Where would you recommend that I take her?"

"Anywhere but Paraiso de Los Falsarios," said the Swamp Fox, naming an island that belonged to their mutual acquaintance Arthur "Drop Dead" Cimarosa. The island's name was Spanish for Crooks' Paradise.

"Why is that?"

"Rita's whale-watching cruise will be passing offshore," said Louie. "Although this blockage persona would not actually be thrown into her path, it is possible that Rita might glimpse her from the boat and be offended."

"I will take this advice under advisement," said Hal, and ducked as his friend finally stopped procrastinating and gave the ball a gut-crunching whack.

It was much too hard a whack for a ball being hit atop a twenty-seven-story hotel-casino belonging to Chester "Grampa" Orion.

Grampa, who had had a fixation on privacy ever since he caught the FBI trying to bug his bathroom, had built himself this private golf course three years ago. For safety purposes, he'd initially tried using whiffle balls, but the building had a distressing habit of swaying, not to mention that, at this altitude, the balls blew up and hit Grampa in the mouth.

At long last he'd reached the conclusion that the only possible means of scoring a hole in one with a whiffle ball on top of a skyscraper was to play on an unusually calm day with the assistance of an earthquake that rolled east to west. Grampa switched to real golf balls.

A high mesh fence managed to snare most, but not all, of them. The general public remained unaware of the situation, but the valets at Grampa's Emporium had taken to wearing football helmets in the hotel colors of black and blue.

The ball arched skyward, clearing the mesh fence by a

good six inches, and curved down toward the parking lot in a brilliant arc.

"Four to one it gets a Lexus," said the Swamp Fox as they hurried to the fence.

Hal had also seen that there were a large number of these cars in the parking lot today. "I am not taking your odds," he said.

"Too bad," said the Swamp Fox as they reached the fence. Each grabbed a pair of binoculars, which were hung there for the entertainment of golfers, and focused on the lot below.

Louie got his adjusted first. "I am glad you did not take that bet. I got one car jockey and a woman in a red beret."

Ricochets were rare but not unknown. Few were so foolish as to bet on them.

Although the valet's helmet must have deflected most of the force of the ball, the woman in the red hat lay sprawled on the pavement as if disinclined to move. This provided Hal with the opportunity to reflect on the fact that he had agreed to golf with Louie here today because he was watching for this very woman.

Melanie Mulcahy, according to his sources, had been scheduled to meet someone downstairs for brunch half an hour ago. The red beret was her trademark.

Apparently she had been stood up or her date had given offense, because she was leaving earlier than he had expected. Hal would have volunteered to teach a lesson in manners to this unknown, rude luncheon companion, but the fortuitous coincidence of Melanie Mulcahy being knocked into the twilight zone had just solved a key problem for him.

"Gotta go," he told Louie.

His companion watched Hal's tall, sturdy figure stride toward the elevator. He smiled to himself, even hummed a little something from *Evita* about money rolling in.

After the elevator went down, Grampa Orion strolled from his penthouse apartment. He was a large man with small eyes, thick eyebrows and a roseate nose. At eighty-five, Grampa moved with a jaunty step, ever ready to dance the tango or dodge flying lead.

"Well?" he asked the Swamp Fox. "Do you think he suspects anything?"

Louie shook his head. "Not a chance, Grampa. The man is too smitten with this dame Rita. Also, I warned him away from Paraiso, so we do not have to worry about him showing up there."

"Good," said Grampa, picking up a pair of binoculars and peering at the crowd gathering in the parking lot below. "We would not want the Iceman to lose his temper with us, now, would we?"

MELANIE MULCAHY AWOKE with such a headache. Keeping her eyes shut, she sniffed the air, but detected neither smoke nor gunpowder.

If what had hit her was a bomb, it had gone off some time ago. By now, the entire war might be over.

"Did I miss another one?" she asked.

"Another what?" asked a deep baritone that was probably male. She thought about looking, but decided she wasn't quite ready to let light crash into her eyes.

"War. Bomb. Whatever."

"Golf ball," said the voice.

"In the middle of Las Vegas?" Now that she thought about it, Melanie recalled that she had just been stood up by a source. This particular individual, the owner of a pawnshop, had claimed to have information about a series of jewel heists at charity events that Melanie was investigating.

The last she could remember, she had been crossing the parking lot outside Grampa's Emporium, which wasn't near any golf course. And then...blackness.

Vaguely, she had the impression that someone had roused her, poked her and taken her blood pressure, and that she must have gone back to sleep.

But why was this room rumbling and quivering as if about to perform an unroomlike act, such as moving? Perhaps, she thought, she was not lying in a room but in a vehicle.

"Where am I?" demanded Melanie, and did two foolish things. She opened her eyes, then sat up.

Fireworks sputtered and spat directly into her brain. Melanie's head throbbed all the way down to the base of her skull.

Some merciful soul clapped a bag of ice over her forehead and eased her so that she was propped against the arm of a couch. "I hate this," she said.

"You will need at least a week for rest and recuperation. Do you feel nauseated?"

"Should I?"

"Only if you have a concussion. But the doctor did not think so."

"The doctor?" She blinked, trying to make out the man sitting beside her on the couch. At first she thought her vision had blurred, and then she realized the room was jolting again.

It was a narrow, rectangular room, plushly but stiffly furnished with a velour couch, a corner desk and several velvet chairs bolted to the floor. The walls were covered with dark red paper embossed with roses, heavy drapes blocked the windows and a small bar had been built into one corner. The place reminded her of an old time railroad car, but there was no passenger-rail service to Las Vegas anymore.

"The house doctor at Grampa's Emporium inspected you," said her companion, answering a question Melanie had almost forgotten asking.

"How long ago?" she asked.

"A couple of hours," said the man.

"You haven't answered my first question," she said. "Where am I?"

"In the care of someone who wishes to preserve you from a dangerous situation," said the man she now recognized as the most feared mobster in Las Vegas.

Hal "the Iceman" Smothers. Via the grapevine, Melanie knew that he had a spotless reputation. This meant that every one of his victims had disappeared without leaving so much as a spot.

Since retiring from the thug-disposal profession, he had built the Ice Palace Hotel, an establishment whose revenue per square foot exceeded that of any other casino in Las Vegas. He was obviously operating a front, but no one had been able to figure out for what.

It was a situation fraught with possibilities. Melanie might have to change her plans. Besides, at the moment, she couldn't remember what her plans *were*.

Shifting the bag of ice to shore up the side of her head, which was threatening to blow out, she did her best to assess this gangster who was regarding her with such tender concern.

He was strongly built, even muscular, which might be expected in a former hit man. She knew the guy to be in his mid-thirties, not very old for having achieved such distinction, although being only twenty-eight herself, she considered he was getting up there.

The weird thing was that, from this angle, he didn't look half-bad. He had a full head of brown hair and matching brown eyes. His face was squarish with a thin white scar above the right eyebrow and an indentation in the left cheek that might have been another scar or maybe a confused dimple.

Her attention kept returning to those powerful shoulders, which looked constrained beneath his silk jacket, and that broad chest, and the little twist to his hips that indicated he knew how to dance. Given his propensity for winning wives, he must be a pretty good lover, although he obviously wasn't such hot stuff as a husband.

Melanie wondered why she was lying here speculating about how it would feel to make love to Hal "the Iceman" Smothers. She made it a rule to keep business and pleasure strictly separate, and since fate had been kind enough to throw her way a man she would very much like to investigate, she had to classify him as business.

Enter one prospective Pulitzer Prize nomination, or at least a sale to a magazine that paid in actual dollars. Exit one pair of sexy hips and a hard, knowing mouth.

The word *investigate* reverberated through her swollen brain. It rang a bell, or was that just another throb of pain?

Oh, Lord. Now she remembered what her plans were.

"What time is it?" demanded Melanie.

"Around two."

"I have to go to a party tonight." With infinite gingerliness, she eased herself up into a sitting position.

Melanie was relieved to see that she was fully dressed in her black leggings, red-and-white-striped sweater and the short black jacket she'd picked up in Paris. Only her red beret and ebony boots had been removed, and must be around here somewhere.

"I do not think you are in any shape for a party." Hal reached down and scooted her hips so she could sit more comfortably. "Please excuse the familiarity. A gentleman would not handle a lady in this manner under normal circumstances, but you are an injured person entrusted to my care."

Melanie wasn't sure which revelation startled her most: that the Iceman had taken her under his care, or that he considered himself a gentleman.

"Look, let's put our cards on the table, shall we?" she said. As a casino owner, she figured, he should grasp the metaphor.

"You wish us to be frank," said the Iceman, still wearing that melting look.

"Right. My name is Melanie Mulcahy and I'm…self-employed. I've got work to do, and if I don't, I won't make any money, so take me home, okay?"

Melanie chose not to mention that her self-employment took the form of freelance muckraking. This was not a popular profession with men of his persuasion.

It was not a popular profession with her wallet, either. Maybe if she had the patience to attend city-council meetings and write human-interest stories about lost dogs, she could draw a steady paycheck. But Melanie loved the thrill of the chase more than anything except maybe a byline.

"I fear I cannot take you home at this time," said the man. "However, you can rely upon me to compensate you for any lost income. I am Hal Smothers, the owner of the Ice Palace Hotel."

"I know who you are, but I've got to—" She stopped, realizing that she had missed her plane to Los Angeles, anyway.

It had been her intention to catch a cab from the L.A. airport to the docks at San Pedro, where she would crash a farewell party aboard the small cruise vessel *Jolly Roger*. She believed that it was the next target in the series of jewel heists she was investigating, and which she believed were linked to Margarita Samovar.

After the party, Melanie planned to stow away, having been unable to afford a cruise ticket. But then, she doubted Rita would have sold her one, anyway. Rita had been hostile to Melanie for some time, having gotten wind of the way she was asking questions.

However, she could hardly explain this to Hal Smothers. He was a crook, and therefore more likely to sympathize with Rita than with Melanie. For all she knew, he might even be involved in the robberies and had deliberately taken her out of commission.

Come to think of it, that brunch invitation from the pawnshop owner could have been a setup. Someone had conveniently arranged for Melanie to visit Grampa's Emporium and put her in the path of a small projectile disguised as a golf ball.

And then Hal Smothers, the deadliest hit man in the West, had laid hands on her. She felt a moment of sheer terror. It was thrilling.

Melanie had slogged through a rain forest once to confront a band of guerrillas, only to find them posing for pictures with the cast of "Baywatch."

She had parachuted into a central Asian nation in the middle of a civil war, gotten stuck in a bog and been rescued by a computer repairman who was servicing the rebels' fax machine.

The kind of adrenaline-stirring peril that had made a hero of Ernest Hemingway had won nothing but anonymity for Melanie Mulcahy. Not that she regretted a thing; she loved the excitement, and trusted that someday it would lead to fame.

Maybe, at last, she could have both. She was going to hook up with Hal "the Iceman" Smothers and use this vicious pirate for all he was worth. It was no more than he deserved.

The room began to shake again, slowed, and then picked up speed in a way that made her head quake. They were, Melanie could see, definitely occupying a private railroad car. Now that her head was clearing, she remembered seeing Hal Smothers on TV, buying such a car at a charity auction.

"Excuse me," she said. "How can we be riding in a railway car when there is no more passenger service to Las Vegas?"

"I prefer this classic mode of transportation," replied the Iceman. "It is inconvenient not to have the traditional engine in the front and rails beneath us, but I have improvised."

Melanie turned and brushed aside the brocade curtains. To her astonishment, she found herself staring across an interstate highway at rugged high-desert scenery.

"You put the railway car on a truck bed?" she hazarded.

"A large semi equipped for a wide load," Hal responded cheerily.

"You travel this way often?"

"Once in a while," said the Iceman. "When I wish to

have privacy and when there is no airport close to my destination.'' He owned a private jet, she recalled.

Where would he take her that did not offer an airport? ''So tell me,'' she said between gritted teeth. ''Where are we going?''

''I have been giving this much thought,'' said her companion. ''Where can I take a lady with a lump on her head, who needs rest and pampering?''

''Where indeed?'' said Melanie.

''I have decided,'' said the Iceman, ''on a little island that has been unrecommended to me but that provides pleasant accommodations along with privacy. It is called Paraiso de Los Falsarios.''

Crooks' Paradise. That sounded just about perfect to Melanie.

2

HAL WAS HAPPILY surprised that Melanie Mulcahy had accepted his offer of a week's vacation without screaming or trying to jump out of the railway car.

He would not want to distress a lady. And he was coming to the reluctant conclusion that Melanie fit into that category.

She gave no sign of being the shrill, backbiting annoyance described by Rita. He could not picture this pretty lady disrupting the Rescue the Whales charity cruise and offending its donors.

In fact, when Melanie stared at him through her slightly tilted eyes the color of cocktail olives without the pimientos, he felt a distinct melting sensation in those parts a man does not mention in polite company. He had also seen her looking at his shoulders in a nicely assessing manner.

However, Hal had yet to converse with this woman when she didn't have a lump on her head. It was possible that perhaps the golf ball had scrambled her personality.

Furthermore, it would do Melanie a great disservice if Hal developed any interest in her of a personal nature. He had seen the dented condition of her car when he arranged to have it towed to his garage.

She might possess nonstop legs and an impish face, but what this attractive person lacked was money. Hal didn't want to perform one of his classic removals on her—in the event of alimony.

He would make sure to arrange for separate bedrooms at the resort. There was always plenty of room at Paraiso de Los Falsarios, so that should be no problem.

"Tell me about this place we're going," said Melanie from where she lay decorating the couch. "And why exactly you feel obliged to take me there."

The why of the situation was not a matter Hal cared to reveal, so he chose an alternate explanation. "You were injured on the property of one of my dearest friends, Grampa Orion," he said. "I wish to spare him a possible lawsuit."

"From what I've heard, he's crusty and disagreeable," she murmured. "You're sure he's a friend?"

Hal didn't wish to be rude to this lovely person, but he could not let such slander go unchallenged. "Grampa has been a substitute father for me, as my own old man perished at a young age."

"Somebody shot him?"

"He ate a particular type of Japanese fish that does not care to be eaten," said Hal. "As he was in Grampa's employ at the time, the Orion family engaged my mother's secretarial skills. This provided us with a livelihood."

Not being the sort of man to bare his emotions, Hal chose not to explain that Grampa and the elder members of his gang were like a quarrelsome but lovable bunch of uncles. He had fond memories of Thanksgiving dinners around Grampa's table, listening to the men trade amiable insults about each others' cooking.

Sammy "Cha Cha" Adams, money launderer and owner of the small cruise ship *Jolly Roger*, had personally taught ballroom dancing to the young Hal. And Grampa, at the request of Hal's mother, Eloise, had broached the facts of life to the growing boy with the aid of a tattered hygiene pamphlet.

At Eloise's funeral when Hal was nineteen, Cha Cha, Grampa, "Drop Dead" Cimarosa and the Swamp Fox had served as pallbearers. On rainy days, he still got an ache in his shoulder where they had each clapped him by way of consolation.

"And you're so grateful that you decided to sweep me away to parts unknown?" It might have been a note of seduction that he heard in the lady's voice. That, or skepticism.

"I acted on the inspiration of the moment," Hal improvised. "Also, Paraiso de Los Falsarios is very picturesque. I am given to understand that you are a writer of sorts. Perhaps you will be moved by the surroundings to compose a poem."

"I'll very likely be moved to compose something," Melanie agreed in that melodious purr. "Now, what about this island? I've never heard of it."

Naturally not, Hal mused. "It has, in recent years, come into the possession of an associate of Grampa's, Drop Dead Cimarosa, who has long aspired to own an atoll in the Caribbean. Preferably one with banks on it."

"I can understand that. But...well, excuse me, but I always check my facts." His guest scooped her purse from the carpet and sat up straighter on the sofa.

Hal wished he dared reach out and help shift her hips again. He had enjoyed doing that earlier, but the lady was, sad to say, looking stronger and healthier by the minute.

"This is peculiar," said Melanie. "The Caribbean lies to the southeast, and we are headed northwest." She held up a small round instrument.

Hal could not believe it. Most women carried a compact, but this one had brought a compass. "Do you get lost frequently?"

"All the time," she admitted ruefully. "In some of the strangest places. Now tell me how we can reach a Caribbean island by going northwest from Las Vegas?"

"That is the question Drop Dead asked after he won it in a poker game," said Hal. "It seems his opponent had exaggerated. The island is small, rocky and north of San Francisco."

"How far north?" asked Melanie. "Is it in the United States?"

"It would be, if anyone knew it was there," he admitted. "Drop Dead built a resort, but he has been careful not to advertise it. Word of mouth only. And it has a very…select clientele."

"You mean it's an unlisted island? A law unto itself?" Melanie pursed her lips, which already had a bee-stung fullness. Hal wondered whether she wrote romance novels and, if so, whether she might considering using him for research purposes.

On the other hand, he could only imagine how furious Drop Dead and the rest of Grampa's crime family would be if their offshore hideaway were to be glamorized in some novel. "It is a mostly legitimate resort and has no need of law enforcement," he said.

"When do we get there?" asked Melanie.

Hal glanced at his watch. They were hurtling along at about eighty miles an hour. "A few hours," he said.

"Then I think I'll take a nap." Giving him a sweet smile, Melanie snuggled down among the pillows and closed her eyes. Her long legs, clad only in thick black tights, pressed lightly against his hip.

Her vicinity was rapidly rendering his body uninhabitable. Grumpily, he moved to a chair, but this only gave him a better view of her long, coltish body and small, lively breasts.

Ashamed of his ungentlemanly ogling, Hal relocated to the corner desk and set up his notebook computer. He was working on a new spreadsheet-based video game, Tax Invaders from the Planet Zog, that made accounting fun. It should net him yet another fortune.

THEY ARRIVED at the island near twilight. As the sun sank below the horizon, it streaked the western sky with all the colors of a punk rocker's hair.

Melanie stood on the prow of the ferryboat, staring at a puzzling sight. Overhead, the heavens glowed picturesquely. But straight ahead, mist swathed what appeared to be a barren clutch of rocks.

Never before, in all her travels, had she encountered such a surrealistic vision. Above, a pink and violet sky. Below, a black lump in the ocean, surrounded by fog.

"There's nothing there. Or at least, nothing I can see." She shivered inside her jacket, which offered little protection against the icy breeze. Fortunately, the cold air also took the sting out of her lump.

"That is the beauty of it." Hal Smothers stopped behind Melanie, his feverish heat enveloping her like a blanket. What fool had named him the Iceman?

"You mean it's always like this?" she asked.

"Perpetually in a fog," he agreed.

"And somebody built a resort on it?"

"It was a sublime act of wishful thinking," he admitted. "At least we should not be troubled by excessive company."

Melanie saw right through him. A top-flight criminal like Hal wouldn't isolate himself for a week in the middle of nowhere with a woman he believed to be a poet. Not even to prevent a lawsuit against his friend Grampa.

The charity cruise that Melanie had missed should be heading past here tomorrow or the day after. Hal could be in cahoots with Rita, planning to stash the jewels once she swiped them from the wealthy patrons.

There had been three previous heists. One had taken place on a charity skiing tour of Switzerland, one during a mystery weekend in Quebec and the third at a costume ball in Juarez, Mexico.

The common denominator was that Margarita Samovar had organized all three events. This intriguing fact had come to Melanie's attention because she made it her job to peruse the Internet for tidbits about unusual crimes.

So far, neither the mainstream press nor the police had seen the similarities among these far-flung robberies. Now Hal might provide another piece of the puzzle. If he was laundering booty through his hotel-casino, that would help explain his extravagant income.

Perhaps, foolishly, he had brought Melanie along to provide some sort of alibi. Well, she would testify all right, but not in the way he intended.

The ferry pulled alongside a wharf. There were no other ships around, not even a sailboat, just a rectangular dock jutting out a few dozen feet atop wooden pilings. Once you arrived at the island, Melanie realized, there was no easy way to remove yourself.

"How often does the ferry run?" she asked as they got off. They were the only passengers.

"Whenever someone radios the ferryman," said the Iceman.

Melanie got the clear impression that he was not about to loan her a shortwave in case of emergency. Oh, well. She would figure out how to leave when the time came.

Having reached the base of the pier, they stood facing a wall of fog. Nothing penetrated it; not a building, not even a phone booth. There was certainly no hotel van waiting to meet them.

Hal hefted his suitcase and stared glumly at the fog. "This is what comes of not having a reservation."

Melanie was glad she didn't have any luggage. "How far is it?"

"It does not matter, because you are in no fit condition to walk." Hal regarded her ruefully. "Your lump has outgrown the ball that inspired it."

Melanie decided not to reach up there and feel for herself. She had a notion it might hurt.

"Well, if I can't walk, how are we going to get there?" she asked. "Is it far?"

Hal didn't answer. Instead, his eyes got narrow and pouchy as he peered into the mist. For the first time since she'd awakened in the train car, he really looked like a criminal.

What if the resort didn't exist? Melanie felt a rush of fear.

Rita had been suspicious of her for over a week now. Assuming she and the Iceman were in cahoots, he might have brought Melanie here to make the long swim to China. If that was his modus operandi, no wonder his victims had never been found.

On the other hand, if Hal Smothers was known for anything besides his efficiency as a killer, it was his soft spot for women. Melanie decided the situation left her no choice.

"Put your bag down," she said.

He clunked it to the ground. "Do you feel faint?"

"Very faint." She sagged against him. Close up, the

man smelled nice. He was wearing the usual gangster-issue cologne, spicy with a hint of musk.

Two strong arms seized her elbows and maintained her at approximately a seventy-five-degree angle, according to Melanie's calculations. Her cheek was resting against Hal's neck, but her pelvis was in Outer Siberia.

"Could you hold me a little closer?" she whispered. "I'm cold." But not as cold as she would be if he pitched her off this pile of rocks, she thought as she eyed the distance to the retreating ferryboat.

Carl Lewis might be able to jump across the rapidly expanding stretch of water. Melanie would prefer to take her chances with Hal.

"I apologize for my lack of foresight." The gangster gave up trying to keep her at arm's length and gathered her against him. He felt hard, all the way up. "It is an unfortunate fact that even cellular phones do not work on this island."

"And they call it Paradise?" As she whispered the words, she blew a series of puffs into his ear.

The man shuddered. "It is not far," he managed to say. "Would you like me to carry you?"

"Yes, please!" Wrapping her arms around his neck, Melanie gave a little hop, and was pleased when he caught her in midair. The man was nothing if not coordinated. "You don't mind leaving your luggage?"

He threw back his head and laughed. This gave her a chance to inspect the indentation in his cheek, which she decided was of natural origin. "From where would a thief come? Where could he hope to hide?"

"I see your point," she said.

Then a problem occurred. To be precise, Melanie's investigation of Hal's cheek interfered with his face's inclination to return to its normal position. In choreographic terms, he looked down just as she looked up.

If you are going to distract a gangster, you must take advantage of any opening. Besides, Melanie was feeling a delicious thrill at being held so elegantly, so easily, so powerfully by a deadly killer who shuddered when she blew in his ear.

She tightened her grip on his neck and pressed her lips against his. His mouth was hard, just as she had imagined, but also hot.

Very hot. Before she could make a strategic duck to one side, his tongue advanced into her mouth and he tightened his grip around her back and under her thighs.

Being held horizontally, Melanie discovered, had its disadvantages. In the first place, it was impossible to back off.

In the second place, the man did not have to maneuver very far to progress from kissing her mouth to trailing his tongue down her throat, to nuzzling inside her partly open jacket toward two rapidly responding feminine orbs.

She had to admire the Iceman's grace. Not once did he stumble or lose his balance.

With the litheness of a dancer and the command of a weight lifter, he shifted her position so that her head tilted away and her back arched toward him. The man was not wasting any time.

No wonder he had been able to land three wives. He had probably consummated their marriages while still kneeling with a ring in his hand.

This was not what Melanie had had in mind. She had wished to promise him anything but give him the slip.

Instead, she gasped into the fog as his virile tongue invaded the scooped neck of her sweater and prowled almost the whole way to one straining peak. At any instant, his mouth would close over it.

The most peculiar part was that Melanie couldn't find it within herself to resist. The man deserved applause.

He certainly deserved more of a reward than a shove in the face and a kick in the *cojones*. But did he really deserve a free mouthful of something she considered exclusively hers to bestow?

Never mind, he was already there. After one tantalizing lick, Hal Smothers mouthed her nipple with heartfelt appreciation.

Her breathing speeded up. If Melanie had been cold, that moment was now history.

She actually liked the way she felt. Good Lord. Who would have believed the man could be so gentle and so desperate, all at once?

Something was moving through the fog, not far away. A low rumble reached her ears.

"Uh, Hal!" Melanie tried to tug her sweater into place.

With a low moan, he released her, but only to take a breather. Then he burrowed in again, looking for the other one.

"Hal!" She squirmed a little harder.

"Mmm?" Reluctantly, he came up for air. In the misty half light, she saw that he wore a dazed expression, as if he too had just been bonked by a golf ball.

Quickly, she straightened her top. "I think our ride is here."

He made a snuffling noise that was somewhere between clearing his throat and choking with embarrassment, then lowered her. Upright again, Melanie swayed a moment before catching her balance.

The incident had happened so quickly that she might almost have imagined it. Was it true? Had Hal Smothers just bypassed her shields before she could even sound a red alert?

The big guy turned to load his suitcase into a black 1930s limo that had stopped a short distance away. The driver, a wizened antique who might have been the car's original owner, waited on the far side of the hood, smoking a cigarillo.

"Good thing the ferryman called me." He gave Melanie a wink, or at least that's what it looked like in the mist. "A pleasure to meet the blushing bride."

"I never blush," she said, and got in the back seat. Good heavens, the man thought she had walked down the aisle with this lug!

Well, Hal Smothers *was* known as the marrying kind. If she were a grasping sort of person, Melanie might consider a quickie wedding, followed soon thereafter by a set of thumbscrews skillfully applied by her lawyer.

But she was not. Heaven knew, Melanie had no great love for men. In her experience, they either wanted to tag along on her adventures or preached the stuffy idea that women shouldn't parachute into war zones.

They nattered on about her long legs, spent too much time gazing into her green eyes and generally bored her to death. Mr. Fastest-Tongue-in-the-West was probably no different from the others.

But she maintained a fastidiousness about ethics. On her personal scale of justice, honest mistakes could be forgiven, and people were expected to take custody of their own broken hearts. That did not excuse deliberate exploitation, by either sex.

Hal Smothers might be made of money, and it might be ill-gotten, but if Melanie Mulcahy ever chose to put her hands in his pockets, it would not be for the purpose of removing his wallet.

HAL RODE to the Casa Falsario in a state of semivertical arousal and acute shame.

He had snatched Melanie in order to win the affections of the lovely Rita. It was not to be supposed that the future mother of his children would appreciate him rooting around in another woman's sweater, regardless of what he found there.

True, Melanie had practically thrown herself at him, but she was suffering the effects of golf-ball ricochet. It was only natural that she should feel dizzy, and seek comfort from her male protector.

And, blast it, he *was* her protector. He had deliberately removed Melanie from her habitat, and until he returned her, he bore full responsibility for her safety.

Everything that had been intact must remain that way until her return. And a gentleman was required to assume that everything about a lady was intact.

But...was it? inquired a roguish part of his brain. Had she not returned his kiss and wriggled appealingly in his arms? Had she not blown in his ear and gasped with pleasure as he...as he...

Hal folded his legs tighter and gritted his teeth. Best not to think about it.

His thoughts returned to Rita. She had claimed that Melanie intended to disrupt her charity cruise. He was finding it harder and harder, however, to picture Melanie as a stealth agitator from the whaling industry.

Worse, he was beginning to wonder whether Rita was as suitable a marital prospect as he had imagined. She owned several sweaters, but he had never been tempted to poke around in them. And he wished he had checked out her claim that it was customary to send a three-year-old to boarding school.

The fog thickened as they approached Casa Falsario.

Then Hal realized that he was observing the arrival of nightfall.

It being September, and the clientele of Casa Falsario being sketchy at best, he had little hope of encountering a festive atmosphere. Most likely they would sit alone in the dining room, eating bowls of thin soup slopped in front of them by a shuffling ex-con.

However, he reminded himself, there was really no need to stay more than a day or two. He had promised Melanie rest and relaxation, but she did not seem the restful type.

The mission had been accomplished, Hal realized with decidedly mixed feelings. This very evening, the *Jolly Roger* would depart from Los Angeles, sans Melanie, and he would have earned Rita's deepest thanks.

He tried to picture the woman with whom he intended to share the rest of his nights, her raven hair spread on the pillow, her pale blue eyes blinking at him from within their raccoon-like nests of makeup.

It was no use. The hair he saw was light brown and short, barely covering a large lump. The eyes were a peculiar shade of green with narrow pupils, like a cat's. The figure was slimmer, the smile more generous.

Hal wanted to take Melanie Mulcahy to bed. Several parts of his body were already seconding that motion.

But as a suitor to Rita, he could not. As Melanie's protector, he could not. As a gentleman, he must keep his head high and the rest of himself low.

The limo creaked to a halt in front of a Spanish-style building. All that was visible of the rest of the compound was a white stucco wall stretching in both directions, its paint flaking from the harsh sea air.

The wall existed not so much to keep anything out as to make the patrons feel at home. Over the years, most of them had spent considerable time behind walls of one sort or another.

On the far side, Hal knew, the resort fronted the island's coast, a sheer bluff tapering to a rocky point. Atop the rocks sat a lighthouse whose glow, diffused by fog, was intermittently visible even from here.

"Hey," said Melanie, "this place really exists."

"You thought otherwise?"

"I had my doubts." She unfolded her impossibly long legs. "Aren't people going to think it's odd, me checking in with no luggage?"

"Not around here," Hal said. "Also, in case I forgot to mention it, I will be happy to buy any necessary items at the gift shop."

"This place has a gift shop?"

"Duty free," he said.

"Smuggled?"

"You are a little too smart," said Hal.

He tipped the driver, gripped his bag and led the way into the lobby. It was a small plain room with terra-cotta tile on the floor, smudged paint on the walls and a battered wooden counter running along one side.

Hal pushed a button. To his surprise, Arthur "Drop Dead" Cimarosa himself slouched in from the back room.

Usually, Drop Dead did not put in personal appearances because in the event of guests who did not know him, this had a less than salutary effect. Drop Dead was not only ugly, he was said to have a Medusa-like effect on susceptible individuals. Also, Drop Dead had a nasty temper and, despite his seventy-two years, a quick trigger finger.

Melanie stared across the counter at this balding man with a face like a gargoyle. "Pleased to meet you, Mr. Cimarosa," she said.

Drop Dead, who was extremely nearsighted but too

vain to wear glasses, leaned to get a closer look. His face cracked into a smile.

"Good-looking dame," he said. "One of the fellows expecting you?" In Hal's direction, he tossed, "Beat it, driver."

"This isn't the driver," Melanie said. "Don't you two know each other?"

"Of course," said Hal, but did not extend his hand because if Drop Dead was in a bad mood, he might not get it back.

The island's owner turned his attention to Hal. He squinted, he frowned and then he coughed. "You? Here?"

"I realize we lack reservations." Hal made a pseudo-Italian gesture with his hands. "We need only two rooms for a couple of nights. I do not see why that should be a problem."

Drop Dead grumbled as he poked through a card file. "Sorry, no room." He did not sound sorry.

"Oh, come on." Melanie leaned against the counter in a manner that emphasized her lovely sweatered globes. "I'm exhausted and I just got beaned by a golf ball."

"Also she might have to sue Grampa," added Hal. "We would not want that."

"The lady," said Arthur Cimarosa, "can have the bridal suite. You can get lost."

He handed Melanie an oversize metal key and snarled, or maybe he was smiling. Then he stumped off.

"Is he always like that?" she asked.

"Only when he is in a good mood. Otherwise, he tends to shoot first and check IDs later." Still puzzling over Drop Dead's behavior, and choosing to ignore the latter's instructions to depart, Hal picked up his luggage and led the way into the courtyard.

Something odd was going on. Why had Drop Dead been so displeased to see him? Was Casa Falsario really full in the off-season?

And how was Hal going to remain a gentleman while staying alone in the bridal suite with Melanie?

3

AT THIS EARLY HOUR, for twilight was dawn by Las Vegas standards, the courtyard sat deserted. It was a modest circular patio with cracked pavement, at best a sort of open-air lobby and happy-hour retreat.

Tonight it looked far from its best. In the haze, a few wrought-iron tables loomed like skeletons, and a mottled bunch of geraniums drooped in a planter box.

"This place doesn't appear fully booked," Melanie said. "How many rooms are there, anyway?"

Hal had come here twice before, once for Grampa Orion's eightieth birthday and again for Sammy "Cha Cha" Adams's marriage—sadly, short-lived—to a saxophone player. Drop Dead had stood in for the minister, since being the owner of an island was somewhat like being the captain of a ship.

However, as a businessman, Hal liked to get the lay of the land. He had made it a point to scope out the place.

"There are four individual rooms and two suites," he said. "Also a conference room." He pointed to a small freestanding building beneath a large palm tree.

He did not add that, to his knowledge, the place was never full except during special occasions. If anything was afoot, Hal had not been notified of it, and this was making him uneasy.

But maybe it was mere coincidence that so many people had descended on the island at one time. Such things were known to happen.

"What about that strange-looking man at the desk?" Melanie asked. "Where does he stay?"

"He lives in the lighthouse," said Hal.

"Really? How romantic!"

Hal could not imagine anything about Drop Dead that would be considered romantic. However, such a notion might be expected from a writer of poetry. "Perhaps so."

"These suites have two bedrooms, right?" said Melanie.

Hal had not gone inside either of the suites, but now that he thought about it, why should there not be two rooms? "Let us hope so."

Indeed, he *was* hoping so. Fervently.

As they walked, a low *whoosh* came to Hal's ears. Then came another *whoosh*, followed by a *whump*.

"Shuffleboard," he said, following a curved walkway out of the courtyard. Sure enough, the moment they turned a corner, the bright flatness of a shuffleboard court appeared to their left.

Beyond it, the fog held so thickly it was impossible to see the ocean, although they could hear the crash of waves below. In the darkness, the court appeared as a rectangle of light, or perhaps of the light-fingered.

At one end of it stood an elderly couple and a younger, pudgy pair. Joe and Violet McAllister were the hustlers of the shuffleboard circuit who, when they got tired of stiffing their fellow senior citizens for spare change, came to Casa Falsario to rest.

Their son and daughter-in-law had been straight-arrow citizens until the daughter-in-law was arrested for feeding a parking meter. When her husband threw a quarter at the arresting officer, he too hit the slammer. Although misdemeanants did not qualify for independent visitation to the island, they were allowed to come in the company of her parents.

If these were the sort of people occupying the premises, Hal had nothing to worry about. The McAllisters generally stayed in the presidential suite and minded their own business, unless they smelled a good confidence game.

"Those folks don't look like gangsters." Melanie sounded disappointed.

"They are low-grade malefactors," explained Hal. "The bridal suite is this way."

He took her arm and felt her sway against him. Perhaps her injury was worsening, he thought with a trace of guilt. He hoped to get her settled quickly for a rest.

Although the doctor had found no evidence of concussion, brain swelling might develop later. If Melanie wasn't feeling chipper by later tonight, Hal would have to relocate her to a hospital.

It puzzled him that he felt reluctant to remove her from the island. Why should it bother him that, once they hit civilization, he would probably never see the lady again?

True, she had a passionate nature and a vivacious intelligence. He was finding her company more pleasant by the hour.

But she was the wrong woman. This time, he didn't need a bullet in the shoulder to convince him. The sight of her dented car had been enough.

They reached the unit marked Bridal Suite. Hal was about to fit in the key, when he realized the door stood slightly ajar.

Drop Dead's cleaning woman, Pixie LaBelle, who had served a long jail term for fixing a beauty contest in which the loser turned out to be the district attorney's daughter, might be at work. Cautiously, Hal nudged the door open with his foot.

"Hello?" he called. The front room, however, stood empty.

"What's that?" Melanie indicated a metallic gizmo on the floor that looked as if it had been built from an Erector set.

"Perhaps some sort of security device," said Hal. It didn't appear threatening, so he stepped inside.

"It's growling," said Melanie.

Hal thought it sounded somewhat like an electronic slot machine about to cough up the goods. "Possibly it generates white noise to help people sleep."

"We're next to the ocean," Melanie said. "Who needs white noise?"

"We will ask the proprietor," Hal said. "Tomorrow."

The growling subsided. With a doglike burp, the security device fell silent.

They entered the square living room, which was furnished with a cracked leatherette couch and two industrial-looking chairs reputed to have been sold as scrap when Alcatraz closed. Over the window, thin cheesy curtains hung unevenly from a rod.

A chipped shelf supported a television set circa 1960. Despite its antiquated appearance, Hal knew that Drop Dead showed great movies, since he stole the satellite signals of all the major cable companies.

Melanie took in their surroundings with a disapproving frown. "This isn't exactly the Ritz."

"It is designed to resemble a prison rec room," Hal explained. "Drop Dead likes his guests to feel at home."

"I feel a little too much at home," she said. "The only things missing are sheets on the windows and sand on the floor."

"I beg your pardon?"

"Never mind." With a sleepy stretch that highlighted the soft roundness of her upper torso, Melanie indicated the doors on either side. "Unless I'm mistaken, there *are* two bedrooms. You want left or right?"

"Right will be fine."

Before he could offer to help her get situated or fetch toiletries from the gift shop, Melanie walked into the room on the left and closed the door.

Feeling bereft, Hal stood alone. He wished now that he had taken his guest some place with luxurious furnishings, room service and only one bedroom.

Grimly, he picked up his suitcase and turned right. Inside his room, Hal flipped on the light and then stared in dismay.

A computer had been set up on the nightstand. The floor and bed were littered with men's clothing and printouts showing columns of numbers.

Worn jogging shoes lay far apart on the floor as if kicked off at random; indeed, he thought he detected scuff marks where they'd hit the wall. What manner of individual had made such a mess?

Still gripping his luggage, Hal retreated. "Melanie?" He headed for the other bedchamber.

Before he got there, she popped out, wearing a flimsy camisole that barely reached her thighs. "I'm going to turn in before dinner, okay? Don't bother buying me a toothbrush. I'll make do."

Hal felt a fierce possessiveness toward this helpless and seminude female of whom he had taken custody. "You should not step out in public like that."

"This isn't public." Melanie's smile took on a bedroom allure. "Besides, it's the only thing I've got to sleep in."

"The other room is occupied." Hal regarded her apologetically. "I do not suppose there are two beds in there, by any chance?"

"No." She shrugged. "I'm tired and my head hurts. If you want to lie down too, I doubt I'll even notice."

She retreated, leaving Hal with a painful dilemma. As a gentleman, he could not take advantage of her. On the other hand, neither could he leave the suite, even if he wanted to.

A strange man who threw his clothes on the floor occupied the opposing room. Sooner or later, he would return.

When he did, he must not find Melanie alone and unguarded. And while Hal had slept on many a couch in his day, the one from Alcatraz was most assuredly as hard as a rock.

Gritting his teeth, he followed his companion's wake into her room. To his astonishment, she already lay tucked beneath the covers, by all appearances sound asleep.

With a mutter of resignation and not a little sneaking disappointment, Hal began to unpack.

IN THE DREAM, Melanie ran through a minefield with ammunition whizzing around her. Adrenaline pumped through her veins, and, laughing, she caught one of the bullets in her teeth.

Nearby, she spotted a hut and headed toward it without knowing why. As she entered the yard, it rearranged itself into the tiny house in Empire Lake where she had grown up.

The walls leaned and the roof was little more than a tin sheet. There had been no body of water in Empire Lake since the Late Jurassic, and there was no empire, either. Only California dirt and scrubby desert growths and a patched-up shack with torn sheets for curtains and scrawny chickens that pecked at her bare feet.

Melanie tried to turn back to the battlefield, but an unseen force pulled her through the scarred door.

Inside, she found her sister Wendy, a bandanna wrapped around her hair, mopping the floor and looking old before her time. On the back porch, she could hear her two brothers arguing over a card game.

Melanie was six years old. She wished her mother would come back, but Mommy was gone and Wendy was only twelve and Daddy wouldn't be home from work until late.

Irritably, Wendy shoved the mop into Melanie's hands and went to start dinner. "When you're done mopping, set the table," she said. "Then help me fold the laundry, and after that..."

Melanie couldn't breathe. She had to get out or she would suffocate. But the door was latched too high to reach, and yellow dust sifted through the windows. A racking cough burst from her, followed by the hopeless sobs of a child who knows something is wrong but can't identify it.

Then, miraculously, two arms closed around her and a grown-up shoulder appeared beneath her cheek, and someone whispered, "It's all right," over and over.

The dream had never turned out this way before. Melanie wasn't sure she wanted to wake up.

"No one's going to hurt you." Daddy never talked like that. He was always too tired. "You had a bad dream."

She curled against a man's chest, a very sturdy chest in which she could hear the reassuring thump of a heartbeat. If she pretended to be asleep, maybe he would hold her like this for hours and hours.

Melanie inhaled deeply of gangster cologne. It smelled like a real, secure, "Happy Days"–perfect home.

Home? She had no home. Or rather, the world was her home.

After working her way through Cal State Fullerton as a waitress, she'd sent out résumés and gone to a few interviews. But the prospect of sitting at a computer churning out routine stories made her feel as if she was back in Empire Lake.

She'd begun freelancing for an alternative newspaper and, later, a couple of hip magazines. The money was barely even adequate, but her expenses were low and her energy boundless.

Soon Melanie was scoping out ever-riskier assignments. Wherever danger lurked, she could be found, a tape recorder in one hand and a sleeping bag strapped to her back.

She yawned. At least if she had to snuggle up to a guy, she told herself, it suited her reputation to have picked a hit man.

Still lazily unwilling to stir, she blinked her eyes open and glimpsed the room through Hal Smothers's armpit. How odd. The door appeared to be gliding open.

Something crept in, low to the floor. A spiny metallic thing jerked along like a giant cockroach from another dimension.

A scream rose in Melanie's throat but she caught it midway. She refused to panic. "Give me your gun," she said raspily.

"Excuse me?" Hal's baritone rippled through her body like cello music.

"I'm going to shoot that thing."

He rolled over, letting cool air wash across Melanie's skin. "Good Lord, what *is* that?"

"Shoot first and dissect later," she grumbled, sitting up. Her head must have grown while she slept; it felt like a bowling ball. "I'm not sure I can aim. You do it."

"I regret that I do not believe a bullet to be the ideal solution." The bed creaked, and his large masculine figure paced across the floor toward the invader.

"*Rrrrrah! Rrrrrah!*" With a hollow noise like a dog yapping from two miles down a sewer system, the gizmo skittered backward.

"It is not alive," Hal announced. "It is the object we viewed in the living room."

"Then why is it barking?" Melanie wondered if she was still dreaming, after all. Then she wondered whether the dream came with aspirin. It would be nice if she could get rid of this headache before she woke up.

"I believe this to be a robotic approximation of a dog." Hal bent to scrutinize the thing, which stopped backing up and began to whine.

"What's it for?" Melanie eased from the bed. "By the way, do you have any painkillers?" To be on the safe side, she added, "Legal ones?"

"The doctor provided a bottle of pills, which you will find on the bedside table." Hal stared at the mechanical dog. "It appears to be thinking over the situation."

Melanie reached for the bottle and, without bothering to read the label, swallowed two of the pills, dry. "Then it's one up on a real dog."

She came around from the side to get a better view of the thing. No matter where she stood, it looked like something a child might make from an Erector set.

The robot snarled, and Hal straightened quickly. "Well, if it is a pooch, I wonder what it eats. I hope the answer is not us."

The dog advanced. Hal took a step back. With a blissful

yowl, the thing hurled itself forward and clamped its metallic jaws around his leg.

With a string of curses in which the names of Eliot Ness and J. Edgar Hoover figured prominently, Hal shook his leg, then grasped the attacker and pried it loose. It let out a series of high-pitched yips.

"Hey! Whoever's in there, don't you dare hurt that—" A skinny young man wearing nothing but thick eyeglasses and a thin towel pelted into the room. At the sight of Hal holding the fake dog, the man stopped dead.

His jaw dropped. He nearly dropped the towel, too. His thin, freckled face paled to the color of cheap vanilla ice cream.

"Oh my gosh." His voice rose to an unexpected soprano on the word *my*. "Just, uh, forget I said anything, okay? I mean, did it hurt you, Mr. Smothers? Gee, I'm really sorry."

The Iceman's eyes narrowed. His mouth tightened. His chest expanded. Before Melanie's gaze, he changed from an easygoing companion to a scarred, ruthless killer contemplating his next victim.

In that moment, she realized that she really, really wanted him. Maintaining her journalistic objectivity was going to be the hardest thing she'd ever done.

MANY THINGS became clear when Hal got an eyeful of Chester Orion III in a bath towel.

First, that these towels must have come from Alcatraz, too.

Second, that neither the end of adolescence nor four years at engineering school had improved the appearance of Grampa Orion's only grandson.

Third, that there was definitely something afoot at Paraiso de Los Falsarios. Chet Orion never came to this island alone.

Grampa must be involved in whatever was going on. Also Drop Dead and the Swamp Fox, who had warned Hal off, but, as he now realized, not because Rita's cruise would be passing offshore.

Could there be any doubt that the other senior members of Grampa's crime family—John "Bone Crusher" Nichols and Sammy "Cha Cha" Adams—were also here? That would account for the occupancies of all four single rooms.

With the probably coincidental visitation by the McAllisters, that spelled one full house. For Hal Smothers, there was no room at the inn, or so his false friends had believed.

He did not think that they guessed the awful truth about him, that he was not like them. Judging by the sheer panic in Chet's eyes, they believed him to be too deadly, too bloodthirsty to trust with their new endeavor.

He had to find out what was going on. Hal's reputation and his self-respect demanded that he take charge of the situation and make these double-crossers regretful.

"So," he said, "you have all come here without me. An interesting situation, would you not say, young Master Orion?"

Even Chet's freckles were squirming. "It's not what you think, Mr. Iceman," he said. "It's not, like…I mean, it's all legitimate."

"Legitimate?" Hal arched one eyebrow. He knew how to do so in such a way as to convey skepticism that could rapidly accelerate into murderous rage.

"Really!" In the young man's throat, a well-defined Adam's apple made a couple of quick elevator trips. "You know I've been studying at MIT. Grampa's been waiting all this time, hoping I'd come up with something good, and I have! I mean…"

Chet had said too much already, Hal could see. But then, the boy had never had a stomach for confrontations.

As a teenager, he had shown no aptitude for crime. But he was smart. So Grampa had financed a college education in the hope that Chet would find a way to turn the latest technology to criminal uses.

The Orion crime family believed that life was passing them by. They longed for the golden age of gangsters, before the international business conglomerates had taken over most of Las Vegas.

Hal's greatest fear had been that this aging gang of cutthroats would actually develop a plan. It might, in turn, require him to participate in some criminal action.

He craved their admiration and respect. He enjoyed their rough-edged camaraderie and even their overcooked turkeys and underspiced stuffing. But he did not wish to have to break the law to get it.

Chet said he had come up with something. And, now that Hal thought about it, he had not heard Grampa mention Chet in a long time. If Grampa had been deliberately keeping quiet, this meant the kid really might be on to a good idea.

"So everyone has come here to meet with you privately, have they?" he muttered. "It is like old times, a gangster summit."

Scarcely able to breathe, Chet nodded.

"Without me," snarled Hal.

The youth started to nod again, then shook his head. "No! Mr. Palmetto said you were otherwise occupied. I'm sure they wouldn't—I mean—oh, gosh, Mr. Smothers, you aren't going to ice me, are you?"

In truth, Hal's nickname did not derive from his reputation for putting people on ice. He had gained it as a clumsy preteenager one very cold winter when he was playing an impromptu game of ice hockey on a frozen pond.

With a stumble, a fall, a slide and a crunch, Hal had crashed through the ice into the freezing water below. There he had thrashed and struggled while his companions had simply watched him and laughed.

They had failed to realize that Hal's clumsiness derived from the fact that, in only a few months' time, his bean-pole body had bulked up from an influx of natural tough-guy hormones. They, however, had taken notice of this when he had heaved himself up out of the ice and had pitched them, one by one, into the water.

He had made sure they all emerged safely, but no one had ever dared to laugh at him again. Now it seemed the members of the Orion crime family needed to learn the same lesson as his other faithless pals.

"Does this mean you are inviting me to the summit?" he said in a low voice.

"Uh, yeah. Sure!" Chet resumed breathing. "But, uh, what about her?" He indicated Melanie. "Who's she?"

Hal felt a prick of dismay. He could hardly abandon his charge. Nor could he drag her, headachy and complaining, into a tense meeting with a pack of wolves.

"I'm his gun moll." Melanie struck a pose with attitude to spare. "Wherever Hal goes, I go."

Gratitude surged through him. She was definitely sharp. If the whaling industry didn't need her to write press releases or disrupt charity cruises, they could always use her as a harpoon.

"Well, I guess that would be all right, then," said Chet.

4

WHEN THE THREE of them marched into the hardboard-paneled conference room and the scarred, mottled faces of the gangsters swiveled toward them, Melanie saw a side of Hal that she hadn't seen before.

He seemed, if such a thing were possible, to tower even higher. To grow like the Jolly Green Giant looming over the Happy Valley. Or, in this case, the not-so-happy valley.

Dismay radiated from the gargoyle features of their hulking host, Arthur "Drop Dead" Cimarosa. Beside him, the dapper, sixtyish Sammy "Cha Cha" Adams, owner of the *Jolly Roger* cruise ship, gave a fidgety smile and glanced nervously at the chairman of the board, Chester "Grampa" Orion.

From the head of a long table, Grandpa sat staring fixedly at his perspiring grandson. Melanie could have sworn those small eyes beneath heavy eyebrows didn't blink, not once.

Of the other two men, she recognized one as Louie "the Swamp Fox" Palmetto. Save for his pointed teeth and skin as pitted as an outlying moon of Jupiter, he might have passed for an ordinary businessman.

The fifth man she had never seen before. With his stiletto-thin mustache and thick, rippling arms and hands, he matched the description of John "Bone Crusher" Nichols, Grampa's enforcer, who was said to have once killed a rival with a strenuous handshake. At the moment, he looked as if he would like very much to shake hands with Hal.

Melanie's fingers itched to snatch a notepad from her purse. Such a pantheon of underworld lords hadn't been seen since the days of Al Capone, and she wouldn't wish to miss one little detail in the story that she was going to write. Or the book. Or the miniseries.

She was weighing the risk of extracting the pad when Hal said, "Melanie, take notes."

"Notes?" growled Grampa.

"My secretary," said Hal. Confidently. Sternly. Massively. Then, over his shoulder, he gave her a glance of pure teddy-bear hopefulness.

He had taken quite a risk; he did not know that she carried a pad, or whether she would choose to cooperate. But so boyishly mischievous was his expression, in that moment unseen by the other gangsters, that Melanie would have taken notes on her fingernails if necessary.

"Yes, sir," she rapped out, and snatched her pad into position.

Grampa's glower fell on his grandson, who had moved slightly ahead of Hal. "You did not advise us that you were bringing guests."

"Uh…" Chet hugged his oversize portfolio like a shield.

Hal pulled out a chair, turned it around and planted one foot on it as he confronted Grampa. "It is not the fault of young Chester that I have taken you by surprise. It seems to me it is you, my old friends, who owe me an explanation for holding this summit in my absence."

"Summit?" said Grampa.

"Absence?" inquired Cha Cha.

"Hey!" The Swamp Fox spread his hands in a gesture

of appeasement. "It was our innocent belief that you were otherwise occupied."

"On some business of Rita's," added Bone Crusher. "You always was a pushover for broads."

"Anyway, who cares?" growled Drop Dead. "We don't owe you nothing."

Melanie's ears pricked at the mention of Rita. So her surmise was true; Hal did have some involvement in the woman's scheme.

What might have been a flare of triumph, however, was doused by a shower of dismay. Hal and Rita were an item? It made perfect sense that one crook would crave another. And it made Melanie furious.

The man was wasting himself. His melting brown eyes and nonstop body deserved better than that makeup-laden, sticky-fingered dame Rita. And Melanie would make sure he figured that out, right before she dumped him.

"This is not a summit," said Grampa. "It is an informal meeting with my grandson to offer him good wishes in his new business venture."

"And possibly to raise capital," said the round-headed, round-faced Cha Cha, with a smile that flashed and vanished like a card in a magician's hand.

"So we are talking business." With a fluid motion, Hal swung the chair around and sat in it. Offhandedly, he gestured to Melanie to take the seat beside him.

Chet remained standing. A tinge of color returned to his freckled face, but he continued to clutch his portfolio and a shopping bag as if his life depended on them. Which, possibly, it did.

"A legitimate venture, of course," said Grampa.

"Nuttin' that would interest you," said Bone Crusher.

The way they were regarding Hal, they were all—with the possible exception of Drop Dead—afraid of him.

These big, tough gangsters lived in fear of a man who had held Melanie in his arms as softly as an angel.

But then, she reminded herself, Hal was a pushover for broads. No doubt he'd held Rita with the same tenderness, and maybe done even more interesting things beneath her sweater.

The thought made Melanie feel hot and cold at the same time. Ruthlessly, she brushed away her jealousy. She didn't want a man, she wanted adventure. And adventure was what she was sitting right in the middle of.

"As a matter of fact, I would be very interested in a legitimate business deal," Hal told his two-timing friends.

Grampa made a tent with his fingers and tapped the tips together with staccato rapidity. "We are doing this only as a favor to my grandson. He has come up, I believe, with some technology that could earn decent profits for an honest man."

"Who you callin' an honest man?" rasped Drop Dead.

"No need to take offense." Cha Cha reached out as if to pat the gargoyle's gnarled hand, but apparently thought better of it.

"We are all, as you know, Hal, virtually retired anyway. It is merely a matter of raising capital to give the lad a start in life," said the Swamp Fox.

He, Melanie recalled, had earned that nickname after he successfully set an arson fire in the middle of a flood. He was absolved in court after the jury learned that he had been hired by a group of little old ladies to torch a strip joint. The fact that the strip joint had failed to pay its protection money was excluded from evidence by the judge, who later retired to the Bahamas.

"So." Grampa quirked one eyebrow at his grandson. "Show us what you have."

Eagerly, the young man opened the portfolio and removed several drawings. After clipping these to an easel set up in the corner, he plucked the metallic dog from its shopping bag and set it on the scuffed floor.

Melanie had to wiggle around to see the drawings. In the one on the left, stick figures were scrubbing and sweeping inside a tube. The sketch on the right showed futuristic cars veering along a maze of overpasses while their drivers read the newspaper and dined on lobster.

"Robots!" declared the young man, his voice rising an octave on the second syllable. "They're going to revolutionize our lives!"

A sharp yip cut him off. Chet frowned down at his mechanical dog, which responded by sinking its metallic teeth into his trousers leg.

With a grimace, he reached down and switched it off. "A security device," he said. "It's just a toy, really. To build something more sophisticated, I'll need money."

"You were talking robots?" prompted his grandfather.

"The wave of the future!" With a flourish, Chet pointed to the first sketch. "Miniaturized robots will enter our bloodstreams and do everything from battle germs to repair our genes. And look at these robotic cars—they drive themselves!"

Remembering her job, Melanie took notes. *Little bloodsuckers.* She glanced at the sketch of the motorists. *Drivers reading and eating—what else is new?*

"Is someone not already testing a prototype for robotic cars?" asked Hal.

"Yeah, but they require a special roadway setup that's prohibitively expensive," Chet said. "I think we can make something practical for the roads that already exist."

"Getaway cars that drive themselves." Grampa brightened. "Who would have thought of that?"

"But curin' the sick?" scoffed Bone Crusher. "What's that gonna do to our reputation? Already we gotta worry about the Russians and the Japanese makin' us look like wimps."

"Maybe they could fight fat," suggested Cha Cha. "There's a lot of money in fighting fat. I happen to know that Mrs. Noreen Pushkoshky spends fifty thousand dollars a year fighting fat, and where she leads, every dame in Beverly Hills follows."

Melanie remembered seeing the name N. Pushkoshky on the list of charitable souls taking Rita's Rescue the Whales cruise. The widow of restaurateur Vladimir Pushkoshky was indeed wealthy enough to have her arteries scraped by robots if she wanted to.

"Robots schmobots," said Drop Dead. "It's a dumb idea."

"Robots can go into fires and rescue people!" Chet's enthusiasm overrode his natural timidity. "They can handle toxic substances! Help parents keep an eye on their kids!"

"Picture this." The Swamp Fox leaned across the table. "We get a contract to operate private prisons. Then we use the cons to make robots, okay? Only like we use some kind of mind-control ray so the robots absorb everything the crooks know about how to break into bank vaults!"

"Mind-control ray?" Chester Orion III gaped at him. "This isn't science fiction! I'm talking about a real business venture here!"

"The kid has good ideas." Hal sat back in his chair. "Count me in."

Silence descended upon the room. It was broken a minute later by Grampa, who thumped his fist on the table and shouted, "I knew it!"

"Knew what?" asked Hal.

"That you would try to muscle in! Take over the racket!" roared the king of the crime family, his oversize nose turning even redder than usual. "Who put this kid through college? Who gave him his genes? Anything he invents, it's mine!"

Chester Orion III snatched the two drawings from the easel and stuffed them into his portfolio. "No, Grampa," he said with more starch than he'd probably ever shown before in his life. "It's mine."

With that, he turned and stomped out of the room. The reverberations must have activated the mechanical dog, because it yipped and scurried after him.

Hal gave a long, lazy stretch. "Well, Grampa," he said, "it appears we may be bidding for the same project. What say we join forces?"

Unwilling admiration flickered in the old man's face. "You always was a tough customer," he conceded. "You talk my grandson into coming back to the conference table tonight, and we'll see."

"Consider it done," said Hal. "Now, is anybody else hungry?"

Grumbling and muttering among themselves, the other gangsters agreed that maybe they were and maybe they weren't. Then they all got up and rushed toward the dining room.

Left alone with Hal, Melanie closed her notebook. Before she could tuck it into her purse, however, he lifted it neatly from her hands, ripped out the scribbled-on pages and shredded them into the wastebasket.

"Hey!" she protested.

"A wise guy leaves no paper trail." After returning the notebook, Hal took her elbow and assisted Melanie to her feet.

"You really are interested in a legitimate business op-

portunity, aren't you?" she asked as he towed her toward
the door. "Why not just come out and say so?"

"Because they would not respect such a man," said
Hal.

"And that matters to you because Grampa is your substitute father?" she said. "Aren't you a little old to be
trying to win his approval?"

"'Honor thy father and thy mother,'" he said. "There
is no cutoff age for the Ten Commandments."

He sounded sad, and she remembered that both of his
real parents were dead. She had never imagined that a
thing like that would matter to a criminal.

Melanie hurried alongside as he paced through the
bleak courtyard toward the dining room. Although her
watch indicated that it was after 6:00 a.m., only a weak
amberish light sneaked past the gathering clouds that
showed through a break in the fog. "What about 'Thou
shalt not steal'? Not to mention 'Thou shalt not kill'?"

A sharp wind whipped away his answer. She caught
something about "a matter of interpretation."

Despite an itch to argue further, Melanie held her
tongue. After all, she herself had not spent a great deal of
time honoring her father, except in absentia.

It had been half a dozen years since she'd seen Dad.
Wendy wrote that he was enjoying retirement and even
dating occasionally, and that he spent every Sunday afternoon playing with her kids.

Melanie couldn't picture her drawn, weary father playing with anyone. Or dating. Or holding her the way Hal
had done when she awoke from her nightmare.

Why had this gangster shown such tenderness toward
her, anyway? Her skin tingled with the memory of how
it felt to be held against Hal's hard body. Even now, in-
haling his musky tang gave her a tipsy sensation.

She hadn't expected him to be so quick-witted, either. He always seemed to be one step ahead of the other men, but never arrogant. One step ahead of her, too; he'd caught her off guard when he'd confiscated her notes.

When they entered the dining room, a new and far less pleasant odor slapped her brain. It made her wonder how half a dozen gangsters, not to mention the family from the shuffleboard court, could sit around looking as if they planned to eat something.

At least someone had attempted to spruce up the room with wallpaper, but Melanie wished they'd chosen something other than gray and black stripes on a mustard background. Neither did she care for the black pull-down blinds hanging crookedly on the casement windows.

"What *is* that smell?" she asked.

"Prison food." Hal eyed the trencher-style tables and the backless benches. "Where would you like to sit?"

"At a McDonald's," said Melanie. "Or we could send out for Chinese. Know anyplace that delivers by helicopter?"

Nearby, a couple of gangsters glanced up. No longer restrained by the formalities of a summit, Cha Cha called, "Honey, the best seat around here is on my lap!"

"I saw the dame first!" growled Drop Dead.

In the corner, a solitary Chet Orion gave a halfhearted wave. Before they could respond, a waiter in a black-and-white jumpsuit shuffled through a swinging door and plopped a couple of trays on the tables. The food looked and smelled like week-old leftovers doused with ketchup.

Chet turned green. Grampa pulled out an embroidered handkerchief and covered his nose.

"Where's the kitchen?" Melanie demanded. "Never mind. I can see for myself." Ignoring the puzzled stares of the other diners, she headed for the swinging door.

Trust men to sit back and eat swill. If there was one thing she knew, it was how to cook guerrilla-style. And since Casa Falsario came as close to a war zone as anything she'd experienced, she intended to fix breakfast herself.

HAL ARRIVED in the kitchen in time to see a pair of tattoo-laden ex-cons staring in disbelief at the shapely figure of Melanie Mulcahy. A long column of ash dropped from one man's cigarette into the stew, or hash, or whatever he was cooking.

"Got a clean pan?" she asked.

Both close-cropped heads shook no. Shouldering past the cooks, Melanie rummaged through the cabinets and came up with a crud-encrusted cast-iron skillet. "Wash this," she ordered.

Reluctantly, one of the men complied, grimacing as he scrubbed. "It's a cryin' shame to waste all this good grease."

"There's plenty more where that came from," said Melanie. "Where are the eggs? Got any onions? How about cheese?"

The other ex-con thrust out a hunk of bluish-gray cheddar through which peeped a few patches of orange. He grinned as if expecting her to withdraw in a fit of squeamishness, but Melanie grasped the cheese, rinsed off a cutting board and began hacking away.

"You can trim this stuff and the cheese is fine," she advised Hal and the welter of diners who crowded in to watch. "With peanut butter, you have to throw the whole jar away, because peanut mold causes cancer."

The gangsters shuddered.

In no time, Melanie sautéed the onions, cracked a couple dozen eggs and whipped up a giant omelette. "This

works better with ostrich eggs," she advised. "They're
big enough to feed an army. Wild-bird eggs are the hardest because they're so small. But you have to make do
with what you've got."

Everyone looked impressed.

Hal had never met a woman like this before. Melanie
had no fear, and she wasn't putting on airs, either. Unlike
most of the dames he knew, she actually seemed to live
inside her body.

Against the drab, steely kitchen, she made a splash of
color as she whisked about in her red beret. Her conti-
nental insouciance went oddly with her sometimes coltish
movements, yet he was rapidly becoming convinced that
tall thin women with short brown hair were the loveliest
creatures on earth.

Soon the diners were filing back into the main room,
each carrying a plate of eggs. Melanie herself didn't depart until she had inventoried the kitchen and given the
ex-cons directions on what to prepare for dinner.

"You mean, eat them oranges?" one cook sputtered.
"I thought they was for decoration."

The other shook his head. "I never heard of nobody
draining no fat."

"Live and learn." Handing a plate to Hal, Melanie
marched through the swinging door with her own omelette.

Hal couldn't take his eyes off her. He was grateful
when Chet finished eating and departed, so the two of
them could sit alone.

He didn't want to share Melanie's company with anyone else. This was odd, because most dames aroused in
him an urge to socialize with as many people as possible.
It was hard to recall a single moment that he and Rita had

spent in private, aside from the one in which she requested that he get rid of Melanie.

"So," he said as they ate, "you have a certain familiarity with kitchens?"

"They inspire some of my best poems," she said.

"Care to recite one?"

Her mouth, however, was filled with eggs, and she waved off the question. Hal did not mind. He almost thought, at this moment when he was staring at Melanie, that he might compose poetry himself.

Your hat is red
Your eyes is green.
Youse the prettiest dame
I ever seen.

He was definitely not going to recite *that* in front of Grampa Orion's gang. It was bad enough they were eyeing him and Melanie speculatively; he could feel the Swamp Fox's smirk.

The chump must be wondering what Hal planned to do about Rita. The truth was, he had no idea.

To distract himself, Hal said, "Is this the most unusual place in which you have cooked?"

"Not by a long shot," said Melanie.

"What is?"

"Peru," she said. "In the middle of a hostage situation on a chicken farm. The rebel leader caught me hiding in one of the coops."

"Why were you there?" Hal asked.

"A person has to be very aggressive in the pursuit of poetry," Melanie replied. "It is fortunate I could cook or I might have become a hostage myself."

"I do not believe I have heard of Peruvian rebels taking hostages on a chicken farm," he admitted.

"The hostages sneaked out while we were eating dinner." A small sigh issued from her well-defined lips. "It was not the kind of situation that makes the front pages. The back pages, maybe."

Since they had finished their food, Hal repeated his offer to buy whatever she needed at the gift shop. Melanie considered briefly. "I would like a toothbrush."

"As many as you need."

"One will do," she said. "As long as it's red."

When they left their table, half a dozen pairs of eyes followed them. More than that, if you counted the McAllisters, who broke off debating the fine points of cheating at shuffleboard.

"She looks like a model," said young Alice McAllister with a sigh, watching Melanie.

"The way men stare at her," said her mother-in-law, "she would make a terrific decoy at a senior citizens' convention. What do you think, Joe?"

Hal didn't hear the answer. He didn't want to hear it. Although he subscribed to the principle that thieves should confine themselves to ripping off their own kind, he did not think of the elderly as fair game for anyone.

As far as he was concerned, the McAllisters should retire. However, it was not his place to give advice to other members of the underworld.

The gift shop lay adjacent to the dining room. From the courtyard, a small display window was visible through metal bars, but it was empty. Hal knew that cigarettes and cigars were vended one at a time, prison-style, and he could only hope the toothbrushes were not pre-honed to a knifepoint.

Inside, a wrinkled granny sat on a stool, crocheting a

scarf at least two stories long. This was Pixie LaBelle, who doubled as the cleaning lady.

Before organizing crooked beauty contests, she was reputed to have run a bawdy house in San Francisco. That must have been a very long time ago, Hal reflected, and yet Pixie still had a mischievous way of sizing up a man that implied she hadn't entirely lost her touch.

"Help you?" she croaked.

"Toothbrush?" asked Melanie. "Red, please."

The elderly woman surveyed the dusty shelves. Although the merchandise was enclosed in plain brown cartons that appeared indistinguishable to Hal, she quickly found the item requested.

"You'll be wanting this, too." Pixie handed Melanie a plastic-shrouded green dress that might have been spun by a spider. "I can tell it will fit, dearie."

Fine, stretchy mesh was punctuated by a few strategic patches resembling miniature doilies. Hal's throat went dry as he pictured it clinging to Melanie's curves.

"I never wear dresses," she said.

"It's been here for years," explained the older woman. "Waiting for you. Hal will be happy to pay for it."

"Of course," he said.

"Well—thanks." Melanie frowned at the dress as she took the hanger. "I guess I'll find some use for it."

She could wear it tonight, Hal mused as he paid. It would throw the other gangsters off their guard. He refused to contemplate what it might do to him. "Ready to get some rest?"

"Seems like I just did that." Melanie rubbed lightly at her beret. "But my head's hurting again. And I *am* kind of tired."

As they strolled back to their room through nippy, moisture-laced air, Hal realized that he enjoyed taking a walk with Melanie. He enjoyed the sound of her voice, and the sound of her silence, too.

He had never especially liked any of his wives; he had always looked on marriage as a mutual-aid package. But the inescapable truth was that he did like Melanie.

He wondered what it meant.

IT MUST HAVE BEEN her injury that made Melanie feel so light-headed. Or perhaps it was the stormy weather and the sense of isolation. Adventures usually happened under circumstances like these, and she was ready for one.

In addition to feeling as if her feet might leave the ground at any time, she found herself enveloped in warmth. The way Hal had looked at her back there in the gift shop had set her pulse racing.

She could tell he'd been picturing her in the dress. The realization that he wanted to see her in a revealing costume was the main reason she'd accepted it.

Not that she necessarily intended to wear the garment. Men were always ogling Melanie, and mostly she found them annoying. So far, she hadn't found Hal annoying, though.

He treated her like a lady. Not a sex object, not an acquisition, and not an intruder, either. Men who weren't fawning over Melanie were usually pitching her out of places where she wanted to snoop. Thank goodness Hal hadn't done that yet, but then, he didn't know she was a reporter.

With a yawn, she leaned against his firm shoulder. Somehow, she knew it would be in exactly the right place to connect with her head.

When he scooped her into his arms and carried her to their suite, she nestled against him contentedly. Of course, she was going to get revenge on him for being Rita's henchman. She would punish him by…by…well, somehow or other.

If she could only keep her eyes open long enough.

HAL DREAMED of swimming in a warm ocean, through an undersea castle that resembled one of Vegas's more ornate casinos. Here and there he caught a flash of silver tail or a glimpse of flowing light brown hair, and realized it was a mermaid.

From nowhere, she shimmered toward him, and slid against him with a fluid curling motion. He wrapped her in his arms and pressed his face against her hair, which smelled of herbal shampoo.

In some portion of his brain, he remembered that people lost their sense of smell while asleep. Therefore, this could not be a dream. Therefore, he had better wake all the way up before he did something he would regret.

Hal spiraled into consciousness and discovered that he was indeed holding a woman in his arms, although the hair was short and she had no tail. He also found that he was fully equipped for all the acts of which men are capable, and particularly for one act which would be difficult with a mermaid but not at all difficult with Melanie Mulcahy.

Primal instincts, no doubt dating back to the aeons when his ancestors really had prowled the seas, vied for supremacy. Against the accumulated urges of millennia, what chance did the thin veneer of civilization have?

Even as Hal reminded himself that Melanie was under his protection, his hips began to shift rhythmically against her derriere. His arms tightened around her and he nibbled at her neck.

She responded by stretching like a cat. He traced his

open palms along the front of Melanie's body and felt her nipples harden beneath the circular pressure. As a low moan escaped her, he shifted her tighter against him.

His entire midsection swelled with primitive need, and yet he could not, would not hurry this joining. Never before had the act of lovemaking and procreation flowed so naturally for Hal.

Always before, there had been distinct, almost disconnected phases: the courtship, in which champagne, chocolates and jewelry played a large role; the preliminaries, somewhat awkward until nature took over; the stimulation and release of climax; and then afterward, the hope that, this time, his wife had forgotten to take her birth control pills.

Birth. Control. The two words rang unpleasantly in his mind.

How could he have forgotten that unprotected sex led to children? Which he wanted, but did Melanie? And if his ex-wives had squeezed him virtually juiceless even without issue, how much more thoroughly could a wife take him to the cleaners if there were a little junior in the picture?

Hal's mind formed an image of Rita Samovar, raccoon-circle makeup, raven-dark hair and all. It was not a stimulating sight, but a reassuring one, nonetheless.

He had refrained from making a complete check of Rita's financial assets, as this would not be a gentlemanly thing to do, but he had obtained a credit report. This showed that his intended wife made large purchases and paid for them promptly, supporting her contention that her inheritances had left her well fixed.

Melanie, on the other hand, drove a car so beat up it was difficult to tell where the dents ended and the surface began. Melanie wrote poetry, a notoriously ill-paid profession. Melanie was beautiful and smart and fresh and bold, and she was the last woman on earth Hal would want to have to remove from the world of the living if she stiffed him.

He must adhere to his original plan. He must choose a wife who would not need to skewer him with that most despicable of weapons, a divorce attorney. He must allow Melanie to go on living and breathing and driving her dented car, because he could not bear the prospect of doing otherwise.

A kind of deathlike numbness settled over Hal. It felt as if he were coated with Teflon, and he could no longer touch or be touched by anyone.

The drumming of rain on the roof came as a welcome counterpoint to his gloom. Nor did he mind when someone tapped at the door and the voice of young Chester Orion called, "Excuse me, Mr. Smothers? Could I talk to you?"

MELANIE FINALLY understood all the hoopla about the tango. Now she knew why it had been the subject of numerous foreign movies, several championship ice-skating routines and an entire Julio Iglesias CD.

The sensual rhythm set her spirit aflame. The heat of a man's body percolated into hers, although oddly he seemed to be behind her, which must be some new variation. The voluptuousness of the dance ripened her breasts until they felt ready for harvest. Ah, the tango.

Beneath its spell, she was even willing to disregard experience, which had taught her that surrender was indeed synonymous with defeat. But surely that would not be true this time, not when she was dancing with Hal.

Then she woke up. Into cool air and a suddenly empty

bed. Rain pummeled the roof, and Hal, wrapped in a white robe, was opening the door to Chet Orion.

Melanie felt her cheeks flush with embarrassment. Of course, Hal probably didn't realize he'd had any effect on her. But *she* knew that she'd allowed herself a terrible moment of weakness.

Life had taught her that she could rely on no one but herself. What if she got pregnant, and Hal left her? What if she ended up in a dusty shack in the desert like the one where she'd spent her childhood?

Worse, what if Hal took over her life and treated her like a cosseted pet? If she could yield to one moment of weakness, might she not be tempted to accept a lifetime of captivity?

During her junior year in high school, Melanie had answered an ad for a local beauty pageant with a fifty-dollar first prize. The couple sponsoring it were promoters looking for girls to appear in corporate-training videos and cable-TV commercials.

Melanie, wearing a homemade prom dress, had marched with a handful of other entrants across the bleak stage of the local men's-club auditorium, and she'd won. The couple offered to take her to Los Angeles, train her and pay her well.

One of Melanie's teachers made some phone calls and reported that these people appeared to be legitimate. They could give her a start on a modeling, and possibly, an acting career.

She didn't want to model. She certainly didn't want to act. But the lure of earning money and getting away from Empire Lake at the age of seventeen had clouded her better judgment.

Melanie could still see her father's creased, weathered face as he spoke to her that evening. "Honey," he'd said, "you're a good student. Your teachers say you can get a scholarship. Hang in there one more year and go to college."

Maybe it was because he'd called her "honey" for the first time in memory. Maybe it was because her father believed in her. Somehow, Melanie had found the strength to refuse the modeling contract, and she'd never looked back.

Now, however, she felt the tug of temptation when it came to Hal. Not that she wanted to give up journalism, even if she did sometimes have to do temp work to make ends meet.

She didn't want to be a gangster's tootsie, either. Yet there were moments when Hal presented a tenderness that was almost irresistible.

What if they made love, and he asked her to come home with him? Wouldn't it be lovely not to have to keep moving her credit-card balance around to get the best rate and not to have to eat noodle soup three days ruming?

He hadn't offered her a cozy love nest, but he might. Before he did, Melanie needed to shore up her resolve.

She didn't have time for self-indulgence or for romance, either, she told herself firmly. What she wanted was to get the goods on Rita, and, if Hal was involved in the heists, on him, too. Then she could earn her own money and spoil herself with no help from him.

She sat up in the crisp air and saw young Chester's eyes fly to her camisole. He turned scarlet and averted his face. "Uh, Mr. Iceman," he said, "I need your advice."

"We will adjourn to the living room." Hal stepped from the room.

"Count me in!" Throwing back the covers, Melanie hopped out, grabbed her black jacket and followed.

HAL WISHED that Melanie would get dressed. Her skimpily clad presence was distracting young Chet, not to mention the effect it was having on Hal.

Then he remembered that her only choice of clothing lay between a sweater over leggings, scarcely more modest than what she wore now, and a clingy green confection woven by spiders. He had a feeling that would be even worse.

"I think I should go home, don't you?" asked Chet.

"Unless home is somewhere on this island, no," said Hal.

The young man wiggled uncomfortably. "The truth is, I don't have a home. My parents are dead and I was planning to live at Grampa's Emporium, but I guess that's not going to work out."

"I do not think you should write off your grandfather so quickly." Hal wished he had a masculine relative who would dote on him as Grampa Orion doted on Chet. It hardly seemed fair that, by a mere accident of genetics, the boy should fall heir to love that Hal had failed to win in so many years of trying.

He had believed, during the outpouring of good fellowship following his mother's death, that Grampa saw him as a son. The first time he was given a murder contract, by "Uncle" Drop Dead, it had seemed like more of an initiation rite than a cold business deal.

Gradually, however, Hal had discovered that he occupied an uneasy position with Grampa's gang. Maybe he was a little too smart. Or a little too efficient at getting rid of his targets.

The men gave him contracts, encouraged him to buy a small casino and applauded as he built it into a large hotel. They still invited him to Thanksgiving dinner. But he felt as if he were always proving himself.

Until this trip, Hal had believed that the gangsters simply were not sure how to classify him, because of his independence and the fact that he never revealed the details of his business dealings. Now he was beginning to realize that they feared and mistrusted him, and perhaps always would.

But it was not Chet's fault. In fact, Hal was finding that he liked the boy. It was also true that he had promised to bring the youth back to the conference room tonight, and that he did not wish to fail Grampa, whom he still regarded with great affection.

"Robotics is my life," Chet went on, carefully averting his gaze from where Melanie sat on the sofa with her long legs crossed. "It has great commercial possibilities. Why does Grampa keep trying to turn everything into a racket?"

"When a man grows old," Hal said, "he longs for the glories of his youth. Your grandfather yearns for the golden years of Prohibition, when gangsters ruled and reputations were made."

"But you're not like he is, Mr. Smothers," Chet said. "We should work together. With your investment capital and my know-how, we could make a fortune. If Grampa would help me, that would be fine, but I don't think it's going to happen. So I'm asking you to be my partner."

"Me?" It surprised Hal that the young man would single him out for such an invitation. Had Chet guessed that the Ice Palace Resort was merely a front for a legitimate computer-programming operation? How could he have divined such a thing, when Hal had worked so long and hard to hide it? "I am as much a gangster as the rest of them."

"Maybe more so," added Melanie. "Certainly he's never been accused of being overly *charitable*." She seemed to be hinting at something, but Hal could not figure out what it might be.

Chet's shoulders slumped. With his hands clasped between his knees, he formed the picture of misery. "I won't build getaway cars. And I can't work with people who believe in mind-control rays. I need someone who knows what he's doing, like you."

Hal agreed that robots might revolutionize society and could reap a huge profit. But if he stole young Chet away, he would break Grampa's heart. The man had shown Hal kindness, and he would not repay it with treachery.

"It may be possible to make your grandfather see the light," he said. "Many gangsters also operate legitimate businesses."

"Name three," said Melanie.

Hal eyed her suspiciously. The shrinking of her lump appeared to be having a deleterious effect on her personality. Perhaps Rita had been right about her, after all.

In any case, he believed one example would suffice. "I myself have dabbled in the computer field from time to time. Although I would not wish the fact publicized."

"Why not?" Chet asked.

"Yes, why not?" Melanie leaned forward.

"It is a matter of loyalty," Hal said. "I would not wish to embarrass my friends."

"You mean they'd be embarrassed to know someone honest?" asked the lady with the piercing olive eyes. "Never mind. No one can accuse you of being that."

Hal was about to protest that he had never been dishonest with *her,* until he remembered that he had in fact abducted Melanie under false pretenses. "What we must do," he said instead, "is to develop a strategy for this evening's conference. A way to make investing in a straightforward business palatable to Grampa."

"You think you can turn people with nicknames like Drop Dead and Bone Crusher into legitimate businessmen?" asked Melanie.

"If anyone can do it, it would be someone called the Iceman," replied Chet, perking up.

Power surged through Hal as he took control of the situation. "I am willing to set myself up as the bad guy. To give the impression that I attempted to steal you away, but that you would prefer to work with your grandfather."

"You don't even want a piece of the action?" Melanie asked in surprise.

Hal sighed. This could be a very large action. Bill Gates, too, had started with nothing but good ideas and a quick mind. What if robots proved as big a hit as personal computers?

"Naturally, I would like some share of the investment," he said. "But not if it requires alienating Chet from his grandfather."

Melanie's lips clamped together. He could have sworn she looked touched.

"I don't like making you out to be the heavy, but if you think that's a good plan, I guess it's okay." Chet's face scrunched, which had the effect of making his ears stick out more than usual. "I owe Grampa a lot. But I'm not letting any of those thugs muscle in. They don't know squat about running a business."

"Once you secure your funding, you can hire a chief financial officer," Hal advised. "I may have one or two recommendations, but we will leave the details for later."

"What if Grampa doesn't go for it?" Chet asked. "What if his pals get ugly?"

Hal doubted that Drop Dead could get any uglier. But he gathered the young man was referring to behavior, not appearance.

"Well," he began.

Melanie stretched sleepily, which gave momentary prominence to her lovely breasts. Despite his determination to keep his mind on the subject at hand, Hal couldn't help being reminded that she was nearly naked beneath the camisole. As for Chet, his eyes bugged out.

"There," she said.

"There what?" Hal wondered if she had said something profound while shifting her body. If so, he had missed it.

"You see what men are like," Melanie replied. "If I wear that teeny-weeny green dress to the conference and things start to turn nasty, I'll just kind of flash myself around. Not very feminist, but effective."

"Underhanded," Hal said admiringly.

"You'd do that for me?" asked Chet. "But won't you get cold?"

"Good point!" Melanie smiled. "Besides, it'll be even more effective if I'm wearing a coat and I snap it open at a crucial moment. Either of you fellows got one I could borrow?"

Hal and Chet nearly tripped over each other in their race to their closets. It was gratifying when Melanie selected Hal's full-length trench coat. It looked a lot better on her than it ever had on him.

Grimly, he forced his attention elsewhere. He would need all his wits about him tonight.

It was possible that, in saving Chet's relationship with Grampa, Hal would permanently antagonize the man he had struggled all his adult life to please. The fact that it would reinforce his own reputation as a shark proved little consolation.

It was only as they were leaving the suite that he wondered why Melanie had decided to help him. Maybe, he thought, she wasn't quite as bad as Rita had painted her, after all.

MELANIE SCARCELY noticed the chill evening air or the downpour on the way to the dining room. Snuggled inside the coat, with Chet holding an umbrella over her and Hal, she felt only a refreshing bit of spray on her face.

As directed, the cooks had prepared a meal of crisp bacon, boiled potatoes seasoned with parsley and butter, and orange-and-carrot salad. Melanie made a point of sending her compliments to the chef, but other than that, her mind was in such a whirl she could hardly concentrate.

Why would Hal "the Iceman" Smothers put himself on the line as a favor to Chet? Was there some nefarious motive behind his decision to forgo potential profits?

She knew him to be a ruthless murderer and a vile henchman of Rita Samovar's. At least, he had some connection to the woman, according to what Bone Crusher had said last night…or was that this morning?

Gangster upside-down time, and the opaqueness of Hal's motivations, were rendering her less than sharp-witted. As she finished her meal, Melanie wished she could sink back into that dream about the tango.

A gust of wind hit the side of the building and set the dishes rattling with a shock so strong it felt like an earthquake. The Swamp Fox and Cha Cha, she noticed, both ducked under their table, then pretended to be searching for dropped napkins.

Hal slipped one arm around Melanie. In the dampness, his thick brown hair had become unruly, and his heavy tweed jacket smelled like Earl Grey tea. He reminded her of a nineteenth-century English adventurer, the kind she'd always wanted to drag into bed.

"Are you all right?" he asked. "That was quite a jolt."

"It startled me," Melanie admitted, allowing herself to be snuggled. "I don't suppose they get hurricanes around here, do they?"

"The water's too cold," Chet informed her.

"They just get storms from Alaska," Hal said.

"You could have fooled me." But Melanie didn't mind the prospect of a deluge. When she lived in the desert, the occasional flash flood was the only excitement they ever got. Storms like this invoked a painfully pleasant nostalgia.

Grampa kept eyeing Chet and Hal. That old man didn't trust anyone, Melanie reflected. He would have made a good reporter.

Finally he stood up, and the other gangsters followed suit. "Here we go," said Hal. "Show time."

Melanie pulled the coat tighter as she imagined what it would be like to show off her skimpy green dress to a half-dozen leering men. Although a seasoned observer of other people's actions, she'd never deliberately made a spectacle of herself before.

Well, she would only do it if the talks broke down. For all their sakes, she hoped that wouldn't happen.

GRAMPA WAS NOT TAKING this well.

When Hal revealed that he had offered to go into business with Chet, the old man glowered and a hush fell over the room. The only sounds were the pounding of rain and the rasp of Drop Dead breathing through his nose.

"But I, uh, wanted to talk to you first," Chet said. "About raising some, uh, venture capital."

Grampa's face got so red, Melanie feared he might suffer a heart attack. "You think I do not see through you two louses?" he roared. "You are in cahoots!"

"No, Grampa," Chet protested, but not very forcefully.

"A blind man could see it," snarled Drop Dead.

Bone Crusher nodded grimly, his stiletto mustache wiggling at the ends as if eager to stab someone. "Your own flesh and blood has turned on you, Grampa. The little weasel is tryin' to squeeze you for dough, and then he and the Iceman is gonna steal the profits."

Hal wore a hooded expression, like a hawk. To Melanie, he had never appeared more dangerous, or more desirable. "Are you accusing me of something, Mr. Nichols?"

Before Bone Crusher could reply, Cha Cha spread his hands placatingly. "Nobody's accusing anybody. The men are just counseling Grampa to be cautious. After all, we did see the two of you talking at dinner."

"Thick as thieves," growled Drop Dead.

"I object!" said Chet.

"This is not a trial," muttered the Swamp Fox.

"Well, it feels like one!" The young man, who had remained standing when the others took their seats, began to sway angrily. "I love my grandfather and I wouldn't cheat him! I resent anybody saying that I would!"

"Big talk," grumbled Drop Dead.

"You gotta admit, you have been awful palsy with the Iceman," said Grampa. "But I will give you another chance. Let us say you and I go into this robot business."

"Okay." The swaying stopped.

"Of course I gotta bring in my buddies for a piece of the action," Grampa said.

"Like, just for investment purposes?" asked Chet.

"Do we look like bankers to youse?" Drop Dead had stuck his glasses atop his beaked nose, but he was right, Melanie thought. He still didn't look like a banker; he looked like a gargoyle wearing specs.

"My friends are my family." Grampa gestured expansively. "We do everything together."

"You wanna work for us, you better accept the situation, and quick," added Bone Crusher.

"I'm not working for anyone," Chet said. "I'm talking about an equal partnership."

"Equal to who?" sneered Drop Dead.

"Yes, kid, we do not see you putting up money," said the Swamp Fox.

"I'm the brains of this operation," said Chet with more spunk than Melanie would have given him credit for. "If my grandfather wants to be my partner, that's fine. Otherwise, I'm going in with the Iceman!"

Grampa gritted his teeth so hard Melanie feared he might have emergency need of a dentist. Finally he said, very stiffly, "You reject my terms? To hell with you, you ungrateful pup!"

Tears glistened in Chet's eyes but he stood his ground. "The same to you, Grampa!"

Bone Crusher sprang to his feet and whipped a pistol from his belt. "Nobody talks that way to Grampa!"

Around the table, men reached into their jackets. Even Hal made a subtle move toward a pocket.

"*Now!*" cried a little voice inside Melanie. She didn't dare give herself time to think. Instead, she jumped onto the table and yanked open her trench coat.

"Hey, fellas!" she said. "Let's not fight about this! Let's party!"

Everyone stared at her as if she'd just grown reindeer antlers. Melanie had never been so humiliated in her life.

She was almost grateful when lightning turned the world white and then, with a shrieking crunch like a ship knocking over a lighthouse, a tree fell on the conference room.

6

PANDEMONIUM REIGNED. Melanie gathered that the roof had collapsed, but at first she attributed its failure solely to the accumulation of water now drenching her.

Then a thick, shaggy trunk crunched down, knocking off Drop Dead's glasses with a swish of palm fronds as it fell across the length of the table. "I can't see!" roared the gangster.

No one paid attention to him. Chet was vaulting the fallen palm tree to reach his grandfather, while the other gangsters fled like drowned rats.

Except Hal. He lifted Melanie off the crazily tilted table and began kissing her passionately. "I am glad to see you are not hurt," he said gruffly, between kisses.

Melanie could feel her soaked dress beginning to steam from the heat. With the walls groaning around them, she had the notion they ought to flee, but when Hal's tongue connected with hers, she forgot everything else.

The man overwhelmed his surroundings, and her senses. Earl Grey tea and gangster cologne were a heady mix, she reflected as she wound her arms around him.

It was a relief to finally have the freedom to touch that thick hair of his, and rub her cheek against the slight roughness of his jaw. Under such circumstances, a natural disaster became irrelevant.

Someone bumped into her. "Get me outta here!" roared Drop Dead.

Reluctantly, Hal released Melanie. "Just a moment, Mr. Cimarosa. I will find your specs."

Despite the imminent danger of the walls collapsing, Hal searched the floor until he found the glasses. The nosepiece had been severed, but, using one half as a monocle, Drop Dead regained a measure of calm and accompanied them outside.

In the courtyard, the elderly man headed toward Grampa's room on the other side. Through the window, they could see Chet helping his grandfather dry off.

Rain was sheeting down as if the sky gods had decided to upend their buckets. Bolts of lightning jagged behind veils of mist and the sonic booms called thunder reverberated through an unseen sky.

"Fabulous." Melanie stared about her in delight. She'd never experienced such a violent storm, even in the desert. It was almost as exciting as a battlefield.

From behind, Hal's arms encircled her. A gust of wind lashed them, and she felt his hips press into her derriere. It reminded her of a dream, or had that been a dream, after all?

She swiveled against him and held up her arms. "Let's tango," she said.

HAL HAD NEVER seen anything as beautiful as Melanie Mulcahy in a tempest. Wild light sparked from her eyes and, in her clingy dress of green seaweed, she came as close to being a mermaid as he ever hoped to meet.

Another thunderclap detonated and, laughing, Melanie danced against him. It occurred to Hal that this might be dangerous, standing here like a pair of lightning rods, and then he wondered who was in greater peril, them or the lightning.

This woman loved danger; he'd seen that risk-taking

hunger in the eyes of Las Vegas stuntmen, and, in his younger days, had felt it twist in his own gut. But in Melanie, right here and now, he could see it transmuting into intense sexual desire.

As a gentleman, he ought to bundle her off to some place where temptation would not dare to intrude. Unfortunately, he could not imagine where such a place might be.

He could picture only their suite, and their room, and their bed. And as he thought of them, Melanie led him there.

They were so wet that he hardly noticed when they escaped the rain. He scarcely heard the thump of the bedroom door shutting behind them, either.

All he saw was the trench coat crumpling around Melanie's ankles, revealing the next-to-nothingness of her dress. The green mesh caressed her delicate bosom and played peekaboo with her golden skin.

Hal could have sworn he heard music, but perhaps it was only the rain lashing the roof. In any case, it set Melanie to undulating as if she were indeed performing the tango, a dance into which he himself had been inducted several times in Las Vegas.

But never like this. Those earlier times, the woman's eyes hadn't connected with his, luring him in and then deliberately breaking the connection when he came close. She certainly hadn't drawn him to the edge of a bed and whirled close enough for him to feel the softness of her breasts before she slipped from his grasp.

It was a game that reawakened the hunting instinct in Hal. He knew instantly that his tactics must be adapted to suit the prey.

Melanie could not be approached directly, or she would whisk away, her laughter floating in the air. He could not seize her, either, any more than a man could grasp a mermaid.

But Hal knew how to wait just long enough for his prey to wonder if he was ever going to stir at all, and then make a subtle move that entranced rather than frightened. Now, the loosening of his tie drew Melanie's fascinated gaze.

He pretended to fumble as he unworked the knot, and felt her palm smooth the silk cloth. When he glanced up, she withdrew quickly, then watched to see what he would do next.

He removed the tie, laid it over the back of a chair and straightened it infinitesimally, as if keeping it wrinkle-free were the sole purpose of his existence. Melanie bit her lip and remained standing half a dozen feet away.

Casually, Hal unfastened his jacket. He deliberately missed the second button.

"You skipped one," said Melanie.

"Did I?" He quirked an eyebrow as if it hardly mattered.

"There." She came closer; he could feel the warmth of her breath on his chest, through the fabric. Her attention was focused on that one button, and he could have grabbed her as she unworked it, but he didn't.

What had begun as a prelude to lovemaking could easily end instead with a painful kick in the groin if she disliked his technique. The only thing that would prevail with this woman was the belief that it was she who set the pace.

"Men are so helpless," said Melanie as she stood back to admire her handiwork.

"Thanks." He removed the jacket and placed it over the back of another chair, aligning the shoulders precisely.

After studying it for a moment, he picked off a tiny bit of lint and dropped it into the wastebasket.

"Are you always this careful?" asked his observer.

"Attention to detail pays off in larger ways," he said. "Has that not been your experience?"

"I never noticed," she said. "Is that how you, er, disposed of your—your targets?"

"By laying them over the back of a chair?"

"No, I mean, by—well, being finicky about details."

Come to think of it, she was right. "Exactly," he said. "I leave nothing to chance."

Her breathing quickened. It was the sense of danger closing in, Hal recognized. Well, she hadn't seen anything yet.

His hands went to the buckle on his belt. It was a very refined, very expensive belt, and if it ever jammed, the manufacturer would probably crawl over from Italy on his knees to apologize. Melanie, however, did not know that, and so Hal tugged it for a moment and then gave a small shrug of disappointment.

"Stuck," he said.

"I could get it open," she said.

"You are welcome to try." He dropped the words into the air with what he hoped was precisely the right tone of indifference.

She edged closer, regarded him from beneath a veil of lashes and then touched the silver design at his waist. Hal remained motionless, or at least the visible portion of him remained motionless.

Melanie hesitated. He wondered what sort of man she was used to, and decided he didn't want to know.

Besides, there was no room in his brain to waste on rational thought as her fingers played around his midsection. The gentle plucking raged through his nervous system.

Hal stood firm, lordlike, keeping his face a mask. Any sign of desire might be seen as weakness, or perhaps a threat.

Melanie eased the buckle open. "There." She took a half step back.

"The zipper is stuck, too," Hal said.

One corner of her mouth winched up. "Is not."

"Do you always leave a job half done?" he asked. Still that cool tone. With Melanie, it was the only lure that might work.

"You think you intimidate me?" she asked.

He released a sigh of strained patience. "I think you are mostly bluff."

"I'm not afraid of you, Hal Smothers!" she burst out.

"Prove it."

"I could strip you right down to—"

"Brave words," he sneered. His body ached with longing, but he did not stir. A single move and his target would flee across the room.

"Watch me." Her face agleam with mischief, Melanie came closer and touched the top button on his shirt.

From beneath his nose wafted the fragrance of spring blossoms. It cleared Hal's sinuses and jolted into a long-dormant corner of his brain, which was the only part of him not already on its feet and cheering.

He wanted to take her in his arms, as a man ought to do, to caress and tease and awaken her. But this woman craved conquest, and he was more than willing to allow himself to be conquered.

Melanie slipped loose the shirt buttons, one by one. As she moved lower, Hal feared she could not help but note his arousal. Still, he held himself in check, allowing her to loosen his cuffs, pull his shirttails free and bare his torso.

As she tossed the shirt atop his jacket, Melanie eyed his bare chest appreciatively. Hal had no false modesty; he worked out daily in his private gym, and knew he was well-toned. He also knew that the bullet scar on his left shoulder did nothing to detract from his appeal.

Her finger traced the white mark. "How did you get this?"

"Does it matter?" said Hal.

"You could have been killed."

"But I was not."

"Did one of your victims—I mean..." The words trailed off.

"I suppose she considered herself a victim." It had been between his second and third marriages, when Hal wooed a French perfume heiress. He had pressed his attentions with a bit too much ardor and jarred the tiny jeweled pistol in her clutch purse, which fired.

The lady apologized profusely and even hinted that, should Hal care to renew his attentions after being released from the hospital, he might find her receptive. He, however, had been sufficiently dissuaded by the reception he had received the first time.

"Care to see another scar?" It was on his right thigh, a memento of a bicycle accident when he was twelve, but he did not intend to reveal the truth about that one, either.

"It's, uh, down there?" she asked.

"Does that bother you?"

"No!"

"Then help yourself," he said.

Melanie stared back at him, stunned and exhilarated.

"Yes!" she cried, succeeding in unfastening his pants. When she pulled them down, Hal knew he could no longer disguise his advanced state of yearning. Relying instead on distraction, he pointed to his scar. "There it is."

"That's nasty," Melanie said approvingly. She crouched, with the gossamer dress creeping up to hip height.

Hal could hardly restrain himself. Once in motion, he was known for his sheer velocity, as he had demonstrated to Melanie at the pier. However, he was not fool enough to undertake such action with his pants around his ankles and his feet encased in shoes.

"In bad weather, it still hurts," he lied shamelessly.

"It does?" She cupped her palm over the scar, which had not yielded so much as a single twinge in more than twenty years.

"It is throbbing right now," said Hal, which was more or less true, depending on how you interpreted "it."

"How awful." Melanie regarded his thigh enviously, as if wishing she too sported war wounds.

"Excuse me," he said, and stepped out of his pants, leaving his shoes behind as well. Now he was ready for action.

Melanie did not appear to realize that she had changed from huntress to hunted. "Does this help?" she asked, and her mouth closed over his scar.

Did it help? Did bottle rockets help calm the Fourth of July?

Colored fountains leaped and shimmered through Hal's brain. "Oh, lady, it sure does," he said, and, swooping down, caught her by the waist and hoisted her in one smooth motion onto the bed.

MELANIE WAS NOT SURE how she went from applying first aid to being launched into the air. She considered filing an official protest, and decided that would be not only futile but foolish.

Because, in truth, she didn't mind at all that her perceptions had just gone topsy-turvy and that Hal had vaulted from a statue into a human dynamo. Before she could even figure which way was up, she lay flat on her back with her wispy dress around her waist and the low-cut neckline pulled down, pinioning her arms and baring her breasts.

With an ease that astounded her, Hal positioned himself over her, his mouth probing down her throat to the straining peaks of her breasts, his hands roving along the insides of her thighs and gently removing her panties.

He had her completely within his control, and, to Melanie's astonishment, she loved it. It had happened so quickly that there had been no need to yield; besides, she knew she had created this situation.

It was she who had disrobed and tantalized him. Only a complete nitwit could have remained unaware of his burgeoning male need, and she was not such a hypocrite as to lead a man on and then deny him.

She wanted him. Wanted him to go right on claiming her nipples and stoking her inner fires. Wanted him to…

And then he stopped. One minute he was compressing her breasts to near ecstasy while one knee skillfully separated her legs, and then he lifted himself away.

"Hal?" she said.

He reached into a drawer in the bedside stand. "A gentleman must be prepared." Swiftly he rolled the transparent protection over himself.

"I thought being prepared was for Boy Scouts," she said.

"They should not need to be prepared in this manner unless, like me, they are over twenty-one," he responded.

Now suitably attired, he proceeded to enter her without so much as a by-your-leave.

For an instant, Melanie thought they had been struck by lightning, so sheer and blinding was the pleasure that riveted her. When Hal drew himself away, she reached up to clutch those slim hips and bring him back again.

"I may be known for my speed," he said, "but there are occasions when a man does not wish to jump to conclusions."

"Mind if I do?" asked Melanie.

"Be my guest."

She arched toward him, thrilled when their mouths met, delighted when she felt his body begin to pump. They connected with a jolt in an unbroken circuit, the electricity flowing through them at white heat.

She had always believed that when it came to making love, men should be rated like ice skaters: one score for technical merit and another for artistic impression. But in Hal's case, it was impossible to distinguish technique from artistry.

The hard vigor with which he thrust into her was like the heat of battle, or, at least, the way Melanie had always imagined a battle should be.

She flamed against Hal. His tongue found her nipples; his soft hair brushed her chest. She hadn't realized she could be sensitive to so many textures at one time.

Then everything came into focus deep within, in a place that only he could reach. A place that Melanie had guarded without realizing it.

A great wonder blossomed within her, spreading to encompass her entire being. Hal must have felt it too, because his shaft intensified its driving, and his muscles tightened, and she felt his wild shudders, as if the joy was almost too sharp to bear.

He groaned and cried out, and then she realized that some of those noises were issuing from her own throat. It was impossible to tell which sounds were whose, any more than she could distinguish his elation from her own.

As he sank against her, Melanie clutched this big hunk of a man, this gangster, this marauder, and wondered how soon they could do this again.

HAL GATHERED Melanie close as cool air settled in around them. Beneath the covers, they lay safe, even as the wind whipped at the walls of their love nest.

Slowly, the afterglow of sex fused with his longing for closeness. He could no longer separate the pleasure of her company from his desire for a home.

Through the mists of deep-seated satisfaction, a discovery rose into Hal's consciousness. The realization shocked him to the depths of his complacency.

Cupid had shot him with the wrong arrow.

He loved Melanie Mulcahy, not Rita Samovar. He had never loved any woman until now, had never even imagined what real love felt like.

Birds sang and rainbows flourished and valentines throbbed on lace-wrapped boxes of chocolates. Hal felt himself sinking hopelessly into a bog of sentiment.

But he must think clearly. For one thing, they were surrounded by gangsters who did not wish him well. For another, Melanie did not strike him as the type of dame to fall into a swoon upon receiving a declaration of love.

Most of all, he did not dare to marry her. His reputation had already been tarnished by the depredations of his previous wives. Melanie, being the poorest of the lot, would also no doubt expect the most.

One more hit on his good name, and Hal would lose the respect of Grampa Orion's gang. He might even need to dispose of someone to reestablish his reputation, and that someone would be Melanie.

He could not bear it. He must make a preemptive strike to prevent such an eventuality.

A premarital arrangement might be feasible, but an unscrupulous attorney would shoot it as full of holes as the hit men had done to Bugsy Siegel. Hal racked his brain for an alternative.

"Let us make a deal," he said at last, sitting up.

With a yawn, Melanie hoisted herself beside him. The covers draped picturesquely around her bosom. "A deal?"

"You cannot deny that you felt it," he said.

She draped one forearm suggestively across his thigh. "I certainly did."

Hal was grateful that the darkness hid the color that sprang to his cheeks. He could not see himself blush, of course, but he recalled that embarrassing sensation from adolescence, and the ragging it had provoked on the part of other youngsters who were not yet acquainted with his talent for giving ice baths.

"I refer to a sensation in the coronary region," he said. "Of an emotional nature."

"Are you trying to say you're in love with me?" Melanie asked in amazement.

Hal cleared his throat. "I am fond of you."

"Well, good," she said. "Can we do that again, then?"

"As often as you like," Hal said. "Once we draw up the contract."

He had not been aware that she was moving in any way, until he noticed how still she had grown. "Contract?"

"The specifics are, of course, negotiable," he said. "An initial lump sum and annual maintenance payments, with large increments and trust funds for each child. Does that sound reasonable?''

"Are you trying to buy me?" she asked.

Suddenly rain began to pound on the roof like drumbeats. Lightning flared and thunder rolled. But inside the room, a deathly hush reigned.

"I am suggesting a traditional arrangement in which the male cares for the female who produces his children," he said.

"You forgot the fur coat." Her voice had a brittle ring.

"Any species you like," he said.

"And the sports car."

"A station wagon would be safer," Hal mused. "But that can wait until after the birth of the first child."

"I hate fur coats," said Melanie.

He knew he was in trouble. "You were not negotiating in good faith?"

"I'm not for sale," said the woman of his dreams.

Hal stared at her in dismay. "Arrangements of a financial nature are a man's responsibility to the woman he…cares for. To protect her. To reassure and comfort her."

"Do I look in need of reassurance and comforting?" growled Melanie.

Lamplight raised emerald highlights in her eyes and transmuted her skin to spun gold. Her spiky brown hair and long slim body gave her a waiflike air that, Hal knew, would make any man want to cherish her.

But most men were not as steadfast as he. Or as well able to provide for a mate.

"You are a creature of passion and fire," he said. "I would treat you like a queen."

"Which queen would that be?" she snapped. "Anne Boleyn or Marie Antoinette?"

Hal could not believe that Melanie had misunderstood him so thoroughly, or that she was reacting with such disdain. Most ladies of his acquaintance would by now be bargaining for the highest possible down payment.

Never before had he met a woman who did not wish to be kept in luxury. He sometimes suspected that he had been deliberately taken advantage of, but that was better than to abandon his principles.

His sense of honor had always required him to offer a marriage license along with the fancy accoutrements. However, it was this same sense of honor that demanded he protect Melanie from the danger she would incur if she went the same mercenary route as his previous wives.

"I apologize if I have offended you," he said. "I am simply proposing a contract that would be advantageous to us both and would safeguard the future of our children."

Melanie flung off the covers and drew herself up, which had the effect of chilling and inflaming him at the same time. "I'm not letting any gangster put out a contract on me, and I'm not having any children, either!"

She jumped out of bed and began scrounging around for her clothes. Hal had never felt so torn. He knew better than to attempt to restrain her in any way, and yet he could not allow her to leave.

He considered blustering, begging or stony silence. Firing a gunshot into the ceiling might gain her attention, but as usual he had put no bullets in his gun.

"I am certain there is some way that we can resolve this issue to our mutual satisfaction," he said.

"Sure we can!" She yanked on her underpants and reached for her leggings. "You go stuff yourself and I'll watch!"

She was magnificent when angry, Hal reflected. It was her very unpredictability that delighted him.

He swallowed hard. A lump of conflicting emotions stuck in his throat, like an elephant inside an overly ambitious snake.

He was, Hal decided, allowing himself to yield to adolescent emotions because the lady had caught him off guard. Surely this emotion that he imagined himself to be feeling was a delusion. If love existed, it would have found him long before the age of thirty-six.

Let Melanie pull her camisole into place and tug on her red-and-white-striped sweater. If she did not notice that it was inside out, why should he tell her? Let her yank on the black jacket, too, and stick her shapely feet into her boots.

Let her leave, if she chose. Why should he care? The hard lump burning inside his throat, Hal thought, was nothing that a dose of antacid and a few beta-blockers couldn't remedy.

He felt calm again. He could handle anything.

Then the earth shook.

At first, Hal thought this was some new and unwelcome side effect of being in love. Then he saw Melanie stumble and heard a chair crash to the ground.

"Earthquake!" she cried. Then, more hopefully, she asked, "Bomb?"

"I am not sure." It took Hal a moment to register that the shaking had stopped. In retrospect, he assessed that he had felt one large jolt, following by earnest trembling.

Springing to his feet, he grabbed a pullover sweater and jeans from the closet. Whatever had happened, it was too powerful to ignore.

Rounding the bed, Melanie opened the blinds and peered into the inky night. "Something's changed."

Sudden alterations that followed large bumps in the night were unlikely to be good news, Hal reflected as he donned his windbreaker. "Can you be more specific?"

"The lighthouse is gone," Melanie said. "It's a good thing Drop Dead is with Grampa or he'd be gone, too."

Crossing the room and leaning over her, Hal studied the billowing, rain-pricked fog. Indeed, the dull luminosity that had previously hinted at the boundary of the island was missing.

"It was equipped with a rod for lightning, so that cannot be the cause," he said. "It must have been the wind."

Below him, Melanie stiffened. "I don't think so." Her voice had a stunned ring to it.

"No?" said Hal.

"I think something hit it," said the woman who had just enchanted his bed and left his nerve endings in a state of advanced agitation. "Look, there are little lights out there."

"Where?" He frowned.

"Don't you see them?"

Narrowing his eyes, he made out a row of pinprick lights in a straight line near where the tower had been. They looked like windows in the ocean.

"It is a ship," Hal said in surprise.

Then he remembered which ship had been scheduled to pass offshore tonight. A modest-size cruise vessel whose row of lighted portholes would be about that size, if memory served from the last time he had sailed on it with its owner, Sammy "Cha Cha" Adams.

But right now he did not think of it as belonging to Cha Cha. Tonight it was Rita Samovar's ship.

7

MELANIE FELT infinitely cold. What ship could this be but the *Jolly Roger?*

She had hoped to stow away in its hold, and now it had come to her. Perhaps beaching it was part of Rita and Hal's plot to rob the passengers, but the possibility that she had caught them dead to rights provided no satisfaction.

Couldn't the ship have stayed at sea an hour longer? It seemed unlikely she and Hal would ever see eye to eye, but they might at least have fallen into each others' arms and enjoyed a rematch. Now that Ms. Samovar had docked, albeit in a somewhat unconventional manner, the choice was no longer Melanie's.

She told herself that it would be foolish to care about a man who transferred his affections from one object to another at the drop of a ship. She reminded herself that Rita had been there first—wherever "there" might be—and had the prior claim; but this was not, after all, a matter of waiting in line at the post office.

It did not even help to reflect that Melanie had felt a flash of prescience: when the tree fell on the conference room, she had formed a mental image of a ship hitting a lighthouse.

So what if she could finally sell a story to a tabloid? Claiming to be psychic was hardly the sort of tactic calculated to boost her reputation as a journalist.

And that's what she was, she told herself, moving from the window to throw on the overcoat. A reporter. Which meant she needed to investigate the scene of the disaster.

Hal zipped up his windbreaker. "Let us go."

"To the lighthouse?"

"You need not come, of course."

"Try and stop me!"

"Do you know first aid? There could be injured—"

"I passed my cub-level test in guerrilla warfare, okay? Let's move!" She led the way.

In the suite's living room, they encountered a bedraggled Chet, who had just come in. When Hal explained that a ship had run aground, the young man insisted on accompanying them.

"How is Grampa?" Hal demanded. "He might catch a chill."

"He and Drop Dead are playing cards in his room," Chet assured them. "They keep accusing each other of cheating. He'll be fine."

"Where are the others?" Hal shouted over a whoosh of wind as he opened the door.

"They ran for cover when they heard the crash," said the young man. "But I imagine they'll want to check out the lighthouse soon enough."

"Good," yelled the Iceman. "We will need them."

To do what? Melanie wondered as they ducked into the deluge. Plunder the ship and rob the passengers?

From the guest list, she recalled the names of Beverly Hills society matron Noreen Pushkoshky and chain-store owners Gerard and Bitsy Germaine. What chance did someone named Bitsy have against people called Bone Crusher and Drop Dead?

Melanie shuddered to think of the helpless, jewel-draped guests at the mercy of hardened bandits. There was, after all, no law enforcement on this island.

They staggered through layers of mist and blinding rain. Fortunately, the island was not large and they soon reached the point where the lighthouse had stood.

Glass and twisted steel littered the shore. From here, looming through the fog, they could see the *Jolly Roger*, tilted in an impressive if small-scale imitation of the *Titanic*.

On the lower deck, Melanie spotted a couple of crew members attempting to launch lifeboats. But the captain—if memory served, his name was Yolo Bowers—where was he?

A scream from behind them made her swivel in alarm. Atop a rise, she made out the dapper figure of Cha Cha hopping up and down and shrieking into the wind. "My ship! My ship! What have they done to my ship?"

Bone Crusher and the Swamp Fox, who flanked him, each seized one arm and urged him down the slope. Melanie could almost have felt sorry for the man if he hadn't been such a crook.

"What should we do, Mr. Smothers?" asked Chet.

"We need to get the passengers and crew to land." Hal studied the yawning wreckage. "Some of them may be trapped or injured, or in shock. How deep is the water here, do you suppose?"

The other gangsters made tepid protests about allowing noncriminals onto the island, but Drop Dead was not present to protect his domain. Also, as Hal pointed out, the only alternative would be worse: to summon the Coast Guard, which would no doubt do something as unsporting as putting Paraiso de Los Falsarios on its charts.

Despite the grumblings of the others and the hysterical cries of Cha Cha, Hal and Chet managed to determine

that the water was no more than hip deep where the ship
had stuck. Nevertheless, the waves were rough and could
be dangerous for very young or old passengers, or those
susceptible to shock.

By shouts and gestures, the two men on shore coordinated the rescue with the crew, who shepherded the passengers into the half-dozen accessible lifeboats and lowered these one at a time. Accompanying crew members
rowed the boats to the surf line.

There were about a hundred well-heeled guests, Melanie estimated, although these sodden, frightened people
didn't look well-heeled at the moment. The assorted staff,
including two who identified themselves as the chef and
a beautician, appeared almost as distraught.

Lightning jagged through the clouds, intensifying the
dying ship's air of menace. One woman screamed re-
peatedly until brought ashore and wrapped in a blanket,
and several children were crying.

Although the *Jolly Roger* might overturn at any moment and crush him, Hal waded into the water to assist
the passengers from the lifeboats. He appeared to give no
thought to his own safety as he carried a baby for its
mother.

Melanie could scarcely tear herself away from the valiant image of Hal Smothers braving the churning sea. It
gave her a fluttery sensation in her stomach.

How could she part with the most exciting man she'd
ever met? But somewhere on this ship lurked another
woman, with whom he had a prior entanglement. And the
contract he had offered Melanie was nothing short of insulting.

As the seagoers staggered ashore, she guided them up
the hill toward the dining room. This seemed like the best
place to establish a shelter.

She still didn't see Rita. Had the woman been injured? Or had she already escaped with the guests' valuables?

Grimly, Melanie focused on getting the passengers settled and, with the aid of Pixie LaBelle and the tattooed cooks, heating soup and boiling water for tea. The McAllisters rounded up blankets for the shivering shipwreckees, while the wizened limo driver, Luigi, applied Band-Aids to the wounds of the female passengers.

A second wave of guests arrived a few minutes later. Two men supported the staggering figure of a white-jacketed man in a captain's hat, while two of the women were assisting an equally rubber-legged, uniformed redhead whose name pin proclaimed her to be Helen Malatesta, M.D., the ship's doctor.

Captain Yolo Bowers had a chiseled face that looked as if it might have fallen off Mount Rushmore. With his high forehead and vein-free nose, he did not strike Melanie as the type to sail three sheets to the wind, and yet here he was, bellowing "Avast, me hearties!" and getting his feet tangled up as he tried to stand unaided.

"Drunk," sneered a short, thin man who resembled newspaper photographs Melanie had seen of the wealthy Gerard Germaine.

"Something was wrong with the wine," interjected his tall, large-boned wife, Bitsy. "Noreen Pushkoshky says she had just one glass at the captain's table, and she's in the same state."

Her husband's indignation died. "Well, if Noreen says it, it must be true."

So someone had spiked the captain's wine, Melanie mused. She could guess who had wanted him out of the way, and why.

But had crashing onto the rocks been Rita Samovar's

intention? And had Hal approved a plan that endangered so many people?

EVEN THE SWAMP FOX could not have started a fire in the middle of this storm, Hal thought as he assisted another boatload of damp cruisers to shore. He was pleased to note that key crew members remained at their posts until every passenger departed. It was a tribute to ship discipline.

Yet their captain had already been hauled up the hill, sloshed to the gills. And his first officer, a baby-faced man with an air of perpetual surprise, was being dragged to shore warbling "Row Row Row Your Boat," and forgetting the words. How could the ship's leaders have become so inebriated?

"Excuse me, are you in charge here?" asked a young woman. Since Cha Cha had retreated inland to sulk, Hal nodded. "I left my diamond necklace in the safe. Someone should bring it out before the ship sinks!"

"I hope it is insured," he said.

"Well, yes," she admitted. "But it has sentimental value. My third husband gave it to me."

Hal could understand such feelings. "I will do my best."

However, the passengers deserved priority. It took another fifteen minutes for Hal to locate the ship's purser and ask him to liberate the contents of the safe.

"I'm not going in there alone!" the man protested over the ship's ominous creaking. "I could be trapped. And if anything gets lost, people will blame me."

Standing amid the waves, with water sluicing into his face from above, Hal gazed blearily around. He had made a promise to the young lady, yet he could not leave his post to accompany the purser.

"You!" he shouted toward shore.

Two figures turned toward him, their unlovely faces barely discernible in the murk. Bone Crusher and the Swamp Fox had been keeping their distance from the teetering vessel, but had at least helped by pointing new arrivals toward the resort compound.

Under normal circumstances, Hal would be loath to entrust jewelry to either of these crooks. However, the two men were continually jockeying for Grampa's favor, and therefore unlikely to cooperate with each other, even in a profit-making endeavor. Furthermore, the presence of the purser should help to ensure propriety.

"If you gentlemen would be so kind, the purser would appreciate your help in retrieving valuables," shouted Hal.

Two scarred and pitted faces mirrored astonishment, and then shook negatively.

"Get over here!" Hal yelled. "Now!"

He knew they had nothing to fear from him. Thigh-deep in water, lashed by the storm, he had no means of restraining either of them. Furthermore, each was quite as lethal as he was; more so, in fact.

But Hal had learned long ago that a vicious reputation was a more effective weapon than any handgun, or possibly even than an AK-47, unless it was also affixed with a folding bayonet. In any case, when he put a gruff edge on the word *Now!* the two heads changed direction and nodded stiffly.

The grumpy gangsters joined him in midwater to get the details of their assignment. Then toward the ship slogged the unlikely trio, with the purser leading the way.

The passengers had all gotten off and the crew members were now disembarking. Hal directed them toward the dining room, secure in the knowledge that if anyone could feed and warm so many lost souls, it would be Melanie.

Even in the wind, rain and roiling surf, his body warmed at the memory of what had transpired between them. He did not know if what he felt was love, but it produced a most satisfactory glow.

Where had he gone wrong in making his offer? Her objections, it seemed to him, had centered on the presumed mercenary nature of the contract, and on the having of children.

When it came to financial arrangements, Hal was prepared to be flexible. But not about children.

A short time ago, when he held that baby in his arms, he had marveled at the strength of the life force in its tiny, wriggling person. A whole human being was encapsulated there, a whole lifetime of mangled phrases and good-night kisses and...

"What have we here?" demanded a clarion female voice with a fake British accent. "I do believe it's the Iceman himself! Hullo, Hal."

As Rita Samovar threw her arms around him, her oversize purse banged Hal in the hip. In her soaked mink coat, she smelled steamy and feral.

"I am glad to see that you have survived the catastrophe," he replied.

She swished backward a step and gestured dismissively with one hand. "I find it quite stimulating, really. So, have you done as I asked?"

Hal could not immediately grasp to what she was referring. He was too busy wondering, as he studied Rita's thick smudged makeup and self-satisfied expression, how he could ever have taken this woman seriously. Also, he suddenly felt certain that sending three-year-olds to boarding school was not at all customary.

"As you asked?" he repeated.

She glared at him. "About Melanie Mulcahy!"

A foreboding fell over Hal, greater than any concern regarding the ship. If Melanie were to learn that he had brought her to this island at Rita's request, any hope of resuming their closeness would be lost.

"She did not crash your voyage, did she?" he replied by way of skirting the issue.

"No."

"It was not she who disrupted your cruise?" he demanded.

"Certainly not!"

"Then you should be satisfied."

With a massive groan, the ship pitched toward them. Horrified, Hal remembered that he had sent three men inside to retrieve belongings.

Vaguely, he became aware of Rita fleeing toward shore. Then, to his tremendous relief, he saw the purser and the two gangsters waddling toward him beneath the overhang of the ship.

At any moment, the vessel might decide to get on with the job of overturning. Hal reached for the purser's hand and pulled the man to safety, with the gangsters sloshing behind.

Barely had they scrabbled onto the rocks when, with a massive rumble, the *Jolly Roger* rolled onto its side. The impact sent a miniature tsunami lashing the shore, and, from some distance inland, aroused a distraught and heart-wrenching wail from the unseen throat of Sammy "Cha Cha" Adams.

"What a shame," chirped Rita. "All those people lost their belongings."

"Not entirely." Hal turned to the purser. "Was your mission accomplished?"

"Well, we got there," came the reply between chattering teeth.

"Got where?" said Rita.

"To the safe," snapped the Swamp Fox. "Only, somebody beat us to it."

WHAT A LOT of spoiled children, Melanie reflected as she supervised the serving of soup to the passengers. She'd never heard so much whining in her life.

The soup didn't please them; neither did the hard chairs or the damp air. And, although their motive had presumably been charitable, they made sure to complain about the high cost of their tickets.

Well, she thought grimly, tonight there would be no cabin service, no chocolates on their pillows and no midnight buffet with pastry puffs and fruit tarts. They should be grateful for dry land, threadbare blankets and Pixie's two-story crocheted scarf, which a family of four had wound around themselves.

The passengers finally piped down as exhaustion and reality set in. They were no longer on a pleasure trip, but they were alive.

Melanie inventoried their conditions and found nothing more troublesome than a few sprains and scrapes. The worst injury on the island appeared to be her own lump, and it had shrunk to a vague unevenness of the scalp.

That was a good thing, since there would be no immediate rescue. For reasons that might be related to power fluctuations, the resort's radio had ceased to function. Luigi the chauffeur, who doubled as handyman, swore he had done his unsuccessful best to fix it.

Once the soup was served, Chet departed to check on his grandfather and Drop Dead. Quiet fell over the dining hall.

The sound of rain slanting against the roof was interrupted only by the first officer and the captain, who had progressed to singing "Row Row Row Your Boat" in rounds. The occasional "Oompah-pah" was supplied by Dr. Malatesta.

In one corner, the Germaines attended Noreen Pushkoshky, who kept trying to jump onto a table and strip off her clothes. Although middle-aged, the society matron retained a striking figure and, in Melanie's opinion, demonstrated considerable professionalism in unrolling her stockings and winking at the crowd.

It was the general opinion, she gathered, that someone had spiked the wine at the captain's table, but so far no one but Melanie suspected who it might be. She wondered when Rita would turn up.

And where was Hal? She hoped he was all right, and then she decided it would be better if he drowned. No, it would be best if Rita drowned, and Hal…and Hal…

Melanie pictured him again, steadfast amid the chaos of the shipwreck. He didn't act like a criminal who had set up a dangerous situation in order to fill his own pockets. Besides, why should Hal covet a few baubles, when he owned the most profitable casino in Las Vegas?

Maybe he wasn't in league with Rita. But if not, why had he chosen this island on which to instigate Melanie's recuperation?

Sternly, she forced herself into the kitchen to check on the cooks, who at her suggestion were arranging canned fruit salad in little bowls. With ruthless honesty, she admitted that she was looking for an excuse to clear Hal of evildoing because she wanted to lure him back into the bedroom.

She wanted to press her nose to his shoulder and inhale essence of gangster. She yearned for his powerful grip as he swooped her onto the bed, and the rapid thrusts as he claimed her. Her nipples tightened and her core sizzled just thinking about him.

Melanie distracted herself by bustling into the pantry and assessing the supplies, which were ample. When she checked, she found the freezer well stocked, too.

The one thing that puzzled her was the absence of a back door from the kitchen. "How do they take the trash out?" she asked Pixie.

The elderly lady pointed to a chute. "Down the hatch."

"Doesn't it violate some kind of code—scratch that." There would, of course, be no health inspectors in a crook's haven. "It seems kind of claustrophobic."

"There used to be a door," said Pixie. "Until Drop Dead caught the cooks sneaking sides of beef out to their chums in a motorboat. The previous cooks."

"Isn't there supposed to be honor among thieves?" Melanie murmured.

"Everyone was shocked," agreed the old woman. "Can you imagine being so crooked you aren't even allowed onto Paraiso de Los Falsarios? Sometimes I wonder what the world is coming to."

A stir from the front room drew Melanie's attention. Having earned her way through college as a waitress, she expertly lined her arms with little bowls of fruit salad before shouldering open the swinging door.

A new group of arrivals dripped puddles onto the worn linoleum. Her attention riveted on the broad-shouldered Hal. His eyes shone a burnished brown, and, even in his drenched state, he towered, larger than life, over the dining room.

Then she noticed the woman beside him.

Margarita Samovar might have been a little wren of a woman if not for the miracle of plastic surgery. According to Melanie's research, the woman's face had been sculpted from nose to cheekbones to chin, her fat suctioned and her tush lifted.

In addition to surgical improvements, she wore heavy makeup and high-heeled boots beneath her long fur coat. And no one over thirty-five had hair that shade of coal black unless it was dyed or false.

Where Hal was firm and well-defined, Rita appeared blurry, like a shape-shifter who couldn't quite make up her mind. But that did not seem to bother her companion, who had looped one arm around her waist.

Melanie's stomach twisted as she busied herself distributing the fruit bowls. It didn't make her feel any better to discover that her suppositions about Hal's friendship with Rita were true.

From behind Hal stepped a man in a muddy white uniform, whose bar pin identified him as Purser Ignacio Grenoble. "Someone's robbed the safe!" he cried. "It wasn't me. I have two witnesses!"

Bone Crusher clasped his hands overhead and brandished them like a victorious boxer. The Swamp Fox merely nodded to indicate he, too, could testify to the purser's innocence.

"What do you mean, robbed it?" demanded a young woman seated at a table. "Where's my diamond necklace?"

"Someone must have stolen it!" boomed Mr. Germaine as his wife frantically rebuttoned the blouse that Noreen Pushkoshky was attempting to shed. "One of those three, I wouldn't be surprised."

The gangsters' mouths dropped open. "Us?" gasped Bone Crusher.

"Steal from a charity cruise?" said the Swamp Fox. "We would not stoop to such a thing. And if we did, we would at least have replaced the jewels with respectable imitations.''

Drawing himself up, the purser glared daggers at Mr. Germaine. Finally the short man relented. "I could be mistaken. But we need to get out of here. Has anyone called the Coast Guard? Where are we, anyway?"

Luigi glared, and one of the ex-cons went into a coughing fit. Pixie made a choking noise.

"A private island," said Hal.

"I didn't know there were any private islands around here," murmured Bitsy.

"That," said Hal, "is what we mean by private. I am sure you can understand that some people prefer to avoid crowds."

Several of the passengers nodded. "When people think you have money, they can be so pushy," said the young woman who had lost her necklace.

"Being prominent is stressful," agreed Mr. Germaine. "But how do we get home?"

"The normal mode of transportation to the mainland is by ferry," Hal said. "However, the radio with which to summon it is not working at the present time."

Mr. Germaine produced a cigarette-pack–size cellular phone and put it to his ear. He shook it, tapped it and pushed the buttons frantically. Several other guests, Melanie noticed, were doing the same thing, with equally unsatisfying results.

In the corner, Noreen Pushkoshky stopped trying to undress and squinted at Rita. "Wasn't she—didn't she—"

"It is I who organized the cruise," said the black-haired woman, with a vague attempt at a British accent. "And I take full responsibility for getting to the bottom of this."

Melanie supposed that, at this point, she ought to reveal

what she knew about Rita. On the other hand, if she did, she would have to explain that she herself was a reporter, a disclosure that might not sit well with Hal's buddies.

Or with Hal.

She was mulling over the merits and demerits of telling all, when she found a pair of raccoon eyes trained on her. Rita's face mirrored shock, dismay and calculation.

Okay, so the woman hadn't expected to see Melanie here. But did she have to look so outraged?

Rita's next move, however, was disarming. "Until we can nab the evildoers," she announced, "I shall make myself useful." With a purposeful stride, she cut across the room. "How can I be of assistance?"

Melanie rallied. "You could help me get more fruit cups."

"Certainly!" A mass of dark hair swished by, but halted as Pixie emerged from the kitchen with a tray of that very item. The two cooks also came out, carrying slotted spoons and industrial-size cans of refills.

"Splendid!" Rita grabbed some bowls and shoved them at Melanie. Under her breath, she gritted, "I told Hal to get rid of ya. Now keep yer mouth shut or he'll do it for real!"

I told Hal to get rid of ya.

If someone had punched Melanie in the nose, it couldn't have hurt more. Puzzle pieces chink-chink-chinked into place like cherries on a slot machine.

So this was Hal's motive for sweeping her away. He'd done it to keep her from getting on board that ship. He'd done it for Rita.

Had sleeping with her been part of the bargain? She doubted Rita would ask her boyfriend to go to bed with another woman. In fact, it was apparent that Rita hadn't expected to see Melanie on this island at all.

That was small consolation. Hal Smothers had used her. From the very beginning, his motive had been to please this ripoff artist.

What had he meant when he offered Melanie a contract? He obviously didn't plan to marry her, although he was well known to enjoy walking down the aisle. Most likely he wished to keep a tootsie on the side while he claimed Rita as his bride.

It was the worst insult Melanie had ever endured.

When she gained enough control over herself to meet Hal's puzzled gaze, she could feel herself thrumming with rage. This was war.

8

RITA HAD NOT WASTED a moment in blabbing, Hal could see. Judging by the expression on Melanie's face, she had learned why he really brought her to this island, and she would never forgive him.

He wanted desperately to be forgiven. He yearned to yank open his chest and reveal the sincere beatings of his heart, like some ancient Aztec captive. Come to think of it, things had not gone so well for the Aztec captives, but he was game to try.

However, there was another, more pressing matter that he must sort out. That was the subject of Noreen Push-koshky.

In her current inebriated state, the Beverly Hills socialite was making little sense to anyone. It would only be a matter of time, however, before she became coherent enough to remember a piece of Hal's personal history that he profoundly wished would remain hidden.

How could a man get into trouble with so many dames at one time? Hal supposed it might be a record of some sort. It was not the type of record that one wished to see inscribed in the Book of Guinness, however.

At that moment, to his horror, Noreen's expression cleared, as if a pair of windshield wipers had scraped away her inner fog. "I remember now!" she cried, and pointed directly at him.

There was a rustle as everyone in the room turned to stare. Hal's heart sank.

Slowly and stiffly, the leader of the Beverly Hills elite swiveled, her finger sweeping the room until it aimed at Rita. "She poured the wine!" declared Noreen. "And she's the only one who didn't get sloshed!"

"You had better be careful, Mrs. Pushkoshky," warned Rita. "You could be sued for slander."

Apparently, whatever drug had been imbibed along with the wine was beginning to wear off all around, because the first officer, after plucking a strand of seaweed from his shirt, announced, "I saw her too! Row, row, rowing out of the purser's office as we gently hit the rocks! Merrily, merrily, merrily patting her purse as if it were a dream!"

"The man's out of his mind." Rita took a step backward, which put her next to Melanie.

"Let's have a look in your purse then," said the purser.

"All in favor?" The captain gazed blearily around the room. All hands went up.

Beneath her makeup, Rita's face turned white. In that moment, Hal saw how utterly and coldheartedly he had been used.

Rita had never had any interest in him. Her goal in this business had been, not the raising of charitable moneys, but the acquisition of stolen property.

He could not fathom why she had wanted him to remove Melanie, but he would figure that out later. Right now, the most important thing was to restore the stolen goods to their rightful owners.

And, thank goodness, Rita was opening her purse compliantly. Even smiling a little—

—as she whipped out a pearl-handled revolver, pressed

it to Melanie's temple and said, "If any of ya jerks move, I'll plug the broad fulla lead."

Everyone froze, except the captain, who was barfing quietly into his cap. Horror and dismay transformed the faces of the passengers, while Bone Crusher and the Swamp Fox registered repugnance at Rita's actions.

She yanked her hostage backward, and the two of them disappeared through the swinging door. Suddenly, to Hal's astonishment, all his other troubles evaporated.

Compared to saving Melanie, nothing else mattered.

AS RITA SHOVED her into the kitchen, Melanie noticed things that had never seemed important before.

Such as the fact that Drop Dead had fortified this place as a last refuge in case he ever got cornered. Not only was the back door sealed up, but there were bars on the windows and three dead bolts to secure the swinging door. There was even a peephole through which one could survey the activities in the dining room.

It made sense that, if a gangster had to hole up, he would do it in the presence of food and drink. Luck certainly seemed to favor Rita, that she should have chosen this one place into which to flee.

But if there was no way in, there was also no way out. Rita couldn't escape, and neither could her hostage.

It was fabulous. Melanie had been trying for weeks to get an interview, and now her subject was stuck with her for the duration.

"Would you quit pressing that gun into my temple? You're giving me a headache," she said.

"Ya been givin' me a headache for weeks!" snarled the dark-haired woman, her ersatz British accent forgotten. After a moment's reflection, however, she released

Melanie and waved her backward with the gun. "How'd ya do it?"

"Do what?"

"Talk Hal outta killin' ya?"

Melanie wondered if the golf ball might have had lethal intentions, but such a method in so public a place didn't fit with Hal's reputation for subtlety. Nor had he forced her to make the long swim to China when he had the chance.

She sat at the scarred table, smoothed out a crumpled bit of butcher's paper and took a pencil stub from a cracked cup. "Why would Hal want to kill me?"

"Like I said, I told him to get ridda ya." Rita pressed her eye to the peephole, then whirled as if expecting to find Melanie creeping up from behind. "What're ya doin'?"

"Making you immortal."

"Immortal? Ya mean incarcerated, don't ya?"

"Well, you *did* try to have me killed," Melanie said.

"Ya brought it on yourself, ya pest," Rita told her. "Ya shoulda expected somebody to put out a contract."

"You paid him?"

"Naw. He don't do hits for a living no more." Tossing her mink over a coatrack, Rita revealed a busily patterned pantsuit with a clashing vest. Upon close inspection, she still resembled a collection of mismatched parts. "I like the guy, though. He's my kinda man. A crook."

Melanie jabbed the paper so hard she tore a small hole in it. "So you two are—" she could barely force herself to say the word "—lovers?"

"Whaddaya take me for, a chump?" Rita blew air disdainfully from her cheeks. "Nobody sleeps with the Iceman unless they wear the white dress first. Everybody knows he's a sucker for doin' the honorable thing."

He certainly hadn't tried to do the honorable thing with Melanie, but she couldn't afford to think about that now. "How come you drugged the crew? Didn't you realize the ship might crash?"

"I was countin' on it." Opening the industrial-size refrigerator, Rita surveyed its contents. "Do they got any bagels and cream cheese around here?"

"Not that I've noticed," Melanie said. "You mean you wrecked the ship to cover the fact that you were sneaking jewels out of the safe?"

The woman removed an enormous jar of pimiento-stuffed olives. "Is it my fault Cha Cha was stupid enough to hire an honest crew? I never figured on that."

"Is that where you got the combination to the safe? From Sammy Adams?"

"Well, he's the owner, ain't he?"

So Cha Cha had been involved in ripping off his own passengers. He obviously hadn't expected to lose his ship in the process.

"How do you plan to get out of here?" she asked.

With her fingers, Rita fished out a couple of olives. "Cha Cha better figure out a way. He's in this up to his neck, ya know."

"Isn't he more likely to strangle you?" Melanie asked. "Besides, everybody knows you took the jewels."

Setting aside the jar, the woman went hunting through the pantry until she returned with a large can of marinated artichokes. "I got enough stashed to hold me for a while. But it's too bad about Hal lettin' me down this way. I was thinkin' maybe I could work in a temporary marriage and get fixed for life."

"He asked you to marry him?" *It doesn't hurt,* Melanie told herself without conviction.

"He was workin' up to it, I could tell." Rita stopped

searching for an opener and attacked the can with an ice pick.

Someone pounded at the door with resounding thuds. It appeared to be more an expression of frustration than a serious attempt to break through, however.

Was that Hal? Melanie wondered. And who was he more worried about, her or Rita?

"He's in love with you?" she asked.

"Love?" A series of tiny holes in the can lid oozed vinegary marinade. "Naw. He wants kids. See, I got one that's stuck away in a boarding school, so he knows I can do it."

"Hal wants kids badly enough to marry you?" No wonder he'd brought up the subject of children to Melanie. But he hadn't offered to marry *her* for them, not that it would have made any difference.

"Yeah. As if I'm stupid enough to go through that again!" With the help of a knife, Rita pried open the can and began digging out artichoke hearts. "I'd rather have some lug shoot me than go through labor!"

Melanie paused with her pencil in midair. "Really?"

"Ya want any of these?"

She was about to refuse, but they smelled good. Besides, Melanie was famished. "Sure."

Only after she said it did she remember that Rita hadn't washed her hands. Melanie might have ingested her share of dirt over the years, but something about the other woman struck her as particularly slimy.

To her relief, Rita used a large slotted spoon to remove the contents and dropped the artichokes onto plates. "Mosta them dames is too finicky to eat like this."

"If it isn't in a can, I don't recognize it as food," Melanie said as she dug in with a bent fork.

"I'm almost glad Hal didn't ice ya," Rita said.

"Thanks," said Melanie. "Now tell me about child-birth."

THE ARRIVAL OF Cha Cha, near-hysterical and drenched from the storm, threw a monkey wrench into Hal's attempts to organize a large-scale rescue effort for Melanie.

The captain and first mate were stumbling over each other trying to explain how Rita had drugged them so that no one was at the helm when the storm hit. Bone Crusher and the Swamp Fox stared in dismay as it became clear that their buddy, while nearly deranged over losing his ship, showed no surprise about the robbery.

Their chum had not only stolen from charity, he had been partly responsible for bringing a bunch of outsiders onto their secret island. It was a betrayal of almost unthinkable magnitude.

As for Noreen Pushkoshky, she gave Hal a broad wink and retreated to the comforting arms of her friends, the Germaines. He could take a small amount of comfort in the fact that she chose not to betray him.

But his main concern was Rita. What was she doing to his angelic lady inside the kitchen?

A dame who would stoop so low as to rob a charity cruise would not hesitate to plug an innocent woman. He had to rescue Melanie, even if she refused ever to speak to him again.

He had brought her to Paraiso de Los Falsarios and thus was responsible for her. Worse, he was discovering with every passing moment how much he loved her.

Hal could not rely on his distracted friends for assistance, nor on any of these shivering, griping passengers, either. Even the captain and first officer, presumably men of action, remained too befuddled to be of use. He must dope out a solution himself.

The dining room was part of a larger building, which included the shop and the front lobby. They were connected by an attic, Hal presumed, but how did one access it?

As surreptitiously as possible, he beckoned to Pixie. In her matron's uniform of a black blouse, full-length black skirt and white apron, she resembled a deranged Puritan far more than a former madam, but she moved at once to his side.

"How do I get into the attic?" he asked quietly.

Her rheumy eyes brightened. "Follow me!"

They slipped out of the dining room. A portico deflected the bulk of the downpour as they made their way to the gift shop.

Thanks to the storm, the air had become even mustier than before. Pixie switched on the single overhead bulb, picked up a flashlight and led Hal through a labyrinth of freestanding metal shelves.

The shop, narrow and deep, resembled a storage room more than a store. Hand-lettered misspellings announced the contents of the upper level of boxes: Umbrellas. Sun Gasses, prescrip. Sun Gasses, desiner. Sun Gasses, plane.

"Why so many boxes of sunglasses?" he asked. He doubted the guests would need them in the perpetual fog.

"Oh, Grampa brought 'em," said Pixie. "He was always complainin' about all the lost-and-found stuff people left at his emporium. Drop Dead figured we had plenty of extra room. Might as well fill it with somethin'."

"I don't suppose you sell many gifts here, anyway," Hal mused.

"Naw," she said. "I suggested startin' my own cathouse. You know, crooks get lonely, too."

They reached an inky recess. A cord hung from the ceiling, indicating a trapdoor to the attic.

"I trust Drop Dead did not approve," said Hal, who would prefer to see misguided young ladies given honest employment.

"He don't care, but I couldn't find nobody to come live here," Pixie said. "We don't even have a hostess at the front desk on account of most women can't stand the isolation."

"I can see their point." Hal pulled on the cord and opened the trapdoor. Unfolding the attached ladder, he said, "You would not by chance have a chart of where the other outlets are, would you?"

"There's a way out in the kitchen," Pixie said, handing him the flashlight. "But I don't know exactly where."

"I have not noticed it, either." Hal had a habit of inspecting ceilings because armed thugs had been known to drop from them. "However, it may very well be tucked away in some corner. Thank you for your assistance."

"No problem." The elderly woman smiled. "I'll tell the others you're takin' a leak."

"Only if they ask," said Hal.

"THAT BAD, huh?" Melanie said when Rita was finished.

She had never imagined that labor and delivery could be so exciting. Or that a hospital could feel so much like a war zone.

This opened new vistas for her. Not that Melanie was ready to relinquish the possibility of parachuting into countries so remote they had to steal their cable TV. But that didn't mean she couldn't expand her scope of operations.

"Hal don't understand," Rita explained. "He thinks the kids just pop out and look cute. He wants to be a daddy."

"You think he would play with his children?"

The woman shrugged. "Even gangsters have weaknesses."

Melanie remembered how gently Hal had carried the baby from the shipwreck. And the tenderness with which he'd lifted her from the tilted conference table, and, earlier, comforted her in the railroad car.

Melanie's own father had been overworked and uninvolved. Although she knew that families could be warm and loving, she'd also read that children were often doomed to repeat the patterns of their upbringing.

She'd never allowed herself to imagine having a real home, cradling babies, then watching them take their first steps and stumble into their daddy's arms. What if it was possible? What if that Daddy might be Hal?

But he hadn't offered her marriage; he'd made a business proposition. Melanie might not have much experience with happy families, but she knew they weren't based on financial contracts.

The door shuddered again as if someone was kicking it. The passengers must be getting restless. "Maybe you should hand the jewels through the door," she said. "They might let you go if you do."

"Give up my loot?" Rita stared at her in disbelief. "I went to a lot of trouble to swipe it. They got a lot of nerve, wanting it back!"

"I don't see how Cha Cha's going to be able to help you get away, then," Melanie told her.

"Ya better cross your fingers he does," Rita said darkly. "Yer still my hostage. Come ta think of it, you oughta be locked up in the pantry."

"The pantry?" Small places didn't panic Melanie, but neither was she overly fond of them.

"Yeah." Rita waved the gun. "I don't wanna have to

worry about ya sneaking around when my back is turned. Get in there!''

Melanie could see there might be an advantage to absenting herself from the scene if the irate passengers broke in. "Okay." She scraped back her chair, pocketed the butcher paper and went into the pantry.

There was no lock on the door but she could hear Rita piling things in front of it. In the darkness, Melanie felt along the wall. Her fingers encountered a light switch, and she flicked it on.

The pantry formed an L leading back into food-crammed depths. The aisle was wide enough to turn around in, and, judging by the assortment of jars, tins and packages, she didn't have to worry about starving.

But she would rather not stick around long enough to need another meal. And so, when Melanie rounded the corner of the L and a cord brushed her cheek, she did the logical thing.

She opened the trapdoor and made her way up the ladder.

ATTIC EXPLORATION was not one of Hal's fields of expertise. Having lived most of his life in apartments, he had been deprived of the experience as a boy, and had never had a chance to compensate until now.

Unfortunately, Drop Dead's attic was not the smooth-floored extravaganza of children's fantasies. There were no steamer trunks to open and no widow's walks revealing dramatic vistas.

Except for a small platform bordering the trapdoor, there was scarcely even a floor, only narrow beams running between fat insulation pads. The attic stretched a considerable distance, but it was so low-roofed that Hal had to crouch.

Rain clapped overhead, as if someone were beating a drum next to his ear. In the stuffy air, his body temperature soared as he crawled toward the kitchen.

But he didn't care about physical discomfort. He had to reach Melanie before she got hurt.

What was it about a pair of uptilted, olive green eyes that made them suddenly more vital to him than any other pair of eyes in the world? Why did the mere thought of her smile set his heart thudding?

In the past fifteen years, Hal had removed half a dozen people from the world. He had never missed any of them and, knowing their pasts, doubted that anyone else had, either.

Not only that, but he also didn't miss any of his ex-wives. Or former girlfriends, especially the one who shot him through the shoulder.

But the thought of anything happening to Melanie was intolerable. So firm was his determination that Hal managed not to cough when dust tickled his throat, and not to curse as, crawling on hands and knees, he slipped and mashed a sensitive portion of his anatomy against the beam.

From a distance, he could hear people talking in the dining room, their words blurring into gibberish. Then he heard something else, a scritching noise that came from right here in the attic.

He paused to listen. Not scritching, he decided, but rustling, and it was moving from the kitchen area toward the dining room.

Passing a support post, he saw a shaft of light define a rectangular opening. Someone had indeed entered the attic.

If it were Rita, why would she be traveling toward the dining room instead of in some safer direction? Besides, he couldn't imagine the unathletic Ms. Samovar moving with such stealth.

Altering course, Hal went in pursuit of the new arrival.

MELANIE WISHED her face didn't keep breaking through spiderwebs. It made her wonder where the spiders were.

She didn't enjoy crawling along narrow boards, either. Her discomfort eased when she reminded herself that gymnasts performed leaps and flips atop beams no wider than this, although usually not with bongo drums beating directly above their heads.

Below and ahead, she could hear people talking in the dining room. Melanie had a facility for sorting words out of mumbling, and despite the rain she was able to make out "Cha Cha," "key" and "go get." It sounded promising.

Then she saw the flashlight beam. Someone had joined her in the attic.

Her first thought was, *Rita.* The newcomer, however, was off to one side, not behind her.

Melanie squinted. Unfortunately, the light hit her directly in the retinas.

Deciding not to wait around for bad news, she kept moving toward the dining room. There was most likely another trapdoor there; if not, she would have to risk putting a foot through the ceiling. She could at least make her presence known before this intruder reached her.

Easing forward, Melanie started to put her weight on the next beam. It groaned ominously, a noise all but covered by a burst of rain.

As she weighed her options, she realized that the newcomer had made more rapid progress than expected. "Melanie!" The low, gruff voice sent prickles down her spine.

Hal. He'd come to save her.

Or had he come in search of Rita? A fist squeezed in Melanie's chest.

"You ratsoid!" she hissed as she backed away.

Hal prowled toward her at a right angle, approaching until she could smell his smoky masculinity. "Why do you call me a rat?" Hurt edged his voice.

"You and Rita!" she replied in a stage whisper. "You were planning to marry her, weren't you? All you offered me was a lousy contract!"

He ducked his head. It was a gesture full of boyish appeal, and also had the effect of ruffling his thick brown hair so that she ached to run her fingers through it. Gangsters, Melanie reflected sharply, were not meant to be so cute.

"It is not as it seems," he said. "I was attempting to protect you."

"From who?"

"From me."

"By keeping me as your tootsie?"

"Tootsie?" His chiseled features reflected surprise.

"Isn't that what you thugs call a mistress?"

"We are not thugs," he answered coolly, "and I do not regard you as a mistress. I consider you a beautiful and sensual woman who would not wish to be kept on a leash."

"That's why you didn't ask me to marry you?"

He hesitated. "It is more complicated than that." The Iceman sighed. "I am willing to be flexible on the subject of wedding bells. However, I must know if you still do not wish to have children."

Although she was reconsidering her views on the subject, Melanie preferred not to say so. After all, she did not

even know if she *could* have children, and if that was all
Hal wanted, where would it leave her if she couldn't?

The only possible justification for marriage was true
love, and true love does not alter when it infertility finds.
''Who knows?'' she said.

''Yes,'' muttered Hal in uncharacteristic confusion.
''Who knows?''

A large, warm hand closed over hers. Tendrils of fire
curled through Melanie's body as she remembered in intense visceral detail how it felt to remove this man's
clothes and be swept away by him.

His face came within inches of hers, holding her fixed
within his spell. His hard mouth angled onto hers, and her
lips parted, and they came together where rafter joined to
rafter.

Melanie knew in an instant that she wished to perform
the ultimate act of gymnastics on a beam, and that the
man she wished to perform it with was Hal. Only a few
laws of physics stood between them, and surely those
could be dispensed with for special occasions.

Directly beneath them, she became aware of the chattering coalescing at one point, as if people were gathering
at the entrance to the kitchen. Idly, she wondered if the
passengers were going to break in and capture Rita.

Thank goodness for the closed pantry door. Even after
the kitchen was raided, it would take a while for anyone
to discover where Melanie had gone. Knowing Hal's
lightning proclivities, the two of them should have earned
their gold medal before then.

Carefully but swiftly, Hal twisted until he lay flat on
his back atop his perch, and lifted Melanie onto him. She
landed on a support of tightly packed muscle and iron
male readiness. Balance was a tricky matter, but she had
always yearned to walk a high wire.

Until now, however, she had given no thought to the partner with whom she would walk that wire. She could not deny how strongly she felt attracted to Hal, the only man of her acquaintance who would even consider making love in such a situation.

Strong hands caressed her breasts through her sweater. Her entire body poised for action as she bent to kiss his waiting mouth.

Something jolted the beam. Once, twice. Melanie grabbed for a handhold, but the only thing she found was Hal, who was in turn grasping the wood beneath him.

Below, the kitchen door rammed open. Not far off, the weakened beam gave a cataclysmic shudder.

This section of attic began to sag. A sudden shift proved the final straw for the struggling Hal as he lost his grip on their support.

With a half twist in a piked position, the two of them slid off the rafter and crashed through the insulation into the dining room below.

9

HAL WAS NOT entirely surprised to find himself plunging through space. He had been in freefall ever since he met Melanie Mulcahy.

Could he seriously be considering marriage to a lady who had no discernible wealth of her own? A female who might not even wish to bless their union with children?

Yet money scarcely mattered, when he had no intention of divorcing this woman. As for children, well, he would have to give that subject more thought after he hit the ground.

Fortunately, he did not hit the ground. What he hit was Captain Yolo Bowers, who had become so relaxed under the effects of Rita's spiked wine that he folded meekly on impact.

Melanie, in turn, fell upon the first officer. He had spread his arms wide to emphasize his singing, and caught her with a force that brought him crunching to his knees, on the downbeat.

By great good fortune, only a small section of ceiling rained down into the open doorway. The rest of the attic held. After making sure that no serious injuries had occurred, Hal turned his attention to the tableau at hand. Frozen in place at this unexpected arrival were a knot of passengers led by Cha Cha, Bone Crusher and the Swamp Fox.

Only a few feet away, trapped in the kitchen, stood a

defiant Rita Samovar. Her pearl-handled gun had been transferred to the custody of the purser.

"We are pleased to learn that the hostage did not meet an unsavory end," said the Swamp Fox. "That would have been another blot on Cha Cha's record."

The usually perky money launderer hung his head. "I am sorry I conspired with this Jezebel," he said. "The jewels will now be returned, and I have suffered the consequences of my misguided actions. The *Jolly Roger* was my greatest treasure, my dearest love, and she, this heartless, calculating wench…"

"Hal," said Rita meaningfully.

He regarded her sternly. "Yes?"

"Will you not assist me?" She tapped her foot against the linoleum. When he didn't respond, her accent took a left turn. "Gimme some help here, Hal."

Disbelief stilled his tongue. The woman had used him, and endangered the lady he loved, and ruthlessly betrayed her own partner in crime by crashing his ship. Yet she expected Hal to leap to her aid?

He felt Melanie's gaze rake him. Everyone else was watching too.

It was not Hal's way to turn his back on a former friend, even one as faithless as Rita. On the other hand, she could scarcely expect to get away with her ill-gotten gains. "First return the jewels," he said.

Overripe lips pursed in displeasure. "Says who?"

Hal met her glare with steely resolve. "If it is your intention to seek mercy, you must make restitution to those you have wronged."

The woman's eyes narrowed and her neck shortened, as if she were becoming a reptile. "I wouldn't yammer about wrongin' people, if I was you."

Did she refer to his decision not to eliminate Melanie?

"You requested that I remove a certain person from your path, and I did."

"Yeah? Did I ask you to bring her here?"

"That was my idea," he conceded. "It seemed harmless at the time."

"You hear that?" Rita asked the assembly. "It was his idea. She don't belong here."

"Yeah?" snarled Bone Crusher. "When a dame is built in a particular manner, we ain't fussy about her bona fides."

"It has never been required that a gangster's guest have a criminal record," added the Swamp Fox.

"She may not have one herself," warned Rita, "but this tootsie can send ya right to the slammer."

With a gulp of dismay, Hal wondered if Melanie might be underage. But no; he had taken the precaution of confirming her identity via her driver's license while she lay sprawled in the parking lot, and it gave her years as a healthy twenty-eight.

"Miss Mulcahy is not jailbait." Recalling a certain previous discussion, he added quickly, "She is not a tootsie, either."

Rita smiled the smile of the self-satisfied. Or of those who have a spare weapon in her purse, possibly in the order of a nuclear bomb. "Hal, ya better help me out here. If ya know what's good for ya."

"You keepin' secrets from us, Iceman?" Bone Crusher's mustache quivered menacingly.

"That would not be wise," said the Swamp Fox unnecessarily.

"I? Secrets?" His mind raced. Exactly which of his secrets could Rita have uncovered? And what did they have to do with Melanie? "I have no secrets that involve this young lady."

"Maybe not," said Rita triumphantly. "But what ya don't know definitely *can* hurt ya."

Melanie, Hal noted, wore an expression of resignation on her lovely face. "I'll spare you the suspense." The woman of his dreams sighed. "She's trying to tell you that I'm a reporter."

There was a painful pause.

"Society reporter?" asked Cha Cha hopefully.

"I'm afraid not," she said. "I'm Melanie Mulcahy, freelance investigative reporter."

"Melanie Mulcahy?" said the woman passenger sans diamond necklace. "I've seen your byline in the *World News in Brief!*"

"The what?" asked several people.

"It's something I found at my dentist's office. Kind of a throwaway."

"You mean you write for a living?" asked Noreen Pushkoshky.

"They pay five cents a word," said Melanie. "You call that a living?"

Hal could not speak. The full horror of what he had done broke over him in a storm surpassing the one outside.

Melanie was a composer neither of poetry nor of press releases. She had mentioned South American rebels and hostages; who but a reporter would hide in a chicken coop to get a story? Why had he not questioned her further?

He had erred massively.

His feelings for Melanie, profound as they might be, were no longer his most immediate concern. Loyalty to his friends, to Grampa and his gang, was the law by which Hal lived.

And he had betrayed them. Brought a snoop to their secret island and put them at risk of exposure. His betrayal ran far deeper than Grampa's decision to exclude Hal from their summit meeting.

For years, he had lived in a house of illusions, and now the entire structure might be undermined by one painful truth of which he had not even been aware.

But Melanie had known. Melanie, the woman he loved, had taken advantage of him. Although it was not her fault that he had brought her to Paraiso, she had seized upon the opportunity to treat him as a chump.

That was exactly what he felt like. A fool.

"So," he said to Melanie, "you care nothing for me. I am for you merely an object to be used in your pursuit of a headline."

Her mouth quivered, but she lifted her chin defiantly. "I didn't ask you to bring me here."

"She did not ask you to bring her here," repeated the Swamp Fox in a low voice.

"I paid for *my* mistake!" cried Cha Cha. "What about him?"

"A reporter? Really?" said the tall woman beside Noreen. "I've always wanted to write my autobiography. People tell me I've led such an interesting life. Do you ever collaborate?"

"Only if there's money in it," said Melanie. "Mostly I prefer to work alone."

Hal understood now exactly how ridiculous he had made himself, offering to build a love nest for this newshawk. She possessed no mating urge beyond a passion for scoops, no fondness save for the next hot story.

The realization hurt him deeply. He had begun to consider that perhaps his devotion to Grampa would never be returned and that he might be wise to begin realigning his loyalties. But to the outside world, as personified by Melanie, he could see that he remained nothing but an object of scorn.

He had been raised in the world of gangsters. It was still the world where he belonged.

"Mr. Iceman?" The Swamp Fox crooked an eyebrow. "It is your obligation to dispose of this problem. Otherwise, we will have to do it for you."

Angry as he felt, Hal could not leave Melanie to the untender mercies of his comrades. Ultimately it was his fault for bringing her here, and if his heart became damaged goods in the process, that was no one's business but his own. "I take full responsibility," he said.

"For what?" demanded Melanie.

"For—" A movement on the far side of the dining room drew his attention. The door opened to admit a breathless, red-faced Chet. "Is something wrong?"

"It's Grampa!" Chet said. "He's having a heart attack! Drop Dead's trying to do CPR, but I think he's making it worse."

Hal's mentor, his father figure, lay desperately ill in this isolated place. His mind went white and clear as Arctic tundra.

"We will not let him die!" Hal announced. "We will put aside our petty quarrels and save Grampa."

"Well, you'd better save him fast," said Noreen, "because Rita just scrammed out the garbage chute."

IN A MATTER of minutes, Melanie's feelings underwent enough climactic turning points to fill the front page of the *New York Times*.

One second she was bursting with passion, with a need to feel Hal deep inside her. Next came the thrill of falling, followed by pleasure at the way he had stood up to Rita.

He had made it obvious, or so she believed, where his allegiance lay.

Then at the mention of one itty-bitty word—well, two, really, ''investigative reporter''—he had abandoned her. That was all it took, a minor declaration of her occupation such as one might list on a credit application without giving it a second thought, and *bam!* Hal had turned back into Mr. Tough Guy.

Melanie wished she did not feel this small twinge that might almost be taken for guilt, that she had gone to bed with the man under the pretense of being a poet. How could she be blamed for the fact that, given the opportunity to observe a gangster summit, she had leaped at the chance?

Everyone knew that the Golden Rule did not apply to reporters. It did, however, apply to gangsters.

She was on the point of telling Hal that he was a crook and a killer who deserved to be deceived, when Chet came barreling into the dining room with his disturbing news. Then Rita took it on the lam.

The change in Hal was stunning. He straightened, determination armoring him like a knight.

''You!''—pointing at Cha Cha and the wizened Luigi—''Get the doctor sobered up, I don't care how much hot coffee it takes!

''You!''—to Bone Crusher and the Swamp Fox—''Find Rita!

''You!''—it was Chet's turn—''Get the radio working!

''You!''—to the McAllisters—''Keep the passengers entertained! And if you turn up with one extra nickel in your pockets...''

''Don't worry.'' Violet McAllister shuddered. ''We saw how much everybody hates Rita. I never thought about it that way before. I mean, it was just kind of a lark.''

"What was a lark?" asked the lady-minus-the-diamonds.

Before anyone could reply, Hal clapped his hands for attention. "And you!" He fixed Melanie with a glare. "Did the cub-level test for guerrilla warfare include CPR?''

"There's no such test. I made it up," she confessed, and was saddened to see, from the dismay on his face, how low she had fallen in his esteem. She really ought to stop lying, she thought glumly.

"I know CPR," said Noreen. "My late husband, Vladimir, had a heart condition." Except for a slight dilation of the pupils, she seemed to have recovered from Rita's potion.

"You come with me! Move out!" barked Hal, and, to Melanie's amazement, the disorganized clot of people sorted itself at once. Off went the designees to their appointed tasks, and the passengers allowed themselves to be shepherded back to their seats.

All because of Hal. In his windbreaker and jeans, he radiated a primitive vitality far removed from the Las Vegas high life. Stripped of his expensive suits, without the genteel manners, he was transformed into a hunk of unrestrained masculinity.

For the first time since she had contemplated making the long swim to China, Melanie found him frightening. And, therefore, utterly desirable.

Was it possible, she wondered as he steered her and Noreen outside, that he might truly be the man for her? That she had let slip from her grasp, and her bed, the one mate who would never bore her?

Cold, rain-laced air refreshed her as they dodged across

the courtyard toward Grampa's room. But inside Melanie's chest beat a heart filled with darkness.

Her experiences with men had been limited by her fierce desire for independence, but she had not reached her late twenties without making some observations of the male of the species. It was her conclusion that a man might grant his affections freely, but once his interest waned, it never revived.

Hal's feelings for her had not so much waned as been obliterated. The odds of restoring them were somewhat less, she calculated, than the odds of her ever again attempting a new move on a balance beam, even though—why hadn't she thought of this before?—it would subsequently be named for her.

She didn't suppose gymnasts of the future would ever brag to each other that they had once performed a Mulcahy with their boyfriend. Nor did she fool herself into believing that Hal would ever again bestow on her his smoldering look of love.

That loss chilled Melanie more effectively than the storm. The cold didn't leave her even when they entered Grampa's room.

They were greeted by the daunting sight of a gargoyle perched on the floor, arching over a prone figure as if to feed. Then she heard the reassuring sound of the gargoyle grunting, "One two three breathe! One two three breathe!"

Hal dropped to one knee. "Grampa?"

Drop Dead shook his head, nearly dislodging his glasses, whose broken nosepiece had been taped together. Below him, the prone figure gasped for air. "He's in bad shape."

"Let me try." Shoving the gargoyle aside, Noreen bent

to the task with far more vigor than the aging gangster had shown.

"Who...?" Drop Dead squinted at the society matron suspiciously, but his glasses were askew.

"One of the passengers," said Hal. "Melanie, rub Grampa's hands. Try to get his circulation going."

"She could rub *my* hands," said Drop Dead as he sagged onto the bed. "She could rub a lot of things."

"Rub them yourself," growled Hal. "Besides, you have obviously not heard the bad news. Melanie is a reporter."

"Yeah?" growled Drop Dead. "Well, spell my name right. That's Cimarosa with a *C*."

Melanie rubbed Grampa's hands for a while, but she kept getting in Noreen's way, so she quit. Hal didn't so much as glance at her.

Still, there was quite an interesting story developing here. A shipwreck on an island, a jewel thief on the loose, a desperate attempt to save a life.

Hesitant to drag out her notebook, Melanie began committing details to memory: the spare, prisonlike room with its chenille bedspread and fly-specked walls; the intent faces of the participants; the way Drop Dead was ogling her chest. And Hal's slim hips and graceful movements as he paced.

She also didn't want to forget the unruly clump of hair sticking up at the side of his head. Or his voice, gruff but loving, as he addressed Grampa. "Come on, you old curmudgeon!"

After today, she realized, she would probably never see Hal again, unless it was in the course of pursuing a story.

She could handle it. Loving and losing; big deal. The only person she could rely on was herself, now as always.

"One two three breathe!" said Noreen Pushkoshky, still CPRing. Grampa coughed and choked.

The door banged open and three people tried to crowd through it. Or rather, two men tried to enter and the woman in the middle wiggled and thrashed to get away.

Finally the Swamp Fox and Bone Crusher dragged the unwilling woman into the room. She had small, angry eyes and a squarish face mapped with incipient wrinkles. Dishwater-blond hair lay matted against her head, and a belted shirtwaist dress gave her the look of a Depression-era housewife.

"Pixie found her in the gift shop," grunted the Swamp Fox as he dodged an angry kick.

"A stowaway?" Hal frowned at the newcomer.

"Naw! Wouldja believe, it's Rita!" said Bone Crusher. "Hey, lady reporter, get a load of Rita Samovar without her wig and face paint."

"What a disguise!" said Drop Dead admiringly. "You'd think she was a normal dame."

"Rita?" Hal stared in amazement.

Tears of humiliation glittered in the woman's eyes, but she stopped trying to kick her captors and drew herself up. "Okay, ya lugs, so this is what I look like. Big deal! Don't forget, I'm the one who told ya about that snoop. You guys ain't the ones I robbed, so let go of me!"

"Take her purse away," said Hal.

Gingerly, the Swamp Fox unhooked the pocketbook from Rita's shoulder, and gazed at it speculatively. "You know, we could divide up the jewels. It would not be as if we were the original ones who pinched them."

"I don't think it violates no ethics," agreed Bone Crusher.

"Those belong to my friends!" Noreen might have protested further, but Grampa broke into a fit of coughing so severe it threatened to turn into convulsions. Hal knelt beside him worriedly.

"We would have to shut up this society dame. And, of course, the reporter." As the Swamp Fox tossed the purse onto the bed, he, Bone Crusher and Drop Dead got a narrow look on their faces that did not bode well. Rita began to smile.

Melanie was mulling over escape routes when someone outside the door called, "Make way! Coming through!"

The gangsters parted grudgingly, admitting Cha Cha, the limo driver and the disheveled redheaded physician. "Open wide and say ah!" announced the gleeful Helen Malatesta to no one in particular.

Melanie wondered if the doctor had drunk more than Noreen. Or perhaps she was simply less accustomed to being slipped a Mickey.

"You call this sober?" snapped Hal.

Cha Cha shrugged. "It was the best we could do."

"Dr. Malatesta!" Hal pulled the giddy woman over to where Noreen continued administering CPR to the sputtering Grampa. "We got a heart attack patient here! Help him!"

The physician dropped to her knees with a crunch. "Ow."

"I'm getting tired," said Noreen. "Can you take over?"

"Why would I want to take over?" asked the doctor.

Despair gave Hal a wild air, and for a moment Melanie feared he might try to shake the woman into sobriety. "A man's dying here!"

"Yes, so get Mrs. Pushkoshky off him!" sang out Helen Malatesta.

Noreen stopped pushing and puffing, and plopped onto

the floor next to Grampa. As soon as she did, he sucked in a couple of deep breaths and sat up.

"Well, it is about time!" he huffed.

"The doctor just got here," Hal said.

"It don't take a doctor to see I choked on a piece of hard candy!" shouted Grampa. "You bozos have been pounding and blowing on me till I thought I'd pass out!"

"You mean you didn't have a heart attack?" Noreen asked weakly.

"Not until you nearly gave me one!" snapped the gangster. He hoisted himself to his feet, using her shoulder for support.

"The first rule of CPR," said Dr. Malatesta, "is to determine whether the patient is breathing and has a heartbeat."

"Is that so?" said Drop Dead.

"You could have killed him!" Hal said.

"Don't blame him!" Grampa shuffled into the bathroom, and they could hear him gulping down a glass of water. "My fool grandson went into a panic when I started choking. The young idiot!"

"I have to go. I have patients waiting!" With that, the doctor wobbled out the door, followed by Luigi, who gave a small wave in parting.

Melanie tried to dart after them, but two pock-faced gangsters barred her path. "Hold yer horses, tale-teller," said Bone Crusher.

"Leave her alone." Hal rubbed his forehead wearily. "If there are any consequences to be taken, I am the one responsible."

In spite of everything, he was protecting Melanie, which made her feel bad for having tricked him. Maybe it would help if she offered not to write about her experiences in Paraiso, but hadn't she decided to stop lying?

The Swamp Fox eyed him warily. "We would not wish to get on the bad side of the Iceman, but it behooves me to point out that there could be more than enough consequences to go around."

Cha Cha glided a couple of steps toward the bed. Noreen, seeing that Rita's jewel-filled purse remained in danger of confiscation, took a flying leap backward and sat on it.

This put her virtually nose to nose with Drop Dead. Aligning his lopsided specs, the resort owner gawked at her as if he had just received the shock of his life.

Thickly, he muttered something that sounded like, "Yes, yes, Nanette."

"Uh-oh," said Hal under his breath. After all the things that had gone wrong in the past few hours, Melanie could not imagine what would elicit such a comment.

Grampa chose that moment to emerge from the bathroom and get his first clear look at Noreen also. He too did a double take.

"So," he said, "the dead live on."

Melanie didn't know what he meant, but she understood one thing: that the gangsters were regarding Hal in a very different manner.

They didn't look afraid of him anymore. They looked downright nasty.

10

HAL CLEARED his throat. "Technically," he said, "I fulfilled my contract with Mr. Cimarosa. I 'got rid of' Nanette Del Rio."

He doubted the argument would carry much weight. Gangsters rarely appreciated technicalities.

Fifteen years ago, Noreen Pushkoshky had been Nanette Del Rio, better known as Yes Yes Nanette, a stripper at the Las Vegas Filly Follies. She had been keeping company with one of Drop Dead's friends, the Follies' bookkeeper.

This unworthy boyfriend embezzled the box-office receipts and disappeared after planting evidence on Nanette. To preserve herself from the unjust suspicions of the district attorney, she had squealed about a small off-site betting establishment owned by Arthur Cimarosa.

This disclosure had resulted in considerable discomfort to Drop Dead, who was forced to close the betting parlor and suffer financial losses. He resolved to take the customary countermeasures by bumping off this loose-lipped peeler.

On his first attempt, Nanette tossed Drop Dead out of her dressing room onto his back, dislocating his hip. On his second attempt, in an alley, she snatched the gun from his hand and shot him in the big toe.

Unable to walk properly for some time afterward, Drop Dead hired Hal Smothers, then a twenty-one-year-old kid trying to make a name for himself, to complete the job. It had been an offer he could not refuse.

Now here was that same stripper, long reputed to be dead. Hal's big, dangerous secret had just been spilled at the worst possible time to the worst possible people.

"You got ridda the dame?" Drop Dead grumbled.

"Obviously not in the precise permanent sense."

"What about the others?" asked the Swamp Fox.

"What others?" Melanie asked in confusion.

"You ain't never killed nobody, has you?" Bone Crusher fisted and unfisted his hands as if preparing them for use.

Hal had nightmared about this moment for fifteen years, ever since he first removed Yes Yes Nanette from the visible world by turning her into Noreen Ames, later Pushkoshky. His entire reputation in the gangster community was based on his unequaled success as a hit man, and it was a lie.

"I believe it is inefficient to use more force than necessary." He deliberately kept his tone mild.

This pack of wolves was ready to pounce. Judging by Rita's smirk, she would be more than happy to lead the attack.

Hal knew he was a good enough fighter to get himself out of here, and possibly off the island. But there were innocents involved. Noreen, for one. And, above all, Melanie.

Even though she had used him, her well-being was Hal's responsibility. More than that, he was head over heels for the dame.

He knew he should reject her with the utter coldness that glinted in the eyes of his erstwhile friends. But he could not help it; he loved Melanie, even though no gentleman would pursue a courtship that was clearly unwanted by the lady.

Her safety must be his first priority. Therefore Hal did a thing that, under other circumstances, he would have considered cheating.

He pulled out his gun.

"Although I have never killed anyone to date, I am willing to turn over a new leaf," he said. "Starting now."

Cha Cha paled and Bone Crusher scowled. The Swamp Fox studied him speculatively. Drop Dead chewed on his lip and, apparently liking the flavor, bit off another strip.

Noreen had the good sense to head for the door behind Hal, taking Rita's purse with her. Melanie hesitated as if loath to miss any of the goings-on, then reluctantly followed.

"You will not get away with this," said Grampa.

"I am already getting away with it," Hal responded with more confidence than he felt, and backed out the door in the wake of the two women.

MELANIE DIDN'T KNOW what to think. Her hit man was a fraud, but a clever one. And he radiated authority as he stood up to those cutthroats.

Apparently she hadn't been the only one keeping secrets. Discovering this fact made her feel both off balance and reassured at the same time.

Out in the wet, wild air, they swung by the dining room. "Noreen, return the jewels to their owners immediately," said Hal. "I do not think even Bone Crusher will pull trinkets from the ears of passengers. Also, Drop Dead does not allow thievery on his island."

"I never thanked you," Noreen said. "You coulda killed me fifteen years ago. Instead, you gave me a new life."

"And you gave me an idea of which I have made good use." Hal's mouth twisted wryly. "It is amazing how many people will jump at the chance to become someone else."

"Particularly when the alternative is a pair of concrete pumps," Noreen said. "Not that I am a slave to fashion."

They deposited the society matron among her friends, who listened eagerly as she began confessing her shady past. "Let us go see if Chet has activated the radio," said the Iceman, and took Melanie by the arm.

As they walked together, she wondered if she should seize this moment to tell Hal how she felt about him, but then she realized that she didn't know how she felt. Except that an undeniable velvety sexuality was blossoming inside her at his touch.

How could she want a man who wasn't dangerous? How could the slightest pressure of his fingertips make her yearn to rip off his windbreaker and make love to him in the middle of the courtyard, in the rain?

She must, Melanie thought, be suffering the aftereffects of her head injury, or maybe of staying on an island where time had no meaning. She no longer even knew whether it was day or night. Nothing seemed real except Hal, and he was the most counterfeit person she'd ever met.

They reached the lobby, where they found Chet squatting behind the front desk, fiddling with the dials on a two-way radio and listening to staticky babble. "The lightning fried a few connections but I've sort of got it fixed," he said. "You wouldn't believe the junk that passes for tools around here. Ever try using a wrench that used to be a nutcracker?"

"Transmutation is the specialty of cons," said Hal. "The last true alchemists are found in prisons."

"Who should I call?" asked the eager young man. "Just say the word, Mr. Iceman!"

Hal crouched beside him. "Honesty compels me to inform you that there have been certain revelations about me."

"Honesty compels me to inform you that the rooms are bugged," said Chet.

"You heard the whole thing?" Melanie couldn't believe it.

"In its entirety," admitted the youth.

This raised a disturbing possibility. "Is my bedroom tapped, too?" she asked.

"Only the single rooms and the front rooms of the suites seem to be rigged." The young man indicated a row of switches.

"I presume you also know that your grandfather is no longer in need of medical assistance?" Hal said.

"Yeah." The young man sighed. "I'm sorry I went off the deep end. When I saw him choking, I jumped to conclusions. He was already mad at me for blowing the business deal. Now I guess he'll disown me for sure."

"If he does, he is a great fool," said Hal. "And I have never taken your grandfather for a chump."

In the Iceman's face, Melanie saw a longing to be forgiven, as Chet would be. But she also saw resignation that their relationships with Grampa were in no way comparable.

She thought about her own father, and the fact that he now played with Wendy's children as he had never played with her. She was surprised to feel a prick of envy. It made her sympathize with Hal, although she was trying hard not to.

"So, who do we call?" Chet asked. "Don't we need to turn Rita over to somebody? And Cha Cha too."

Hal straightened. "Rita must face the music," he said. "But I think Cha Cha has suffered fit punishment. Besides, to call in the Coast Guard would only punish the innocent."

"You mean, Drop Dead?" Chet said. "After all, he's the one who owns the island."

"He's not exactly innocent," Melanie said.

"He has committed no crime," corrected Hal. "Recently."

"You think we can get the passengers ashore and Rita into jail without people finding out about this secret island?" she asked. "I don't see how that's possible."

"It will take a lot of effort." Hal's clear brown eyes fixed on her. "And the cooperation of the press."

She cringed. Never before had Melanie landed an exclusive story of such juicy proportions. How could she give it up, merely in the name of preserving this oddball sanctuary?

Yet, in a world where the Internet blurred the differences between Tahiti and Cleveland, while deep in the rain forests the monkeys played Donkey Kong video games, did she really want to disturb this last piece of uncharted territory?

"I've spent months researching Rita and the way she's been ripping people off around the world," she said. "I'm going to do everything in my power to get that story published. But I could fudge a little on the exact location of the shipwreck."

"Some rocks off the coast," suggested Chet.

"Passing fishermen snatching the passengers and crew to safety," Hal mused.

"Then leaving before they could be interviewed," Melanie added.

"You think everyone will cooperate?" asked the young man, plucking nervously at the radio.

"We have won a concession from the press," said Hal. "Now it is the turn of Grampa Orion's gang, who, after all, have the most to gain by assisting in this collusion."

"Would Rita keep her yap shut?" Melanie asked. "I mean, her mouth?"

"If we make it worth her while," Hal murmured with the distinctive low intonation used by gangsters when their trigger fingers feel itchy. "I must present my case to the gang."

"You're going back to Grampa's room?" Chet asked. "You're going to face those guys again?"

It would, Melanie realized, be both easier and safer for Hal to summon the Coast Guard. Yet his allegiance to his friends ran deep.

"You, Chet, will monitor the room, and should there be an unfortunate outcome, call in the seagoing gendarmes," said Hal.

"You bet." The young man's ears wiggled uncomfortably, but resolution shone from his face.

"Be sure to take your gun," Melanie said.

Hal patted the bulge in his jacket, then removed it and handed it to Chet. "It was one thing to draw it in self-defense. Now I am returning voluntarily. To do so at gunpoint would be a hostile act. You keep it."

Chet stared at the weapon. "I wouldn't know how to fire it."

"You will not need to," said Hal. "It is not loaded."

He had saved them by bluffing, Melanie realized with a start. But this time, when he went back, there would be no bluff. He was going to stare death in the face.

In that moment, she realized that she desperately wanted to make love to Hal one more time. To be scooped off her feet, and held in his arms, and tossed and flipped like pizza dough in the hands of a master chef.

She wasn't sure she wanted a man for a lifetime. But she needed that moment of belonging to Hal, that intense excitement with a core of tenderness, more than she had ever needed anything.

Just once more, she told herself. Then, surely, her mind would clear, her independence would reassert itself and she could go her merry way.

However, while she was making this discovery, Hal departed. Knowing the speed with which he operated, she supposed that by now he had already reached Grampa's room.

Without another word, Melanie left Chet manning the radio and went after him.

HAL WALKED into Grampa's room with his hands held in front of him, palms outward, to signify that he came in peace.

He hoped he wouldn't leave in pieces.

"You have a lot of nerve," said Grampa, not without appreciation.

The faces of Drop Dead, Rita, Cha Cha, Bone Crusher and the Swamp Fox formed a rogues' gallery as they fixed their attention on him. It occurred to Hal that he had spent years avoiding this moment when he would find himself figuratively naked in front of his friends.

To his surprise, losing the respect of this bunch did not bother him very much. It did not compare to how he felt about the near certainty of losing Melanie.

Still, he would not dishonor himself by betraying his former pals for his own convenience. "If you wish to save the island, you will listen to me."

"We don't need no help," snarled Drop Dead. "This

ain't the worst storm I ever seen. The island ain't gonna sink.''

"In case you have not assessed the situation," said Hal, "our friends Rita and Cha Cha have brought into our midst a large group of the noncriminal element. What exactly were you planning to do with them?"

Drop Dead scratched his head. Bone Crusher cracked his knuckles.

"You raise an interesting point," said the Swamp Fox.

"It was not part of the plan to crash my ship into the lighthouse!" protested Cha Cha.

"The lighthouse?" said Drop Dead. "Somethin' happened to my lighthouse?"

"It's toast," said the Swamp Fox.

The gargoyle blanched. He began to sway and, had he not been sitting on the bed, he might have toppled.

"If I were not a gentleman," rumbled Grampa, "I would pound you on the chest and blow my foul breath into your mouth like you did to me. However, under the circumstances, I extend my sympathies."

"My Albert Payson Terhune dog novels—gone to the briny!" cried Drop Dead. "Where'm I gonna find another copy of *Collie to the Rescue?*"

"Dog novels schmog novels." Grampa waved a hand.

"No, wait." Rita frowned. "Is he cryin'? I hate to see an old geezer cry."

Considering that this came from a woman who rarely saw her own three-year-old son, Hal was not inclined to take her concern as anything but a ploy. "I will make inquiries among rare-book dealers, if you like," he said. "First, we must deal with the passengers and crew."

"I would like to see you make *them* disappear," said the Swamp Fox.

"That will not be possible," Hal said. "However, now

that their valuables have been returned, it might be feasible to secure their cooperation.''

"Cooperation?" said Grampa.

Having finished performing calisthenics on his knuckles, Bone Crusher proceeded to wrestle loud pops from his wrists. "I gotta admit, the lug seems to know how to motivate people. Like they talk about at them business seminars I go to."

"You attend business seminars?" asked Cha Cha.

"We gotta keep up wit' progress." There was a defensive note in Bone Crusher's voice. "Otherwise we would still be killin' people with stone axes."

"In order to persuade the passengers and crew not to squeal on us," Hal said, "we must first agree to turn Rita over to the proper authorities."

"Hey!" said Rita. "They got their doodads back, didn't they?"

Grampa glanced at her dismissively. "Considering that you wrecked a ship and a lighthouse, not to mention sending the passengers' luggage to Davy Jones's locker, you got a lot to answer for."

"I believe," said Hal, "that if we offer to repay these innocent victims for their losses, and give them free annual vacations at our Las Vegas establishments, they might be persuaded to keep their lips buttoned. But we will have to win their trust first."

"You mean, like, be nice to them?" sniffed Drop Dead. "Only a galoot would suggest such a thing!"

"Or a straight arrow," grumbled the Swamp Fox. "By the way, I have been wondering. If you did not ice anybody, how do we know you even run a crooked establishment?"

Hal saw that it was time to come clean. "I do not," he

said. "I design computer software with both business and gaming applications."

Bone Crusher's eyes narrowed to slits. "Tell us at least you don't pay no taxes."

"I am afraid I do," said Hal. "Look, it is no skin from my nose if we blow the lid off Paraiso, since you lugs will never allow me to set foot on its shores again. Do we make nice with the passengers or not?"

"Maybe," said Rita, "somebody oughta just shoot him."

"In which case, young Chet, who is at this very moment listening to us courtesy of Drop Dead's one-way intercom, will call the Coast Guard," said Hal. "And then it will be not only Cha Cha's boat that is sunk."

The entire room held its breath. They knew he had them.

"What about the snoop?" asked Grampa. "That girl."

Hal heard a movement behind him. As he shifted to a defensive position, he saw that it was Melanie.

"'That girl' is going to keep this place a secret," she said. "I've got more than enough dope on Rita and her shenanigans to fill half a dozen stories."

"You mean she done more than this?" asked Bone Crusher.

"Lots more," said Melanie.

Rita tried on several expressions. Innocence. Defensiveness. Spite. Then gave it up and burst into tears.

Drop Dead patted her hand. "Since you was sympathetic to me, I got a soft spot for you. Also, wit' your criminal history, once they let you outta the slammer, you can have a job on the island. As it happens, we got open the position of hostess."

"Me?" said Rita. "Ya know, I always kinda wanted to work at a resort."

"Can she bring her kid?" Melanie said. "The poor little tyke's in a boarding school."

"No, he ain't." Rita sighed. "My ex-husband has custody. I told a fib to impress Hal."

"I always said a dame could make a saphead outta the Iceman." Bone Crusher chortled.

"The Iceman ain't no saphead. I mean, he isn't one," said Melanie. "He's smarter than the whole lot of you."

She stood there, fearlessly facing down a roomful of thugs. Hal knew in that moment that he would not let this woman go without employing every persuasive means in his power.

He had thickheadedly spent the past twenty years trying to earn the friendship of unworthy men and women. As soon as the immediate crisis was past, he knew he must make one final, desperate attempt to win the love of this worthy dame.

He would get only one roll of the dice, and he'd better make it a good one.

THE FACT THAT no one had been shot yet boded well, Melanie thought. Although she loved danger, she preferred it pain free.

In fact, now that she found herself mano-a-mano with a roomful of crooks, she was forced to reassess her craving for perilous assignments. Perhaps there was a limit beyond which even the foolhardy should not go.

After several long and thunderous beats of the heart, she saw heads start to nod. It appeared the gangsters agreed with her assessment of Hal.

"The Iceman makes sense," rasped Drop Dead. "I don't want no government agents turning Paraiso into someplace for sissies."

The Swamp Fox squinted until his eyes nearly vanished

into pouches. Finally, he said, "A man that could hood-wink the lot of us for fifteen years is hardly a lightweight. Also, he has made more money than us crooks, when the laws of gangster economics say it can't be done."

"I'm willing to try things his way." Cha Cha rubbed his palms together. "I vote yes."

"Ditto," said Bone Crusher. Grampa gave a tight nod.

Melanie's knees received an infusion of gelatin at the sudden release from tension. She stumbled, and came up against the reassuringly hard form of Hal.

Standing behind her, he caught her by the shoulders. His warm breath tickled her neck and she felt herself en-veloped by his strength.

Definitely, they needed a rematch. What else could cure this feverish rush of her hormones?

Beneath her rump, she felt his masculinity awaken. So he, too, was having these thoughts in spite of his studied indifference. Or was that simply the way men were built, to respond to a woman no matter what?

A ripple of movement ran through the assembled gang-sters, and Melanie saw them staring past her at the door-way. She turned, but Hal was blocking her way, and she couldn't at first see who was there.

"Uh, fellas?" came Chet's quavery voice.

"We are getting matters straightened out." Hal moved aside, and Melanie glimpsed the young man's flushed face. "I think we will be all right."

"Uh, no, we won't!" Chet's hands flailed in agitation. "I've been monitoring the radio. The Coast Guard picked up some kind of automated distress signal from the *Jolly Roger* and they're on their way."

11

"THEY SAY that into each life some rain must fall," observed Grampa into the horrified silence that followed his grandson's pronouncement. "It is my contention that we have had more than enough rain, both figurative and literal, and I would request that the great Capo in the sky should cease and desist."

That, Hal reflected, was as close to a prayer as the gangster chief ever was likely to utter. Despite his own reverence for the Divinity, however, Hal believed it was incumbent on mankind to put up umbrellas rather than pray for an end to precipitation.

"Is the automatic signal still ratting on us?" he asked Chet.

The young man shook his head. "It was cut off after a few minutes."

"So perhaps the gendarmes do not yet have an exact fix," he mused.

"No, but I've been monitoring their radio. They're convinced there's a whole cruise ship full of people in trouble," Chet said. "As soon as the weather lets up, they're going to send out a helicopter."

"Then we had better arrange for them to find their passengers," said Hal. "Call the ferryboat captain and tell him that he must arrive immediately. He will receive a bonus of ten thousand dollars for each boatload he takes ashore within an hour."

Chet gave a quick nod and vamoosed. He was a most resourceful young man, Hal reflected. As for Grampa's opinion, one could tell nothing from the old man's poker face.

"Do you really think we can keep the Coast Guard from finding the island?" Melanie asked. "I don't see how they can miss it."

"The lug what lost Paraiso to me said a juncture of the earth's magnetic fields bollixes up radio waves," said Drop Dead.

"Kind of like a Bermuda Triangle of the Pacific," explained the Swamp Fox.

"Also," noted Drop Dead, "I use a jamming device."

"Does this mean it is time to make nice with the passengers?" inquired Cha Cha.

"That is exactly what it means," said Hal. "We will need to coordinate their stories with ours. Fortunately, the passengers are in the habit of following the lead of Noreen Pushkoshky, and she is squarely in our corner, unless—" he fixed Drop Dead with a quelling look "—a certain person wishes to renew animosities of the past."

"I am calling off the contract," said the island's owner.

"You are not offended by my unorthodox method of removing Yes Yes Nanette?" Hal asked.

The gargoyle shrugged. "There ain't such a big difference between sending her to Hades and sending her to L.A., anyway."

Bone Crusher, who had removed his shoes, the better to crack his toe knuckles, spoke over a series of minor detonations. "Ya know," he said, "I been thinking about the way you iced them targets. Who else has figured out how to recycle people? I take my hat off to youse."

"Put your hat on," said Grampa. "Also your shoes. And come with us."

The gangsters trooped out toward the dining room, Rita trudging beside Drop Dead. Hal knew he should go with them, but he did not want to miss this moment alone with Melanie.

"I wish to thank you for your support," he said.

It was difficult to gauge the emotions flickering through those green eyes. "I'll go you one further," she said. "I won't even print the fact that you're a legitimate businessman."

"That is very kind," said Hal. "However, now that the cat has been released from the receptacle, I do not suppose there is any point in keeping my occupation a secret."

"I'll only use the information if necessary," said Melanie. "After all, cats do have nine lives, in or out of bags."

It was an awkward, formal conversation to be having with a woman whom Hal wanted to haul into the depths of the now-vacant room so he could demonstrate his bed-clearing techniques. The covers belonged on the floor, and he wished to sweep them there in a manly display of gangland passion.

Then he would like to replay the entire scene with a rose between his teeth and Spanish guitars twitching vaguely in the background. Followed by the Hawaiian rendition with ukuleles and a yellow hibiscus, in this case tucked behind Melanie's ear.

However, experience had taught Hal that men and women were constructed differently, and not only in the obvious sense. What might appear romantic to a fellow—that is, ranting, raving, ear-shattering sex—tended to be perceived by the woman as an act of animal lust.

He did not merely want to turn himself and Melanie into a display of neon electrification. He wished to win her hand in marriage, and for that, he must display restraint.

The question of future parenthood had managed to resolve itself without Hal's conscious effort. He could see now that the only children he wanted to have were Melanie's, and that he would marry her even if she chose to remain unmotherly.

Determined to show no sign of his inner agitation, he extended his arm to the lady. "Allow me to escort you to the dining room."

Her lips pressed together, but he could not judge whether she was displaying disappointment or some other uncharted emotion. In her individualism, Melanie represented territory as unmapped as this island.

"If there is anything else I can do for you...?" Hal said.

Her short, dark lashes gave a startled blink, and her face tilted toward his. He was reminded of their encounter on the pier, and the thrill of tasting that full mouth for the first time.

"Well," she said. "Actually, there is."

"Yes?"

She reached up to trace his cheek. It had been some hours since Hal shaved, and by now the stubble must be sprouting like crabgrass in the springtime, but Melanie did not seem to mind.

"First," she said, "you could kiss me."

As there was nothing he would rather do, Hal seized her by the waist and lifted her toward him. She smelled, he noticed, of rain and mist and canned fruit salad, the kind with cherries in it.

But he had forgotten to shut the front door, and when portals are left open, any manner of creatures may walk through. In this case, the creature came in the form of the wizened Luigi.

"Hey, loverboy," he said. "You better get yer gluteus maximus over to the mess hall. The inmates ain't cooperatin'."

With a forlorn sense of opportunities lost, Hal let Melanie slip from his arms. "Rain check?" he asked.

Melanie glanced out at the dank night air, where only a drizzle was still coming down. "I suppose. Under the circumstances." But she didn't sound happy about it.

It was the fate of responsible men, Hal supposed, to choose duty over love at least some of the time. He must rise to the occasion.

THE SCENE in the dining room almost compensated Melanie for what she had missed in the bedroom. The sight of Grampa Orion's gang making nice with the passengers was priceless.

Children shrieked in terrified delight as Drop Dead poked his face from behind a chair. They pelted him with balled-up paper napkins until he vanished, only to loom again moments later like a figure from a Punch-and-Judy puppet show.

Cha Cha was demonstrating dance steps to a giddy Helen Malatesta, his round face barely reaching her chest as they tipped and tapped their way through the room. Bone Crusher exercised great restraint as he arm wrestled the purser across a table, while the Swamp Fox was helping some ladies light a fire in a metal wastepaper basket to warm themselves.

Judging by the stern expressions on the faces of the people near Noreen and Grampa, however, success was far from assured. Although small in stature, Gerard Germaine made an imposing figure as he folded his arms and planted his legs akimbo.

"I have no intention of deceiving the Coast Guard," he boomed. "I'm shocked that you, Noreen, would ask us to pretend this island doesn't exist."

"But aren't we being ungracious to our hosts if we betray their little secret?" Noreen persisted. "After all, Rita's agreed to confess to the robbery and to doping the crew, so there's nothing to be gained by blabbing."

"I am not a liar," responded Mr. Germaine.

Noreen turned a pleading face toward Hal. "Oh, dear," she said, sighing. "I've done my best, but I'm afraid it's not good enough."

As Hal advanced toward the group, Melanie expected him to deliver the sort of smooth pep talk of which she knew him to be capable. But he surprised her.

"I agree with you," he told the chain-store owner.

Grampa's face reddened with anger. "I knew we could not depend on this turncoat!"

Noreen raised a cautionary hand. "I think we should let the Iceman finish."

"Yes," said the Swamp Fox darkly. "I would like to hear this."

"I have spent my life telling lies," Hal said into a room grown suddenly quiet. "I am not proud of that fact."

"Nor should you be!" harrumphed Mr. Germaine.

"To tell a lie for profit, or ego, or even friendship, is a losing proposition," said Hal.

"Well, here's a how-de-do," grumbled Cha Cha, who stopped whirling the doctor around and stood listening.

"You double-crossin' us?" asked Bone Crusher in disbelief.

"I am giving the morality of the situation some

thought," said Hal. "As this is an unfamiliar activity for me, I am doing it slowly."

Tears glittered in the eyes of Drop Dead, who sat in the midst of a circle of children. "The state and the feds is gonna come in here with all them rules. There goes our fun."

"No more smokin' in the kitchen," said one of the tattooed cooks. "How'm I gonna flavor my barbecue sauce?"

"Yeah, waddabout our election pool?" asked Pixie LaBelle. "Every election, the boys and me, we make bets about which politician is gonna smear the other ones worse. The state don't allow no betting."

Luigi hung his head. "I unhitched the air bag in the limo, on account of I'm so short. I ain't got no permit to do that. They're gonna come in here and arrest me."

Resolve replaced the confusion on Hal's face. "This is not self-interest, is it? We are talking about preserving a vanishing way of life."

"You mean like, a Rescue the Whales kind of thing?" asked Bitsy Germaine.

"We support the whales, in spite of what Ms. Samovar tried to do to us," conceded her husband.

"Is it cowardly," asked Hal, "to lie in order to save an ecosystem that is nearly extinct?"

"Who you calling extinct?" said Drop Dead.

"Us, you fool," snapped Grampa. "He's calling us old fossils."

"Once a way of life is gone, it can never be revived," Hal said. "Think of the Wild West. The gold rush era. The Roaring Twenties."

"Prohibition," said the Swamp Fox nostalgically.

"We will give some thought to your point," said Mr. Germaine, drawing his wife aside.

Everyone looked to Hal. He gave them a weary smile. "At any rate, we must all go ashore sooner or later, and it appears the downpour is letting up."

Suddenly, intensely, Melanie wished it would rain forever. She didn't want to leave this topsy-turvy island behind, even to achieve her dreams of journalistic glory.

She didn't want to leave Hal.

One more tumble in the hay, she told herself fiercely. *That's all I need. Just to clear my sinuses.*

A short time later, Chet came to inform them that the ferryboat was landing. A hustle ensued, during which Luigi volunteered to drive the women and children the short distance to the pier, while the men would walk.

There was no need for the gangsters to evacuate, but, as the owner of the sunken ship, Cha Cha felt it best to be present when a report was made. As the owner of the island, Drop Dead wanted to know immediately how much was disclosed and by whom, so he insisted on going, too.

In the end, all the gangsters went, leaving behind only the resort employees and the McAllisters. Having resolved to retire from crime, these visitors wanted to enjoy the remainder of their final stay on the island.

Technically, Hal explained to Melanie, retirees were not banned. However, the McAllisters had decided to devote their sunset years to the doing of good works as a kind of atonement, and therefore wished to make a clean break from their former life.

It took four boatloads before all the refugees were evacuated, and they passed the time by singing camp songs under the direction of Captain Bowers and the first officer. "It Was Sad When the Great Ship Went Down" proved popular.

As they motored to shore with the last ferryload, Melanie relished the sting of the salt air and the genial humming of her fellow passengers. Beside her, a young woman fingered her restored diamond necklace wistfully.

"It's almost like being on the *Titanic,* except with enough lifeboats and without Leonardo DiCaprio," said the woman. "I don't suppose anybody'll make a movie about us, though."

"Not unless I sell the miniseries rights," said Melanie. She was already trying to figure out how to tell the tale without revealing the existence of Paraiso. An isolated, unnamed coastal town might make a reasonable substitute, she supposed.

Then she stole a look at Hal, who leaned on the railing staring into the darkness. He had a strong profile, with a sensitive quiver at the tip of his nose that she had never noticed before.

He radiated a resigned wistfulness, like a man who has lost his innocence but gained maturity in the process. Melanie was surprised to discover that she, too, felt as if she had left a part of herself on the island.

It certainly was not innocence.

When they reached the landing dock, cheers went up from the passengers already on shore. "I'll ask the boatman to notify the Coast Guard now," said Chet as he lifted a little boy onto the wharf.

Next, he reached a hand to Melanie, and with a hop she landed beside him. The young man straightened, and she realized he had in a matter of hours outgrown his post-adolescent gawkiness.

"I don't know if anybody's thanked you," she told Chet. "You've been terrific."

He glanced toward his grandfather, who stood on the wharf surrounded by his gang. The distance between them stretched like a no-man's-land. "I only wish Grampa were proud of me. But I guess I'll never be the grandson he wants.''

Hal, after assisting the last of the evacuees, joined the two of them. ''I meant what I said about going into business together.''

''You bet.'' Chet shook his hand. From his coterie, Grampa glowered.

The boatman came to report that the Coast Guard had already narrowed its search to their vicinity, and that a cutter would arrive shortly. In the meantime, the passengers packed into the terminal in search of the hot-drinks dispenser.

Melanie remained outside with Hal, staring toward Paraiso. Although it lay only a short distance offshore, it had vanished into the mist.

''Once the gendarmes depart, I will escort you back to Las Vegas,'' said the Iceman.

His formal manner was not encouraging, but, she reflected, he'd responded to her kiss in Grampa's room. Or at least he'd been about to respond when they got interrupted.

The chill in the air reminded Melanie of exactly how hot and exciting Hal's skin would feel against hers. She edged closer, yearning for his attention almost as much as his touch.

But his gaze remained fixed on the sea. Then she saw what he was looking at, a white blur looming ever larger until a Coast Guard cutter pulled to the pier.

Amid the calling of voices and the bustle of docking, a question hung in the air. Namely, would Gerard Germaine, who stood with one arm around his wife, spill the beans or keep the lid on?

Yolo Bowers presented himself to the captain of the

cutter. Melanie caught snatches of his tale of drugged wine and the *Jolly Roger* getting its hull breached.

There were, she gathered, questions about how such a miraculous rescue had been effected and why the cruise ship had sunk so abruptly. The seagoing cop also said he would make sure to note the existence of treacherous rocks on his charts, but that, she supposed, might not be a bad thing, since it would steer future ships clear of Paraiso.

With the *Jolly Roger's* captain and its owner present, and all passengers and crew accounted for, the Coast Guard captain seemed puzzled but not unduly suspicious. Then Gerard Germaine stepped forward.

"Have you something to add?" asked the captain.

The little man drew himself up. Beside her, Melanie felt Hal stiffen. "There is one thing," said the chain-store owner.

They waited, scarcely breathing.

"An attempt was made to steal our valuables," he said. "These have been returned. However, the would-be thief is also responsible for scuttling the ship, and I believe she should be brought to justice."

That was it. No mention of a lighthouse or an island. Not even a complaint about the slow service in the dining room.

"She's right here." Captain Bowers indicated Rita, who stood pouting beside Drop Dead. "This is Margarita Samovar, our cruise organizer."

"She's already confessed her crime," Cha Cha added quickly. "The guilty plea is a cinch."

"No need to stick yer dern nose any further into our beeswax," muttered Drop Dead.

"Is this true?" the Coast Guard captain asked Rita,

who had somehow managed amid all the brouhaha to replace her black wig and reapply her raccoon makeup.

"Not exactly," she said.

Although they were barely touching, Melanie could feel Hal's heart pounding against his rib cage. Or maybe that was her heart. She wasn't sure she could tell the difference.

"Not exactly?" the captain repeated, crooking an eyebrow.

"They ain't tellin' the whole truth." Rita's chin came up defiantly.

"Which part did they leave out?" asked the sheriff of the sea.

"The most important part," said Rita.

12

DROP DEAD SCOWLED. Bone Crusher flexed his hands, and Grampa reached toward a bulge in his waistband.

"What's the most important part?" asked the gendarme.

"I didn't just rip off this ship," said Rita. "I stole a lot of other stuff, too. Ask her." She pointed at Melanie.

A ripple of relief ran through the group, tempered by a few suspicious snorts. But although Rita pursed her lips as Melanie gave the captain the names of law enforcement agencies in Switzerland, Canada and Mexico, she showed no signs of blowing the whistle.

The captain took Rita into custody. Spontaneous applause broke out among the gangsters.

Only Drop Dead appeared sympathetic. "Don't forget, you got a job waitin' when ya get out!"

"I'm countin' on it," said Rita.

Finally the Coast Guard disembarked with its prisoner, and buses arrived for the passengers. After tearful farewells and the provision of markers for free stays in Las Vegas, the erstwhile crew and passengers of the *Jolly Roger* rode off.

The ferryman told the remaining small knot of gangsters that he would be making the trip back to the island as soon as he ate breakfast. The pastries in the vending machines weren't more than a week old. Would anyone care to join him?

No one would.

This was, Melanie realized as the seaman scrammed, a climactic moment of sorts, with Hal facing down, possibly for the last time, his onetime buddies in Grampa's gang. Although the odds of a shootout seemed small, Hal steered her to one side, next to Chet.

She knew she should be quivering with joy, to find herself so close to a potential battle. Instead, she violated every principle of journalistic objectivity by clutching Chet's arm and saying, "Can't you stop them? What if Hal gets hurt?"

"Then my grandfather will have me to deal with," the young man stated, loud enough for everyone to hear.

"I am glad that my grandson has finally found his manhood," Grampa announced. "I am only sorry that it is against his own flesh and blood that he wishes to exercise it."

"That depends on how my own flesh and blood behaves," said Chet.

"As for myself," Hal interjected, "I wish to apologize if I seem ungrateful, Grampa. You provided my mother with a job when she needed one and I have always considered you a friend."

"I had a debt of loyalty to your late father," the gangster said levelly. "You owe me nothing."

"I also wish to apologize for living a lie," the Iceman continued, "but I am not sorry that I refrained from icing anyone."

"You gotta give the guy points for creativity," muttered Bone Crusher.

"It is not exactly his fault that he brought a snoop onto the island, either," said the Swamp Fox, "seeing as Rita set him up."

"He coulda blabbed to the Coasties about the island," conceded Drop Dead. "And he di'nt."

"If he hadn't spared Noreen Pushkoshky fifteen years ago, we would never have won over the passengers," added Cha Cha.

Grampa raised his hands for silence, his thick eyebrows merging into a straight line across his forehead. "You galoots seem to be laboring under the impression that I am angry with our friend here."

"You mean you ain't?" said Drop Dead.

"I am not pleased to discover that I have been the target of trickery." The old man drew himself up to his full height, which made him nearly as tall as Hal. "However, I can see that it was motivated by a desire to please, something that has never troubled my own grandson."

"Hey!" protested Chet. "I came here like you asked, didn't I?"

"You came in search of financial backing," said Grampa. "Which you have received from the Iceman. However, I would also like to participate in this arrangement, now that I know that Mr. Smothers is a legitimate businessman who adheres to the law."

"In other words," Hal said, "you trust me now?"

Grampa grimaced in a manner that, to Melanie, conveyed both agreement and a certain embarrassment. "I did not invite you to our summit because I feared you would muscle in. Now I am willing to participate with you in a business deal. However, you are no longer one of my gang."

"I never was," said Hal, "or you would have invited me in the first place."

The old man gave a reluctant nod. "I believed it was only a matter of time before you formed your own gang. I see now that I was wrong."

"Wait a minute." Chet folded his arms. "You just announced that you're participating in our company. I believe I have something to say about that."

"What is it that you wish to say, then?" asked Grampa.

"I wish to say…yes," said his grandson. "You're in. But we're equal partners, the three of us. And nobody else."

The other gangsters shifted and muttered, but didn't insist on being included. Melanie gathered they were relieved not to have to participate in an aboveboard concern.

"Very well," said Grampa. "Also, you are invited to Thanksgiving dinner at my penthouse, and you will bring pumpkin and pecan pies, none of that sissy apple stuff."

"Done," said Chet.

"I will make the yams," said Drop Dead. "With pineapple."

"Don't forget the marshmallows like you did last year," said Cha Cha.

"Youse a fine one to talk!" snarled the island's owner. "The size of them lumps in the gravy, everybody thought they *was* the marshmallows!"

"Wait!" The Swamp Fox held up his hands. "Let us face a painful truth. Without the Iceman's cranberry-orange relish, it will not be Thanksgiving. I vote that we confer upon him the title of Honorary Criminal."

Everyone looked to Grampa.

He shrugged. "I have no objection."

"Okay, ya lug," said Drop Dead. "Ya get to keep yer island privileges."

The gangsters smiled and slapped Hal's shoulder. Melanie thought he winced a little, but no one else seemed to notice.

"I will make one final concession," said Grampa.

Everyone turned to him in varying states of puzzlement. "Yes?" said Hal.

"I am calling off all the other contracts you artfully dodged," said the gang leader. "Your no-hitter record stands."

"I am relieved to hear it," said Hal, and shook the hand of his onetime mentor.

Then he turned away so quickly that only Melanie saw the sheen of moisture in his eyes. After so many years, Hal had achieved his goal and been accepted by Grampa.

Yet he didn't look very happy. She wondered what could be missing.

THE SCENE that resolved a lifetime of uncertainty had played itself out almost on the periphery of Hal's consciousness.

All of his body, but only part of his mind, had removed itself from the island, transferred to the mainland and conducted this unexpectedly favorable discussion. The rest continued to clasp Melanie with her lips inches from his own.

Although a bed no longer loomed invitingly in the background, he found himself infused with the certainty that the world was full of beds, and haylofts, and other suitable venues. But, more than that, he intended to secure Melanie on a permanent basis.

Steam might rise from his damp clothing, fueled by the fires below. But when the flatbed truck arrived carrying the private railway car, he merely extended a polite arm to Melanie.

Her fingers curled over the muscle of his forearm as they sauntered from the wharf. Each tip burned through his jacket until he could have lifted a set of her fingerprints from his skin. But still he held himself ramrod straight.

While they waited for the driver to set a ladder in place, Melanie stood so close that he could feel the static electricity crackling from her short, defiant hair. "Wait," she said. "Haven't you forgotten something?"

Hal strained to concentrate. Forgotten what? His keys? His wallet? His heart? "I do not think so."

"Your luggage." Melanie's teeth toyed with her lower lip as amusement lit her eyes.

"Oh, that." He had left his suitcase in their suite, since it had seemed bad form to bring it when the cruise passengers were bereft. "Pixie will send it along."

"I see." She gave him a bemused smile and climbed up to the car, displaying those impossibly long, slim legs.

Stifling a groan, Hal followed.

MELANIE FELT like skipping into the railway car. Now at last she and Hal would be alone, except of course for the driver, but he might as well be on another planet.

After staying on an unlisted island undetectable by modern radar, she no longer found their mode of transportation odd. There was simply nothing ordinary about Hal.

His loss of gangster status didn't bother her, and not because of his honorary-criminal position, either. That might give him entrée to what was surely a most peculiar Thanksgiving celebration, but it did not make a woman's adrenaline kick in.

What did stir her juices were memories: Hal facing up to his lethal buddies. Hal tenderly holding a baby as he helped its mother wade ashore. Hal pretending not to notice as Melanie unbuttoned his shirt, then grabbing her.

At the same time, she reminded herself how invigorated

she would feel once this ache was salved. She could go on about her business unhindered by the inexplicable urge to bury her nose in his jacket and inhale deeply.

Freedom. It was the one thing Melanie had always craved. Soon it would be hers again.

And getting there was going to be more than half the fun.

Inside the car, she glanced around in confusion. The walls, which had been covered with old-fashioned embossed wallpaper, were hung with silken draperies. She wondered if this was the latest trend in railway-car decorations.

The velvet couch was still there. That was the important thing.

She settled onto the cushions and Hal slid the door shut, closing out the rest of the world. Although the car was a large one, his powerful frame dominated it.

Melanie propped herself against the arm of the sofa and stretched lazily, aware that the motion thrust her breasts into prominence. The point was to break down Hal's defenses.

"Make yourself comfortable," he said unnecessarily, and went to the small desk in the corner. There he switched on a computer.

This was not part of the plan. Men, she well knew, could lose themselves in cyperspace for centuries without coming up for air.

"What are you doing?" Melanie asked with more waspishness than she intended.

"Checking out a new program," he said.

The man would rather play with his computer than make love to her? She choked down a burst of frustration.

In the suite, he had egged her on by pretending indifference while she undressed him. Perhaps his attention to the computer was simply another ploy.

"Need any help?" Melanie purred.

"No. You relax," he said. "You have been through a lot these past few days."

Come to think of it, she could scarcely remember when she'd last slept. The churning of the engine made her lump throb, and her muscles tensed as the truck lurched forward. Her hip hurt, too, from when she and Hal had fallen through the ceiling.

Digging in her purse, Melanie found a bottle of ibuprofen and took two, dry. That ought to help.

So it did. Before she knew it, she was asleep.

HAL FINISHED reviewing the program for glitches and stared idly at the computer screen, letting his thoughts wander.

Although he remained friends with Grampa, a new chapter was opening in his life. His identity as a businessman had come out of the closet, and people would regard him differently.

Should he be modest and private, like Bill Gates? Outspoken and activist, like Ted Turner? The future seemed fraught with decisions.

Yet Hal also experienced a rising sense of excitement. The cause of it lay snoozing on the sofa, her inside-out striped sweater bunched around her hips and taut across her breasts where the short black jacket lay open.

He would like to wake her with a kiss. To hold her in his arms as he presented his surprise.

But this was no ordinary woman. He had accepted the fact that Melanie Mulcahy, the love of his life, marched to a different drummer. Possibly to a different band altogether.

She did not wish to be pursued, or wooed, or seduced. If there was anything Hal knew, it was that he must wait for her to come to him.

It was the hardest thing he had ever done.

MELANIE AWOKE to the restful sound of the truck rolling along the highway. Stretching and sitting up, she brushed aside a curtain, but all she could see were rocky, rain-shrouded hills.

They could be heading back to Vegas, or Alaska-bound, for all she knew. That would be fine. She wasn't ready to go home yet.

"Hal?" she asked.

He half turned at the desk, a dark figure against the glow of lamplight. Clearing his throat as if dragged from a reverie, he said, "The bar is fully stocked. Juices, snacks...take whatever you like."

He swung back to the computer. Clamping her lips, Melanie went to the small built-in bar and poured herself a glass of cranberry juice.

It would serve him right if she ignored him. But in a matter of hours they would arrive back in Sin City, and she would be left a seething mass of unslaked desires.

She had to take action.

Melanie drained the glass and slammed it onto the counter. "Time for dessert," she said.

The man's head came up and a pair of frank brown eyes met hers. "I regret that we do not have any."

"Yes, we do." She leaned back against the counter and regarded him boldly.

Even sitting down, the Iceman radiated power. His shoulders were wonderfully broad, and her eyes traced the brawny swell of his chest.

She wanted him to stand up and walk away from her

so she could watch the bunching of his buttocks and note the slimness of his hips and the length of his legs. Better yet, she wanted him to walk toward her, but he seemed in no hurry to do so.

"Scoot your chair back," said Melanie.

"It is bolted to the floor." She could have sworn the corners of his mouth twitched, but when she looked again, he wore his usual serious expression.

"You're doing this deliberately, aren't you?" she said.

"Pardon me?"

"I've never met a man," said Melanie, "who could be so deliberately obtuse."

"Who are you calling obtuse?" The words defied her, but he didn't repress a smile.

"You, you big thug," she challenged. "You gangster. You fraud. You couldn't kill a mouse if it ran across your lap and blew you a raspberry."

"I did not realize mice were capable of making that particular noise," he said.

She wanted to shake him. Why didn't he uncoil and speed across the space between them and whip her onto the couch?

Melanie wondered if he was still angry about her occupation. Or if, like shallow men everywhere, he lost interest in a woman once she began to develop an interest in him.

She didn't care. She wanted him, one more time.

"I'm not taking no for an answer." Tensing against the movement of the truck, she crossed and stood over him.

"Who said no?" asked the Iceman.

"I don't see you taking action," she reproved.

"That is because I see no need to."

Melanie leaned down and blew in his ear. The only response was an involuntary shudder.

He still wore the windbreaker, unzipped, and beneath it a pullover. There were no buttons to unwork, so she brushed her lips over his jawline and ran her tongue down the side of his throat.

He swallowed hard.

Reaching to his waist, she tugged the sweater loose from his belt and reached beneath, up to the bare expanse of his chest. She could feel each individual muscle tighten.

How much longer could this go on? she wondered, and slid her hands lower, beneath the belt.

Like a volcano, Hal exploded.

Melanie got an impression of seething heat, and heard a low roar, and then she was lying on the couch, deliciously draped. Her clothes flew through the air along with Hal's.

One of these days, she was going to figure out how he accomplished warp speed. Then she remembered that there weren't going to be any rematches; this was it.

Her blow for freedom. Well, so be it. She intended to enjoy every millisecond.

A hard, probing mouth closed over hers, and Melanie surrendered herself to a pyroclastic flow of sensations. His chest rubbed her breasts. His hands adjusted her hips beneath him. His body covered hers.

They floated atop a column of rising heat. By the time Hal entered her, Melanie felt as if she had been awaiting him for aeons. He belonged there, swelling inside her, melding them into white incandescence.

The rumbling of the truck intensified his thrusts. She wrapped her arms around him and hung on for dear life.

Gasping at the intensity of his sensations, Hal rolled her atop him. Bracing her hands against the couch, Melanie was startled to discover that he could plunge upward with undiminished force.

His lips claimed the tips of her breasts. Lava shot through her as Hal pumped fast and hard.

Melanie wanted to hold back some part of herself, but his mouth had become welded to her breasts, while his eager shaft erupted inside her. She felt herself lit by a blaze that came from the earth's core.

It was a long time before the heat receded. Hal lowered her beside him, one arm encircling her so that she rested against his shoulder, a perfect fit.

It was over, Melanie realized dimly. They had made love, just as she planned.

Now, finally, she would be free of him.

13

"THERE IS SOMETHING I wish to show you," said Hal.

"I think you just showed me," said Melanie.

"That, too," he murmured. "But not again. Not quite yet."

She sighed. It seemed a shame to interrupt their reverie, lying here entwined in classic lover bliss. Independence might be a fine thing, but she was in no hurry to get on with it.

"This will just take a minute," said Hal. "I believe you will find it intriguing."

He swung himself from the couch and reached above her to tug at something on the wall, near ceiling height. Melanie heard the swish of fabric and realized he was pulling apart the hangings.

Her recollection had been right, she discovered as the draperies retreated along a rod: the walls *were* covered with embossed paper. Or at least, that part of the walls visible beneath a display of maps circling the car.

Each map showed a different region of the world and was marked with red symbols and letters. "A geography lesson?" she asked dubiously. "Or is this some kind of weather forecasting?"

"Allow me to demonstrate." Hal retrieved a navy robe, belted it about his midsection and went to the computer. "There is a master that is continuously updated." With a couple of keystrokes, he produced a miniature world map onscreen. It seethed with shifting red symbols. "We have to transfer them manually onto the wall maps."

"What *are* those red things?" Melanie leaned forward to get a clearer glimpse of the graphics.

"I apologize. I intended to give you this." Hal handed her a plasticated sheet on which each symbol was accompanied by an explanation.

C stood for civil war, W for conventional war. A spiral meant a tornado, wavy horizontal lines represented hurricanes and a wavy vertical line signified an earthquake. A drawing of the atom indicated a nuclear accident, explosion or theft.

"What's all this for?" she asked.

"At any given instant, we can run a computer simulation to determine the most calamity-prone spot in the world," he said. "The maps on the walls are not strictly necessary, but I thought you would enjoy being surrounded by danger."

"But—what use is it?" she asked.

"First," he said, "to pick a spot for our wedding. Then the honeymoon. At that time, we can rerun the program and figure out where to build a house."

"You want to find the safest place?" She knew the man was no longer posing as a criminal, but this caution seemed excessive.

"Not at all." Hal tried to lean back, rediscovered the fact that the chair was bolted and folded his arms instead. "The opposite."

"So we can pick the most dangerous place on earth?"

"Is that not what you desire?"

"You dreamed this up for me?" she asked.

"I know how much you love danger," he said. "You have given me the impression you cannot live without it. So, here it is."

He was offering her freedom with a bonus—himself. "You mentioned a wedding?" Melanie couldn't believe she'd heard correctly.

"Also a honeymoon." Hal studied her thoughtfully. "Which region of the world would you prefer? The Middle East is generally unsafe. There are still regions of instability in the former Soviet Union, also."

"You want to have kids, don't you?" she said. "You can't seriously intend to raise them in a war zone."

"I want *you*," he corrected. "You have made it clear that you do not wish to produce young persons. Therefore bombs and bazookas become irrelevant."

Only to a crazy person, she thought. Or a reporter. Or Hal "the Iceman" Smothers in love.

Melanie had never met anyone so special, or so insane. He was like the breath of fresh air she had always dreamed would blow the dust off her shabby childhood shack.

Even the image of home was changing in her mind, getting spruced up, becoming idealized. With Hal in the picture, she could almost see herself raising a family in a cozy cottage with lace curtains and a rose garden.

She would prefer that those curtains not cover grenade-shattered windows and that her roses not be periodically blasted to smithereens. Also, there were a few other matters to clear up.

"Please don't be offended," she said, "but I have the impression, judging from your track record, that marriage to you is a disaster zone all by itself."

A startled expression crossed Hal's sculpted face, and he stood abruptly. Melanie wondered if she had angered him, but when he sat beside her on the couch, he looked thoughtful rather than irate.

"You raise a legitimate point," he said. "The odds

would not seem to favor success, but then, I have never been in love before.''

''Why did you marry women you didn't love?'' she asked.

''I believed that it was sufficient to be in love with the idea of love.'' Lightly, he smoothed back her tousled hair. ''I approached the situation as I would a business problem. I clarified my goals and listed the desired parameters.''

''And sought a woman to suit?''

He gave her a rueful grin. ''Now I have found a woman who does not suit anything but my heart, and I realize that love is the only thing that matters.'' Uncertainty glistened in his eyes. ''Melanie Mulcahy, will you marry me?''

The way he spoke the words, they sounded almost like a song. A song that, she noted with a start, could be sung to the tune of ''Row Row Row Your Boat.''

There was only one man she wanted to row her boat, and that was Hal Smothers. If only he had not abruptly added, ''Of course I will make a generous financial settlement.''

''Do you have to drag money into this?'' asked Melanie.

''You do not wish me to?'' He looked puzzled.

''I don't care about your money!'' she said.

Sadness muted his warmth. ''You are rejecting my offer?''

''No, just your money,'' she said. ''Keep it. I'm marrying you for love.''

Her words hung in the air for an electric moment while Hal's face registered surprise and disbelief. ''You are saying yes?''

''Yes!'' she agreed.

"Of course, you can have stock options, if you wish."

"The only option I want is on your future," she said.

Joy beamed from his face. For a moment, he couldn't speak. Then he pointed to one of the maps. "Central Africa looks good," he said.

"For what?"

"Our wedding."

Melanie laughed. "I don't need danger, either. At least, not *all* the time."

"You have changed your fundamental worldview?" he asked. "That is unusual."

"I still want to see interesting places and meet interesting people," she admitted. "But I think I can live without flying bullets." Not to mention muddy swamps full of unshaven rebels for whom deodorant was a distant dream, she added silently.

"If you don't mind my asking," he said, "exactly what was it about peril that meant so much to you?"

It was a fair question, one that she'd only begun to ask herself. "It made me feel alive," she said. "When I grew up, I felt numb a lot."

"Love can also make you feel alive." Hal's smile made it clear he spoke from personal experience.

Melanie curled against him, relishing his strength and her sense of security. "The strong men I knew always tried to run my life for me. It wasn't until I met you that I discovered what real strength meant. You don't feel a need to dominate me."

"I cannot imagine dominating you," he said earnestly. "You are not a dominate-able sort of person."

"I don't mind leaving a few things up to you," she noted. "Such as where we get married. Just as long as no one's shooting at us."

His arms encircled her. "Does that include the ballroom

of my hotel? I can personally vouch for the excellence of the catering.''

"That would be fine." Melanie thought of something else, something more important than she had ever dreamed it would be. "I want my father there to give me away."

"You have a father?" said Hal.

"Also a sister and two brothers," she said. "Plus nieces and nephews. A whole wedding party."

"That will be wonderful." Hal's cheek grazed her temple. "I only regret that I have no family of my own to introduce to you."

"That could change, one of these years," she said.

"I beg your pardon?"

She remembered what Rita had said about the perils and pains of childbirth. The prospect no longer intrigued Melanie, now that she didn't crave danger.

But she wanted children anyway. Little people to cuddle, and watch over, and give the kind of childhood that she had wished for herself. Children who would grow up with the best father in the world.

"I want kids," she admitted.

"Yes?" He looked as if he might leap up and fly around the room, but all he did was draw her closer. "Yes, truly?"

"Truly," Melanie said. "As long as I can have them with you."

"What about your career?" Hal asked. "Of course, a woman can do both these days, but you would be away a great deal, would you not?"

"Occasionally," she said. "But you know, it used to seem so urgent to become famous, as if otherwise I didn't matter. Now, well, what's important is being happy, and I don't have to be famous for that. I do love interviewing people and writing articles, but I can do those things closer to home.''

"I will buy you your own newspaper,'' vowed Hal.

Melanie shook her head. "Whatever success I achieve, I want to be my own.''

"You *are* serious about not taking my money.'' Appreciation shone in his eyes. "But marriage is a partnership. If you need it, everything I have is there for you.''

She smiled. "The money you can keep. But I'll take everything else you've got, Hal Smothers. You'd better believe it.''

Then she threw her arms around him and kissed him, just to prove it.

HAL COULD scarcely believe his good fortune. Melanie Mulcahy had said yes.

He wanted to write poetry about the gold of her hair, except that her hair was brown. And the sea-deep azure of her eyes, except that they were the color of green olives without pimientos, and he could not think of anything to rhyme with pimiento except, if you stretched the point, Sacramento.

It seemed to Hal that gangsters in love were prone to become saccharine and to drop large amounts in jewelry stores, but he did not mind. He thought he might start with a diamond ring and a pair of earrings to match, and perhaps a delicate ruby necklace, and for special occasions a tasteful tiara of rubies, diamonds and emeralds. Or would she prefer opals?

He decided not to ask. When Melanie was surprised, her eyes got wide and the tip of her tongue flicked over her lips. It was an expression he hoped to see often.

The sun came out by the time they arrived in Vegas. Hal had been so absorbed in watching Melanie sleep and making a few important phone calls that he'd forgotten to order a limo, but there was a cab waiting at the truck storage yard just the same.

He preferred to leave the private rig here rather than have it stop outside the Ice Palace. It was too large to fit in the hotel's courtyard, and Hal had no desire to attract the attention of the tourists who wandered the Strip in an unending stream.

"Yo, Mr. Smothers!" The cabbie hurried over and looked around for bags. This was Monty Montrose, formerly Josh "Ace" Sloggins. "How ya doin', my man?"

"I am fine." They exchanged high-fives. "You have been waiting for me?"

"I picked up your message on my machine and figured I'd come thank you in person." Seeing no luggage, the cabbie hurried to hold open his car door. "Wanted to let you know I did like you said and got my high-school diploma. Also put my savings in that mutual fund you recommended. I got enough now to quit driving and go to college full-time."

"I am pleased to hear it." Hal waited for Melanie to precede him, then followed her into the air-conditioned cab.

"Man, it's a relief not to have to hide out no more." As he got in the front seat, the driver removed his heavy, curly wig and pulled off a fake mustache. "I mean, anymore."

Melanie gave Hal a startled smile. "One of your former hits?"

"One of my most successful," said Hal.

Several years previously, Monty had worked as bodyguard to a cocky young gangster who made the mistake of trying to muscle into Grampa's business. When the gangster underwent a sudden religious conversion and retired to a monastery, Monty had been left to take the flak.

Now that his disappearance from the world was over, he could turn back into Ace again. But Hal had a feeling the young man was happier being the person he had become.

Halfway home, they were sitting at a red light when one of Vegas's finest pulled alongside in his cruisemobile. "Roll down your window, Smothers!" called the copper.

Although the desert heat was, as usual, ever ready to toast the unwary, Hal complied. Along with a faceful of hot air, he received a big grin from Officer Dale Winkins, formerly Mick "Punchy" Ruckowitz.

Once heavily bearded and tattooed, the red-haired man was scarcely recognizable in his clean-shaven state. The tattoos had been expertly lasered off at considerable cost, as Hal knew because he had paid for it.

"Thanks for the message!" called the flatfoot. "But you know what? I just got a promotion, and my wife's due any day now. So…"

"Congratulations!" called Hal.

"You ever get a ticket, come see me!" said Dale, and pulled away as the light turned green.

Melanie grinned. "It's amazing. How many people did you contact, anyway?"

"Oh, half a dozen," Hal said.

"You think most of them are happier with their new lives?"

"I do not see how they could fail to be," he admitted, "seeing as their old lives were of the sort that caused others to wish them dead. However, I am sure they will be glad to visit their friends and relatives again."

"It's like one of those fairy tales," Melanie said,

"where the hero conquers the bad witch, and all her victims turn back into the people they used to be."

"Except," said the cabbie, "that thanks to Mr. Smothers, we don't want to be who we used to be."

Melanie's face squinched as if in deep contemplation. She didn't say anything else until they reached the Ice Palace Resort.

With typical Las Vegas lack of understatement, the vast curving facade had been designed to resemble a natural growth of stalactites and stalagmites reflected in meandering pools of water. At night, the pools turned into colored fountains, while gargantuan white and blue neon letters flashed the hotel's name overhead.

They pulled up to the portico, where a doorman raced to escort them from the cab. Ace/Monty shook Hal's hand and drove away, whistling.

They were in the private elevator going up to the penthouse, when Melanie spoke again. "You know, this would make a great article. Do you suppose I could interview those people? The ones you were supposed to kill but rescued instead?"

"I thought you did not wish to involve me in your journalism career," Hal said.

"Oh. That's true." In the mirrored walls of the elevator, three Melanies smoothed their striped sweaters, which were now right side out. "Besides, nobody would believe it anyway."

"On the other hand," he said, "I would not object if it keeps you close to home."

"Oh, I'm sticking around. I've got plenty of writing to do about Rita," she was saying as the elevator doors opened.

Her mouth worked, but no sounds came out as she regarded the penthouse hallway. Hal hoped she liked it. He had asked the designer to re-create an ancient-Egyptian temple, with a double row of chiseled pillars and, set into wall niches, oversize classic sculptures.

The floor and walls were faced with marble, the ceiling painted in a stylized panorama of the pyramids at Giza. The only thing missing was the Sphinx, which was located around a corner out of sight.

"You live here?" she asked at last.

"My office is at the end of the hall," Hal said. "The private quarters are to our right. To the left are the other administrative offices."

"I see." She swallowed a couple of times.

"I thought you might like a chance to rest." He hoped he had not made a misjudgment. "If you would prefer to return to your own apartment, however..."

"Not at all," said Melanie. "I love museums."

To their right, a door opened, and the housekeeper appeared. She was a motherly woman with the good sense not to make undue inquiries, and, after ascertaining that they would like to rest before dinner, she departed.

Inside his quarters, Hal showed Melanie the sprawling living room, the game room, the gym, the home theater, the formal dining room, the breakfast room, the kitchen—although most of his meals were prepared downstairs and sent up in the dumbwaiter—plus the five bedrooms and the four bathrooms.

He hoped she did not mind the airy modern style. The original living room had continued the theme of the entryway, until one night when, sleepily heading for the kitchen to fix a snack, Hal was startled by a light through a window moving on the face of a goddess and shot her three times before coming fully awake. He had decided to have the whole place redone in blond Danish woods with brass accents.

"Do you think you could feel comfortable here?" he said.

"I already do." She gazed around with interest.

"Naturally, we will clear space for your possessions," he said.

"A laptop and two changes of clothing?" she said. "That shouldn't be hard."

They arrived at the master suite. Silently, Melanie took in the dressing room and entertainment alcove, the bank of mirrors and the oak furniture. Her gaze came to rest on the emperor-size water bed.

"That is where I sleep." As soon as the words were out, Hal felt foolish.

"I see."

"Where we sleep."

"Uh-huh."

"But of course, you already knew that." He had never felt so awkward bringing any of his brides home before. But then, it had never felt like home before. "And this is where, I hope, someday our children will get their start in life."

"I'm not ready for that," said Melanie.

"Take all the time you need," said Hal. "Months. Years."

"Not too many years," she said.

He stopped speaking because he had nothing more to say and because he loved the way the recessed lighting burnished her skin. Also the way she smelled of energy and sunshine. Mainly, the fact that she was here and that she belonged to him.

She gave him a slow, teasing smile. "Well?" she said.

"Well, what?"

"Well, what are you waiting for, Mr. Iceman?" She held up her arms. "They say practice makes perfect."

Time stood still as they flew to the bed, because they were traveling at the speed of light. There, Hal quickly discovered, there was only one thing wrong with what Melanie had said.

Their lovemaking was already perfect. But he decided to keep practicing, anyway.

BONNIE
TUCKER

I Got You,
Babe

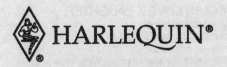

HARLEQUIN®

TORONTO • NEW YORK • LONDON
AMSTERDAM • PARIS • SYDNEY • HAMBURG
STOCKHOLM • ATHENS • TOKYO • MILAN • MADRID
PRAGUE • WARSAW • BUDAPEST • AUCKLAND

Dear Reader,

My Hebrew name, Berakhah, means blessing, and that's how I feel, as if I've been blessed. Okay, so I'm going to get all sentimental and gushy—I can't help it. When my editor told me that my third book, I GOT YOU, BABE, would be one of the launch books for the new Harlequin Duets line, I got that kind of knotted feeling in my stomach that we get when something special is going to happen, something you never anticipated. And then suddenly, there it is, this special something falling right in your lap. I am truly blessed.

Children, too, are a blessing. I knew my third, Jessica, would be my last, and that made her and everything she did seem all the more special. I carried her everywhere, I recorded the things she said and did because I never wanted to forget the day-to-day life I had with my last baby. Little did I know I'd get the chance to remember and recreate several of those moments—some wonderful and some not so wonderful—while writing *I Got You, Babe*.

I'd love to hear from you. Please write me at P.O. Box 16281, Sugar Land, TX 77496-6281.

Bonnie Tucker

Books by Bonnie Tucker

HARLEQUIN LOVE & LAUGHTER
18—HANNAH'S HUNKS
52—STAY TUNED: WEDDING AT 11:00

From the moment of conception until delivery, this book belongs to my editor, Brenda Chin. Thank you, Brenda, for giving me the opportunity to have another baby, without the weight gain.

"Right Stork,
Wrong Address"

Prologue

DIANA SMITH HAD lots of time to think on the airplane taking her from Connecticut to Texas. Three and a half long hours with nothing but time. But that was a good thing, since time was what she thought about most.

She wished she could turn back the clock to the summer she'd been eighteen. Only she knew there wasn't really any point in trying to fix something she couldn't.

Yet, she had to wonder how different her life would have been right now if she had taken that European vacation six years ago, instead of staying home in Sugar Land and working for her father.

So many of her friends had invaded Europe the summer before they went to college. Looking back, she knew she probably should have gone, too. She should have been in Italy, sightseeing, admiring the centuries-old marble statues of cherubs with wings and naked men with little penises that squirted long arches of water into big fountains. She should have been standing in front of those fountains, tossing in her coins and making three wishes.

The thing was, she would've only had one wish—to be home in Sugar Land. That's where Nick Logan was, and where Nick was, Diana wanted to be. She wanted to be able to see him and hope that he'd notice her. And maybe, one day, he'd speak to her, even if it was only to say, hi.

A "hi" from Nick. She'd faint, that's what she'd do. Just plop right down then and there and pass out. After they'd revived her, she'd remember that "hi" and cherish that single word forever and ever.

Diana settled herself more comfortably in seat 2B. The first-class seats were cushy and big. They were perfectly suited for someone like her who wanted to lie back and do nothing but dream. Diana pressed the little button, the seat tilted back, and she closed her eyes.

Dreams. Daydreams. Night dreams. Okay, so she had come to terms with the fact that some girls dreamed about movie stars. Others dreamed about rock stars. Why, she even had a friend, Annie, who was absolutely in love with Teddy Helms, the town's softball coach. Annie was the worst ballplayer. She hated softball. In fact, Diana wasn't even sure Annie knew which end of the bat to hold. Yet, every year, for the past eight, she'd been out there slugging away, and missing. Granted, she had tried to hit the ball. But it was hard for Annie to swing a bat when she was too busy drooling. And drooling was what Annie did, every single year, over Coach Helms.

So, given the mess Annie was, Diana felt that the horrible crush she had on Nick Logan was pretty tame. In fact, it shouldn't have been any big deal. And normally, it wouldn't have been. Except that Nick was Charlie Logan's youngest son, and the Logans and Smiths were sworn enemies. She wasn't allowed to talk to Nick. And she never had. Except twice.

Those were two moments she'd never forget.

Nick Logan was to her what Coach Helms was to Annie. The kind of true love a girl could never have. The stuff Shakespearean tragedies were made from. Diana was Juliet and Nick her Romeo.

She had met him at the Sugar Land Public Awareness Association dinner. That evening, despite the fact that her father, Harry Smith, owner of Smith Construction, and Charlie Logan, owner of Logan Construction, hated each other's guts, the association honored them at an awards ceremony as the two men most responsible for Sugar Land's growth into the twenty-first century.

Of course, what the association didn't realize, and would never know, was that it was Harry's and Charlie's fierce competitive-combative natures, and their extreme hatred for each other, that caused the rapid growth of the little town as each man tried to outdo the other to win contracts to build the biggest and the best buildings. The town's growth had nothing to do with either man's devotion to any civic cause.

At the awards dinner, Charlie and Harry sat at opposite ends of the long head table where they glared at each other like two scarred-up roosters getting ready for a cockfight.

Nick, his older brothers, younger sister and his mother, were seated with Diana at one of the fifty round tables on the floor.

Mrs. Logan, and Nick's brothers, ignored her. His little sister stared at her, and Nick, who sat next to her, talked to her throughout the meal, despite the sharp looks thrown at him by his mother.

Diana knew, even at the vulnerable age of sweet sixteen, that her life had changed forever.

She talked to Nick all evening. She even danced with him once, a slow dance, where they were almost, but not quite, touching. She had fallen in love with him and there would never be anyone else for her because no one could possibly compare to Nick Logan. No one.

So for the next two years she had reminisced about his deep voice, and how it washed over her. She thought how his skin, all muscled and tan from working for his father that summer, would feel touching her. She replayed their one dance over and over again in her mind. She'd imagine conversations they'd have. She'd imagine scenarios where he would one day spot her in a group of people and point her out and say, "Oh, Diana, my love, I've been dreaming about you forever. Where have you been, my darling?"

Of course, she knew it wouldn't happen. It couldn't happen. But dreams never hurt anyone.

Then came the White Envelope Incident.

Diana had worked for her father the summer before college, the same summer she didn't go to Europe. He had been building an apartment complex on Elm Street.

Nick had been working for his dad that summer building a shopping center right across the street from her dad's project.

Diana always waved to him in the morning and at night when she went home. But she absolutely couldn't talk to him.

Diana knew she had the best possible job. She was great at answering the phones, typing envelopes, paying the utility bills. For a bonus she got to watch Nick work on the construction crew across the street. Nick had a way with a hammer, and what he did with a tool belt was almost obscene.

When Nick shucked off his shirt in the summer heat, his skin glistening in the hot, humid air, she about died of heat exposure herself.

His jeans rode low on his slender hips. She wanted more than anything to be able to touch him, to span the warm flesh and hard muscle with her own hands. Her fingers itched with longing to scrape her nails along the sides of his chest, down to his hips, and sink her fingers below. To feel his warm flesh against her skin, to follow the trail her fingers made with her lips, to taste him, to lavish her tongue and lips along his skin, yearning to discover if his skin was soft or hard, salty or sweet.

She even liked when he wore his yellow hard hat over his dark wavy hair. But when he pulled the hat off, and ran his fingers through his hair, she moaned with longing, wishing it were her he was running those fingers over.

Her friends could keep Europe. As far as Diana was concerned, watching Nick Logan was all the sightseeing she needed.

And everything was going so fine, too, until the White Envelope Incident. Her father and Nick's father, along with several other builders, had submitted sealed bids on the Stratford-upon-the-Brazos condominium project.

It had been her job to put the Smith Construction bid in the envelope and take the sealed envelope to the courthouse where it would be held until the day all the bids were opened.

Logan Construction won the contract. That wasn't any big deal, normally. Both companies regularly beat each other out, so she didn't think too much about it.

Until, weeks later, she'd seen the developer, Mr. Stratford at the annual charity fund-raiser benefiting the saving of the Brazos River alligator. He pulled her aside and told her he had opened the sealed white envelope and found a check for six hundred ninety-two dollars and fifty-nine cents made out to the electric company.

Now, Mr. Stratford, being the brilliant man he was, realized immediately that the check wasn't a bribe. The amount was way too small for bribery. Not to mention the fact that the check was made out to the electric company. So Mr. Stratford, one of the most powerful men in the real estate business, forwarded the check Diana had mistakenly put in the bid envelope on to the proper place, and never said a word to anyone about it, until he'd seen Diana at the fund-raiser.

Mr. Stratford understood her total humiliation and embarrassment, and he swore he'd keep her horrible mistake a secret for life, which meant he'd never tell her father— as long as Diana promised never to apply for a job with any company he owned. He even handed her a list, one he'd typed himself so his secretary wouldn't know, of his companies, and asked her to memorize it. Throughout the next six years he'd sent her updates of new acquisitions and told her which businesses she could delete from the list. That man was serious.

So Diana had never told her father about the White Envelope Incident. How could she? How do you say, "Gee, I'm sorry. I was so distracted when I was ogling Nick's butt, I shoved the electric bill in the Stratford condominium-bid envelope, and the bid in the electric-bill envelope. Then I sealed all the envelopes. You understand, Dad, don't you? It wasn't just a plain, ordinary-looking butt, Nick's was a magnificent butt. So if you were ever angry about not getting the contract to build the Stratford condos, don't be. You were never in the running."

From the moment Mr. Stratford told her about the White Envelope Incident, her life had been nothing but one "Incident" after another. And the saddest part of all was that she had never seen Nick again. Except, that is, in her dreams.

1

If Diana had been asked, she could have told the president of Yale that as far as explosions went, the Yale University Lab Incident was insignificant. It hadn't been as bad as the Brown University Incident, nor as damaging as the Oxford Incident. The worst so far had certainly been the Princeton Incident. So Diana couldn't figure out why everybody was getting so riled up.

But riled was exactly the president's state of mind when he had ordered her to remove herself from the university.

Coming home had been nice in a way. Over the last six years she had been to eight universities, and while she was away she'd lost the sense of belonging anywhere. She needed to have a connection to someone, someplace, and the only person who had ever provided her with that connection was her father.

So, on her first morning back home, she woke up feeling on top of the world, glad to be alive, and ready to get on with what was sure to be the next "Incident" in her life.

Diana headed down the hallway toward the kitchen, and wasn't surprised when she ran into her father as he headed the same way. "Good morning, Daddy. Boy, I missed you." She gave him a kiss on the cheek and a big hug. "I'm so glad to be back home."

"I paid Professor Masters up there at Yale to watch out for you, Diana. To make sure you didn't blow anything up again. I forked over good, hard-earned cash."

So much for a good morning, nice to see you. "I know

you did. But maybe you didn't pay him enough,'' she suggested. "Sometimes when you offer to build a wing—"

"You don't think ten thousand, on top of tuition is enough? Any more would be extortion." Harry looked as if he'd explode himself.

"You're right," Diana said, wanting to calm him down. Her father didn't realize these incidents were totally out of her control, and had been since the first one, the White Envelope Incident. "When I leave for Duke, you might want to consider hiring a watchdog to watch over the watchdog that's watching over me."

He stared at her, his mouth slack.

"Bad idea?"

"Come with me, Diana." He turned in the opposite direction, and headed back down the hallway toward the living room. "You and I have to have a long talk."

"Now? I thought we'd get some coffee, and I wanted to see Alicia." Alicia had been their housekeeper since before Harry had made his first million. Diana's mother had still been alive back then. Her mom died when Diana was eight, and Alicia had stayed to take care of her. She was receiving a salary, but she was still part of the family.

"Right now," her father said. "I want to talk about your future. I want to get it over with."

"My future after I get my degree? You want to talk about this now, even though it might not be for another two or three years?" In theory, she only had one year left until she could get her bachelor of science degree. Only, with her, one year could stretch into many.

"No. Your future as of right now. Tomorrow."

The lines on his face seemed more pronounced than they'd been six months ago just before she had left for Yale. She hoped she hadn't put them there. "I'm sorry I worried you, Daddy. That was never my intention."

"Diana." Harry held out his hand.

She grabbed on to his familiar callused fingers the same

way she had as a child. Like a chain-link fence. Sturdy. Dependable. Held to the ground with steel. He had always been her rock. The man who could fix anything, take care of all her little foibles. Her father. Her lifeline.

"You're so creative," he said. "You can do so many things. Did you ever stop and think that chemistry might not be where your talents lie?" he asked.

"Absolutely not." She let go of his hand and stepped back. "I've had more successes than failures. It's only that when I have a failure, my failures are so...so...combustible."

"You always did lean toward the overdramatic." He sighed.

"Overdramatic? Me?" Realistic, yes. Overdramatic, hardly.

He looked grim. "Maybe I've been blinded by my faith in you, and what I always thought you could do. Maybe you hoodwinked me."

"Me?" Her voice rose two octaves. "Hoodwink you? No way." Oh, God, she thought. Had he somehow found out about the White Envelope Incident?

"Sheila says you've been pulling the wool over my eyes for years."

"A-a-a-h." She was still safe. He didn't know. "Now I see where this is going. Sheila." The name of his new wife said it all. Sheila had made it plain at their wedding six months ago that she considered Diana a liability. A tie with Harry's past that would best be gotten rid of. Well, Diana wouldn't let her get away with it. She reminded her father, "I'm your daughter."

"She's my wife."

"Wife number five," Diana scornfully pointed out. Wives were an expendable commodity to her father.

"Now, now, Diana." He sounded conciliatory. "She's only trying to help. Be a nice girl."

"Girl? I'm not a girl anymore, Dad. I'm a woman.

Twenty-four. And as far as being nice, well, Nice is my middle name."

"To some you might be, but Sheila thinks you could be a little nicer."

"Okay, I'll be nicer." Diana didn't have a clue what Sheila was talking about, but there was no point discussing this with her dad. She had long ago learned that arguing about any of his current wives was like a failed experiment. Both seemed to blow up in her face. Her father stayed in love and had complete loyalty to every one of his wives, right up until the divorce.

The only wife who had never divorced him was her mother. Harry had been so in love with Elizabeth, he'd been trying to find another wife just like her. With no success.

He gazed at her in pity. "I only hope I'm not too late. We should have talked after that disaster in Boston."

"You mean the Harvard Incident. I thought you understood that Christine was a good friend."

"*You* have to understand," he said, "that you never take it upon yourself to redesign the chancellor's daughter. I wish your mother were here. I wasn't equipped to teach you social skills."

"Daddy, I was helping Christine. She wanted to try for the blond look. That's all. So I took out my permanent hair-dye formula and mixed up the ingredients. Everything worked fine until she went outside to smoke a cigarette. Everyone knows smoking is bad for you."

"You set her on fire."

"I did not. I was in the house. *She* set her hair on fire, and I was quick enough to get the fire extinguisher and put the flames out. I should have been hailed a hero."

"You were thrown out of Harvard."

"Ingrates," she mumbled. "I explained to her family that her hair would grow back. In time. How could I know that they were going to meet Queen Elizabeth and Prince

Philip the next day? That's the problem, Dad, Americans have an obsession with British royalty.''

"They were meeting the queen of England. They had reason to be upset."

"I've lived in England, so I can say it's no big deal." That had been before the Oxford Incident. The chemistry professor at Oxford had been asking her out for weeks, and she had been turning him down. One day she was working in the lab when he stood next to her and whispered, "Douse the flame." Diana thought he had told her to *arouse* his flame. There was no way she was going to arouse anything about that man, especially not his flame. When she pushed him aside, he knocked into the burner, which tipped and set the chemicals on fire. He had blamed her, of course.

But the way she looked at it, she couldn't really be held responsible for someone else's accent problem. "Christine looked fine," Diana told her dad. "Even if having a shaved head wasn't the look she was after." So the Harvard Incident became history, and she had gone on to Brown University.

"That's exactly my point. Your attitude. It's as if you expect to be thrown out of school, as if you expect failure. I should have talked to you earlier, only I didn't think about it. Not until Sheila pointed out my own failure as a father."

"I won't have you talking like that." Now she was getting angry. "First of all, you're not a failure. Failure is not an option. That's the motto you and I both live by. Remember?"

"There comes a time when you have to admit defeat and move on."

"I'm not ready."

"Sheila says—"

"Sheila's all wrong no matter what she says." Diana had her hands on her hips, and they stood facing each other in the hallway, neither moving. Neither giving in.

"Sheila said I don't have control over the situation."

"You have control. You've always been in control. You and I are in this together. You know that if I'm going to discover something that would make the world a better place to live in, then accidents are a risk. I will make you proud of me."

Diana's ideas had always been sound, her intent sincere. It wasn't her fault that some of her experiments—well, a lot of her experiments—went up in flames.

"Sheila said I coddle you." The way he said it cut her deeply. He seemed so ashamed, and that wasn't her father. He didn't coddle her, either. Sheila had been doing a number on him, brainwashing him.

Diana tried to stay calm. "No one, not even Sheila, can take away the future that I've invested the last six years of my life obtaining. Despite the obstacles, I'm not giving up on my destiny."

"You need to pick a new destiny then," her father said. "It's all been decided." He stared at her long and hard. "You could have been killed in that explosion at Oxford. Then where would I be?"

It took only a moment for Diana to realize Harry wasn't angry with her—he was extremely worried. She gave her dad a hug, and whispered, "Thank you for caring."

"Come on, Diana," he said gruffly. "I want to discuss where you're going from here."

"You know I'm going to Duke next. Nothing about my plans have changed." Then she stepped inside the living room and sank ankle deep in plush, white carpet.

Maybe her plans hadn't changed, but this room sure had. She wiggled her toes. The carpet hadn't been there when she had left for Yale six weeks before. The room now smelled of fresh paint and looked slick with new furniture. She squinted at the brightness emanating from the windows with no draperies or blinds to prevent ultraviolet rays from coming in and bouncing from white wall to white wall, searing her eyeballs.

Gone were the comfortable soft, cotton floral couches, and the big blue-and-yellow-checkered chairs. Gone were the beautiful tongue-and-groove pine floors.

Then her gaze focused on the corner near the back window. Her table and chairs were gone, too. She looked around the room, and they were nowhere in sight. *Don't jump to conclusions,* she told herself. *Take three deep breaths. Good. Now lick your lips. You can't carry on a conversation with dry lips.* She licked them. *Now ask your father. Go ahead. Don't be afraid.* "Dad, did you put them in the basement?"

"What are you talking about?" Red tinged his neck.

He knew what she was talking about and suddenly she started to shake. "My table and chairs. Did you move them down to our storage space?"

He shook his head.

Swallow, Diana. You can't talk if your mouth is all dried out, either. She swallowed. "Dad, where are they?" She pointed to the corner.

Her father's face was splotched with red and his lips moved, but no words came out. Oh, God. No. It couldn't be. If she had been the fainting type, she would've been out for the count.

Instead, she made a conscious effort to remain calm and rational. She had been trained, at least in theory, not to form a conclusion until all the evidence was in. So she stood in the center of a white living room and stared at a white silk plant in a white plant holder that stood in the corner where her table and chairs should have been.

"Where are they?" Diana asked again.

"Those old things." Harry's voice cracked as his arms flagellated up and down. "You didn't need those anymore."

"I—didn't—need—them." She choked on her words, and the palms of her hands went as cold as her heart. Fear.

That's what it was. Blue, frigid fear. "I'll always need them."

When she and her dad had moved from her childhood home into the penthouse at the Stratford-upon-the-Brazos condominiums, they'd agreed that's where they'd put the tiny oak table and two chairs that Harry had made from scratch when she was only a toddler. She and her mother had had tea parties at that table and had colored pictures together there, too. That's where she had learned how to write her name. The table and chairs weren't just any table and chairs. They were special. All her memories of her mom were tied up in those small pieces of wooden furniture. They meant everything to her.

Her mother had died. Now the table and chairs were gone, too.

"Sheila," Harry started. "She didn't think they matched the rest of the room. She said you didn't need them anymore and you'd be grateful to get rid of them."

"You accepted that?" Diana couldn't believe that he'd gone along with Sheila. That he'd do what wife number five had said to do without protecting what belonged to his own daughter. His *only* daughter.

"How was I supposed to know?" he said. "She's a woman, you're a woman. What do I know about women?"

"You should have known. They are—were—mine."

"Sheila said—"

"Sheila said, Sheila said," Diana mimicked. "You know, every time you get married again, your brain turns to mush." Her dad was still in newlywed heaven. The old goat. The randy old goat. Then she caught herself. Looking at her father, she finally noticed that he was as upset as she was. "I'm sorry. That remark was disrespectful and rude."

"I deserved it. Your stepmother threw the whole set out while I was at work," he confessed almost in a whisper, looking over his shoulder, making sure no one else was there.

"She's not my stepmother." Diana was too old to have stepmothers. But if she ever had the chance to *be* a stepmother—or even a mother... But that would never happen, because the only person she would ever consider having children with was Nick Logan, and she knew that if she ever spoke to him, the sky would fall, the earth would crack, the rivers would flood and lice would descend on the hair of every firstborn girl child for generations to come.

"If I had known, I would have stopped her. I didn't know what she had done until the trash collectors had come and gone."

"I believe you." It didn't matter. The damage was done, and the sick feeling wouldn't go away. Yet she was still trying to comfort him when it was she who was feeling empty inside.

"When Sheila started her decorating, I stayed away from this part of the place. It's so white."

"Yes it is." Diana pointed her finger, making a promise. "I'm going to write a book someday, Daddy. I'm going to call it the *Stepmother-In-Training Manual.* Maybe it will save someone else's beloved furniture. And you have to admit, I'm an expert on stepmothers. It'll be a bestseller."

"Diana," Harry said softly. "I am sorry. I want you to know I went to the dump and searched, but I couldn't find the table and chairs. I brought a whole team from my construction crew over there. I did everything I could."

"Oh, Daddy." She went into this open arms, finding what comfort she could. These were the same arms that hugged her when she'd scraped her knees. The arms that had been there for her when she'd come home from a bad date.

Only she found no comfort in his arms this morning. Only an extreme sense of loss.

IT WAS SIX in the morning when Nick Logan opened the front door, and his sister, Cathy, greeted him with a cheerful, "Nicky! You wonderful brother you!" She launched her one-year-old daughter at him, then backed out into the hall again. "You weren't sleeping, were you?"

"Been up for two hours already working on some new plans for the Castillo house." Nick didn't know who was more surprised about whose arms his niece had landed in, Jessica or him. From the look on the baby's face, he had a feeling the shock effect was mutual.

"Aren't computers wonderful things. You can work at work and you can work at home. You never have to not work, once you're connected. Incredible." Cathy came back in the apartment carrying an armload of baby junk. She dropped a car seat on the floor and leaned a portable crib against the wall. "And thank you in advance for helping me out."

"What am I doing?" He held Jessica out at arm's length, as her tiny legs started to kick in the air and her feet, encased in heavy leather walking shoes, scraped his chest and arms. "Cathy," he called out, waiting until she stopped long enough to make eye contact with him. "Let me rephrase the question. What are *you* doing? Moving in?"

She only laughed then headed out the door again. Jessica's face scrunched up, her nose started to turn red and her eyes crinkled together. "Caaaathy," he warned sharply. "She's going to start that crying again."

"No she won't," his sister said when she unloaded more baby things. "Jessie loves you."

"Yeah. As much as she likes getting a shot."

"Don't sell yourself short, big brother. Both you and immunizations are good for her. You're the most perfect brother a girl can have. I mean that, too." Her voice caught.

"Don't get all sentimental on me. You know, to all intents and purposes, I'm the only brother you have." But he wasn't perfect. Not by a long shot. All anyone had to do was ask his three older, perfect brothers, and his perfect parents, and they'd list in chronological order exactly how *un*perfect Nick was.

As far as Nick was concerned, the only thing his perfect family did to perfection was to be unforgiving. When Cathy had told them she was pregnant, they had thrown her out of their house, and their family. Banned from Logan-dom forever.

Nick had always been the rebel son. He alone had stood by her side, helped her through her pregnancy and had been there for both her and his niece afterward. Nick was the only close relative Cathy had besides Jessica. The squirming kid who right at this moment was getting ready to let out one of her famous, "I hate you, Uncle Nick" screams. He made a face at her and, just as she opened her mouth to let loose, he put her down on the marble floor. She wobbled on tiny feet for a second, then got down on all fours and crawled away as fast as she could.

"Isn't she adorable," Cathy gushed, stopping for a second, watching her daughter.

"A real stinker all right."

"Is it her diaper? I just changed her."

"No, she's fine." If you liked ungrateful, noisy toddlers. "What do you need, Cathy, besides storage space?"

Her bright smile disappeared and in its place was a worried frown. "Remember you told me once that if I ever needed anything you'd always be here for me?"

"Sure." He had made the offer time and again. She'd never asked for help though.

"I need you."

"I'll get the checkbook, you fill in the figure. What's mine is yours."

"Not money." Cathy scooped up Jessica and held her close to her chest before she sank down, cross-legged on the floor, holding the baby in her lap. She rubbed Jessica's back, and looked at her brother with the most angelic smile on her face. "Nicky, the most wonderful, incredible thing happened today. I'd been praying, and finally—"

"What happened?" he asked, hoping Jessica's no-account father had finally shown up and was going to start taking some responsibility for his kid.

"L'Ouverture Parfum's finally called. They want to buy *L'Amour.*"

"Hey, that's great." He kneeled in front of her and ruffled her bangs the way he used to do when they were kids. "You deserve this."

She'd been trying, for the last couple of years, to generate interest from L'Ouverture Parfum for the fragrances she'd been creating and selling to local gift shops. She had a good business, with her signature perfumes, colognes, soaps and other products. However, they both knew that having L'Ouverture show interest in purchasing even one of her fragrances could set her and Jessica up for life.

"Thank you. I'm thrilled. I only hope when they buy *L'Amour,* they're interested in a few others from my collections, too."

"You're not going to sell them the *Nicholas X* formula, are you?" After Jessica was born, Cathy had thanked him for his help by creating *Nicholas X.* She had come up with a shaving soap, aftershave, cologne and deodorant that was all his own.

"I wasn't planning to."

"Good, because that stuff drives women wild. If all the men were wearing it, too, no work would ever get done."

She batted at his arm. "You're crazy."

"I'm serious. You have no idea what my life has been like since you gave me my own aftershave. I can't keep the women away."

"You couldn't keep them away before I created *Nicholas X.*" She winked at him. "Anyway, big brother, that formula's all yours."

"That reminds me," he said. "I'm on the last of the

aftershave. So if you don't want me to have to resort to my old standby—'' he paused ''—soap and water, which will put me right back in the ranks of the he-who-is-ignored-by-women group of guys, would you bring some with you the next time you're over here.''

"I will as soon as I get back from Paris."

"You're going to Paris? All alone?"

"Of course." She shook her finger at him. "Why? Did you think I needed my mommy and daddy to hold my dainty little hand?"

"Point taken." He knew Cathy was an adult. She had the baby to prove it. She was a businesswoman. She had obtained a good deal of success, and she was still climbing the ladder. Nick was proud of her. Still, she was his little sister, and she'd always be his little sister. Sometimes he'd forget that she was all grown up. "I know you don't need Mom and Dad to travel with you."

"Good thing. It's not like they know I'm alive." The hurt still tinged her voice. "Or Jessica."

"Forget them."

"Okay. They've forgotten us, we'll forget them." This time she grinned at him. A grin that didn't reach her eyes. Neither one would ever forget what their parents had done. "Can you believe the perfume company executives want to meet me in person. They've sent me a ticket, a driver, everything."

"Sure I can believe it." He said the words quietly, meaning every one. "Those people want to meet in person the woman who makes the stuff that makes guys like me smell so good."

"I know. Oh, Nicky, I don't know how I can thank you for taking care of Jessica while I'm away."

"I'm not taking care of Jessica. I don't remember ever saying I'd take care of her." He stood, and slowly backed away from Cathy. "Where'd you ever get a crazy idea like that?"

"From you. Who else? You told me if I ever needed anything, you'd do it. I need you now."

"I meant money. If you needed money." Starting to panic, he backed up until he hit the wall, which of course made Jessica scream again. "I can't take care of her, the kid hates me. Whenever she's near me, she starts screaming."

"You scared her, that's all. Anyway, that was only a phase."

"A phase that's lasted from the time she was born? I don't think so. Besides, I don't know a thing about babies."

"Neither did I when I first had her. But I managed just fine. So will you. Besides, I'm leaving you with all kinds of instructions. And I'll only be gone a couple of days. I'll be back before she even knows I'm gone."

"Cathy, I have a bad feeling about this whole thing. It's not a good idea." He stuck his hands in his pockets and paced. This would teach him. The next time he offered to help with *anything,* he would have to be more specific about the definition of *anything.*

Cathy stood up and placed Jessica in a contraption that had a canvas seat and a small hula hoop soldered on two pairs of in-line skates. "This is a walker," she said. "Don't let her climb out of it, because if she does, she'll fall down and crack her head open. Not a pretty picture, I can tell you."

Jessica took off sliding down the hallway in her walker. "The first thing I'm buying her is a helmet," Nick said. "And me some earplugs."

"That's a fabulous idea. See, you're doing well already." She stood on tiptoe and kissed his cheek. "Now, pay attention to my instructions."

"I'm paying attention."

"Okay, this is a box of diapers. The box says Diapers and even has a picture to go with the words, so you shouldn't have any problem finding them."

His eyelids narrowed. "Cathy," he warned. "I know how to change a diaper." He never had, but he'd seen her do it, and it looked easy enough.

She gave him a big smile. "See how simple it is? Everything is numbered and labeled. You're going to have so much fun. This is a car seat. And this is a..."

He listened to Cathy with half an ear. From down the hallway Jessica had stopped and looked at him. Nick would swear by the expression on her face, the baby was saying, "Get ready, Uncle Nicky, I'm going to make your life hell."

THREE HOURS LATER, long after Cathy had gone, Jessica had demonstrated just how much hell she could raise.

He had left her to herself, in his bedroom, rolling around in her walker. He thought she'd be safe. He was within earshot, so he could hear her in case she started screaming in pain instead of anger. Plus the master bath was attached to the bedroom. He only had to step out of the dressing area where he was shaving, and he'd be right back in his bedroom, where he could see her.

He'd been right. She was very safe. Instead of screaming, she was making soft, talking noises that no one could possibly understand. When he peeked into the room the first time, his face lathered with Cathy's shaving soap, she was quietly roaming around in her walker, studying all his belongings. She sniffed a few times, then turned her head when she realized he was in the room. She gave him that evil-eyed glare before turning away, ignoring him. Nick took that to be a positive step in their relationship. No crying.

He went back to the sink to finish shaving. The sound of paper ripping didn't register right away, but when it did, he fast-tracked back into the bedroom. "Jessica, no," he shouted as he pulled paper out of her hands, and some out of her mouth. She screamed at him, which made his nerve endings stand at attention. No big deal.

Until he noticed what he held in his hands. His complete collection of the *Sports Illustrated* swimsuit issues. She had somehow rolled herself to his nightstand, opened the door to the cabinet and pulled out the magazines, one at a time.

She screamed louder, sticking her tongue out at him. Nick thought for a brief moment that he should let her finish eating the paper, but then he remembered that the little screaming tyrant had already cost him half the salary he would have paid one of his construction workers, when she was born. No way was she going to be eating magazine print. He was going to protect his investment, if nothing else.

He scraped the wads of wet paper off her tongue and considered it a success that she only bit him twice. He looked at the two puncture holes on his finger. "You hardly drew any blood, Ms. Vampire."

He listened to another scream, and watched a few tears flow, then went into the kitchen in search of a plastic garbage bag to clean up the mess.

"I'm not cleaning this myself," Nick told her, putting the trash bag on the floor. He lifted Jessica out of the walker and put her down on the carpet. "Pick this up and throw it in here." He showed her how to take the scrap of paper and put it in the bag.

Like the other two women in his family, his mother and his sister, Jessica appeared to listen, *appeared* being the key word. Then she turned her back on him and ripped the cover off another magazine.

"That does it." Nick put her back into the walker, and this time he rolled her out in the hallway. "Go, Jessica. Go race to the front door."

She stayed right where she was, in the doorway, and watched him. Nick, mumbling to himself about how a great uncle like him ended up with such an impossible niece, got down on his belly to search under the bed for more papers. That's when he found it.

Nick had thought he could handle anything. Until he

reached under the bed and pulled out the pieces of his broken college-championship football trophy.

He glanced at the nightstand where he always kept it, hoping that what he held in his hand was something else. But no, the top of the nightstand was bare, and he held pieces of the constant reminder that as far as his father was concerned, second in the nation wasn't anything.

He looked across the room at Jessica staring at him from the doorway. She wasn't crying now, just sniffing through her clogged nose.

"Why?" he asked her. "Why did you do this?" She stared back at him with those big blue eyes, eyes so like his sister's, so like his own. And just as calculating as his father's.

As quarterback for the University of Texas, he led his team to the division championship, and ultimately the Orange Bowl. UT lost the Orange Bowl game by one point. Still, Nick had a great deal of pride in the accomplishments he had made that year, both for his team and himself. There had been a parade in Austin that day. A big ceremony when they passed out the trophies, and other honors. Nick had been king of the world, a hero to the school.

"Second isn't first, is it?" his father had said the day he came home with the trophy. "People only remember who's first. It's not second place that goes down in the record books."

Nick gripped the broken-off football player, a miniature replica of the person he had once been. Almost number one.

Maybe for him that was good enough. Nick didn't build shopping centers or office buildings anymore. He did what he had always loved to do, creating the most beautiful and unique homes in the city. And he had a waiting list for his services.

He heard Jessica rolling herself down the hallway, giggling all the way.

"I think you are a little sadistic at heart, baby," Nick called out so she could hear him as he very gently put the broken pieces of the trophy safely away in the top drawer of his bureau. "Because if you aren't, then you have a very strange personality."

Jessica had rolled back into the doorway, as if tearing around in her walker was the greatest game in town. She clapped and giggled then rolled back down the hall again.

Nick finished shaving, threw on shorts and a T-shirt and followed her to the hallway closet. "I'll take you for a walk. I need to release some of this stress you've caused. Then I'll call my secretary and see if she can find you a baby-sitter."

He rummaged through the boxes lining the back wall of the closet until he found his old University of Texas backpack and took it to the room he used as his office. Cathy had placed Jessica's things over the couch and all the available chairs, and had his desk covered with pink paraphernalia, too. The box of diapers sat next to his computer.

Jessica had followed behind him, rolling faster than he walked, tripping her wheels over the backs of his running shoes. All the while, she leaked water from her face and there was no telling what the other parts of her were leaking, too.

He put eight diapers into the backpack and moved the box away from the computer. If he were lucky, eight might last an hour. He carried the portable crib into the spare bedroom and set it up next to the queen-size guest bed. Jessica still followed him, crying sporadically, throwing stuffed toys at him. She had pretty good aim.

"Come on, kid." He took the backpack and went into the kitchen. Jessica stayed behind, rolling up and down the hallway. He packed eight bottles of milk to go with the eight diapers and had zipped up the backpack, when he heard Jessica's earsplitting screams. He ran back to the hall and found her, sitting on the floor, the walker tipped over

on its side. Nick scooped her up in his arms and brought
her back to the kitchen, sitting down in the chair near the
window. He ignored her screams, which sounded different
than they had before. "Quiet down for a second, Jessica,"
he said through his clenched mouth. "I'm checking your
head to make sure it's not cracked."

She only screamed louder.

When he didn't find any damage, and his heart rate had
gone back to almost normal, it dawned on him that Cathy
had been wrong. Jessica didn't break her head open the
way she'd said she would. It stood to reason then that if
she'd been wrong about Jessica breaking her head, she
could also be wrong about other things. Like Jessica having
gotten over her hatred for him.

The baby climbed off Nick's lap and stood herself up on
wobbly feet. He walked back toward the counter and she
followed close on his heels, all the while swatting at the
backs of his legs, screaming nonsense.

"Would you like a cookie?" he asked. He didn't care
what she thought inside that little head of hers, he knew he
was a great uncle, offering cookies and bottled milk. She
didn't deserve him. He didn't deserve the treatment she
dished out.

"Nooooo," she screamed, taking hold of the material on
his jeans' leg and twisting the denim, pinching the back of
his knee.

"Ouch," he cursed, which made Jessica laugh. "The
least your mother could have done was teach you how to
say, 'No, Uncle Nicky.'" He bent down to her level and
handed her an oatmeal cookie.

"Nooooo," she screamed louder as she grabbed the
cookie and chomped down.

"That's what I like. A woman who knows what she
wants and isn't afraid to tell me."

"Nooooo." She smiled at him through her red nose and
watery blue eyes.

He didn't know what to do with her. A baby who cried and smiled at the same time wasn't normal. As soon as she finished the cookie, Nick asked her if she wanted another one.

"Nooooo," she said with another wet smile, holding her arms up toward the bag on the counter.

"Then let's go." He handed her two cookies, one cookie for each hand, then shrugged into the backpack. While she was occupied with the food, he lifted her. As soon as he did, the tears started coming.

After several tense moments, the baby ended up horizontal, as if she were swimming at his waist. She kicked his behind with her legs, and pounded his thigh with her fists. "I'm going to remind you of this when you start dating," Nick muttered. "These are the exact tactics I want you to use on any guy who tries anything."

BY NINE O'CLOCK that morning, Diana was both physically and emotionally exhausted. Then she heard the ominous tap-tap-tap of approaching footsteps.

Her dad, though, seemed to perk up. Where he got the energy after all they'd just talked about, Diana didn't know. But Harry spit into his hands, slicked back his hair and pasted a smile on his face.

"Sheila, my love," Harry gushed, holding out his arms.

Diana rolled her eyes. Her dad hadn't even reached fifty yet. He was still a good-looking man with all his dark brown hair. He could have done better than Sheila-the-Hun.

Harry positively glowed when wife number five floated into the white room, her arms spread out wide, the white bell sleeves of her white caftan flapping in the breeze her entrance had created. And her father called Diana dramatic. Hah!

"Darling." Sheila patted hair that had been pitch-black the last time Diana had seen her, but was now dyed blondish-white to match the room. She blew kisses past Harry's

cheeks, since she was so small—even in her white high-
heel shoes, she still only came up to his shoulder—then
flitted to the white couch where she perched. Diana wasn't
fooled for one moment. A white canary with the heart and
personality of an albino vulture. "Diana, dear, how are
you?"

"I'm fine, Sheila," she said sweetly. She decided then
and there that when she arrived at Duke, the first thing
she'd invent was a chemical to take Sheila's blood out of
white carpet.

Sheila's own eyelids narrowed. "Really? How interesting. I would have thought with all you've been through,
you'd be more downtrodden." She turned away, showing
Diana her bony backside.

Diana wouldn't be dismissed. She walked around to the
side of the couch where Sheila sat, and stood in front of
her, waiting until Sheila finally looked her in the eye. "The
only bad thing I've been through is coming home and finding out you threw away my table and chairs. *Mine,* not
yours." Unshed tears stung her eyes, and gave her the beginnings of a headache, but she refused to succumb to the
pain. She would not let Sheila, the black-hearted wolf in
sheep's snowy clothing, have the satisfaction of knowing
how much she'd hurt her.

"Those old things. I didn't know they had any kind of
sentimental value until your father—" she gazed at Harry
with loving eyes "—told me. Afterward."

She was lying and Diana knew it. By throwing out the
tiny table and chairs, Sheila had found the perfect way to
say, "I'm taking over, and you're out." Diana had been
through enough stepmothers-in-training to know they all
had their own private agendas. Harry's other wives may
have been a little different, but none of them had been cruel
or mean. Diana had liked them all, and was sorry when
each marriage had ended.

Sheila, on the other hand, was mean. And since meanness wasn't part of Diana's personality, she was having trouble coping.

But she'd learn. Diana was nothing if not studious.

"Harry, did you tell Diana about *our* plans for her future."

A sinking sensation gripped Diana in the pit of her stomach. Stepmothers-in-training weren't allowed to make plans for the children of their new spouse. If that wasn't already an unspoken rule, then it would become a written one as soon as she wrote the manual.

"Not yet, Sheila. Come, Diana, sit down," her father said gently. "We haven't had our coffee yet."

She glanced at Sheila. Diana's first cup of coffee was meant to be savored. She couldn't enjoy anything sitting in the same room with wife number five. "I'll have mine later."

Harry's jaw dropped, as well it should have. Diana was never known to turn down a cup of coffee. He picked up a white bell from a white stucco end table and shook it.

"If this is going to be a meaningful conversation, we should both have our coffee now. Right?" His smile seemed weak.

"Okay." She knew the unwritten script. The stage directions said, "Agree."

"Really, Harry," Sheila fussed. "You mustn't drink that coffee in here. You might spill it on the rug. Or the couch." She looked sideways at Diana, and Diana knew who Sheila was really worried about.

"We'll drink in here." Then he bellowed loud enough to carry through the twelve-thousand-square-foot penthouse, "Alicia, bring two coffees and one of Mrs. Smith's teas."

"But, Harry, darling—"

"Coffee will be served in here." This time, Sheila stopped, apparently deciding this battle wasn't worth fighting.

"Thank you, Daddy." Diana stood on her toes and gave him a kiss on the cheek. "For being my dad." She had learned in her psychology classes at Princeton and Oxford, before she'd been asked to leave those schools, that arguing didn't do much good. Now, sentiment, that was another matter altogether. Sentiment could get a positive response. Diana had a feeling that before the morning was over, she was going to be using sentiment a lot.

By silent agreement they didn't say anything else as they waited for the coffee. Diana walked around the living room. All signs of lived-in comfort were gone.

Diana squinted. "This room is giving my eyeballs a sunburn."

Sheila said, "Don't be flippant."

"I didn't think I was," Diana said. She plopped herself down on the white stuffed sofa and immediately sank almost to the floor.

"I could have sworn I'd lost weight at Yale." Crossing one leg over the other, trying to adjust to sitting down with her knees higher than her bottom, she refused even to think she might have gained weight. "I have a theory that having a passion for chocolate-filled doughnuts doesn't put on ten pounds, as long as you set your mind into weight-loss mode. You see, I did this experiment with some of the women who lived in the college's apartments. We each ate five chocolate-filled doughnuts a day, and then we willed ourselves not to gain weight. Only two of us didn't gain. The rest didn't use their minds to will the calories away. Which is why they gained weight. That's when I started working on a pill that turned the properties of chocolate into water."

"Really, Diana," Sheila said. "How your mind works. Silly."

"Not to people who like candy." Her foot buried itself in the carpet and only some red, slightly chipped toenail polish showed through the white wool whorls. She'd bet her life Sheila was a closet chocolate eater.

Alicia came into the room wearing a white dress with a white apron and white lace collar. She served coffee on a clear Plexiglas tray. "Here are your beverages, Mr. Harry and Ms. Sheila. Good morning, Miss Diana."

"What's with this Miss Diana and Mr. Harry stuff? Why are you wearing a uniform?" Diana asked. Alicia didn't wear uniforms. She called Diana's dad, "Hey you, Har." Alicia was not someone who should ever have to say miss and mister.

Alicia's face scrunched up as she nodded in the direction of the stepmother-in-training. "Miss Sheila's idea."

"That's insulting." Diana turned to her father. "Aren't you going to do something about this?"

"Now, Diana," Harry started. "Sheila thinks that a man in my position should have a more formal staff."

Alicia rolled her eyes at Diana as she poured the coffee in a set of new, white bone-china cups. She rolled them again when she left the room.

"We need to think about dismissing that woman, Harry," Sheila said. "She doesn't know her place."

"You do anything to Alicia, and I'll personally see you gone," Diana threatened.

"Well, I never." Sheila tsked, drumming her white-painted fingertips on her white sleeve.

Diana struggled out of the sofa. When she regained her balance, she took the cup of coffee and gave it to her father, ignoring the second cup.

Finally Harry cleared his throat. "You're my daughter. I could never get angry at you. I know these experiments you do will work, eventually. The problem is, most schools don't have the patience to wait until you get it right. Maybe you've been distracted, and that's why things go wrong. It can't be easy pulling up stakes every semester."

"It hasn't been hard. Disappointing though. I thought I'd be further along than this."

"Well, I did do the best I could for you. You know that."

"Of course I do. And I appreciate how you've always been here for me, allowed me to try and fulfill my dream."

Harry put down his empty cup and paced. Diana stood next to the window, looking down thirty stories to the park across the street.

"Sheila thinks that you should switch your major from science to English."

When she saw Harry had a very straight face, and realized he wasn't joking, she said, "English. Surely you're joking," she said. "Daddy, nobody saves the world by majoring in English."

"You're jinxed, sweetheart. Face it."

Diana laughed, only her laugh verged on hysteria. "Oh, Daddy, you're so wrong. So very wrong. I'm not jinxed." But then again, maybe she was. Maybe the problem with her was that she'd been carrying the burden too long about the White Envelope Incident. She knew if she told him the truth, she could lose it all. But she looked over at Sheila, saw her evil grin of satisfaction and knew she was going to lose it all anyway, so it didn't matter.

She drew in a slow, deep breath. "Then again, maybe you're right."

"Of course I am. You see, Sheila thinks—"

"Oh, no, it has nothing to do with Sheila, and everything to do with these condominiums."

"What are you talking about?" It was his turn to look befuddled.

"Oh, Daddy, have I got a story for you. You better sit down." She would tell him, just the bare facts, just enough to let him know why she'd been so distracted. And why chemicals may have gotten mixed up. "It's about these condominiums. And Nick Logan."

"Nick Logan?" he snapped. "That bastard Charlie's kid?"

The way he said Nick's name, Diana knew that all her dreams of being with Nick were just that—dreams. The family hatred ran too deep.

"What about that Logan?" Harry said.

It was too late to go back. She could only hope he'd forgive her. Hope he'd understand that everything that had happened to her in the past six years was directly or indirectly related to that day.

Harry waited, and Sheila smirked. *English*. That stepmother-in-training had a lot to learn about Diana Smith.

Her life had been hell for the last six years, and she knew the exact day it had started. "Remember the summer I worked for you when I was eighteen. Right before I left for the Sorbonne."

"Sure." He poured himself another cup of coffee. "We thought it would be a great way for us to spend more time together before you left the country. I was between wives then, too."

Sheila made a grunting noise.

"Remember how Smith Construction was building an apartment complex on Elm," Diana said, "and Logan Construction was building the office building right across the street?"

"I'll never forget. Their concrete trucks blocked ours. Charlie kept trying to hire all my men by offering them more money. I had to match him. That job cost me big bucks."

O-o-o-o-o-h, Dad, Diana thought. *You have no idea how many millions that job really did cost you. Yet.*

"Remember how Charlie's son Nick was working for him?"

"Not really. Can't be expected to remember everyone."

Diana didn't believe him. No one could forget Nick, and her father probably had every one of Charlie's kids tattooed in his brain. "Well, I remember that I was paying bills that day...."

So Diana explained everything to her father, without going into detail about how Nick made her feel, or what she had wanted to do to him, because she knew no father wanted that much personal information about his daughter's wayward imagination.

"Somehow, the envelopes became mixed up."

"So you fixed them, right?"

"Well, Mr. Stratford, what a nice man, he sent the electric company the check."

"How did he get the check?"

"Because the electric company got the bid," Diana squeaked.

Her dad stood there, his eyes bugged out, his mouth hanging open. So far, he seemed to be taking it pretty well. All things considered.

"There was no way I could know about this in advance, because the project was a closed bid."

Harry made a strangled noise in his throat. But he hadn't yelled. Things were still looking good.

"And that's why Logan Construction got to build the Stratford."

"Diana, do you know what you've done?"

"I thought you'd be happy to know you didn't lose out to Charlie Logan. You weren't even in the running. Doesn't it make you feel better knowing that Logan didn't beat you?"

Harry's face had turned bright red. The words came out slowly and very precisely. "Diana, I had reluctantly agreed with Sheila before, but now I'm positive about this. You will go back to school. You will change your major to English. You will not go near another laboratory again. Do you understand?"

Sheila trilled in, "She has to go to the University of Texas. She can't stay here."

Diana turned on her. "This is *my* home. You can't tell me how to run my life."

"But dear," Sheila purred. "We hold the purse strings, don't we, Harry, darling?"

"This is what I get for being honest?" she said. "My own father turns on me?"

"You will be finished in a year, Diana," Harry yelled.

Diana didn't yell back. She turned to Sheila and said quietly, and with purpose, "Why are you being so mean to me? What did I ever do to you?"

"Really, dear, you just exist." Sheila whispered back, with a smile, so only Diana, and not Harry, heard her speak.

Diana hurried out of the room as fast as she could, but not before hearing Sheila consoling her father. "Don't worry, Harry, Diana will get over her little tantrum."

Diana found small comfort in the darkness of her bedroom, especially after the blinding light she had just left behind. The blue miniblinds were closed, blocking out the morning sun. She let her vision become accustomed to the darkness. She then opened her sock drawer, took out the first pair she touched and put them on. Her suitcases were still on the floor, still packed, and after the conversation with her father and Sheila-the-Witch, they were likely to stay that way.

Never had she felt more alone. Or lonely. Not only had her Rock of Gibraltar disintegrated, but the life she had so neatly planned since she was eighteen was falling apart, too. And this time she was not the one who had initiated the explosion.

From the moment she discovered she'd mixed up the envelopes, she knew what direction her life would take. The fact that it was taking her many more years, and many more colleges, than she had originally planned was of no significance, despite what Sheila insinuated.

Diana knew she would still graduate from a university. Eventually. She knew she would make a difference in the

232 I Got You, Babe

world. Eventually. She would make her father proud, despite his infatuation with wife number five. She'd find a way to continue. Somehow.

She wasn't hopeless or helpless. She could get a job. She wasn't going to blame Sheila for this setback either. That would be too easy, and hating someone took too much energy. No, she'd find a way to help herself, and she'd come out a better person for it.

Diana dug inside the massive black suitcase until she felt a pair of running shoes. She put them on, double-knotting the laces.

Her father was waiting outside her room, leaning against the wall. "You understand, don't you?" He looked worried.

"No." Oh, she understood, all right. She knew what it was like to be so much in love with someone all reason went out the window. That's how she felt about Nick. That's how she got in this mess in the first place.

But Sheila wasn't Nick. She had watched Nick work outside for his dad. She had talked to him that one night when she had been sixteen. She knew Nick wasn't an evil person. And therein was the difference.

"Where're you going?"

"I thought I'd take a walk in the park." She wished he'd take back all the angry words he'd said. She waited, hoping for a retraction. The silence between them was deafening. Finally, she had no choice but to leave him standing there. "I'm going to go, Dad. I have a lot of things to think about right now."

"Here." He pulled out his wallet and shoved hundred-dollar bills into her palm. "Go get yourself some coffee."

"Oh, Daddy." She looked down at the money, took his hand and placed the bills back in his grasp. She smiled up at him, a weak smile, but it was the best she could do right now. When she started to speak, her voice caught in her throat. "I love you."

As Diana closed the apartment door behind her, she could have sworn she heard him say that he loved her, too.

3

THE ELEVATOR STOPPED on the twentieth floor and the doors swooshed opened. When Diana saw who stood there waiting to get on, her heart almost stopped, too.

She hadn't seen Nick Logan, except in her dreams, in six years. Yet she would have recognized him anywhere.

Nick stood outside the elevator in all his six-foot-who-knew-how-much-inch glory, looking better than any fantasy had a right to look.

There had to be something to this power of suggestion, since today, more than any other day in the past, he had been in her thoughts, as well as the topic of conversation.

There was no doubt Nick had changed, matured. Powerful virility had replaced his boyish handsomeness. There was only a faint trace of the youthful guilelessness which had so attracted her to him in the first place. Nick had grown into a rugged virile man. All muscle and radiating heat. The air crackling around him was worldly and experienced, not naive.

His dark brown hair still came below the collar, and even though he had brushed it back off his face, strands fell across his forehead. His eyes, though, hadn't changed at all. They were still the very deepest blue, and against his tanned skin, very intense.

If she ever had any doubt before why she had been so caught up in a memory, she had none now. Nick Logan radiated potent male sexuality. She had been caught in his web at sixteen, more deeply entrenched at eighteen, and now at twenty-four, had no desire to escape. She wouldn't doubt that other women had felt the same way and were hanging off him everywhere he went. Like the one hanging off his arm.

The little girl.

Little girl?

A baby?

It can't be. *Well if it isn't, then what do you think it is?* Nick's baby. *It's a baby, a real live baby.* No. *Yes.*

She couldn't stop staring. While she'd been dreaming about Nick, Nick had become an attached man. Attached to a baby, and where there was a baby, there was a mother. A quiet rage rippled through her. Why did all these terrible things have to happen to her in one day? How much more was she expected to handle?

"I know you," he said. He also looked as if he'd seen a ghost.

Diana's insides knotted. She wanted to press the close button, keeping him and the baby out. She didn't want to face the fact that he was married and had a child. If she closed the door on him, maybe she could forget she'd ever seen him, and go back to her fantasies.

Not likely.

"Diana? Diana Smith. Right?"

She nodded.

He stalled outside the elevator, as if unsure whether to get in with her, which would mean occupying space with the enemy. "That really is you. How 'bout that."

He stepped toward the elevator car.

She licked her dry lips, which made her realize she wasn't wearing any makeup. She'd had a horrible morning, and she knew she had to look as if she'd been dragged through the ringer. All the warnings of her father's third wife, Starr Gazer, the exotic dancer who danced with nothing on except a boa—and not the feather kind, either—had drilled into her about never going out of the house without makeup. Starr wouldn't be caught dead stepping outside, not even to get the morning paper, without blush, turquoise eye shadow, three layers of black mascara and frosty pucker-pink lipstick.

The elevator started beeping and Diana jumped for the open-door button and flattened her back against the wall as Nick entered the car.

His smile was as tight as his jeans. The baby wore pink clothes that went with her wet pink face. The spicy-woodsy scent he wore filled the elevator and sent her senses reeling. It made her wish she could get close enough to sniff his neck, and feel the warmth from his skin as the scent he wore heated.

"Haven't seen you in years," he said.

She held up her right hand and wiggled all her fingers and thumb. "At least six." She had the date imprinted in her brain. She'd never forget that day. That Monday in August. The first Monday. Maybe the second. Come to think of it, it might have been a Wednesday. Well, who cared? Dates were never her strongest point.

"Are you visiting someone in the building?" she asked, staring at the child, unable to look at him, afraid if she did, her feelings of loss and loneliness would be right there in her eyes for him to read. She didn't want to be that vulnerable to anyone.

"I live here."

If she had any hope before of Nick being a single dad, maybe even giving birth himself by immaculate conception, now it was dashed away forever. Only families lived in the Stratford-upon-the-Brazos condominiums. The baby he held looped through his arm, kind of lopsided, looked enough like him that she knew the worst had happened. She wanted to scream at the injustice of it all. While she'd been busy getting thrown out of schools for trying to do something good, for trying to make the world a better place for everyone, Nick had had a baby.

"How wonderful that you live here." *Just shoot me now and get it over with.*

"I think so. The Stratford always held a special place in my heart." He gave her one of those half grins that made her heart do an extra thump.

In return, Diana gave him what she hoped was an "even if you're married and have a child, it really doesn't matter to me" kind of smile. After all, he couldn't know how she had felt about him all these years. And even if he had, it wasn't as if she could have done anything about it. "Hi, baby." She wiggled her fingers again.

"Say hi to Diana, Jessica."

"Nooooo," the baby screamed.

Diana's smile faltered.

"It's not you. *No*'s her favorite word," Nick said.

"I'm relieved to know she's not prejudiced against a Smith. It would have been horrible to pass down the hatred between our families to a third generation."

"Pretty nasty thing, that feud."

She nodded. The Smiths and Logans were like opposing armies of ants. Not just any ants, either, but fire ants. Each family guarding its hill, ready to attack at any moment. "I'm not allowed to talk to you, you know."

"I'm not supposed to talk to you, either."

The baby was sniffing through her stuffed-up nose, and singsonging, "Nonononononononono."

At this moment Diana knew how it felt to walk barefoot through fire-ant hills. "I guess we can make the elevator neutral territory."

"Good idea." He hoisted his daughter, who was slipping down headfirst, back to her original place. The baby had tears rolling down her face.

"Happy baby," Diana said. Boy, could she make an impression. Why didn't she just crawl under the sand and make like a hermit.

"Never happier." His jaw clenched.

What an incredible face he had. Such a loss, him being married. What an awful day. "So, Nick, how've you been?" Could she come up with great small talk, or what?

"Fine." He grunted when the little girl pounded his thigh with her fists. "And you?" he asked.

"Oooh, fine." She grimaced. Such scintillating dialogue. "Fine-fine-fine-fine-fine," she added.

"Great." His grin pinched his lips as the child screamed and beat on the backs of his legs, too.

They landed in the lobby seconds later. As they walked, side by side, toward the revolving doors, Diana said, "My father never told me you lived here."

"Did you expect him to?"

"Not really."

"I moved in about a year and a half ago right after I found out my sister was pregnant."

"Your sister has a baby, too. How nice for all of you."

Diana would have had Nick's babies. Gladly. Life wasn't fair.

Over the years, Diana had felt many things for Nick, but nothing had prepared her for the jealousy raging through her right now. The thought of another woman, having his baby was almost more than she could bear. Knowing someone had been with him in *that* way. The most intimate way a man and woman could be when they wanted to express their love to one another, when they wanted to create a new life from that love.

The pain and loss of what could never be between them were immeasurable.

She glanced at the baby. The poor little girl's face looked like a red tomato with blotches, her nose ran, and her fingers and face were covered in some slimy clear stuff that looked suspiciously like what was coming out of her nose and eyes.

"Your baby's crying." *Oh, good, Diana. Your conversation is becoming even more brilliant, if that's possible.*

"I know." Nick grunted as the child's foot connected with his side again. "She doesn't stop."

When the baby's body tilted downward, headfirst, arms askew, Diana forgot about crushes, fantasies and family feuds and rushed over next to Nick. Instinct made her reach out and grab the baby's shoulders and arms, then help balance her back on Nick's hip again.

"Can you hold Jessica for a second?" he asked. "I need to get all this stuff straight."

"Sure." Diana had never held a baby before, but how hard could it be? Not hard at all, she realized, once Jessica settled in her arms. The baby's tears immediately stopped as Jessica looked at her with big, wet eyes. Eyes just as beautiful as Nick's. "Well, Jessica, you're a cute little thing, aren't you?"

"Nooooo," Jessica cooed right back through a big, watery smile.

Diana laughed as they walked toward the doors, using the pad of her thumb to wipe tears away from under the baby's eyes. Jessica gripped Diana's thumb and stuck it in her mouth. Nick looked at her with his mouth open, his eyes filled with shock. "I use that antibacterial soap on my hands," she said. "I don't think she'll get a Smith disease."

He shook his head, his deep baritone full of admiration. "That's not it. She's stopped crying."

She sure had. Diana didn't want to feel anything special for a child that was not hers and Nick's together. But little Jessica had stopped crying while in her arms. That was a special moment as far as Diana was concerned. She wanted to tell the warm and fuzzy feelings starting to stir around in her belly region to go away, even if that child was chewing on her fingertip, and making relishing smacking noises. Diana didn't want to think that maybe she tasted good enough for a baby to chew on, but wasn't good enough anymore for her own father to love.

That she hadn't been a good enough memory for Nick to hold her close to his heart, as she had held him to hers.

Okay, so she knew it was unrealistic to have hoped that maybe Nick had carried a secret thing for her, too. But, well…a fantasy is a fantasy, and if she had wanted to think that, she could.

But now she had to stop thinking of Nick in fantasy terms. He was married. At this very moment, she held in her arms the product of that union.

Nick bypassed the revolving doors and held the side door open for them. Diana, with a bouncy, laughing Jessica sitting on her hip, went through. She liked the feel of the baby in her arms. "I didn't know you'd gotten married," she said tentatively.

"Me? Married?" he said in disbelief.

"Oh, so you're a single father. Are you raising Jessica on your own, or is this your weekend?"

"I'm not a father. I'll never be a father. Kids hate me. I don't know why, but they do. Look at her."

Diana was so relieved to hear that the baby wasn't his, that she didn't know what to say. "I guess, she's having a bad afternoon."

"She's been having a bad year."

"I just thought—well, you know—you're living in a family building, and she looks like you. I couldn't help thinking—"

"Jessica's Cathy's baby. My little sister's." He cleared his throat. "She's not really my 'little' sister. She's younger than me, but she's not a kid or anything."

"I knew what you meant." Diana let his words, as if they were an afternoon April shower in the Sugar Land bayou, wash over her.

"I remember Cathy from that awards dinner six years ago when our fathers were honored. She was just a little kid back then." Diana smiled wide this time, as wide as she could without lipstick. "Jessica's a precious little thing." Now she could appreciate the baby. She hugged her closer, and Nick didn't act in any kind of hurry to take the little girl back.

They walked across the circular driveway and headed toward the street. Diana could almost pretend that they belonged together—her, Nick and their child. By unspoken agreement, they stopped in front of the eight-foot-tall brass-and-silver Stratford-upon-the-Brazos sign. From where they stood, no prying eyes would be able to see them talking. Namely, her father, or his spies.

Jessica let go of her finger and Diana used her free hand to rub the baby's back. She didn't know why she did that, but the softness of the baby soothed her jumbled nerves. Jessica seemed to like it since she still cooed and smiled and gave a singsong version of "Nooo, nooo, nooo."

"She likes you," Nick said. He wasn't looking at her eyes anymore. His gaze slowly traveled downward over her body.

"Do you really think so?" Her voice came out breathless. The path his gaze took torched her. Her stomach tightened, and her breasts felt heavier, needy. Something she'd never felt before. She had to be imagining the seductive look he gave her. She was sure Nick's perusal was all innocent, because he couldn't know how she had felt about him all these years.

"I know so. Just like I know she hates me." His gaze continued to glide downward.

Diana held her breath, unwilling to break the moment. She tried to keep his sentences straight in her mind but it was getting so hard to concentrate. She was standing here with Nick. The whole idea was almost too overwhelming. "Nobody hates you, Nick," Diana said softly. Some people, she wanted to say, dream wonderful thoughts about you.

"Don't kid yourself. Look at your father."

"Oh, you can't take that personally. He hates your whole family."

"Agreed. But Jessica here is another matter. We're family. She should love me. I gave her cookies for lunch," he said with pride.

"A bribe?"

"Of course." He said the words as if there was no doubt he could buy her affections.

"But, were they chocolate-chip?"

"Oatmeal."

"There's your answer. Chocolate's the key to a woman's heart. You, being a man, may not have known that."

"Do you really think a chocolate-chip cookie would have done it?"

He gave her a boyishly heart-stopping grin. His teeth were so white and straight. Perfect teeth except for a small chip on the front left one. She didn't remember that being there before.

"I know a little about science." If she ran her tongue over that tooth, would it be rough or smooth? "And chocolate has these endorphins, that make women happy."

"No kidding. Thanks, Diana. I'll get some at the grocery store this afternoon. Me and the water fountain over here have to go get some good kid food." He didn't try to take the baby back. "I can't believe it. Jessica really likes you."

"You haven't told her my last name is Smith yet."

"She knows I'm a Logan and she hates my guts."

"Maybe she's on my family's side of the war, instead of yours."

"Considering my family, that's a strong possibility."

"You can't believe that." Diana knew the Logans had as strong a family bond as she and her father had. Or once had.

He didn't seem to agree. "When my sister left for Paris this morning, she gave me a list of instructions. I'm glad

we ran into you because nowhere did it mention chocolate.''

"I used to live there. In Paris. Went to school there for
a short time.''

"No kidding. Paris is a beautiful city,'' he told her, looking as if he'd had a pretty good time there once. He must
not have eaten their steak.

"Beautiful, yes. But the people have a certain—how do
you say?—way of eating that's not normal. Just a warning,
when you talk to your sister, tell her not to put catsup on
any kind of meat. If she does, they may kick her out of
town.''

"No one uses catsup on their food in Paris, Diana.''

"Oh, really?'' Catsup and Paris were sore subjects with
her. While it didn't take away the way she felt about Nick,
she wasn't going to be a doormat either. "I have to dis-
agree.'' She hoisted Jessica a little higher on her hip.
"Would you make a cup of coffee, and leave out the coffee
grinds? Would you make chicken soup, and not use
chicken? Well? Who would eat steak and not put on catsup? It isn't done.''

"The Parisians do it.''

She sniffed daintily. "Yes. And they made me feel very
unwelcome.''

"That's the way Jessica makes me feel. Unwelcome in
my own home.''

Nick looked at Diana's feet thoughtfully, and that curli-
cue feeling in the pit of her stomach was there again. It
grew and expanded, and she didn't know how to get rid of
it except to have Nick kiss her, which she knew he'd never
do and she'd never ask. She was surprised they were even
talking. Then again, she thought of all the explosions she'd
set off over the last six years and she had to question
whether or not he had been responsible for all of them.
Whether she had been so far off in her imaginary world

with Nick Logan that she hadn't been paying attention when she mixed chemicals, or wrote down formulas.

Everything that could go wrong, whether in the lab or in her life, did whenever she thought of him.

"Nice socks," he said.

She looked down at her orange-juice-colored socks. She had limeade-colored ones, too.

"Being a guy, I'm probably the last to know about fashion. But if wearing two different shoes at the same time is what's in style, then I'll have to get Jessica outfitted properly. I know how women feel about those things."

"Two different shoes?" Diana looked at Jessica's tiny little feet. They were encased in the same little sneakers. "I don't know what you mean."

Nick pointed down past Diana's orange-juice socks to her leather-covered feet. Proof right there in the white leather that thinking about him, confessing that morning to her father how she'd switched the bids, had made her do things she normally would never do, like wear an Air Jordan on her left foot and a Reebok on her right. "You know, Nick. This style is so popular that I have another pair at home exactly like these."

"Would you like to go shopping with me and Jessica, and help me find a pair just like those?"

"A Smith and a Logan shopping together?" Oh, what she'd give to go with him, to be in the same car with him, sit next to him, spend the day with him. Diana looked at Jessica, who was smiling up at her, blowing little bubbles out of her mouth.

Reality hit her. If either one of their parents saw the two of them together, they'd both be disowned, disbarred, dismembered. "That's a nice thought, us getting her shoes. Thank you for even suggesting these are a pair. I didn't see what I was putting on this morning. I dressed in the dark."

"It's okay. You should see what I end up wearing sometimes."

If only she could. Diana lifted Jessica off her hip and moved to hand her back to Nick. "You better reclaim this little girl before some relative snitches on us."

"I'm not worried. Are you?"

"A little." *A lot.* "Are you afraid of Jessica?"

"You betcha!" He grinned.

She had to smile right back at him. Nick was as nice a man as she had remembered. She really hadn't wasted all these years thinking about him. Yet, there was no future for them, so in a way, that was bad.

"I can't keep holding her."

"I know." His shoulders slumped and he looked resigned to the fact he was getting his niece back.

"If my father got wind of me talking to you, he'd kill me, and he's so mad at me now, he wouldn't need much of an excuse to carry it through."

"I understand. Believe me. I'm on the other side of the war." He took a deep breath and held out his arms.

Diana placed Jessica in them, feeling his flesh for the first time in years. She had to pull away quickly, before she let her fingers roam over the corded muscles in his arm.

Jessica sat quietly for a few moments, cradled next to Nick's massive chest, sucking on a finger, and looking at Diana through big blue eyes so like her uncle's. For no reason at all, since Nick wasn't really doing anything except holding her, Jessica's eyes began to tear up, her nose turned red and she started to sniffle.

Diana couldn't take it anymore. She'd be the worst kind of person to desert the two of them, when the baby was so unhappy. "Give her back," she ordered.

Nick didn't waste any time, and before Diana could blink, Jessica was once again in her arms. "Thanks, Diana. You're terrific helping me out like this."

"You know, if I listened to what my father tells me about you and your family, I'd be running in the other direction."

"Same with me." His smile got bigger.

"If I thought Jessica could understand, I'd tell her not to give you a hard time."

"Would you really, Diana? Even though I'm a Logan?"

"Of course I would." She wished he was anybody but a Logan. "You didn't make fun of my shoes. I'll always remember that."

"Hey, I'm a nice guy. I keep telling people that, but no one believes me. Isn't that right, Jessica?"

Jessica gave her uncle a genuine smile, which she could do from the safety of Diana's arms. "Aren't you the most unhappy baby?" Diana rubbed her tiny button nose.

Jessica squealed and laughed then grabbed both of Diana's cheeks and pulled. "Nooooo."

"You're such a sweetie."

"So where were you going?" Nick asked, adjusting the backpack. "If I'm not being too nosy for a Logan."

They crossed the street side by side and entered the Sugar Land Park and Wildlife Refuge. A natural canopy of live oak and drake elm branches kept the sun out, and the temperature on the asphalt track cool. Diana tickled Jessica's tummy and baby-talked to her. Not that she understood what Jessica was trying to tell her. That didn't seem to matter to her though.

They came to the first fork in the trail. One way led to the left, the other to the right. Diana stopped in the middle between the two walks.

"You're not going to give her back to me, are you?" he asked.

"You look frightened." She had to laugh at him. Never would she have thought Nick, who looked so big and strong, could look so petrified and vulnerable at the same time. That was a deadly combination to her. She had to get away from him before she made a fool of herself. Fantasy was getting all mixed up in reality. "It was nice seeing you, Nick. Really nice." She gave Jessica's foot one last tickle. "And you, too, pretty little girl."

"Behind that pretty girl beats the heart of a tiger."

"I don't think so. But then what do I know? Try chocolate."

He gave her the thumb's-up sign. "First thing this afternoon."

"See you 'round." She waved and walked away. "Sometime."

Nick had always been her forbidden fruit. For so many years, he'd been the hero in her fantasies. Nick and her on a first date. Nick and her going swimming. Nick and her holding hands. Nick and her with their own baby. Neither her father, nor his, were ever in the picture. She had stood next to him. She had talked to him but had failed to make any kind of lasting impression.

How she wished more than ever that her mother was still alive and that she could talk to her. To be able to ask her what had happened to start the Smith-Logan war. How did it feel to have two men so in love with her that they had been feuding now for over twenty-five years?

Mostly she wanted to ask her mother if the love she had felt for her father was anything like what Diana was feeling for Nick. Was this tingly, giddy feeling, this tongue-tied, stomach-knotting experience really love, or was it just a fantasy being played out in real time?

Diana had to remind herself, with her and Nick there was no such thing as real time. All she could have of him were her fantasies. Fantasies were just wishes to keep a person warm at night when a live body wasn't there.

She marched farther and farther away from him, and with each step became more determined to convince herself that she had to get over him. He'd been a crush—that's all. She was a woman now, and she needed to grow up. She needed to find herself a real man with whom she could have a future. She needed to get herself a life.

"Diana," Nick called out. "Come on back here."

She kept moving forward.

"Please, Diana. We need you."

Oh, Lordy. She would have to get on with her life some other time. There should be once, in every woman's life, when she could take a day to live through a fantasy.

Diana was such a sucker for Nick. At least she was honest enough to admit it to herself. Sucker, sucker, sucker.

Jessica's nose had turned pink and her eyes had started to water, but she wasn't crying. Yet.

"Come and walk with us," Nick invited. "There's no point in going off by yourself when we're here."

"You know that's not a good idea." She was one tough mama. Yes indeed. To think she didn't jump when he had called her back. Nope, she went back slowly. Where the willpower came from, she couldn't begin to guess.

"I'll make you a deal," he said. "If you come with me and Jessica for a walk, I'll buy you lunch." He pointed to the hot-dog vender halfway down the path to her left.

She thought about it for a whole half second, and then held out her arms for the baby. "Don't tell my father, but I can be bribed, too."

"Don't tell mine." He handed her Jessica. "So can I."

They smiled at each other in a conspiratorial way. Life couldn't get any better than this. Not in her book anyway.

Diana held Jessica's rose petal-soft hand in her own and gently kissed the little fingers. "Hello again, pretty baby." She glanced at Nick and knew her heart was on her face, and she didn't care.

4

NICK WATCHED Diana kiss his niece's hand, a Madonna smile on her lips, and knew what it felt to be sucker punched. When she looked up at him, and saw him staring at her, she smiled. When she smiled, he almost lost all the air in his lungs. Sucker punched, that's what it was. No woman had never made him feel as if he couldn't breathe. No woman had ever had the ability to make it so he couldn't think straight.

Then along comes Diana Smith and does it all with a beautiful smile and a kiss to a baby's hand.

"I remember you from the dinner that Sugar Land association had in honor of my father," he said.

"My father was honored, too."

"Sure. He had to have been, or you wouldn't have been there. Do you remember talking to me? I know it was a long time ago."

"Oh," she said, pausing. "I vaguely remember. You were sitting next to me, right? Or was it your brother?"

"It was me. How can you forget me?" *Boy, hit a guy in the ego, why don't you.*

"Of course it was you." She smiled as if she couldn't believe she'd forgotten. "How silly of me. But you know, I was so young—"

"I can't believe you don't remember me that night."

"It's coming back to me. Slowly. If I'm not mistaken, your brother was sitting on the other side of me, right?"

"I suppose." Now that he thought back on it, he didn't remember who had been sitting on the other side of her.

He didn't remember who had been sitting on the other side of him, either. He had been too busy concentrating on Diana. It didn't sit well either that she had remembered who sat on her left, more than she remembered who had sat on her right. Namely him.

"I do remember your mother. She glared at me."

"What can I say? My dad was in love with your mom once. My mother is still jealous."

"My mother died a long time ago. If your mother is jealous, she needs to get over it."

"Easier said than done. She likes being jealous. It makes her feel like a martyr."

"That's sad," Diana said softly, then gave Jessica a hug.

"Are you kidding? She's the happiest person I know, living in her own misery."

Diana laughed, and her laughter reminded him of the tinkling of little bells. He'd have to remember how prettily she laughed and try to get her to do it some more. Sometime.

"We talked a lot that night," Nick said. "I remember that."

"I'm glad you were nice to me, and I'm assuming I was nice to you, too."

"Very nice. After listening to my father talk about your father, I thought any offspring Harry would have would have horns. It was kind of nice to meet you. You were cute back then."

"Thanks," she said almost begrudgingly.

She didn't sound too pleased. She didn't look happy, either, and he didn't know what he'd done. Then he snapped. Good thing he had a sister, because growing up around a girl made a guy like him more sensitive than an average Joe. "You were cute then, Diana, but you're beautiful now."

Her large brown eyes widened, and her mouth parted slightly. She said thank you again, only this time he knew he'd done the right thing. She looked happy again. She sparkled.

They walked farther, going slowly. Neither seemed in any rush to get back. Jessica gurgled her nos, and played with Diana's dark hair, pulling strands out of its ponytail. Nick had to resist the urge to brush the hair off her face. But when a piece got caught in her mouth, he had to stop and tuck the strands back behind her ears. Her hair was soft, her cheeks were soft. Her breath was warm and inviting.

She went on talking as if he'd never touched her. "I remember you now, Nick. I had a very good time that night. You made the evening special for me."

"I have to admit that I started talking to you because it really ticked my mother off. I was young back then, I think about twenty, maybe twenty-one."

"Twenty-two," she corrected almost instantly.

Aha. So she hadn't been totally unaffected that evening. Well, hot-damn. He wanted to whistle "Cheeseburger in Paradise," but didn't know if she was a vegetarian. So he played it cool, 'cause he was a cool kind of guy. "Twenty-two. That's right. You know, Diana, I saw a picture of your mother once. My dad had it hidden in his desk drawer at work. He was on one side of her, she was in the middle, and the person on the other side of her had been ripped out of the photograph. I'm assuming it was your father."

"Probably. I have a photograph in my bedroom with my dad and my mom and someone on the other side torn out. We should compare pictures. That's if we ever see each other again."

"Sure we'll see each other again. Sometime."

"Of course we will." She didn't sound as if she believed it. "Sometime."

And if the truth were known, the way their families were at war, it would be pretty hard. But they'd had this morning, and he enjoyed her company. Jessica obviously loved her company. He wasn't in any hurry to see the morning end. "How old was your mom in that picture?"

"About twenty-one. I'm twenty-four."

"She looked just like you. Exactly. It was no wonder my mother was sending you dirty looks that night. You probably reminded her of your mom."

"I wish I could have been like her, but I'm not. My mother was perfect, and I'll never be." Her voice caught, and she stumbled. Nick took hold of her elbow until she regained her balance. "It's the shoes."

He nodded. He could tell she had loved her mother, and the conversation seemed to bring back memories. He didn't know if they were good or bad. He didn't know many people who had someone close to them die.

"I still miss her," Diana said. "So does my father. He's been trying to find a replacement for her ever since, and he's failed. He's on his fifth wife now."

"No kidding. Harry? Does my dad know?"

She shrugged. "I don't know what anyone in your family knows. I've been going to school, all over the world practically, for the last six years."

"I remember seeing you several years ago. I was working for my dad on Elm Street."

Diana's face had suddenly turned a bright shade of red, and she started taking in deep gulps of air.

"Are you all right?" he asked. "Do you have asthma? Need anything?"

"I'm fine," she croaked. Pointing to a water fountain, and holding Jessica tightly in her arms, she ran over to it.

Once she'd calmed down, she walked back to where he waited for her, and said, "I remember that summer, too. It was right before I went to Paris."

"Sugar Land's such a small town, I would have thought our paths would have crossed sometime. But they didn't. And then of all places, to meet in an elevator."

"It's truly amazing. Almost like fate," she said.

He slung his arm around her shoulders. Jessica gave him an evil-eyed look, but she didn't start to scream. Which was good, because he didn't want to take his arm off Diana.

When he first touched her, she stiffened, and then almost immediately relaxed.

The path through the park twisted in all directions. The squirrels were out in record numbers. The blue jays and sparrows made plenty of noise. Diana smiled at him. "If my father ever found out that you had your arm around my shoulder, and that I was holding your niece, he would get so bent out of shape he'd look like a baked pretzel."

"The same for mine. I want you to know I'm not talking to you because that will make them mad. Even if I think their glass houses could use a few dings."

When Diana's arms begin to sag, he took Jessica. She swatted at his cheek, laughing and crying at the same time. Women. No matter what age they were, they were all the same. Confusing.

Jessica's tears and cries didn't bother him, at least not that he'd admit, but apparently they got to Diana. She stopped walking and held out her arms. Nick didn't need a second invitation. He handed the baby back to her. From a safe distance of at least two feet, Jessica glared at him with her red-rimmed dripping blue eyes and wet clumpy black eyelashes. Her red button nose dripped, and her hands were wet from rubbing all that dripping wet stuff all over her face.

Nick hoisted the backpack higher, and the bottles shifted, which reminded him of what he had been planning to do in the first place. "I've got Jessica's lunch in here, and Mel's over there with his hot-dog cart. Can I buy you the best hot dog this side of New York City?"

Diana's face lit up. "That would be great. Does he have coffee? I'm in desperate need of caffeine."

"One hot dog and one coffee coming up. It's the least I can do for you. You're doing me a big favor."

Diana seemed to hug Jessica closer. "It's been fun," she said softly. Her smile so sweet and innocent. Lovely, that's what she was.

"Hey, Mel," Nick greeted the vendor with a wide slap on his arm. "How'ya been."

Mel looked at Nick and then at Diana and Jessica. "Fine, but apparently not as good as you. When did all this happen?" He waved his arm at Diana and Jessica.

"Nothing's happened."

"You didn't get married and have a baby since the last time I saw you?"

"I saw you last Saturday."

"Oh yeah, that's right!" Mel punched Nick in the shoulder, then gave Diana the eye. "Hiya, doll."

"Hi," she said.

Nick said, "This is my niece, Jessica, and my friend, Diana Smith."

"Only a friend. Well, hot-diggity-dog. Get it? Hot dog?"

"We get it," Nick said.

"Is she single?"

"You don't have to talk about me in the third person," Diana said, smiling warmly at Mel. "I'm very single. Always have been. Probably always will be."

"Well, I can take care of that. No problem."

"Really?" she asked. "How?"

"This hot-dog stand is only a hobby. I also drive a cab. I can take care of a girl like you. What about dinner tonight?"

"Thank you. That is so nice. I think—"

"Hot dogs, Mel," Nick interrupted. "We need some dogs, ol' buddy." Nick didn't like the way Mel looked at Diana. And he sure as hell didn't like that he'd asked her on a date.

"Listen, I don't want to be forward or anything, but you know, I'm kinda new in town—"

"You were born and raised in Houston," Nick pointed out.

"That's not Sugar Land," Diana explained.

"Yeah, that's not Sugar Land."

Nick knew where Houston was. He didn't need Diana

explaining they were located almost right next to each other. That wasn't the point and they all knew it.

Jessica made a valiant effort to lurch out of Diana's arms and into Mel's. Diana handed the baby over to the hot-dog man. The scumbag who Nick used to consider a friend took little Jessica and held her.

His niece, a Logan by birth, a traitor in life, gave Mel the hot-dog man a smile without tears, screams or any two-letter words, namely N-O. Nick, the blood-relative uncle was ticked off to no end. "Can we get back to business here?"

To his own ears, he'd come off sounding slightly irritated. Too irritated. So he cleared his throat. Twice. *He'd* show them he wasn't irritated. Not Nicky boy. Oh, no. He was above all that. Yessiree. "We came here to eat, so give the kid back, will'ya, Mel, and get us our dogs."

"Okay, ol' buddy. No problem. Here she is." Mel handed Jessica to Nick. He opened the silver lid to the steaming dogs, and said, "So, Diana darlin', did you know I was single? I don't want you to think I was askin' you out and I was a married man. I'm not. I'm single and available."

"Nooooo," Jessica screamed.

Nick hid his smile, all the while thinking his niece had great timing.

"Man doesn't live by hot dogs alone. How about you and me, going out for dinner—"

"Nooooo," Jessica screamed once more. Nick grinned ear to ear, then quickly hid it when both Mel and Diana looked at him. He shrugged helplessly, as if to say, "Hey, I'm only a guy, what do I know about babies?" He couldn't have choreographed Jessica's part any better. Although now Nick would never know what Diana's answer would have been.

"Let me take her back." Diana reached for the baby, and Jessica didn't waste time lunging into her arms.

Well, hell, he would have felt the same way, so he

couldn't really fault her. Diana was prettier than him. She was all soft-looking, so she was probably soft-feeling, too, especially to a kid like Jessica. Nick, on the other hand, was all muscle. Muscles were hard. If he were a baby, he'd rather sit on a pillow than a board.

"Hot dog with everything, extra onions for my good buddy," Mel said.

"Hold the onions," Nick told him.

Mel glared. "Sure thing, Nick." He turned to Diana, swept his gaze from head to shoes, and lowered his voice. "What do you take on yours, you lovely specimen of femininity?"

"Catsup," Nick called out. That'll show ol' buddy Mel. In a guy's world, knowing about catsup was as good as staking a claim on a woman. Mel got the message, too.

Then it dawned on Nick what he'd just done. Answering for Diana had been done on instinct, done when one guy moves in on what could be the other guy's territory. He didn't want to stake a claim. Did he?

Ah, hell, maybe he wanted to stake a small claim. A get-to-know-you claim.

When Diana gazed up at him and gave him that sucker-punch smile again, the one that radiated from inside her, he knew he'd done the right thing.

As far as Mel's dinner invitation, he'd bet the profit he was going to make on the Bertling home his crew had broken ground on last week, that she would've said no.

While Nick waited for the hot dogs, several of the grandmothers who lived in the Stratford, all of them wearing hot-pink jogging suits with the slogan Gray Power Club embroidered on the back, had formed a semicircle around Diana and Jessica. "Oh, isn't she an angel?" one lady said, poking her finger into Jessica's side.

"Just a li'l precious pumpkin face," another said.

"My granddaughter is cuter," harrumphed a third. "You remember my granddaughter, don't you, Sylvia?"

"Of course, Gertie, everyone remembers ah…ah… Cherry?"

"Chrysonoe. What's so hard to remember?"

"It's not like a Jane or a Susan."

"Of course not," Gertie sniffed. "Chrysonoe is the name of the daughter of Cleitus. My daughter-in-law told me that."

"I don't know any Cleitus," Sylvia told her friend. "But I do know that it's never wise to listen to any daughters-in-law. They steal things."

"What things?" the first grandmother asked.

"Sons." Sylvia turned and left in the opposite direction.

The women standing there shrugged at the uppitiness of their friend. "I'm not going after her, are you?"

"Not until after I get my hot dog."

Jessica, from the protection of Diana's arms, blew nose bubbles at Nick. In spite of her sniffling, hiccuping, yawning, crying and gulping for air, she acted happy, if that were possible. When she buried her little face in Diana's neck, Nick's own heart squeezed tight. That little kid looked good with Diana. Damn good.

"Jessica, what do you take on your hot dog?" Nick asked.

Jessica's head hit Diana's chin when she jerked it up to look at Nick.

"I don't think she should eat a hot dog. Should she?" Diana asked.

Nick shrugged. Hell if he knew. He'd left Cathy's baby-care instructions at home.

Jessica's big blue eyes were so serious, and her tiny pink mouth was forming a perfect quiet pout.

"Are you allowed to eat hot dogs?" Diana asked her.

The baby smiled for her and said a big "Noooooo." A big, happy no with a big, happy smile. Not a tear to be seen. "I'll share some of mine with her," Diana said.

"You're one lucky son of a bitch," Mel conceded as he

handed Nick the food, all the while casting Diana a look of abject longing.

"You know it."

Nick followed Diana and Jessica to one of the park benches. She sat down, letting Jessica sit on her lap. He handed Diana her hot dog, and opened the lid on the disposable coffee container. "Cream? Sugar?"

"Both."

He fixed her coffee, and left it in the cardboard holder Mel had given him.

"Thanks. For the coffee and the hot dog." Diana unwrapped hers and held it in front of Jessica's mouth. The baby turned her head the opposite direction. "I don't think Jessica's mouth is big enough to take a bite."

"Her mouth is big enough. Don't let the size fool you. You've heard her."

"I'm pretty sure the loudness of her screams has nothing to do with whether or not she can take a bite out of a hot dog. Does she have any teeth?"

He held up two fingers. "She took a bite out of me this morning."

"Oh. That explains why she's not hungry." Diana bit into her hot dog. "Good. Thanks again." She tore off a piece of the bun and gave it to the baby. Jessica shoved it in her mouth and chewed.

"This morning she was screaming at me for no reason. She didn't let up. Every time I got near her, it started again. Then she threw my football trophy and broke that. Maybe if I'd known she was coming, I could have found someone to take care of her. But I didn't know."

"Your poor trophy." Diana had always thought he was the All American type, but didn't realize he had trophies to prove it. He really was out of her league. She took another bite and gave Jessica more bun.

"She likes you," Nick said again.

"I like her, too."

"So, what are you doing the next week?"

"Are you looking for a baby-sitter?" She smiled at him.

"You betcha. Hey, I'll take all the help I can get. So, what do you say?"

"Are you willing to risk your parents' wrath for the sake of a baby-sitter?"

"I wouldn't be risking anything. My parents haven't seen Cathy since the day she told them she was pregnant. They've never seen Jessica. If they knew she was here, they'd stay away."

Diana stared at him wide-eyed. She looked at Jessica and then back at him again. "How can they possibly stay away from this beautiful baby? Do they have so many grandchildren they can afford to ignore one?"

Nick's anger at his parents for the way they had treated Cathy and Jessica felt as sharp today as it had been a year and a half ago. "Cathy had the baby without the benefit of a gold ring," he told Diana. "Jessica is a symbol to them of how their daughter violated their morals. My mother felt a baby born out of wedlock would ruin her social standing. She chose to disassociate herself from her daughter and granddaughter, rather than risk the censure of her friends."

"And your father?"

"He does what my mother wants."

"Has he no backbone? No brain?" Abruptly, Diana reached out and grabbed his hand. "I'm sorry I said that. I don't mean to criticize your father. I took my own anger out on you, and I shouldn't have. Especially you. I need to be more careful, what with your being a Logan." Diana told him about her morning, leaving out the part Nick had played in her past. She didn't think it would be wise to reveal all her secrets.

"I'm sorry to hear that you and your dad are having problems."

"It's nothing that we can't work out. As soon as he divorces Sheila." She smiled at him, but the smile was bittersweet.

"At least your dad keeps trying. My dad is a great businessman. Your dad is a great businessman. But I lost respect for my father when he let Mother throw Cathy out. She needed her parents, and they deserted her. That's when I quit working for my father and started my own company. I couldn't work for him after what he let happen to Cathy. He should have stood up to my mother, and he didn't.''

Nick also needed his parents. He didn't know the first thing about taking care of Jessica. Sure, it might be easy for Cathy now, but he was sure she'd had a rough time in the beginning, especially while trying to run her own business.

''If I could help you, I would, but you're a Logan and…''

''You're a Smith,'' he finished for her. ''So what? Will our parents drop nuclear bombs all over the place if you help me out.''

''I don't think *bomb* is a good word to use around me.''

''Why?'' he teased. ''Are you the kind of girl that has one of those hair-trigger personalities?''

''No.'' Diana took a sip of her coffee. ''I have a bad habit of experimenting with chemicals that cause these little explosions.'' She looked sheepish, and she shrugged her shoulders daintily. ''So, Nick, did you say you had a bottle?''

''Yes.'' He had to shake himself. She blew things up. Diana, that little package of femininity who held on to his niece so gently, blew things up. ''I forgot about the bottle. I've got diapers, too.''

''Well, that's the beauty of diapers, babies, friends and relatives. Guess which word doesn't belong in that group?''

''Diapers?''

''Oh, don't you wish that were true. It's friends. They don't have to change baby diapers when there's a relative around.''

She leaned back in the bench, pulling Jessica against her, and sent him a smug look. Boy, he thought, she was really cute.

Diana took the bottle and gave it to Jessica, who promptly stuck it in her mouth and sucked down half the milk.

Jessica nestled against Diana, with her bottle pushed to the side of her mouth, and sipped a little slower. She batted her eyelashes at Nick. The kid had nerve. As if that would make him forget how she'd treated him for the last year. Diana took another sip of coffee, then said, "So, you're a builder like your father and my father."

"No," he said adamantly. "Like myself. They do big buildings. I do custom homes, specialty homes, one at a time."

"I blow things up, by accident, of course. You build things up. Interesting." She sipped. "How come you live in the Stratford and you didn't build yourself a custom home?"

"But I did, Diana. I built the Stratford."

"No. Your father won the contract. I know. I have an intimate insider's knowledge about Stratford details that would blow your mind. No pun intended on the blow part, of course."

"Of course. I worked with my father on the Stratford. But two years ago I'd been hired to do some renovations. That was my first job after going on my own. The Stratford symbolizes the beginning of my freedom."

"You know, the Stratford symbolizes something for my dad, too. He bought both penthouse apartments and knocked out the walls, redid the whole thing. There's even a swimming pool up there. Do you know why he did all that?"

Nick shook his head.

"Because he was sure your father was going to buy one of those apartments and he wanted to prevent that from happening."

Nick stretched his arm along the back of the park bench and squeezed Diana's shoulder. He started to laugh, the kind of laugh that came from deep inside his chest. "My dad didn't care about the penthouse. He was building a home on the golf course over in Sweetwater."

"Are you saying your parents bought the house in Sweetwater before the Stratford was built?"

"Sure. They had started building it before my dad knew he had won the contract."

"Oh boy. Oh boy." Diana straightened up so fast she startled Jessica. The bottle popped out of the baby's mouth and landed on the grass. Jessica tried to get down to go after it, and Diana let her.

Nick reached the dirty bottle first, which made Jessica cry. "Wait a second," he told her, reaching inside the backpack and getting her another one.

She took the bottle, plopped down on the grass and drank.

When Nick looked at Diana again, she, too, had tears in her eyes. "What's wrong?"

"This is stupid. Their whole feud is stupid. I hate it. You will never believe how the revenge my father tried to extract from your father, the revenge that was no revenge, has personally affected me, all these years later.

"Nick, we moved into the Stratford specifically so your dad wouldn't get that penthouse. Before we moved here, we lived in a nice house over in the lakes area. When I was about two years old, my dad built me this little table and two little chairs. They were wood, and they were so pretty. My mom put decals on them, little bunnies hopping over carrots. My mom and I had tea parties at that table. We drew pictures together at that table. She helped me with my homework in first and second grade at that table.

"One day, I'll never forget this, my mom turned the table over and we both carved our names on the underside, and then my mom carved Diana and Mommy Forever Together."

"She sounds like a wonderful woman. It was no wonder my dad fell in love with her," Nick said wistfully.

"So your father builds the Stratford, and my father buys

the penthouses. And we move in. Then who should my dad meet here about a year ago? Sheila. He never would have met her if we were still living at the lakes.''

"He married Sheila, is that right?"

"Yes. Then, while I was away at school over the last six weeks, Yale this time, Sheila threw out my table and chairs.''

"She did what?"

"You heard me right. Tossed them in the dump. Gone.''

"Diana, I'm sorry. I don't know what to say.''

"Listen, if my father hadn't been trying to get back at your father, this wouldn't have happened. You know, Nick, I've had a few years of bad luck.''

He had his legs stretched out, keeping Jessica, who was still sitting on the grass drinking her milk, cradled between his ankles. As if Jessica knew the importance of what Diana was saying, she didn't make one sound.

"I'm sorry about your bad luck. Is it getting better?"

When she looked at him, and smiled that sucker-punch smile, he had to grin right back. When she said, "Much better," he felt as if he'd been lifted off the ground.

"You know about enablers, don't you?"

He shook his head.

"Enablers are people who allow addicts to continue their destructive behavior. And that's what we're doing. You and I. By going along with our parents' feud, by not talking to each other, we are letting their fight fester. I'm not going to do that anymore." Diana stood up, her shoulders back, her breasts thrust out, her back straight. "Look at how many lives have been ruined."

"My dad did love your mom, and that's what started the feud," Nick said, "but he never would have married my mother if he hadn't loved her. My mom couldn't believe that, and she let the hatred she felt for your mom ruin her life. Growing up in that house, with parents who were at each other all the time, was hell." Nick's tone was harsh, gruff. He refused to allow the pain to show.

"People who hate with such passion love with that same passion, too. Our fathers were best friends at one time. They both strove to be number one," Diana said.

"They were best friends until Elizabeth chose Harry and left my poor dad eating their dust."

"And where would you be, Mr. Nick Logan, if they hadn't? You wouldn't have been born, and I wouldn't have been born. And little Jessica here wouldn't have been born."

"Okay, I can see you and me. But her? I'm reserving judgment."

"You do that. I'm going to be grateful for what happened, and I think the generation that's sprung from this Smith-Logan war should also be grateful, instead of acting so nasty about it. Because if the truth is told, none of us kids would be here today if the parents we had were different."

"You're right. In fact, I'll bring that up to my brothers and sister at our next family meeting."

"Do you really have family meetings?" Diana pulled the blue cloth band out of her hair and let all those brown curls fall past her shoulders, all the while fluffing it out, digging her fingers through to her scalp, and massaging.

When she finished, she shook her head like a little filly, sat back on the bench and again spoke to him in her quiet, soft voice. A passionate voice. A compassionate voice. He'd bet Elizabeth had been just like her. Nick surprised even himself when he reached out and touched her hair. Soft. Just like it looked. "No," he said, mesmerized by the silky feel of her hair. "No one in my family talks to each other either."

"It's no wonder, the way you have the story mixed up."

"What do you mean? I have it right."

"The way I understood the story," Diana said, her voice husky and warm, relaxing him. "My mom's father owned a big construction company. Our fathers were partners in a small construction company. They both courted Elizabeth.

But when she married my father, Harry, her father made him co-owner of the bigger construction company." Diana paused for a moment, reaching down, and stroking Jessica's hair. "Charlie must have felt deserted. Abandoned even. First by Elizabeth, then by his best friend."

"It shouldn't have mattered. He ended up doing damn well for himself."

"They all did."

"So he should get over it and move on."

Diana took a deep breath and closed her eyes. He saw a nerve working in her cheek. This time he gave in to the impulse and touched the ticking muscle with the tip of his finger. Her eyelids flew open, and her smile was once again sweet.

"I miss my table and chairs, Nick."

"I know you do."

"I want to punish them."

He nodded. "Revenge is good."

"I'll baby-sit for you," she said abruptly.

"Are you just saying that because you know I'm desperate and you feel sorry for me?" He didn't know whether to be happy...or worried.

She chuckled. "No, I'm saying that because I feel really sorry for me. I want our fathers and your mother—I'm not going to leave her out of this—to know what we're doing. I want them to be so angry that a Smith is cavorting with a Logan that they'll stop and think about what they've done, and maybe grow up."

"We could tell them that you're moving in with me, and that we're going to get married. We don't have to get married, but if they think we are, that'll make them mad as hell."

She shook her head. Damn, Diana was vicious to a guy's self-esteem. First she didn't remember meeting him, and now she was refusing to consider just telling her father they were going to get married. What was so bad about him anyway? Jessica hated him, Diana could take him or leave him. He rubbed his neck, then casually sniffed the palm of his hand. No, the aftershave was still there. Damn. His *Nicholas X* wasn't working at all with these two females. He'd have to have a talk with Cathy when she got back.

"We can tell our parents that we're living in sin," she announced. "That will really make them mad."

"You want to do that? A sweet girl like you?"

"Who said I'm sweet?" she asked.

"Who do you think you're kidding?" He didn't have to know her that well to know she was, not only a knockout to look at, but a nice person, too.

"Do you think it won't work?" she asked.

"I think it'll work, all right. I'm only thinking of your reputation."

"Oh, Nick, my reputation has been literally blown to pieces," she said with a self-deprecating grin. "I know this whole thing is a risk. I'm willing to give it a try. How about you?"

"Anything worth obtaining is worth taking a risk for. That makes winning so much sweeter. That makes the prize so much better."

"A prize," she said. "I didn't even think about that. You're so good. What's the prize going to be?"

He looked her square in the eyes. "A family."

5

THEY WALKED TOGETHER slowly back to the Stratford. Diana held Jessica, and Nick, whenever he thought he could get away with it, took hold of her arm, or her elbow. She liked it. And the whole time they walked, they talked.

By the time they arrived home, they had their story worked out so airtight nothing could have unraveled it.

Diana hadn't come back down to earth yet. She still couldn't believe that Nick had remembered her from that dinner they had both attended when she was sixteen. All those years ago, and he remembered.

She almost felt bad that she didn't tell him she had remembered him, too. But how could she have told without giving away that she'd been dreaming about him forever? That would have scared him away for sure.

As soon as the elevator stopped on the penthouse floor, even before the doors opened, Nick put his arm around Diana's shoulder as if it were the most natural thing for him to do. Diana had been waiting for it, hoping for it. Dreaming about it, willing those dreams to come true.

They had sat next to each other on the park bench talking for a long time. Jessica had played in the grass, caught all kinds of bugs. Amazing how those little eyes saw so many things.

They had ridden in the elevator together, twice already. They had talked and laughed, and shared hot dogs and coffee. Diana knew they had what some people might consider the beginnings of a great friendship.

Only, nothing had prepared her for how it felt to have his arm around her. Twice in one morning. That alone was almost more than she could bear, it felt so good. Could he see her heart beating through her T-shirt? Could he see the pulse jumping out of her neck? Did he feel the tremors going through her bloodstream, or was all this just so very obvious to her?

She rang the doorbell. Chimes vibrated all around them.

He leaned down and whispered in her ear, "Are you all right?"

"Of course." Maybe he could tell what he was doing to her just by standing so close.

"You're shaking." He gave her shoulder a light squeeze.

Diana realized she'd never make it in the CIA. If it had been on her shortlist of jobs, she might as well have scratched it off. "I'm fine, really. It's only nerves." At least that was the truth.

"Do you have a key to your front door?" He still kept his voice very low.

"The door's never locked," she whispered back.

"So why did you ring the bell?"

"I don't know," she again whispered. "Maybe I'm having brain seizures."

Nick squeezed her shoulder again. "Don't be nervous. I'm with you."

"I'm not nervous. Where did you get the idea I was nervous?" She put her fingertip over her left eye to stop it from twitching. "Remember, this was my idea in the first place. We're going to live in sin. Lovely sin. Luscious sin. Sin is a good thing."

God, she was such a dope. She couldn't believe she was going to tell her father that she and Nick were going to live together. He would have a heart attack. What in the world had she been thinking?

"It doesn't matter what my father thinks, Nick." She

was saying this out loud more to convince herself than him. "It's sin and that's the way I like it."

"Diana, if that's what you want, then sin it is." Nick reached around her for the door handle.

Just being engulfed in his arms was enough to send her heart racing in anticipation. Her mind, the realm of reason, calculated the odds of her fantasy coming true.

Yet, if she turned her head, just so, her lips would be right there, and if he turned his head at the same time, his lips would be right there, too, and together their lips would be so close, so very—

"What are you doing out here, Diana?" Alicia opened the door, and blew her daydream to bits with her loud, New England voice.

"Hello, to you, too," Diana said. "Doesn't she greet guests well, Nick?"

Jessica's eyes got bigger and a smile broke out on her little face. She bounced in Diana's arms. Alicia had captured another fan. In fact, the only one who didn't seem to like Alicia was Sheila, and that woman didn't count.

"What's the matter with you?" Alicia said. "You know I hate that bell."

Diana nodded her head in Nick's direction. "I'm bringing someone and didn't want to barge in on you."

The housekeeper snorted.

However, Nick was so good-looking that Alicia immediately went from disapproval to flirting in the time it took to blink. "Well, well, lookee here. A real manly man."

"Nick, meet the woman who raised me. Alicia, Nick."

Alicia wiped her hand on her apron and stuck it out. Nick grasped her palm, "If you're the woman who raised my Diana, then you're okay in my book." He put his arm back around Diana's shoulder. "You'll sit in the front row at the wedding, and I'll hear no arguments about that."

"What wedding?" Alicia eyed them suspiciously.

"What wedding?" Diana asked. "There's no wedding."

"You ain't gettin' married," Alicia said.

"We're not getting married." Diana glared up at Nick. He was so cute. Was he dense, too? "I told you I want to live in sin. We talked about it all morning. We agreed to live in sin."

"Diana Marie Smith, you bite your tongue," Alicia yelled.

"Nooooo," Jessica yelled, clapping her hands.

"Smart baby," Alicia added.

"Diana." Nick, the voice of reason, who seemed to have forgotten his role in all this, but she liked him a lot anyway, said, "The object is to convince our families to make up, not add fuel to the fire."

"I'm not going to tell them we're getting married because we're not. I will not lie." She was adamant about this. "No way."

He ran his fingers through his hair. She bounced Jessica at her side. They stared at each other. "Nick, I never lie." She may exaggerate—a little, but that's not the same thing. "I'm not backing down on this."

"I'm not either."

"You're stubborn."

"Don't confuse stubbornness with tenacity."

"Same thing."

"Diana—"

"Nick—"

Without moving her head, she widened her eyes so she wouldn't blink for at least five minutes, and said, "Alicia, come over here, please, and take this baby."

Alicia scurried to take Jessica from her arms.

"Now, please close the front door. Nick and I are going to start this all over again and we're going to practice until we get it right."

Nick didn't wait for Alicia. He closed the door himself. Their gazes never wavered as they each stepped back. At least Diana thought they had. Only Nick seemed to be getting closer. He seemed to be crowding her against the wall. "Now, now, Nick." She tried sweetness. After all, she really was a nice person. Everyone thought so. "I don't want to lie to them. We're not getting married. Don't tell them something that's not going to happen." Although they weren't going to live in sin, either, Diana hadn't given up hope.

"I'm going to kiss you, you know."

Her eyelids, already opened wide, popped, and so did her mouth.

"I have to. Just once." He stepped closer to her. "It's something I gotta do. I've been thinking about it all morning. From the time I first saw your socks."

"But, Nick." *Oh, God, Oh, God, OhGodOhGod.* A kiss. He wanted a kiss from her. She'd been dreaming about a kiss for so long that she didn't know if she could handle the excitement now that he wanted one. How had something so simple as a little kiss become so overwhelming? What if she didn't know how? What if she stunk at it? What if she failed the test? What if their lips didn't match up? What if their teeth clanked together? What if—

His mouth reached hers before she could think of any other potential disasters. Soft lips, gentle pressure, strong hands holding on to her shoulders so she couldn't run away. He angled his head without moving his lips from hers. His fingers traveled from her shoulders, skimming her neck, outlining her jaw, her chin, making slow, small, delicate circles over her cheeks. He outlined her lips with his tongue, and she tasted him briefly, wanting more. She opened her mouth for him, giving him what he wanted, taking from him what she craved, and had been craving for years.

And then she knew. The chip in his tooth was smooth.

"Now this time," he whispered, "ring the bell, and tell Alicia we're going to live in sin, if that's what you really want to tell her. But when she doesn't believe you, act as if it's her that's crazy, not us. Got it?''

"Nick? We are going to be living in sin. Right?''

"Yes we are.''

"Do you think this is a crazy idea? Trying to get our fathers together again?''

"Of course not.''

"But Alicia—''

"Diana, you said yourself she raised you. She probably has a better handle on what you're like than your father does. She knows you wouldn't do anything wrong.''

That made Diana feel better. If she could talk the talk about living in sin, she might be able to end the Logan/Smith feud. But she didn't want to lose the respect of those she loved in the process.

Alicia once again opened the door before Diana rang the bell. "Don't you dare ring that bell,'' she said.

"Have you been spying on us?'' Diana crossed her arms and raised her right eyebrow.

"Of course I have. What do you think I am, stupid? How else am I gonna know what's going on?''

Nick kept his arm around her waist as if to lay claim, even though she knew he couldn't possibly be doing that, despite the kiss. That incredible kiss.

She smiled. For a day that had started out as the worst day of her life, it had turned into one incredible morning. She hoped it never had to end.

"Hello, Alicia,'' Nick said, and he winked. "I'm Nick Logan, and Diana and I are going to live in sin.''

"That better make our parents sit up and take notice,'' Diana said. "If that doesn't work, we're going to *say* we're getting married.''

This time Nick gave her a grin that would have knocked her socks off. "That seemed like a good compromise,'' Diana added. "See, I told you the Smiths and Logans can do that.''

"So can Logans and Smiths."

"Ah, I see the pecking order is important to you."

"Nope. Doesn't mean a thing."

"So Smith and Logan is okay?"

"No. Alphabetical order does mean something to me. Logan and Smith."

"I can do the A-B-C order. That's a good compromise."

Alicia looked from one to the other, then handed Jessica back to Nick. "You two are sick. Really sick. I'm outta here."

Diana glanced over at Nick and shrugged. "I don't know what's wrong with her."

He smiled. "She's playing with you, Diana. She's all bark. What does matter is what our fathers think. Alicia," he called to her retreating back. "Is Harry home?"

"He went to work right after Diana left this morning."

"What about Sheila?" Diana asked.

"She went to the spa to get herself oiled and massaged."

"Then we have some time." Nick took Jessica into the living room to watch the football game, and Diana followed Alicia down the hallway to the kitchen. "Can you teach me how to make that wonderful macaroni and cheese you made me all the time when I was a kid?"

"You want to make macaroni and cheese?" the housekeeper asked. "What in the world for?"

"Breakfast for Jessica. You made the best. I want to give Jessica good memories, the kind I had when I was growing up, and you were cooking. I loved your macaroni and cheese. Every time you made it, the sauce was so creamy, the pasta cooked to perfection. All I'm asking is how you did it." Diana had pulled a piece of paper and a pen out of a drawer and was ready to write down the secret to her childhood favorite.

"Well…" Alicia hesitated. "You want to know the secret to my macaroni and cheese."

"If you'll share it with me." Maybe it was a recipe that

had been handed down in Alicia's family for generations. Maybe ethics made it impossible for the housekeeper to share. The thought of never knowing how Alicia had made that wonderful macaroni and cheese, the one meal that brought warm and fuzzy memories that took the sting out of a very lonely childhood, disappointed her. "I guess I can understand if you're not able to do that."

"No, no. I can tell you."

"I'm ready." Pen and paper were poised in anticipation.

"I don't think you'll need that," Alicia said, pointing to Diana's pen.

"I want to write everything down. I don't want to miss one word."

"Go to the pantry. Third shelf on the right."

Diana opened the door.

"Do you see a green box that says 'Macaroni and Cheese'?"

Diana pulled the box off the shelve. "I've got it right here."

"That's the one."

"The one what?"

"That's my family-secret macaroni and cheese."

"No way." Diana waited for a denial. A sign that Alicia was pulling her leg. Nothing. "Are you telling me you didn't add anything to it?"

"That's it. You're going to find that sometimes the best is the easiest. So I'd suggest you follow the directions on the box."

"I can do that," she mumbled. Taken. That's what she'd been. Taken in by soft pasta and creamy cheese.

"You don't sound like you're sure. Because this is me you're talking to, and I know about you and your experiments. I know you like to mix a little here, add a little there. I'm telling you to follow the directions on the box and don't deviate."

"I won't. I promise."

Alicia laughed. "Diana, when you make a meal, do as much as you can by the box, by the can, or frozen. I did, not that your father ever knew."

"I loved your pizza."

"You loved Briggardo's pizza. Best takeout this side of the tracks. You have to understand that you needed me more than you needed a home-cooked meal."

Diana smiled softly at the older woman.

"By the way," Alicia said, "don't marry a man that kids don't like. That baby cries a lot around Nick."

"We're not getting married. We're living in sin."

Alicia rolled her eyes. "Yeah, tell it to the judge."

"Okay, I will." Diana, who had been leaning on the counter, with her chin in her hand, looked at the box of macaroni and cheese and sighed. "I think if I add paprika to this, it will really give the flavor a zing."

6

NICK CARRIED a sleeping Jessica back down to his apartment. Diana unlocked the front door, and followed him to the guest bedroom.

She now knew that once Jessica fell asleep, the baby liked Nick just fine. It was when Jessica was awake she had problems with him.

She also now knew that Nick liked football and football put Jessica to sleep. So if Nick watched a football game, and at the same time held Jessica in his arms, within seconds Jessica would be sleeping, and not crying. Both would be happy and they could consider it quality time together. Besides, they were doing something each of them enjoyed, watching football and sleeping.

Nick laid the baby very gently in the crib. Two tiny fingers found their way into her mouth. Jessica sighed and sucked softly, never opening her eyes.

Diana hovered close behind while he covered Jessica with a yellow blanket and placed a small teddy bear in the crook of her arm.

The portable crib had been set up next to the queen-size bed. The rest of Nick's apartment, from the deep green marble floors in the hall, to the wood floor in the kitchen, said, "I am man, hear me roar." This bedroom, though, was the complete opposite. Everything sunshiny yellow and luminous lavender, lace and ruffles and feminine, right down to the plum carpet.

As if he knew where her thoughts were headed, Nick

said, "This is where Cathy stayed during most of her pregnancy." He spoke softly, as if the room itself dictated a different kind of speech and atmosphere.

Diana watched him while he fussed over the sleeping baby, determined more than ever that she would do everything she could to make things right with their families. Or at least get Nick's parents communicating with their own daughter and granddaughter. Not that she knew what to do, but she knew that she had to do something. And if all her efforts blew up in her face, well, it wouldn't be the first time.

"Where does Cathy live now?"

"I had a piece of property in old Sugar Land that I signed over to her. We put a house on the land, and built a laboratory out in the back. She needed a place to work with her perfumes and soaps. Which is why she's in Paris. A company there is buying her formulas."

"She has her own lab." Diana spoke reverently. Cathy was a woman to be respected.

"It's small, but it's a start for her anyway."

"Did she ever have anything that...kind of..." Diana threw out her arms. "Exploded?"

"Not that I know of."

"Some people have all the luck." Nick's sister mixed chemicals and created beautiful things that smelled good. When Diana mixed chemicals, she ended up with a mass evacuation of the building, and three fire departments in attendance.

If she got a chance to talk to Cathy, she'd have to ask her how she had such good luck in the lab.

"You bet she's lucky," Nick said. "Getting an all-expense-paid trip to Paris was about the best thing that's ever happened to her."

"That, too," Diana murmured. "But I was talking about having a lab."

"She needed that lab. She wanted to stay home with the

baby. She was planning on going back to work. But then we discussed the pros and cons, and we figured that this perfume hobby she had was making pretty good money. If she could do it full-time, she decided she could double her revenue. But she was wrong.''

"I'm so sorry. So did she have to go back to work? I never thought about how hard it must be to be a working mother.''

"Don't be sorry for her. She tripled what she estimated she'd make, and it's going up. Now she employs other mothers, and she provides them with on-site child care.''

"Why didn't she leave Jessica with them?''

"I'm blood.''

Everything was so simple. Blood. Family. The bonds that tied them all together were strong in spite of parents who did what they could to change that. Diana was finding out there were a lot of things she hadn't thought about before. She never thought of herself as a selfish person, she had always wanted to make a difference in people's lives. Yet, for some reason, meeting Nick again, being with Jessica, she was coming to see that maybe not everything she had planned to do to make the world a better place was such a great idea after all.

Maybe what she needed to do was concentrate on something closer to home. Like her family. Like Nick. "You were nice to help her.''

"I wasn't nice,'' he said. "It was in my best interest to see her taken care of. I love my sister, I want the best for her. By doing what I can to help her and Jessica, I'm really helping myself. Trust me, Diana, I was being selfish when I built her the lab.''

"I don't understand why you're saying that.'' She glanced in the crib at Jessica. So sweet and innocent when she was sleeping. Looking at the child, no one would ever figure that she could be so hostile to a man who had been a fairy godfather to her and her mother.

"*Nicholas X,* the best aftershave in the world. That's why I built her the lab. Smell me."

Diana didn't have to be asked twice. Nick bent down a little, she stood on tiptoes and leaned into him, her nose and lips touching the warm skin in the crook of his neck. She breathed deeply and filled her senses with the spicy-woodsy scent that was all male. All Nick.

She took in another breath, her eyelids heavy, her body relaxing. He turned his head slightly, his cheek a gentle caress against hers. His lips were so close, but still miles away. Time didn't move, and neither did she. Was he about to kiss her?

"Should I change her diaper?" he asked abruptly.

Sometimes reality really stunk, she was finding out.

Diana moved away from him. There had to be something wrong with her that while she'd been thinking about kisses, he'd been contemplating diapers. How could that be? Is it possible that all her instincts were so wrong?

Then she remembered Nick had been her dream. She hadn't been his.

"Diapers? When she's sleeping? Why?"

"So she can sleep longer and doesn't get a rash. Cathy said something about that in the instructions she left me."

So while their lips were so close, and she was sniffing his neck, and they were standing cheek to cheek, he had been thinking about diaper rash.

Okay. Her feelings weren't in the gutter. She was fine with this. "You could change it if you want to. Or I could try and do it," she said.

A look of relief passed over his face when she made the offer. Who knew that by saying she'd change a diaper, she'd get his gratitude? "I've never changed a diaper before," she said. "I'm not sure how to do it, and if I do it, I'll probably wake her up, and she'll see you and start screaming. I bet you could do it while she's sleeping and not wake her up."

"Come with me." Nick took Diana by the hand and brought her out of the bedroom and into the hallway. There they were, connected again, fingers entwined. And he was still talking about diapers.

"I don't really want to wake her up right now," he said. "Besides, we need to talk about what we're doing here."

"What's wrong? Don't tell me, let me guess. You want to back out of the living-in-sin part." She just knew it and she told him so, too. "When we were upstairs and you slipped by saying to Alicia 'marriage' instead of 'sin,' I knew you were going to do something that would throw everything we talked about this morning out the window."

"Saying the word *marriage* was a mistake. I'm a bachelor. A confirmed bachelor. Marriage wasn't even in my vocabulary until this morning. I didn't even know if I knew how to pronounce the word. Look at your father, five wives. Look at my father, one wife and years of misery."

"Well…as long as you don't want to back out of the living-in-sin part." She had been so looking forward to that.

"I'm a guy. No guy walks away from sin. Especially not sin that's definitely illicit, like ours would be."

Diana swallowed hard. Even though she'd been dreaming and fantasizing about him, she wasn't easy by any means. Okay, so she could be easy in her fantasy, but that didn't mean she was easy in real life. He had to know that. Didn't he? He was looking at her with hot eyes. Maybe he didn't. "Nick, we have to talk about this."

"That's why I brought you out here. I know I would say I'd do it, and I could do it if I had to. At least I think I could. But the truth is, I've never done it."

Diana's eyes widened. "No, you can't mean what I think you mean. There must be some mistake."

He shook his head. "No, no mistake. I've watched my sister do it, but I've never done it myself."

Diana crossed her arms and scowled at him. "Do you take me for a fool? It's because I'm a Smith, isn't it?"

"No, of course not. I wouldn't lie to you."

"I don't believe you for a minute."

"Believe what you want. Some people are teachers, some people are doers. I'm a teacher. So I can teach you."

"You can teach me, but you can't do it. You want me to do it while you watch. Is that right?"

"That's it. I could try to do it, but I would mess it up, and that's not something you want to mess up. See, Diana, I would watch my sister do it and she made everything look easy. So I know I could instruct you. I would just watch over your shoulder, and tell you what to do. If you follow my instructions, and do it just like I say, which will be the same way my sister does it, then you'll be fine."

"Nick."

"Diana?"

"Do it yourself."

She stormed down the hallway, heading toward the front door and out of the apartment. Fantasies blow up as fast as realities. Shoot.

He came running after her, grabbing her on the shoulder, stopping her from going any farther. "Okay, I'm sorry. If you want me to change her diaper, I will. I won't ask you to do that. Call me a male chauvinist pig, okay? Just get it all out of your system, and we can start over."

Oh boy. She swallowed, licked her lips and swallowed again. No way was she ever going to go near the place where she thought he'd taken her. No way. She gave him her best, I forgive you for being a male, smile. "I would consider it an honor to have you teach me how to change a diaper."

His hand, still resting on her shoulder, squeezed gently. "Thanks. It's not that I wouldn't change it, I would. It's just that she cries, well, you know, you've seen her."

"I'm here to help. Remember?" she asked softly.

He nodded.

They went back into the bedroom, and Diana carefully pulled back the blanket and pulled down the little pink cotton pants.

"Undo the tabs," he whispered from behind. "But get one of those wipe things so you can hose her down."

She did what he said, and Jessica still didn't wake up.

"You have to put a clean diaper on the bed, and fit the top part between her legs, rest it over the stomach." He waited while she did as he instructed. Then, "Okay, now let the sides meet, pull the tabs and hook the sides together."

Diana was getting ready to pull the pants back up, when he told her not to. "She might wake up if you do that."

She handed the dirty diaper to Nick. "I'll agree to change the diapers if you'll agree to flush them down the toilet. I don't want anything to do with dirty diapers."

"You're not supposed to flush them."

Diana pointed to the boxes of diapers. "It says on the box disposable."

"That means you throw them out, not wash them."

She thought about that, and wasn't sure he was right. But she was in his house, and these were his toilets, so she figured he could throw the used diapers in his trash if he wanted to. Personally, if it had been her house, she would have taken the chance on the toilet rather than have a smelly diaper in the room.

"Everything is so simple now," Diana said. "But I guess it's a sign of life, too. Disposable diapers, disposable spouses." She looked at the crib. "I didn't know baby beds were this small. Do you have to buy a new one every few months as they grow? Disposable cribs."

"It's a travel crib. You don't throw it out. And it's bigger than it seems. That should last another year at least."

"There's so much I don't know." And that was discouraging. She didn't like feeling so helpless, but that's how she felt. She wanted Jessica to remember her time with Auntie Diana as a great experience. Auntie Diana?

"Don't look so lost, Diana," he said, breaking into her thoughts. "You did a great job."

"Really?" She brightened at that. She'd take praise anywhere she could find it, but coming from Nick made it all the more special.

"Come on. I'll make you a glass of my special homemade lemonade."

"Powdered, right? You look like a powdered-lemonade kind of guy."

"I'm crushed. In fact, I'm a squeezing-lemons kind of guy." His blue eyes were full of mischief.

Nick was a nice man. He really was. He was handsome, sexy and nice. A deadly combination for someone who had been in love with the fantasy she'd had of him for years. As she followed him back down the hallway toward the kitchen, she started having guilty twinges about letting him believe she didn't remember him.

But she had been afraid if she did, he'd read her mind, her eyes, her body language, letting him know she remembered him all too well.

Then again, maybe some things were best left unsaid. At least for a while.

So Diana, for the second time that morning, leaned on a kitchen counter, her chin resting in the palm of her hand, and watched Nick squeeze lemons. He didn't use some little sissy squeezer either. He flexed his muscles when he squeezed, and he relaxed them when he finished. Flex, relax. Flex, relax. Oh, he was a magnificent squeezer. She sure knew how to pick the guy to dream about.

He handed her a glass full of juice and ice. He drank his in one swallow. "I was thirsty. All that diaper changing about wore me out."

"You did so much work." She sipped her lemonade

slowly, savoring the texture and the flavor, knowing his hands had been on what was now going into her mouth.

"Did you pack your bag?" he asked.

It took a full fifteen seconds—she *really* had to stop zoning out—before she realized he'd been talking to her. "No, I haven't packed yet. I was too busy getting Alicia's recipe for homemade macaroni and cheese."

"Hey, that's great. I lived on macaroni and cheese in college. Only not homemade, we always ate the stuff in the box."

"Well, then, you'll feel right at home."

She walked over to where Nick had taped Cathy's instruction list to the refrigerator door. Four pages of single-spaced typewritten instructions. The words *car seat* jumped out at her. She pulled the instructions off the door and carried them over to him. "I think you'd better go put Jessica's seat in the car, because as soon as she gets up, we're going to have to get her some food, and then I have to get to the bookstore, to buy some material on child care."

"Thank you."

Two simple words, said with the most heartfelt gratitude she'd ever heard. It had been so long since anyone had thanked her for anything. Not even those people at Yale, who should have thanked her for forcing them to build a new lab, had thanked her. Yet here was Nick, a Logan, and he was thanking her for changing a diaper and helping him take care of his niece.

Now, if only things went smoothly from here. The one thing she didn't want to do was blow them out of the house. She might as well ask and get it over with. "Nick, you don't by any chance have a gas stove, do you?"

7

"I'M NOT BEING PREJUDICED when I say this. But Jessica is the smartest baby I've ever met."

"Sure she is," Nick absently agreed as he placed the car seat in the back seat of the Bronco and leaned in. He figured securing the seat should be pretty easy. All he had to do was lift the handlebar, or whatever they called that thing put on a car seat for the express purpose of letting kids bang their hands on so they can drive unsuspecting uncles crazy. Then, when the handlebar was all the way up, he'd pull the seat belt out of its resting position, and take it as far as it would come out. Once he had a lot of excess seat belt, he'd weave the strap through the steel rods on the bottom of the car seat, then click the seat belt into place.

The job was so simple anyone could do it.

Five minutes later, he wasn't so sure.

"You know," Diana said chattily. "I talk to Jessica and she understands exactly what I'm telling her. It's amazing." She paused. "Are you having trouble?"

"Amazing," he mumbled. Even more amazing was that Diana noticed that he was having a hard time. He couldn't say he knew too many women who were that observant. Sure, it didn't make his situation any easier the way Diana held Jessica, face out, giving the kid free kicking access to his rear end, which, Jessica being Jessica, used to her full advantage.

"I'm so glad you agree with me," Diana said. "I wish you could have seen her while I was getting her dressed today. For the second time, after I spilled the baby powder, she told me she was tired of pink clothes. So then I put her in the yellow clothes, but she spilled her milk on that, which was probably better, because blue is really her color. And anyway, she was getting tired of changing.''

"Nooooo," screamed Jessica giving Nick another kick.

"Tired." He'd get the seat belt halfway there, then it would lock up on him. "I'm working as fast as I can, Diana. She can sleep in the car." He'd have to release the belt, let it go all the way back to the starting point, and pull it back out again.

"Sleep? She had a pretty good nap earlier. I don't think she needs sleep. What I think she's tired of is saying the word *no*. Now, that 'no' she said before doesn't mean 'no' like you and I would think a 'no' means. It's not a negative response by any stretch of the imagination," Diana explained. "I know this because she told me when I was changing her clothes that she's hungry. What Jessica's really saying is that she's so excited that you're taking us all out to eat. Now, now, Jessica, stop kicking Uncle Nick."

"Hungry? I was, but not anymore. Losing my appetite. I guess you two are, though." He'd been working that seat belt, and it wasn't cooperating. The handlebar slipped from his grasp and hit his head just as he almost had the seat belt in place. "Three times the charm," he said under his breath.

"Oh, absolutely. That's why the third outfit, the blue one she's wearing, is so nice. Because I also believe three times is the charm."

"A charm, huh?" Did she think a charm would work? Well, why not? At this point, he'd try anything. "Diana, if you have some kind of magical charm that you can use to get this seat in, then I'm all for it."

"I know she's charming," she went on, seemingly oblivious to what he'd just said. "And smart, too. And I'm not saying that just because she's your niece. Okay, wait.

Maybe I should qualify that statement. If you were to question me closely, I would have to say I don't know any other one-year-olds. But I don't see why that should figure into the overall equation about how smart she is. You didn't have to know Albert Einstein to know he was a genius."

Jessica started kicking again, harder this time.

"Albert Einstein died before you were born. How could you know him?" Nick grunted after each word, which coincided with each kick. He didn't think the manufacturer of car seats could possibly have meant getting the seat hooked up to be this complicated. "Shouldn't she be getting tired of this game?"

"I don't know. I really need to get to a bookstore. There's so much I'd like to learn about what she's doing and why she's doing it. For instance, do you think they'll have a Berlitz tape that will either teach an adult to understand baby talk, or teach the baby to speak words that we can all understand? I want something instructional that can teach me how to communicate with babies."

"Instructions, that's it!" He backed out of the car. "Diana, you're a genius." He pulled her to him and gave her a big kiss on the lips. "Thank you."

Jessica squirmed between them, but that didn't matter. He kissed her once, now he had to kiss her one more time. Mandatory, just like the instructions. This time he got stuck on Diana's lips, her soft, tender, provocative lips. When she parted her mouth, he took that as an invitation to enter and explore.

Until he got kicked in the wrist. "We need to teach her about kicking the hand that feeds you."

Diana's brown eyes widened, her pink lips were slack. He liked her that way. "I'm going to get Cathy's instructions. Be right back." He jogged in the direction of the parking-garage elevators.

"Nick," she called out.

He turned.

"I have Cathy's instructions with me. I can't go anywhere without her instructions, because I'm afraid I'll do
something wrong." He came back to her, and she handed
them over to him.

"Diana, I have to tell you, one of the reasons I think this
idea of yours is going to work, is that we listen to each
other." He'd never be able to tell her how much that meant
to him. "I like that."

"It works both ways. You make me feel as if what I say
is worthwhile."

"It is." He flipped through the four pages, and didn't
see anything that told him how to get the seat belt pulled
out and wrapped through the bottom of the car seat without
getting hit by the handlebars. "But, a picture is worth a
thousand words, and these instructions aren't worth the paper they're printed on."

"I can try to get it in," Diana offered.

"Sure, if you think you can." He was man enough to
let her try. He knew she couldn't do it, though. After all,
he was the one who could build a building with his bare
hands, raise a roof in a single day. Diana was a thinker. A
scholar. He respected that about her, but thinking didn't get
a car seat hooked in. For that, a person needed brawn, not
brains.

Diana climbed into the back seat with Jessica, and sat
her down next to the car seat, then backed her way out
again.

"I've assessed the problem and I've figured it out."

She was cute. Going along with whatever she said was
easy on the eyes and ears.

"Nick, installing this car seat is a two-person operation.
Can you hold up this handlebar for me so it doesn't hit my
head?"

Diana leaned half her body into the car again, and Nick
leaned over Diana. Nice. Soft. Rounded in all the right
places. "What do you want me to do?" He didn't think it

mattered whether she got the seat belt through the car seat or not. He liked leaning over her like this. He could stay this way for a while, and it wouldn't bother him at all.

The truth was, he really couldn't do much else anyway, because standing up straight at this moment would almost be an impossibility. "So, Diana—" His voice sounded an octave higher. He cleared his throat and tried again, deeper this time. "So, Diana, what do you suggest?"

She moved backward out of the car, and stopped when she ran into him. He knew the second she felt the reaction he'd had to her. She stiffened, too.

"I, ah…ah…figured it out," she said. "If you would hold up the handlebar for me, I can push the seat belt through the bars."

At this point, he'd do whatever she wanted. He leaned farther in the car, and lifted up the bar while she threaded the seat belt through the rods on the bottom of the car seat.

"Okay," Diana said.

He took a deep breath.

"Nick, you can get up now."

No, Nick couldn't. Not until his body stopped reacting, and he cooled down.

Diana turned her head. Her ponytail swung down, almost to the floor. Big brown eyes stared into his soul. "Nick?"

He knew what she was going to ask, and he wanted the same thing. All he had to do was say, "Yes."

"Thank you."

"I'm the one who should be thanking you."

"There's nothing to it, really. It takes two people. It's not something you can do by yourself."

"I wasn't planning on doing anything like it myself." The very thought didn't appeal to him. What he had in mind was a two-people operation.

"So, do you think we should tell Cathy to give more specific instructions next time?"

"Instructions?" He didn't know what she was talking

about. He didn't need instructions. "If you feel you need instructions, Diana, I could teach you anything you want to know. Let's leave Cathy out of this. She doesn't need them. She already knows how."

"Are you sure?"

"Positive."

"Well...if you insist."

It seemed as if Nick had known Diana all his life. He was that comfortable with her. Talking about sex with any woman could be tricky, yet with Diana, the honesty and understanding they had with each other pretty much amazed him. This living in sin could get serious and he was glad to know they were in complete agreement with each other. He smiled at her. They were in this together. Partners. They would succeed.

Then he felt Jessica's foot connect with his head.

"Jessica! What are you doing?" Diana placed her hand on top of the toddler's moving feet just before they could gain momentum for another round.

All those feelings, a mixture of tenderness and sin, he'd been having while he leaned over Diana were pretty much overwhelmed by the pain in his forehead inflicted by the miniature football player in blue. Nick backed out of the car. His hands spanned Diana's slender hips as he helped her back out, too.

She came out pulling Jessica across the back seat. "Let's put her in the car seat and get to the restaurant. I bet she's starving and that's why she's acting up."

"Hungry or not, she doesn't need a reason to act up with me."

"Nooooo," the baby screeched, trying to get her feet free again.

"You see. Did you tell her to do that?" Nick demanded.

"Of course not. Why would I want her to kick you?"

"I don't know why. I don't even try to guess why

women think some of the things they do. You all have these
secret girl codes.''

Nick looked down at Jessica's feet, which were still kicking wildly. Hard to believe such little things could inflict
such pain. He looked at her now-smiling, grinning face.
''It's no wonder she's hungry. The kid's been doing step
aerobics for the past thirty minutes. Kick my stomach, step
on my head, kick my stomach.''

''You know she didn't mean it.''

''Do I, Diana?'' He knew he sounded sarcastic, but he
had finally gotten to the point where he didn't care anymore. His ego, his head and his gut had taken a beating.
''Do I really?''

Jessica bounced in Diana's arms, her head bobbing up
and down.

''See,'' Diana said with pride. ''What did I tell you? She
knows what you said, and she's telling you that not only
is she hungry, but that yes, she's been doing aerobics, too.
You are so brilliant, Nick.''

''I give up.'' He sighed. He put his arms around Diana
and gave her another kiss. This one on the tip of her nose.
''I don't know how your father's wife could possibly be
doing all those things to you. I wish there was a way to
make it up. You don't deserve any of it.'' And she didn't.
Diana had been given bad breaks all the way around. He'd
do anything to try to fix it for her. Anything. Even if it
meant putting up with Jessica just to keep Diana around
for a few days.

Nick took Jessica from Diana's arms, and placed her, as
she kicked and screamed all the while, in the car seat. He
moved fast, and strapped her in quickly. For him, at least,
it was almost painless. For Jessica? He wasn't so sure.

Nick held Diana's elbow and guided her toward the front
of the Bronco, holding open the passenger-side door, helping her in. She seemed just as light and delicate as Jessica.
Just as soft. But unlike his niece, Diana was very compliant.

He closed the door and walked to the other side of the car, whistling "I Got You, Babe."

Diana heard him whistling, recognized the song, and her heart about exploded.

She knew for sure Nick liked her in the physical sense, because she had backed into him and felt his desire. She knew he liked her mind, because he asked her questions, and listened to her answers. Really listened, not just half listened as if he were trying to formulate what he would say next. She knew he liked her emotionally. Perhaps that was the most important part of all. The way he held her elbow, or dropped a kiss on her forehead for no reason except to kiss her. Those were the best kind of kisses. Even better than any passionate kiss could be, because they were spur-of-the-moment, *I just care a lot about you* kind of kisses.

Diana also knew that when her father found out about her and Nick, all hell would break loose. Yet, that was the plan all along. Nick was a big man, even bigger than her father. Still, she had to wonder how he'd hold up against a father's wrath.

She glanced over at him as he drove. Large, tanned hands held lightly on to the steering wheel. She could still feel those hands on her cheek. Strong, callused and tender. They were an incredible combination, just as she had always imagined they would be.

Nick would hold up well against her father, she decided. He was Charlie Logan's son, and despite the feud, Diana knew he had come from good genes. After all, Charlie couldn't be all that bad. Not if he had loved Elizabeth. Anyone who loved her mother was okay in her book.

THEY HAD ARRIVED at ¡Otra, Otra! in the middle of the business-lunch crowd. By Diana's way of thinking, these people all needed to be back at work and not out eating.

Apparently, others didn't see it that way, and ¡Otra, Otra!

was packed wall to wall with people holding frozen margaritas.

As they waited in line, Diana kept a tight grip on Jessica, who had started to squirm. Until Nick came back with packages of soda crackers.

"Do you want one?" Nick asked.

"Nooooo," Jessica screamed, batting at him before she grabbed the cracker and shoved it in her mouth. She gave him a big smile then turned to whoever was on her left and shot the wad of crackers.

"Nick, did you see her aim?"

"I played football in college," he said. "I think she takes after me."

"Give her another cracker."

"Jessica, do you want this?" He held up the soda cracker.

She took it from his hand without a word and bit down.

"You're not playing football here, don't spit."

Jessica made little munching noises before she buried her head in Diana's neck.

"I love when she does that."

"She looks good on you," Nick told her.

"You know, I didn't think of this before, but I'm good with this baby. I've been trying so hard to find something I'm good at, something that I can do to change the world, and I will—uh-oh—where did it go?" Diana looked over her shoulder. Another cracker ball missiled and landed. "Let's move south," she said, heading straight ahead.

"That's north."

"Nick, don't sweat the small stuff."

Jessica grabbed another cracker from his hand. "I know I'm precise, but I have to be," Nick said. "In my business, being off even one centimeter can throw the whole house off."

"I'm precise, too." At least Diana thought she was, most of the time. She truly believed that when things went wrong, it had been because she'd been thinking about Nick. And since she was with him now, she didn't have to think about him, she could just be—

So why was she arguing over north and south? Who could tell the difference inside a building anyway? She was just about to point that out, too, when the lady who had been Jessica's target turned around and stared hard.

"Sheila!" Diana tried to sound enthusiastic, and not sick. "What a surprise." Where there's a Sheila, there's a Harry. "Jessica," Diana whispered. "No more crackers."

Nick held up his hand. "Here, Jessica, have another."

"What are you doing here?" Sheila asked, wheezing through her nose. All those white-paint fumes probably had done permanent damage.

"Waiting in line." Diana stood as straight as she could, standing over Sheila by a head. There was power in size, she thought, giving her father's fifth wife the same sweet smile she reserved for door-to-door salesmen. "And you?" *You little Napoleon Bonaparte–complex person.*

"I was supposed to meet your father, but I know once he knows you're here, he's not going to want to stay. You've disappointed him greatly, Diana. You should be ashamed."

Diana felt herself shrinking, until Nick reminded her, by circling her waist with his arm, that he stood by her side. He empowered her with strength of mind and character, and she didn't know how or why he was able to do that with a simple touch. Maybe that was a good thing, maybe it wasn't. But for now, he had her gratitude.

"Diana, aren't you going to introduce me?" Sheila asked. "To your friend."

"Nick, Sheila. Sheila, Nick."

"Don't tell me," Nick said. "You're the interior decorator. Is she the one, love?" He pulled Diana closer to his side.

"She's it."

Sheila's mouth twisted. "Your father's here."

Okay, Diana. You can do this. She looked up at Nick's beautiful eyes. She loved those eyes. He winked at her at the same time she was winking at him.

"Diana," Harry said. "You joining us for lunch?"

Nick nodded slightly, and so Diana agreed. She figured they probably wouldn't get as far as the table together.

Jessica had chewed another cracker, and once again Sheila was the target, only this time, Jessica hit the front of Sheila's white dress, instead of the back.

"That child is evil and has no manners. Give her back to whomever she belongs to," Sheila demanded while she swiped at the front of her dress. "Oooh, this is disgusting..."

"She's my niece."

"And who are you?" Harry asked.

"Nick Logan." He held out his hand, which was ignored.

Diana smiled up at Nick. He was so calm. So respectful. Her father, on the other hand, had that look on his face again, the one that turned his complexion red and splotchy. His hatred for the Logans ran so deep.

"What are you doing with him, Diana? You know better than to speak to a Logan."

"Nick's not part of your fight."

"He's a Logan. That's enough."

Nick had given Jessica another cracker. She chewed and chewed this one, and Diana felt sure she was going to actually eat it. But this time she opened her mouth, stuck out her tongue and let it drop, right on Harry's shoe. They all looked down at the same time. It was Harry who got kicked in the face by Jessica's swinging leg.

"Who is this child?" he bellowed, shaking off his shoe and rubbing his head.

"My sister's."

"Diana, will you tell that Logan boy that I'm not talking

or listening to him. When I have a question, I will come to you. If you wish to defer to him, that is your choice. But for every moment you're with him, consider that one less day of college. So I ask again, who is this child.''

"Daddy, you can't bribe me. I don't need your money. And even if I did, I'd like to think that I have more backbone than that.''

"Diana," Nick said, admiration deep in his eyes, genuine affection on his lips. "I'm proud of you."

"Are we going to eat, Harry?" Sheila asked. "They've called our table."

"Are you still inviting us to join you?" Diana asked.

"You've got to be kidding. I won't eat with a Logan."

"It's too bad, Daddy, because Nick and I are, well, we're—" She took a deep breath, tightened her hold on Jessica, and felt Nick squeeze her waist. She hoped that squeeze was for encouragement and not as a signal to stop, do not pass go, do not collect the possibility of a future with Nick.

So, she stared her father in the eyes and just blew out the words. "Nick and I have decided that the two of us, well—we're going to live in sin."

8

THEY SAT at the kitchen table in Nick's apartment, the three of them, Nick with his fork and Jessica with her fingers suspended in midmouthful, waiting for Diana, who could only look around the table and say, "So—"

Diana's gaze darted back and forth between identical blue eyes. She took a deep breath, let out a big sigh, lowered her head and continued to cut her chicken into small pieces just as she had just done for Jessica moments before. Three-quarters of the way through cutting, she finally realized that what was done was done and there wasn't a thing she could do about it.

She put her knife and fork on the plate and folded her hands in her lap. Leaning forward a little, she asked, "In your honest opinion, Nick, and don't hold back, on a scale of one to ten with ten being high, how mad do you think my father was?"

"At least a fifteen." A forkful of black beans went in his mouth.

Diana broke into a huge smile, clapping her hands together. "Really? Oh, that's so wonderful, isn't it? I thought so, but I wasn't really sure. I needed confirmation."

"He reacted just like we thought he would." Nick took a tortilla, helped himself to more meat and topped it off with salsa, sour cream and guacamole. He rolled the tortilla and took a big bite and chewed with relish. "They outdid themselves today. This is good stuff."

¡Otra, Otra! had stupendous take-out food, the very best

Diana had eaten. The people who ran the restaurant must have had a good-neighbor take-out policy since they had filled fourteen-inch tinfoil containers with enough food to last three days, maybe four. Diana thought that was great since she didn't know how much macaroni and cheese she'd be able to disguise as rotisserie ravioli rossetti, or sunset spaghetti surprise, which was not to be confused with shocking sunrise spaghetti—two totally different ingredients. Both main ingredients were macaroni and cheese, but sunset was made with tomato soup, and the sunrise with raisins, cinnamon and butter.

Jessica bounced around, as much as a baby who was strapped in a high chair could bounce. She tore apart tortillas and munched on fajita chicken. She had tears running down her face as she jabbered to her little cut-up pieces of food, but she wasn't screaming.

Nick was on his third helping of mesquite smoked chicken, beef and vegetables, topping everything off with melted garlic butter.

Diana ate slowly, savoring the company, wishing meals like the one they were sharing this afternoon could go on forever. She knew better than anyone how short forever lasted. She knew she'd better enjoy each and every moment they shared because without her even realizing it happened, the very next moment everything could be gone, just *poof!*—up in smoke. "A fifteen," she said. "That's great. Better than I even hoped."

"Okay, maybe I exaggerated. You can give or take one or two points."

Diana pursed her lips, nodding. "I think this is good. Real good. Don't you?"

"The plan was to get your father so angry at you he could throw a steel girder. Okay, we succeeded. We did a great job." He took another bite.

Diana's hands went slack, her fork dropped to the plate.

"Oh, no, Nick. That's not what happened. We have to do the whole thing again. This plan didn't work at all."

"Of course it did." He gazed at her encouragingly. "I was there, I know it worked."

"He was supposed to get angry at you, remember. And your dad was supposed to get angry at me."

"Diana, I know anger when I see it. I'm telling you, when you told him we were living together, your father about hit the ceiling. If I had a daughter who told me she was living with some bum, that bum would be dead meat."

"Really?" This part made her happy. Nick was thinking in terms of children. His children.

"Of course, I'm not planning on getting married, and I'm no bum, so that scenario doesn't apply to me. I'm just saying how I'd feel if I were in your father's position."

"I understand." She nodded knowingly.

"No, I can tell by the look on your face, you don't."

"What look? I'm not looking like anything. Of course I understand what you're saying. I don't agree, but I understand."

He grabbed her hand. "Diana, listen to me. When I tell you Harry was angry at you—not me, he was angry at you."

Oh, Lordy, right now she wanted to move their hands closer to her mouth and kiss his knuckles, then turn his hand over and kiss the palm, and then his wrist, and then the inside of his elbow, and up and up until she got to his mouth.

She'd kiss him deeply, and thoroughly, and drink in all that was Nick. Maybe now she could advance the fantasy, and dream about her and Nick having children. About the fun they'd have getting them.

She hadn't let herself imagine a relationship developing to that point of seriousness between them. She hadn't fantasized past the dating and making love part before today because she had always known that even talking to Nick the way she was doing now was such an unattainable goal. Yet, it had happened. So who knew what else might happen?

"So you see, Diana," Nick was saying, "Harry wouldn't waste any time being angry with me. I see that now. To him I'm a nothing. I don't exist. So pushing me into his face, making him come to terms with a Logan again, would make him angry at you. He doesn't want to face the fact that we're alive and kicking. He wouldn't want to be reminded."

She knew in her heart he wasn't right. Still, there was this little flame of a doubt, and if there was even one little flame, no matter how small, she had to douse it. "I would say the same thing to you if it was your father we saw today and I didn't want you to be disappointed. Only, I didn't realize how hard it would be to tell my father. You know, I'm his only daughter. I didn't think about a daughter saying to a father, 'Hey, Dad, I'm living in sin.'"

"We're not living in sin, Diana." His intense gaze sought her eyes, searched her face. "Yet."

But tonight they would be, and by tomorrow— A tingling thrill raced up her spine. She looked down at her plate, breaking the lock he had on her. She had to think. "Now it's your father's turn. First thing tomorrow, you'll call him, and tell him about our arrangement."

He shook his head, taking another bite of his fajita.

"Why not?" she asked. He had to. This had to work out.

"Because something just dawned on me. It's a given that no matter what we do together, both fathers will be angry. However, your dad was ready to shoot nails from an electric nail gun right into my heart for touching you."

Diana nodded. "That's because I'm a daughter, remember?"

"Exactly. And that's also exactly why my dad won't care. Living with someone isn't marrying them. Marriage is permanent. Living together is temporary. My dad would say, 'Have a good time, son, use protection.' At this moment your dad is upstairs on the thirtieth floor figuring out a way to make me sing soprano.''

Diana shook her head and gazed at him in sympathy. He was so wrong. "Nick, my dad is still at ¡Otra, Otra! eating lunch. Nothing, not even the idea of his daughter living in sin, is going to affect my father's appetite.''

"Oh, Diana, you of little faith. Your dad wants to cut off my male parts and hang them up to dry. It pains me even to think along those lines. That's the difference between the father of a son, and the father of a daughter.''

"No way would he want to do that.'' Her dad wasn't sadistic. Just hungry. Once he ate his lunch, and had time to think about things, he'd be reasonable. Especially if he had sopaipillas for dessert.

"I wouldn't want to test out his anger.''

Okay, so her father did have a lot of tools. Saws, a hatchet— "I didn't think about that before. This is now an emergency and we didn't think of a contingency plan. It's really too late to drop the whole thing, because it's all been set in motion. What am I supposed to do, go to my father and say it's a joke? He'd never believe me.''

"Not that.''

"I want them talking again. I want these families at least on a cordial level. Nick, if my dad and your dad could at least renew their friendship, maybe my father wouldn't be searching so hard for someone to take my mother's place.''

Jessica squealed, banged on her high-chair table and stuck her fingers in her mouth. Nick went to the refrigerator and took out three bottles of milk, setting them on the tray.

"I didn't think of this before, but everything is coming together. My father lost his wife and his best friend. He's lonely,'' Diana said.

"I'm not suggesting we stop. I'm suggesting that we modify the plan. This morning when I told Alicia we were getting married, yes, it was a slip of the tongue. I'm not getting married, you do understand that?''

Diana rolled her eyes. ''Of course I understand. Here, have a taste of this.'' She put some chicken on a fork and pushed it toward him. He opened his mouth and took the chicken off the fork with his lips. She wanted those lips on her lips, but her lips on the fork he just touched would be almost as good. Not quite as good, but a start.

''However, the more I think about it, the more reasonable it sounds as far as what we tell my father.''

''A parent wouldn't be angry if we were to get married. Marriage is a good thing,'' Diana said.

''For ninety-nine point nine percent of the population, that's true. Then there's my father. If I tell him you and I are getting married, he'll go crazy. Because you're a Smith and marriage to a Smith is as bad as my sister having a baby out of wedlock. Like I said, marriage is a permanent institution.''

''So's a baby.''

''Look at my parents, married forever, miserable forever.''

''Look at Jessica. She's a part of them, whether they like it or not.''

''Like I told you, they've ignored her, and my sister.''

There was a real heaviness in her heart for him and for Cathy. Diana at least knew her father had loved her mother. That thought always kept her secure at night, as if her mother, like a guardian angel, always watched out for her. Nick didn't seem to have that. Diana guessed that without knowing a mother's love, a person couldn't grow up feeling whole.

Nick was a good man. She knew that from the moment she'd met him. She might have spent a good deal of that summer before the White Envelope Incident ogling his behind, but she also saw the way he'd gotten along with the men on the crew. He didn't act like a rich man's son, lording his position over the men. He'd been right in there working and sweating with the rest of them. That's what made him so much fun to watch.

His parents needed to be taught a lesson, and she was just the one to do it. If she had to return to her fantasies when these few days were over, then at least she wanted to go out with a bang, no pun intended.

Nick took another mouthful of fajita. Diana played with her food, moving it around the plate with her fork. Jessica dumped two bottles on the floor, and drank milk out of the third one. When she finished, she threw chicken pieces at Nick and screamed at him, while tears rolled down her cheeks.

He caught the chicken pieces midair and stuck them in his tortilla. "I was a quarterback once upon a time," he said when Diana complimented him on his catching ability. "I also played outfield in college baseball."

"That's why Jessica's feet kick all the time. See." She pointed to Jessica's oscillating legs.

"She gets the athletic ability from me. She gets her temper from my mother. If she turns up talented, she'll have gotten that from Cathy. Smart, my other brothers."

"What did she get from her father?" Diana asked.

"Life."

"That's a lot, Nick. Even if he's not here, that's a precious gift."

"Responsibility is an obligation that goes with that gift." His eyes turned a deep, stormy blue. "I'm not spending the night here." Nick took their plates off the table, dumping them in the sink. He brought back the coffeepot and set it on a towel. "Because I'm a responsible guy, and I'm not going to see you compromised."

Diana smiled at him. Things were going excellently. "I want to get this straight. You're afraid to stay here tonight, even if we don't sleep in the same bed."

"We shouldn't spend the night in the same house. Your

father would think we had sex. I don't want him to think that.''

"But we won't." Although she'd sure try to change his mind.

"Diana, I'm wearing *Nicholas X*. Of course we will if I stay here. It never fails.''

Diana's grin widened. Poor Nick was running scared. This was great. Never had she even imagined in her wildest fantasy that he'd be affected by her, too. "Don't you trust that I can control myself?''

"Not when I'm wearing *Nicholas X*," he said matter-of-factly.

Diana had Nick's number and it spelled 1-900-I-WANT-U-2. Never in her life would she have imagined that he'd be afraid to spend the night with her. Afraid of what their own natural instincts would lead them to do. "I understand." He couldn't run forever. "Where will you be?''

"I'm going to the office. There's a couch there with lumps made for my body. Before I go, I'll call my dad and tell him the good news about the wedding. In the meantime, can you get me a picture of you to take with me to work?''

"It's upstairs." She pushed away from the table. "I'll hurry back.''

Nick looked over at Jessica and for the first time realized what a mess the kid was. Food was everywhere. Two bottles of milk were dumped on the floor. Green guacamole was drying on her face and arms.

He untied her from the chair and lifted her out by the armpits. She was wet from the collar of her little T-shirt, to the tips of her shoes. He carried her at arm's length to the sink. She cried all the way over there, but she was shivering, too, probably more from the air-conditioning hitting her wet clothes than the idea that she was being held by him. Her sobs were punctuated with rattling shivers. "I don't know what I ever did to you to deserve this kind of treatment," he told her. "I wouldn't confess this to anyone, monkey face, but your rejection hurts. Right down to the bones.''

She didn't care. She didn't stop crying, her little red nose ran, and she rubbed fisted hands all over her face, spreading the slimy stuff.

He ran water in the sink until it was warm, then he dumped her in there, clothes, shoes and all. "I don't know why nobody thought of this before," he told her. "Washing kids and clothes at the same time. I wonder if I can get a patent on the idea."

He took the sponge and wiped her down. He used the sprayer to wash her hair. After he got all the juice from the chicken and the guacamole off her shirt, he peeled it over her head. Next came the shoes. They didn't look so good—maybe leather wasn't something he should have put in the water. Too late. He took off her socks next, then those little jeans. By now Jessica had calmed down enough to sit in the sink. She slapped her hands in the sudsy water that had risen to her waist, sending bubbles flying.

Her sobs had turned to laughter, her "nos" to a singsong tune that sounded suspiciously like that commercial where all the cats sing "meow."

He undid her diaper, and if it had been wet before, five minutes in a sinkful of water really weighed it down. He opened the trash compactor and threw it in. "You know what?" he said. "I should have thought this out a little bit better."

Jessica responded with a splash. He wiped his eyes.

He looked around the kitchen for something he could reach without taking his hand off Jessica's shoulder. The best he could come up with was the dish towel hanging under the sink.

He lifted Jessica a little, so her bottom wasn't over the drain anymore, and the water began to go down the pipes. Jessica seemed just as happy playing with the leftover bubbles.

Nick dried off her face and upper body. He helped her stand up, and miracle of all miracles, she held on to his shoulders and hardly screamed at all. He dried her bottom and legs, and was left with one naked baby and no diaper. "That's not a problem. Until I can get the diapers, you'll use this." He put the dish towel between her legs, and knotted the ends at her side. Not the best, not the worst, either. All in all, he was pretty damn proud of his accomplishment. He couldn't wait for Diana to get back.

He didn't have to wait long. Jessica sat at his feet, eating an oatmeal cookie. And Diana thought chocolate-chip was the way to the baby's heart. Oatmeal was the only way to go.

Diana skidded to a stop halfway between the kitchen entryway and where he stood. Her eyes were wide as she gave the flooded room a tour with her gaze. "What happened?"

"I helped."

"Pardon?"

"Look at Jessica." He pointed down to the newly washed kid with the dish towel diaper. She shone with cleanliness, and new cookie crumbs. He'd get those in the morning.

"Nick, did the pipes leak?"

This time he looked around. He scratched his ear. He rubbed his chin, which after a day's growth, scratched his hand. He gave her what he hoped would be an I-screwed-up-big-time grin. "I knew what I was doing," he told her with supreme male bravado. "I thought I'd help."

"Listen, you know what? This is exactly why we need to go to the bookstore tomorrow. I don't know what I'm doing, and even if you do know—" she threw out her hand taking in the room "—accidents happen. If we don't get some professional help, we're going to end up with a bigger mess than we started with. Where's your mop?"

"I'll get it, Diana. Why don't you take Jessica and put a diaper on her, and I'll clean up in here."

"You don't have to offer me an olive branch twice." She picked up Jessica and hurried out of the room.

Nick saw the picture Diana had left of herself on the table. It hadn't been taken in Texas, he could tell that by the leaves turning colors, and the snowcapped mountains in the background. She smiled for the camera, her hair long and flowing down her back. He stuck the picture in his back pocket and wondered who had taken it, and if he should be jealous.

NICK HADN'T WANTED to leave Diana and Jessica. Well, he could give or take Jessica, but he really didn't want to leave Diana that night. He had to, though. He had no choice.

Living in sin was one thing, but actually doing the *living-in-sin* part was something else again. When he had helped Diana hatch this plan, he'd made a vow to keep his hands to himself. Diana was bright, funny, and most of all, she was a sweet innocent caught up in this Smith-Logan mess. As long as she stayed in his home, he wouldn't be staying with her.

Nick had found out as the day went on that while the vow was easy to make, it wasn't as easy to keep. Diana was the kind of woman a man longed to touch. Why, he felt like a martyr leaving the apartment tonight, with her looking after him with those big brown Bambi eyes and him not wanting to go but having no choice. He refused to give Harry any more fuel to throw into the Logan family fire.

So after he had cleaned the kitchen, he left Diana to care for Jessica. Diana had said, "Say bye-bye to your Uncle Nick, Jessica." And of course Jessica had said, "No," which is what he had expected. But Diana came back with, "No, dear heart. You have to say, 'No, Uncle Nick the coward.'" To which Jessica put both her tiny hands on Diana's cheeks and said, "No," even louder.

Nick drove to his office, knowing that even if Diana thought he was a coward for leaving and not spending the night with her, at least Jessica didn't. Of course "no" was Jessica's standard answer for everything. Still, it would look mighty good if he could put down on a recommendation inquiry, *"Nick Logan is a courageous man, willing to take chances,"* which in essence is what not being a coward meant.

He had tried to explain that to Diana, but she didn't get a real grasp yet that for Nick sleeping at the office was about the most courageous move he could make. He liked her too much to compromise her, which is exactly what would have happened if he'd stayed. She deserved better than that. He respected Diana. He considered himself a gentleman. Most of the time.

Before he left home, he had called his father and told him he and Diana were getting married. Charlie did what Nick expected his father to do, threatened to cut him out of the family. It was nice to know that if Nick had been getting married to Diana, instead of setting up this elaborate scheme to get their fathers talking again, this was what he could expect.

Harry threatening to cut Diana off this afternoon. Charlie threatening to cut him off tonight. Those two men were of the same ilk. No wonder they hated each other.

Diana could hope for a reconciliation between the men, but he didn't see it happening. He wasn't about to burst her bubble though. She had too much of herself tied up in it. Until she realized that there would be no reconciliation between the families, he wasn't going to rock the boat. He knew that if he and Diana were in fact living in sin, her father would never agree to any kind of peace agreement.

So until peace either came, or Diana came to the conclusion that it would never come, he and Diana would have to spend their nights apart. For Nick that also meant very frustrated days spent in her company. But he wouldn't have it any other way.

Nick knew there wasn't anything either one of them could do about the family feud. It had gone on too long, there were too many feelings of anger and bitterness, and he had no control over what the fathers of the families did. He could only control himself.

He drove into the parking lot of Nicholas X. He had named his company after the products his sister had made for him. He owned several acres of land in the far corner of Sugar Land. There he'd built a warehouse, a small office building, as well as several other buildings.

He flipped on the floodlights to the storage unit behind the warehouse where he kept all the extra scraps and pieces of wood. He pulled the antique oak boards he had taken from an old house he'd renovated, and brought them inside to the area he called the center. This is where he and his craftsmen did the smaller, more precise custom work that couldn't be done on-site.

Nick took Diana's picture out of his pocket and set it on the table. Taking out a new automatic pencil, he clicked until fresh lead appeared. He pulled a piece of white paper off the shelf and laid it flat on the table. He had just turned on the overhead light, when he heard a car pull up.

Nick went to the front door, turned on all the floodlights outside and waited. A man got out of a big, dark sedan and walked toward him. His walk, his shape as familiar to Nick as his name. "Dad."

Charlie brushed passed him, entering the center. "I haven't been out here in a while," he said. "Not since you first had the buildings up."

"I know." Nicholas X wasn't number one. There was no reason for his father to investigate his business, since there wouldn't be any competition from his end.

Charlie walked the perimeter of the room, stopping in

front of the drafting table. "I came to talk some sense into you."

"There's nothing to talk about."

His father stared at the tabletop. "I came to tell you what a mistake you're making. You can't get involved with the Smith family."

"Diana and I have nothing to do with your fight." He sounded passionate. If Diana had been here, she'd have been proud of his performance.

Charlie picked up the photo. He brought it to his face, slid his glasses to his forehead, squinted one eye and looked closer. The room was so silent, not even the crickets dared to chirp.

He slowly lowered the picture, and pushed his glasses back down again. "Elizabeth."

"That's Diana, Dad."

"She looks like Elizabeth. Two of a kind."

"Her mother died. A long time ago."

"I know that. I've been to see her."

"I don't understand."

His father reached into his breast pocket and pulled out a handkerchief. He wiped his forehead and the back of his neck, then put the handkerchief back. "The cemetery. I bring flowers. Not often. Maybe once a month. Maybe twice a month. Certainly no more than once a week. Your mother doesn't know."

"She won't find out from me."

His father's expression didn't change, but then Nick didn't expect it to. Charlie would expect his son to keep his secret. Charlie might bully him, he might disown him the way he'd disowned his own daughter, but as Cathy had told him earlier, they were blood. He trusted Nick.

"Your Diana is a beautiful girl."

"I know." She wasn't "his" Diana though. He had to wonder if this scheme was a betrayal of trust. Probably, but it was for everybody's own good.

"Not as pretty as her mother," Charlie said. "And probably not as nice either."

"She's beautiful." He meant that. "And nice."

Charlie's face formed a scowl. "Does she have a hankering to experiment with things?"

"What do you mean experiment?"

"Elizabeth was perfect, mind you. The only mistake she ever made, of course, was when she married Harry the dog. But before she married him, she was going to school and she had the worst luck there. She used to write me all about it. She'd put these chemicals together, experimenting, and things would happen. There was a small fire one day. There was a little explosion another time."

"Are you kidding?" He couldn't believe this. He wondered if Diana knew.

"Hell, no, I'm not kidding. Get that smile off your face. It's not funny. Harry and I were best friends. I asked him to watch over Elizabeth while I was in the army, and this is how he watched her? She wrote and told me she had almost burned herself and Harry was going to save her from harm. The next thing I know, they had gotten married. He brainwashed her."

"From what Diana said, Elizabeth loved Harry."

"How could she have loved him when she loved me? There's no comparison."

"Dad," Nick had to ask, even though he wasn't sure he wanted to know the answer. "Didn't you love Mom?"

"Sure I did. Even after Patricia found the letters from Elizabeth and started tormenting me. Your mother became a bitter woman. I keep hoping she'll change." The lines around his father's eyes deepened, and his lips locked together.

Now Nick knew what he was dealing with. And he wasn't optimistic. Sometimes it was easier to fix a business deal gone sour than it was a broken heart.

His father didn't stay long after that. When he left, Nick

sat down at the drafting table and began to sketch his own version of what he thought Diana's small table and chairs looked like. He even drew little bunny rabbits hopping over carrots. He knew his staff artists would be able to paint those onto the chairs. He figured it would take him one night to cut the wood, and another to put the whole set together.

He didn't intend for this new set to be a replacement for the table and chairs her father had made for her over twenty years ago. He only hoped that maybe it would take the sting out of losing something that meant a lot to her. Lately, it seemed as if they were all losing things. Like the picture of Diana that his father had folded into his handkerchief when he thought Nick hadn't noticed, and taken with him.

Nick didn't begrudge his dad the picture. But what he did want now almost as much as Diana was to end the cycle of hate. He figured he could start right here with a small table and chairs.

9

DIANA WOKE UP the next morning to the sound of little Jessica chattering to herself.

She rolled over and peeked out of one eye. Jessica stood in the crib holding on to the handrail, having a conversation with herself. "What are you trying to say, Jessica? That you think Uncle Nick should be here to wait on us hand and foot, and give us his undying devotion and love? Well, I know for a fact, you already have his love."

Jessica bounced on the mattress and babbled louder, her gibberish punctuated with giggles and little lip-smacking noises.

"I'm telling you, Jessica, you shouldn't play so hard to get with him. There comes a time when a girl just has to give him a kiss and say, 'Let's be friends.'"

Diana liked being roommates with Jessica. Unlike the ones she'd had in college, Jessica wouldn't be borrowing her clothes or stealing her boyfriends, if she had any, anytime in the near future. And for at least the next twelve years she wouldn't be hogging the phone or the bathroom.

"Are you ready to get dressed?"

Jessica squealed in delight.

"Is that a 'Yes, I am, Auntie Diana'?" Diana got out of bed and stretched. She reached over and took both Jessica's hands in her own. "What do you say? You think you'll wear the purple ball gown today, the one you wore at dinner with that Leonardo DiCaprio babe? Jessica, you have good taste."

Jessica squealed again, and with their hands held together, waved both their arms.

"Oh, no, Jessica, dear," Diana said. "First of all, you mustn't settle for Leo, unless he's your Prince Charming. If he's not your Prince Charming then you must wait." Diana lowered her voice. "For me, your Uncle Nick is Prince Charming. He's so wonderful. He's the only one I've ever dreamed about, Jessica, and if it weren't for you, I wouldn't be in this situation. I owe you, big time. What do you want? A college education? A Mercedes-Benz? Every Beanie Baby that's every existed? Anything."

Jessica let go of Diana's hands and clapped, teetered backward then grabbed back on to the handrail for balance. While smiling at Diana, she put one chubby little leg over the railing and tried to hoist herself over and out of the crib.

"No, Jessica." Diana gently placed the baby's leg back inside the crib. "You stay there. Save the acrobatics for the health club."

"Hello in there," Nick called from the other side, knocking on the door.

"Jessica," whispered Diana. "The lord and master has come home." Diana's heartbeat went into overdrive.

"Everyone awake? Decent?"

"Kind of." Diana had on the shirt she'd worn to bed, and Jessica was in a diaper. They were both decent but barely.

"Coming in. Coming through." Nick opened the bedroom door and the sight before him made his body surge with a thousand-watt jolt of electricity.

It wasn't that he'd never seen women half-dressed before. He'd seen his share. He'd even seen his share less than half-dressed, and more than quite a few completely bare. It's just that he'd never seen Diana half-dressed. She wore a man's blue oxford shirt. And nothing else.

She was leaning over the crib, standing on tiptoe. The

shirt rode up the back of her thighs, the hem skimming the bottom of her pink lacy underwear. The kind that women like to wear, and men like to dispose of quickly. A creamy rounded buttock showed just enough to make a guy's imagination take a flying leap and his male counterpart stand at attention.

When she leaned farther into the crib, more of her bottom came to view, and the front of his jeans got tighter. His voice cracked as it had when he went through puberty, which is exactly how he felt.

"Hi, Nick. Are you ready for breakfast?"

She couldn't possibly realize how hungry he was right now. She couldn't be doing all that bending over on purpose just to drive his testosterone into some crazy boogie-on-down-tonight dance. "Diana, you're not upset that I didn't spend the night here, are you?"

She leaned even farther into the crib. He saw more bottom, causing him to break out in a cold sweat. He heard a muffled, "No."

She straightened the sheet on the opposite side of the crib. He leaned his head down for a better view. She stretched her arm out, and said, "Why would you think that?"

"No reason," he mumbled, cursing his own nobility.

"I understood why you did what you did. I think it was extremely wonderful of you."

Strands of hair got loose from her ponytail, falling over her cheeks and down her neck. She turned her head to look at him, without standing back up. Even more of her became visible to his hungry gaze. And boy-oh-boy was he ever hungry. Three of her top buttons were undone, allowing the front of the shirt to gape open. The plump tops of her breasts played peekaboo with his vision. Light from the window silhouetted the rest.

He shoved his hands into his back pockets to keep himself from walking over there and undoing the rest of those buttons.

"Did you have a nice sleep," she asked him, "over there in your office?"

"Not as good as I would have had here in my own bed, but it was something I had to do for the sake of this mission we're trying to accomplish," he said self-righteously.

When she finally straightened, the front of her shirt came together, which kept her breasts from playing peek-a-boo with his senses. He could breathe again.

The shirttail hit her legs at a conservative mid-thigh. She shouldn't, by all rights, look sexy. But she did. Very sexy. The bedroom didn't help either, smelling of sleep and woman and baby powder. No wonder his testosterone level had jumped as soon as he'd entered the room.

Diana lifted her arm to swipe some hair off her face. The movement made the shirt hike up again. His body reacted immediately with the urgency of a man who desperately needed a woman. One particular woman. Diana.

Her eyelids, still heavy with sleep, widened just a fraction. She knew what he wanted. It would be impossible for her not to know. Her own body responded to the silent signals he had passed to her. Her tongue ran over her parted lips, her breathing came a little faster, her nipples hardened through the shirt.

His fingers buzzed with the urgency to touch her, stroke her. He wanted, needed to be stroked in return. All this talk about sin, about not sinning, did something to him. He was better off just doing it, and not thinking about it. Because once he had decided to be a saint and deny himself her, that's all he could think about. Diana and sin.

Anyway, he'd never make it as a saint.

She sifted her nails through Jessica's fine hair, pushing the baby's bangs off her forehead. Like everything else about Diana, he liked to watch her hand move, too. Such delicate fingers, yet he knew they were strong and capable.

"How did you sleep?" he asked.

"Wonderfully. Jessica and I were just talking, and she wants breakfast, too."

"What does Jessica want for breakfast?"

"Something good, like macaroni and cheese, and canned fruit, and maybe some canned vegetables."

He scratched his neck. That menu put a damper on his frustrated libido. Frustration he wouldn't have right now if he were given free rein to sin if he wanted to. "What about bacon?" he asked. That was the kind of meat made for a man.

"That's way too greasy."

"Not for me. Bacon and eggs, now that's what I call a real meal." A man's meal.

"I'm not going to make bacon and eggs, but if you want to, you can."

"No. Heating up the kitchen isn't what I have in mind." Heating up Diana though, that would work. He moved closer to her. Nearer to her warmth.

"Jessica and I want macaroni and cheese." Diana lifted Jessica out of the crib. The shirt hiked higher with Jessica sitting on Diana's hips, her legs straddling Diana's waist.

Nick was sure Diana didn't realize she was being exposed. He pointed. "Diana." She'd probably be horrified to know that he could see not only her pink lace panties, but also the dark patch covering her womanhood that the panties barely concealed. "Diana," he tried again.

"Now, Nick, no bacon. Trust me, you'll love my macaroni and cheese. It's an old family recipe. Listen, I have a favor to ask you. Nick? Nick? Are you all right?"

"Diana, put Jessica back in the crib." He had to get his mind away from what he and Diana wouldn't be doing with the part of her he was now seeing.

"Why?"

"Just do it." Better yet, maybe a little sin would be a good thing.

As soon as she put Jessica back down, Nick pulled her to him, lowered his lips, and didn't even think about the consequences. "This is to thank you."

She opened her mouth—only before she could speak, he kissed her, hard and deep, his tongue probing, circling, searching, reveling in her sweetness. He heard her moan. He heard Jessica through the fog that had become his brain, saying, "no, no, no." With each no, he pulled Diana closer, thinking "yes," enjoying the feel of her breasts, full and warm, against his chest. Her hand reached up, her fingers lightly grazed the back of his neck. She kissed him back with as much burning desire as he felt. He inched her toward the edge of the bed, and that's when she started to pull away. "No?" he asked.

She looked at Jessica. "No."

"Not ever?"

"Maybe sometime."

"Promise?" He lowered his lips to hers again, brushing them gently, wanting more. "I can promise we'll enjoy ourselves," he murmured.

"Is that all?"

Nick broke the kiss. He needed to look in her eyes to see if she felt the same kind of need he did. He ran his finger down her neck, following the contour of her shoulder, and the length of her arm to the rapidly beating pulse in her wrist. Her skin was so soft, her scent, that of a woman ready for lovemaking.

She looked at him, not as a woman wanting to have a good time, but a woman who wanted something more. Something like commitment, or marriage, or both. The very thing he had realized when Jessica came screaming into his life a little over a year ago, that he'd never be able to give to any woman. Children. How could he be a father to a child who screamed at him? He couldn't take the chance that he'd be an outcast in his own home. He had no choice.

Diana would have to know. "I'm a man who has been put here to give you pleasure, but I don't do commitment."

He watched as the desire that had burned so bright, slowly diminished. He was saving her from himself, and he should feel proud of what he had done. Instead he felt like dirt. "Commitment means marriage and kids. Kids hate me. I won't have children."

"How do you know kids don't like you?" she asked.

"Look at Jessica. What more proof do I need?"

"That's one child."

"Doesn't matter. They're all the same." Every time he was around Jessica and other kids, they all cried. There was something about him children didn't like.

Diana took in a deep, steadying breath. "If I could convince you otherwise, would you change your mind?"

"You won't."

"All right then. I won't try."

She had a determined set to her lips, so he knew she had every intention of doing just that. Trying. Didn't these women read the advice columnists? Every one said women shouldn't try to change a man. Men don't change. Ever.

Diana shivered, then hugged herself. "Listen, I forgot my robe. Can I borrow one of yours?"

He gazed at Diana, her breasts outlined under the shirt, her legs from small, trim ankles to shapely calves to slender thighs. When he looked at her just the way she was right now, he could jump right back to the kiss they shared, and damn commitment to hell. He could still feel her mouth on his lips, the way her body molded to his, the urgency of their hands working each other's flesh and muscles.

The way Nick saw it, he had two choices. He could either do the gentlemanly thing and admit he had a complete collection of silk robes, every relative and ex-girlfriend's favorite Christmas gift to him. Or, he could do what he wanted to do. He opted for the latter. "Sorry, Diana. I don't own a robe."

"Not one?" Her eyes widened in disbelief.

No wonder he liked her so much. She was one sharp babe.

"Not a one." He shrugged, shaking his head.

She gave him that you're-pulling-my-leg look, and said, "I can't believe that."

Well, hell, neither could he. But he made his bed, and now he'd have to lie in it. He hoped, not alone for long. "To tell the truth, if I were sleeping here, when I woke up in the morning I'd put on these jeans for the sake of modesty." He stared deep into her big, brown Bambi eyes. "Your modesty, not mine."

"Thank you." Her voice trailed off.

"I sleep naked. And, if there's no one here, I walk around the house naked." He gave her a lazy-eyed look and deepened his voice. "Sometimes, Diana, I walk around the house naked when there is someone else here."

When he saw her mouth slacken and her eyes widen, he knew his words had sunk in. He said, "I'm going to take a shower, see you at breakfast." He left her staring after him with those huge eyes. He'd done the job. For the rest of the day she'd be thinking about him and her naked. He sure as hell knew that's what he'd be thinking about.

ALL DIANA could think about was Nick and her naked together. Maybe having no commitment between them wouldn't be such a bad thing. In her fantasies she and Nick eventually got naked every time they were together anyway. But this was real life, and, she told herself in her most stern talking-to voice, she was a good girl who needed a commitment before getting naked. Even the "let's go steady" kind would be acceptable.

As soon as Nick left the room, Diana put Jessica on the floor, and ran for the bathroom. She splashed cold water on her face and neck. That wasn't enough. She splashed more cold water on her wrists and down the cleavage be-

ween her breasts. That man had her burning up. She dried
herself off.

She went back into the bedroom and found a pair of
nylon running shorts in her overnight bag and put them on.
She couldn't believe how cool and calm she had acted
when he'd come into the bedroom. What she had really
wanted to do was run up to him, put her arms around his
shoulders, lean her body against his so she could feel every
hard muscle and ripple of his chest, then give him a long,
slow kiss.

Mostly she wanted the kiss.

No, she wanted to feel him.

No. She wanted to touch him and have him touch her.

Okay, a kiss to start, and then the touch. And then what
did she do when he did kiss her and touch her? She had
stopped him. Was she a crazy fool? Oh, Lord, yes. She was
going positively crazy with wanting more.

Diana had to sit down to let her heart rate slow. She'd
been dreaming about making love with Nick forever. She
now knew the sad truth of the matter. When it came time
to actually acting out a fantasy, she was all "think" and
no "do." If she had been more of a doer and less of a
thinker, she would have thrown herself down on the bed
and let her fantasy man make love to her until they were
both exhausted.

Instead, she'd just stood there and kissed him. Then
when he offered her the golden goose, she actually thought
about her future, and what her future would be like without
him in it, and she'd thrown the opportunity away. What
was she anyway? Stupid? This was a fantasy come to life,
and she had become her old moralistic self.

Now was not the time to start thinking about commitment. Now was the time to start acting out her fantasy. She
would, too, the next time. And there would be a next time.
She'd make sure of it.

Diana dressed Jessica, and together they walked hand-in-hand to the kitchen. "I'm going to make you and Uncle Nick a breakfast the likes of which neither one of you will ever forget. He'll be dreaming about having this breakfast with me for the rest of his life. You sit here." Diana put Jessica into a sitting position on the floor near the table, out of the way of where she'd be preparing the food.

Jessica stood up and scrambled five feet away. Diana carried her back and helped her sit where she had sat her originally. "Let me give you something to play with." She handed her a wooden mixing spoon that had been on the counter. "Now pretend this spoon is a whip. Here, whip it around."

Jessica took the spoon, which was almost as big as she was. She looked it over, then twirled it in her hand a few times as if she was trying to figure out what it was used for. It didn't take long for her to start banging the spoon on the Italian-tile floor. "Good girl, Jessica. You're so smart," Diana crooned.

"Now this." She handed the baby a heavy plastic mixing bowl. Again Jessica turned it over, put it on top of her head, took it off again and finally stuck the spoon inside. She looked up at Diana as if to say, "Did I pass the test?"

"Well, you did very good," Diana said. "However, if you want to do really great, you need to think in a more abstract way. For instance, remember we said the wooden spoon is a whip. Right?" They both nodded their heads. "But you can pretend this bowl is awful old Professor Percival Penleigh from Princeton."

Jessica tilted her head, hanging on to every word. Diana had never had such an attentive audience.

"Professor Penleigh had me thrown out of school just for doing a simple experiment. For some reason the flame got a little out of control and—well, it doesn't matter. I transferred to Brown shortly thereafter. The thing is, Jessica, I really liked Princeton, so I want you to take care of Old Professor Penleigh for me."

Jessica hit the spoon on the bowl with a terrible bang and looked up for approval. Diana clapped her hands. "O-o-o-o-h. That's a good one, Jessica. Now don't hold yourself back. You go girl!"

That's all the encouragement Jessica needed. She was off and banging, giving that plastic bowl everything she had. Each smack was music to Diana's ears and she danced and sang a well-known, brazen college ditty to the beat of the pounding spoon.

When Diana finished singing, Jessica dropped the spoon and bowl and clapped. Diana bowed. "Thank you, thank you very much. You're a fine audience."

She heard more applause from behind her. She turned and bowed for Nick, too.

"I didn't know you were so talented." He came all the way into the kitchen.

"I didn't know you were watching." Diana went into the pantry and pulled the box of macaroni and cheese and one can each of corn, carrots and green beans off the shelf, putting them on the counter. She filled a pot with water and set it on the stove to boil.

"I'm always watching." Nick leaned against the counter, pointing to the cans of vegetables. "Is that stuff breakfast?"

Diana nodded. It was hard to speak with him this close, and her body still tingling.

She had thought her life had been fairly interesting before yesterday. She had thought herself fulfilled in her friendships, and her career choice. At least as soon as she got out of school and had the chance to have a career. There was something thrilling about working in laboratories. Always being on the verge of discovering something new. Something that could change the world.

Yet nothing, absolutely nothing, compared to what she felt when she was near Nick. Absolutely, positively electrifying.

"Are you finding everything all right?" He pushed the cans around.

"Yes."

"You don't have to go to all this trouble, heating up cans of vegetables, making macaroni and cheese. Instead, I'll take you and monster mouth out to eat. No bacon and eggs will do. Pancakes. Doesn't that sound good?"

"Sure it does. But vegetables with macaroni and cheese are much better for you."

"I didn't know that." He sounded doubtful.

"Sure you did. Plus, there's no reason to eat pancakes for breakfast, just because people have been doing it for hundreds of years."

"You don't think tradition is a good thing?"

"Nick, if it were, would we be standing here this morning talking about breakfast?"

"Sure we would."

"No, we wouldn't. Because I'm here to break family tradition. You know what I just realized?"

"You changed your mind and opted for pancakes?" He looked at her hopefully.

"No. We're having a beautiful breakfast, full of aesthetically pleasing colors and textures. You're going to love it."

"I can think of things I'd love better." He looked into her eyes with longing, and when he gazed at her lips she could swear she felt as if his lips were touching hers again, kissing her, opening for him. He finally looked away and she could almost breathe normally again.

"You don't want these." He took the cans from the counter and put them back in the pantry.

"What do I want?"

Nick reached for her, pulling her closer to him, tangling his fingers in her hair, lowering his lips to her neck, and nibbling his way down to her shoulder. "This."

Diana closed her eyes, moaning softly, leaning her head

back, giving him more access. He had given her another chance to let him know commitment between them didn't matter. Even if it did, she would put that aside, and take the chance that he'd realize she was important to him. She had to use the opportunity now, or maybe lose it forever.

She couldn't lose. She wanted to give him the same kind of image to think about, something that would drive him crazy with desire, with longing, like the one he had left her with in the bedroom. The one of them naked together.

She moved even closer to him, barely touching his body, but touching all the same. The tips of her breasts burned against his chest, her stomach and legs became weak from grazing against his.

She moved back slightly staring into his eyes. Her voice all husky and wanting asked, "Are you going to treat my body like one of the homes you build? Like something that needs to be stroked gently with a paintbrush, and lovingly molded to fit the owner's needs?"

That's all it took for Nick to draw her flush to him, kissing her hard and raw. His tongue glided into her mouth, exploring, seeking, working its mystical magic on her senses. He must have known her legs had become weak, because he leaned her against the counter for support. His hands slipped under her shirt, kneading her waist, her ribs, inching higher. His thumbs skimmed the soft, tender skin beneath her breasts, feeling their weight, rubbing over her sensitive nipples. She leaned into him, wanting more, much more. She felt his erection against her very core, and rotated herself around him, clinging to his shoulders, feeling him shudder, listening to the masculine sounds coming from deep inside him. She knew she gave him as much pleasure as he gave to her, still that wasn't enough. She wanted more of him. She needed him buried deep inside her. Fantasy wasn't good anymore. She wanted the real man.

Diana heard Jessica laughing, somehow, through the fog of passion floating in her brain. She realized the sound had gotten farther and farther away. She slowly, regretfully, broke their kiss. Before he could recapture her, she looked down to where Jessica had been. Then her world tilted. "Where is she?"

"Who?"

"Jessica."

"She *was* right here," he said, pointing down where Jessica had been.

Diana glanced all over the floor but didn't see Jessica. She looked at Nick. He didn't seem too steady after their kiss either. "Where did she go?" she asked.

They heard the baby chuckling at the same time, and both scrambled around the kitchen's island and headed through the doorway, and a short distance down the hall, following the laughter. Diana spotted Jessica just as she was putting a little moth in her mouth and closing her lips. "Stop! Jessica! No! Don't eat that!"

Jessica's little body gave a startled jump when Diana shouted her warning. The baby looked up at her, wide-eyed, a tiny white wing hung between her lips.

"Oh, Jessica. We don't eat insects."

"No, we don't," Nick seconded. "We eat snails."

"Don't give her any ideas." Diana glared at him as she pulled the bug out of Jessica's mouth. She had to stop herself from running the baby over to the sink and washing her mouth out with disinfectant. She forced herself to contain the anxiety coming over her. "Jessica, please say you pulled off the moth's other wing and it's on the floor someplace. Please don't tell me you've eaten it." Diana tilted her head toward Nick and whispered out the side of her mouth. "Do we need to call poison control?"

"What for? Eating a bug? I probably swallowed hundreds of them—now, Diana, you don't have to wipe your lips off. I didn't eat one before I kissed you."

Her hand dropped. "It's not nice to make fun of a worried caregiver."

"Oh, come on." Nick acted all smug as if being a man made him the insect expert. "You know when you're a kid eating bugs is a fact of life."

"Not my life. Anyway, the point is, what if the moth had insecticide on it?" She could be self-righteous, too.

"She didn't eat it, did she?"

"I don't know, where's the other wing?"

"Don't worry about it. She'll be all right."

"I have to worry. When you asked me to watch her, you gave me the worrying responsibility, too."

"All right, you win. I'll get the number of poison control and call," he said like a long-suffering male. "I'm only doing this to prove she's okay."

"Thank you, Nick." Diana stood back up and hugged him. Heartbeat to heartbeat. Rigid muscle to softer flesh. His very strong sex zeroed straight toward her womanly center. She leaned further into him, needing to feel his closeness, his hardness, his warmth.

He rubbed his palm on her back and drew her even closer. "Thank you for caring, Diana. Not many people would."

"It's my responsibility."

"Is that what it is?" He rested his cheek on the top of her head.

"Yes." He felt so good. He smelled even better. She closed her eyes, and just let herself take him in. "For now."

"For now," he repeated, dropping his arms, stepping away. "I'll call poison control."

Diana scooped Jessica up and hugged her, too. "Just between us girls, if anything good comes out of this I'll name our firstborn after you."

She returned the baby to the kitchen floor where she'd been originally and gave her back the bowl and spoon. "I have another idea. We'll have a moth funeral, and then eat breakfast. We'll bury the moth in dirt, not in your belly.

Insect protein is good for some people, but I have a better breakfast planned for you.''

"Pancakes?" Nick asked when he came back in the kitchen.

"Haven't you given up on those yet?"

"I'll never give up."

"Okay, live in your fantasy world." Diana certainly had lived in her own for a long, long time. "Is Jessica going to have to have her stomach pumped?"

"She's fine. I thought I heard you planning something else for her."

"We are. We're going to have a funeral for the moth. You've got this wonderful ivy sitting right here by the window. Do you think we should pray?"

"For pancakes?"

"Nick! Get over it. You'll eat your carrots and like them."

"They're canned."

"I know. They're as good as fresh. Alicia told me I grew up on them, and look at me now." She spread her arms wide, and gave him a good view of her body.

"You've convinced me. Bring them on."

"All right. That's what I like to see, a man who knows what he wants and isn't afraid to say so." She turned to Jessica. "Say bye-bye to the little mothy." Diana took Jessica's hand and waved it at the planter. "Bye-bye."

"Bye-bye," said Jessica.

"Diana, did you hear that?" Nick shouted in her ear.

Ouch. "Hear what?" She had jumped back, which made Jessica bounce in her arms, causing a string of giggles.

"Jessica said bye-bye." Nick lowered his voice, his excitement turning to stunned awe. "Two new words. Bye and bye."

"I'm positive that doesn't count as two."

"Bye-bye is two," he said adamantly.

"On second thought, it sure is." The way Nick said bye-

bye, made her think night-night. Kiss-kiss. Hug-hug. Oh-oh. She gathered her wits and stomped on her jumbled electrodes. "Babies do that, Nick. They say bye-bye." She cleared her throat to get her voice back to normal. "So do grown-ups."

"Jessica's one and only word is and always has been *no*. She can say no with different expressions, she can say no in different languages even. At least we think they are, no one can really understand her." He shrugged those massive shoulders. "But you got her to say bye-bye. Diana you're a miracle worker."

"Thank you." Getting a compliment from Nick was better than when she discovered her chocolate calorie-buster pill had the possibility of working.

"Throw on some shoes." Nick hurried out of the kitchen. "I'm taking us all out to celebrate. How about pancakes?"

"Nick," she called after him.

He stopped in his tracks, looking back at her with a devious expression across his handsome face.

"I'm being conned aren't I?"

"Do you want to be?" he asked.

She smiled at him. "Sure. Let's go."

10

AFTER DIANA AND NICK had finished eating breakfast, *and*
Jessica had finished decorating the carpet, walls, her clothes
and the hair of the man sitting in the booth next to her,
Diana insisted Nick drive to Barrington's Bookstore.

"I told you Cathy called and she'll be home day after
tomorrow," Nick said. "There's no reason to go to the
bookstore anymore."

"That's all the more reason to go. You don't want anything to happen to Jessica in the last few days you have
left, do you?" Diana placed her hand on Nick's biceps.
"That moth scared me." Now she understood how Professor Penleigh felt about the fire. Devastating.

"It was only a little moth."

"You know what I mean," she said.

"Listen to me, Diana, it's silly the way you're getting
all worked up about this. It's not that important. You know
the government even allows a certain amount of insect re-
mains in your food, like your cereal."

"No, I didn't." Diana squinted her eyes at him. "That
is so disgusting. I can't believe you're telling me this."

"It's the truth."

"Well, then, it's a good thing I don't eat cereal." She
crossed her arms under her chest. "Anyway, you're missing
the point."

"And that is?"

"What would you do if it had been a tarantula?"

"Taken her to the hospital."

"Or a black widow spider?"

"Taken her to the hospital."

"What about a mosquito carrying Saint Louis encephalitis? And without the books, we wouldn't know what to do."

"Same thing. Taken her to the hospital."

"Fine. Where's the hospital?"

"They're all over the place."

"Would you pay cash? Have insurance?"

"All right, Diana. I understand you're worried. And I know that all those things can happen, but they're rare. I don't think those spiders even live in our area. I'm not sure they even live in Texas."

"Maybe they do, maybe they don't. But you know, Nick, I don't have good luck with things. It would be my bad luck that something bad would happen to Jessica while I was watching her, and then I'd never forgive myself. This will help me be less worried."

"I don't mind going. I only think it's a waste of time."

"What would you rather do?"

He sent her a you-know-what grin. "Not a thing. My day is yours."

"In that case, I have to go to the grocery store—"

"Not quite what I had in mind, but since we do need cereal, I'll be sure and check the insect by-product on the package label. But I'm putting my foot down on the macaroni."

"Is that a no more for real, or just a no more for maybe?"

"For real. I'm going to have food brought in."

"I'm not going to argue with that. Did you invite your father to our party of five, or will it only be three?"

"Not yet. By the way, I have some news that might make you feel better about your luck." Nick proceeded to tell Diana about her mother's experiments, and ensuing mishaps.

"Are you saying my mother and I did the same thing?"

"Seems like that's the case."

"And so it wasn't the White Envelope Incident. These things would have happened anyway." Fate. Destiny. Written in the book of life.

"What white envelope incident?"

"Nothing. I was just talking to myself."

"No you weren't. Are you going to tell me?

Diana handed Jessica a soda cracker. "There's nothing to tell. I'm going to write to every president and every dean of every university I've been asked to leave," she said as they drove to the bookstore. "I'm going to tell them that I am sorry for what happened, and that I understand their pain."

"So you're not going to tell me," Nick said. "That's okay. I can wait."

She smiled at him and squeezed his arm. "Thank you."

When they arrived at Barrington's, Nick insisted that he hold Jessica. This was good. Jessica didn't scream much, although she had tears streaming down her face. Diana didn't know if it was Nick, or whether there was actually something wrong with the child. She hoped she'd find some clue in one of the books.

Diana walked up to a man in a Barrington's uniform, and asked, "Excuse me, can you tell me if you have a book about how to take care of a baby?" She pointed to where Jessica and Nick had been standing only seconds ago. Now there was empty space. Great. Where could they have gone?

The salesperson looked at Diana with red-veined bloodshot eyes that even wire-rim glasses couldn't hide. Diana repeated the question.

Finally he uttered, "Yeah. We have books." He went back to stocking shelves.

She waited a few moments for him to complete his answer. When he didn't, she asked, "Can you tell me where?"

Without looking up, he pointed in the general direction of the ceiling. Diana read the signs, and spotted "Children."

Diana said, "I know those are children's books. I'm looking for books that tell about how to raise a child."

This time he waved his arm to the opposite side, where another sign said Child Care and Diet. It was no wonder she hadn't seen it. The sign had been hidden by another that read Sex and Impotence.

"What's that supposed to mean? You diet so you can have sex, then you have children and become impotent?"

His jaw slacked. "Huh?"

She left him and went searching for Nick and Jessica somewhere in this monster three-story building. "Where are you, Jessica?" she called out very softly. The tall bookcases and the quiet atmosphere made Barrington's seem more like a library than a bookstore. She tried a little louder. "Yoo-hoo, where are you, Nick?" Okay, this was a typical man thing. He said he'd go shopping then he disappears. She figured he probably took Jessica outside. She knew if Jessica and Nick were here together, she'd hear Jessica a mile away.

Diana stopped at the child-care book section. Oh, Lordy. What was she supposed to do now? How could there possibly be this many books? How could she possibly figure out which was the best? She thought about going back and asking the salesclerk. Bad idea.

This was silly. All she needed was a book that had, One Year Old in the title. Something to tell her what they ate, when they went to sleep and when they woke up. Something to tell her how many words should be in their vocabulary, besides the word *no*. How much crying they're supposed to do. Something about the psychology of a normal one-year-old. If Jessica was normal.

Diana pulled Cathy's list out of her purse. Her instructions were fine to a certain extent. The problem was, they were more for a person who had some experience with children and babies.

The books were filed in alphabetical order, and not by subject matter. She had to go through each book, one by one, until she had a pretty good selection. Gathering them together, she decided to circle the store one more time in case Nick and Jessica were still there.

NICK KNEW Barrington's pretty well. When he worked for his dad, they had built the building. Since that time, he liked to come in on Sundays, buy coffee and a paper, and sit outside.

He hadn't been over to the children's play area since the bookstore had opened.

Now, as he stood on the outside of the little carpeted arena, he could see in action what he'd been told in theory would work. Barrington's had hired college students who needed early-childhood-development credits to work and watch over the children as their parents shopped.

The play area was crowded and Jessica squirmed in his arms, only too eager to get down. As soon as he put her inside the arena, she half walked, half crawled to a wire structure with wooded balls looped throughout. She promptly attacked the thing, and seemed happy and content doing just that.

One of the mothers standing around pointed to Jessica and asked if she had a cold.

"No," he said.

"Her nose is all stuffed up."

"Allergies." That seemed like a good thing to say. Everyone in Texas had allergies. Conversations centered around which brand of decongestants worked best. Everyone in his family had had allergies when they were young.

Besides, he'd rather say Jessica had allergies than she hated his guts.

The mother next to him nodded in understanding and started a discourse on her own son's allergies. Nick tried to look interested and nodded in what he hoped were the right places. What he had learned since Cathy had given birth was that a baby gave every stranger in the vicinity a license to become a mother's, and now apparently an uncle's, best friend. They offered advice whether he wanted it or not.

Where was Diana?

He let the lady drone on and watched Jessica leave the wire-and-wooden-balls toy and toddle over, on shaky legs, to where some other kid was quietly reading a book. She plopped herself on the carpet and grabbed the book out of the kid's hand. "No," she screamed at him, then scooted on her bottom in a half circle, giving the poor little boy whose book she stole her back. "Bye-bye."

The other child walloped Jessica. Jessica turned around, slinging the book at him. "Nooooo! Bye-bye."

The incident happened so fast Nick barely had time to get into the arena and retrieve his niece before she gave the boy a black eye with the corner of the book.

The little boy repeated, "Mine...mine...mine," as he grabbed one end of the book.

Jessica held on to the other end, yelling, "No...no... no."

Nick had expected tears from Jessica or the other kid, but none flowed. So maybe this was the one-year-old version of sharing. Her saying "no" and him saying "mine" really meant, "I'll take what you have because I want it, and you'll have to deal with it, sucker."

Nick stood over them as they duked it out over a raggedy book for barely a second before they both took deep breaths, and looked up at him. He could see their expressions change from one of baby-to-baby indignation to baby-

to-baby "let's gang up on the big guy." He could almost
see them formulate the words "Who are you, jerk-face?"
Then their faces scrunched up and the waterworks started.

"I didn't do anything," Nick said, gesturing helplessly
to the mother with all the advice. "Honestly."

She gave him a disgusted look and walked away.

"Thanks a lot, kids," he muttered. He had to get out of
the play-pit, and take Jessica with him before any more
damage was done. But since he'd gone in, he'd become
surrounded by a mob of thirty-pound rug rats, crying, and
beating on his legs with whatever they were holding. He
grabbed a few wooden blocks away from them, which only
intensified the screams.

How did a guy escape from these tiny hellions?

He looked around. There was no help in sight. The day-
care worker was on the phone with her back to him. So
much for qualified staff.

"Help," he called out. The children's cries escalated. He
would have thought that if the kids hated him so much,
they'd leave him alone. Instead, it looked as if they were
ganging up on him. They were crawling all over the place
like ants.

He had to get out of there. "Diana!" He bellowed this
time, not caring whom he disturbed. No more Mr. Nice
Guy. He was a desperate man.

The college girl on the telephone looked at him, held her
finger to her lips and sneered. Then she went back to her
telephone conversation.

He couldn't believe it. "Lady," he shouted. "Get me
out of here."

She turned again, glaring at him before rolling her eyes.
Finally, she said something into the phone and hung up.

Behind him he heard familiar laughter. His muscles
tensed and his heart beat faster. How come Diana had the
ability to do that to him?

"Are you stuck, Nick?" Diana asked sweetly.

"I can't move. They're beating up on me." He didn't know what it was about him that made kids hate him. "I'm a nice guy," he growled downwind.

Diana's soft laughter didn't help. He watched her carefully place an armload of books on the stair, then enter the arena, stepping daintily around the children, saying, "'scuse me, 'scuse me." Soon she had cleared a pathway through the forest of toddlers. "You can come out now, Nick."

He looked behind him. All clear. He lifted Jessica and carried her and her freshly exercised lungs, out of the arena.

"If you take my books, I'll take her," Diana offered.

Jessica had her arms wrapped around his neck and her head buried under his chin, all the while sobbing. He didn't deserve this. When Cathy was pregnant, she must have had some heart-to-heart talks to the baby in her belly. She must have told Jessica some mighty terrible stories about the other three Logan brothers, and somehow the baby had him confused with them.

Nick didn't want to give her up though. But for the sake of everyone else in the bookstore, he had no choice. He unpeeled Jessica and gave her to Diana. He paid for the books and met them at the car.

As he drove toward the Stratford, Jessica gurgled happily in her car seat, and Diana flipped through the books he'd bought her.

"Are you looking in there for the proper way to feed a one-year-old?" he asked. He didn't think soda crackers, milk and water were it. Last night, more of her food landed on the floor than in her stomach.

"Food...food. Hmm...let's see."

"See what?"

She flipped to the index of one of the thicker books. "I'm wondering." Her fingernail clicked her front tooth. "Schedule...schedule. Hmm...yes, this is mostly a feeding schedule for babies. It says here that babies can be breast-fed for a long time, and that breast-fed babies are healthier. I remember hearing that a woman who had adopted a child, an infant, put the infant to her breast, and after a while milk started flowing. I find that hard to believe. Still…''

Nick didn't know, but all this talk about breasts was making him hot. He kept thinking of Diana's breasts, and how they'd looked under the shirt she had worn this morning with the sun coming through the window.

''We shouldn't talk about this in front of Jessica.'' Little did Diana know she was on the verge of another Incident. One where his libido went up in flames.

11

NICK STRAPPED Jessica into the high chair, then slid the tray toward the baby until it clicked in place. He leaned down to kiss her forehead. Her tears started immediately, although slowly at first, then more and more, until her nose became bright red and her sobs turned to hiccups.

He backed away, and Diana could tell by the look on his face that he was hurt. She felt the same frustration he did. She had been going through the books she'd bought, and so far she'd found no reason why a child, or children, she amended, remembering the crowd in Barrington's, would hate one man in particular.

The strange part about the whole thing was that even though Jessica always cried when Nick came near her, she seemed to also seek him out. It was as if she wanted his company, then made both their lives miserable when she had it.

"I don't get it." Nick looked at the baby and Jessica looked back at him with her wet eyes and red nose. "I'm a nice guy." He turned to Diana as if needing to make sure she knew that. "I am."

"I know you are. You went to the bookstore with me and braved a sea of anklebiters out for your blood. Then you went to the grocery store with me where you were subjected to more humiliation."

He grimaced. His fingers jerked through his hair. "Do you believe this? All I did was go to the cooler to get some ice cream, and that kid, out of nowhere, attacked me with that mini-shopping cart. Why do they make those things?''

Diana shrugged.

"How much do you want to bet I'm black-and-blue on the back of my calves?"

She wouldn't mind checking. "Did you want to pull down your jeans and have me look?" she asked innocently.

Nick's eyes crinkled, and the smile on his face turned decidedly wicked. His hands went for the snap on his jeans. Diana ran over to him, put her hand on top of his and said, "Stop."

"I thought you were going to check me out for damage."

"I was joking."

"It's not nice to joke about things like that, Diana. Not to a man who is spending his nights on a couch at the office."

"I know. I'm sorry. I couldn't help myself. The words just popped out, and…"

He put his finger across her lips. "Shh. It's okay. I couldn't help it, either. You're too easy to tease."

"That's bad."

"No, that's good." He lowered his mouth to hers, and captured her lips, lightly putting pressure on her. She opened for him, and he drank while she poured.

And Jessica screamed.

"Jessica," Diana said. "Is mad."

"Jessica," Nick breathed. "Is always mad.

Diana had never realized before what a pothole a child could be in the road to seduction.

Nick moved back. "I'm getting very frustrated."

"I know, I know," Diana said, rapidly patting herself where her heart was. Then she chuckled. "I wouldn't be surprised to see your face on a Wanted poster in Barrington's."

He grimaced. "Thanks, Diana. Let me tell you how much I appreciate your sympathy."

"Oh—" she waved her hand "—it's not a problem."

He shook his head, picking up the *Wall Street Journal* from the counter.

"And we can't forget the grocery store. How many times can a grown man get attacked by children in the same day?" She burst out laughing, remembering Nick's horrified expression.

"Very funny."

"And of course the story will get repeated and repeated. Maybe the *Sugar Land Times* will pick it up, and, if you're lucky, you can get into Tillie Mae Tuttle's column. Then you'll know you hit the big time."

"No—no." He held up his hands in mock horror. "Not that. Not Tillie's column."

"And think how good that will be for your business." Diana giggled.

"Diana, stop. You're killing me."

"You couldn't afford this kind of publicity."

"You're right. I can't."

She nodded with a smile. "The theory is that any publicity is better than no publicity."

He nodded back, with a frown. "They don't know my name, do they?"

"Maybe not." She thought for a moment. "Do you think we should go back and start over?"

"I don't think so." He looked relieved.

"I want to tell you how much I appreciate you taking me out, even though I knew you didn't want to go. I didn't know those kids would attack you, though. See what you might have missed?"

"I couldn't let you go alone. You needed me there to watch Jessica while you shopped."

"Now don't get all male on me, like I couldn't do this without you. The truth is, you didn't want to take the car seat out of your car, and put it in mine."

"Damn! You found me out." He didn't look happy. "I thought you'd think I was a hero or something."

"I do, Nick," she said softly. "After what you've been going through with Jessica, I think you're the best kind of hero. I want to help figure this problem out. There's already too much fighting in this family."

"Now *that* I agree with."

"You know, it's probably something so simple that we can't see because it's so obvious."

Diana circled the island in the center of the kitchen. Jessica pounded on the tray and said, "No, no, bye-bye, no."

"I marked on your calendar that Jessica said a new word," Diana said.

"Two new words." Nick brought the *Wall Street Journal* to the breakfast table.

"Two. Cathy'll be sorry she missed it." Diana knew if she had a baby, she'd be sorry she hadn't been there. "Hungry?" she asked Jessica. "Is that a silly question or what? It's almost dinnertime. Of course you're hungry." Diana took out an apple from the refrigerator, peeled off the skin and sliced it, then handed Jessica a good-size piece. "This should keep you busy until I make you a great big to-die-for dinner."

"Dinner?" Nick asked, turning a page.

"I'm going to make her dinner."

"I thought we agreed to order out."

She waited until Jessica started gnawing on the apple slice. "I still have what I was going to make for breakfast. When I was little, I loved it when Alicia cooked things for me, so I wanted to give Jessica at least one good memory."

"Are we back to the macaroni and cheese?"

"You bet. Don't groan, okay? It's disconcerting."

"Was I doing that?"

"Yes. Which reminds me, speaking of cheese, did you ask your father if he was coming over tomorrow?"

"He said yes. Did you ask yours?"

"He said yes. Did you tell him my dad was going to be ere?"

"Sure did."

Diana found a child's dish that had been sectioned into uarters and had little suction cups stuck on the bottom. If he unscrewed the little cap in the center of the dish, and lled its hollow interior with warm water, it would keep he food warm. Since there wasn't anything Diana needed) keep warm for any long period of time, Diana filled it vith water, and stuck a carnation in the center.

While Jessica gnawed on her apple slice, Diana made the nacaroni and cheese, just the way Alicia had told her to, y following the directions on the box. And she didn't even dd any secret ingredients. Bland, she was sure, but she ad promised Alicia, no paprika.

She cut up a fresh peach into bite-size pieces and ar-anged them in one section of the baby's dish. The maca-oni and cheese went into another section. She opened a an of peas, zapped them in the microwave, then smushed hem down into the third section. The last section she filled vith mashed strawberries and whipped cream.

Diana stood back and admired her work. Presentation neant so much when it came to epicurean delights. In the ast she may have had a few explosive episodes, but she ure did have a flair for the aesthetic beauty of food. Jessica vould eat this up if only for the way it looked on the plate.

Diana licked the bottom of the suction cups then forced he bowl down onto the high chair's plastic table. Jessica :langed two spoons together squealing "No-no-nooooo" n excited anticipation. The back of the spoons only :macked the top of Diana's hand twice. They hardly even nade a dent. Or a black-and-blue mark. Just a little purple.

"Enjoy your food." Diana stepped back, placed her ands behind her back, rubbed the pain she tried not to feel nd waited.

Jessica lowered her head to the plate, getting whipped

cream on her nose, then lifted her face and gave Diana a big, beautiful smile. In no time at all, the baby dug in with ten tiny fingers, and Diana's heart swelled with pride at the success of her first home-cooked meal.

"Nick, this is working out so perfectly. Look at how she's eating."

"Great. Should we order Chinese for us?"

"Sure. We can eat when she's sleeping."

Diana had started to put the dishes in the dishwasher when the first spoon hit the floor. She went over to pick it up. Jessica's hands dived into the food and immediately smeared it on her face. Very little actually made it to her mouth. Her fingers dipped in again, and pink strawberries, golden peach pieces, macaroni and cheese and whipped cream went flying to the sounds of her laughter and "no-no-no-no-nos."

"Nick! I'm in trouble here." Diana grabbed a sponge and dish towel and went down on the floor, crawling around, picking up food. "Eat, Jessica, eat," she ordered.

"No-no-no-no," came the response.

Nick grabbed a trash bag, and as quick as Jessica tossed the food down, he gathered it up and put it into the bag. But no matter how fast he worked, Jessica rained food on top of his head even faster. "Eat, Jessica," his booming baritone ordered.

"No-no-no-no-no," she screamed in return, her little legs kicking under the high chair's plastic table, managing to land a few good ones before Nick could retreat.

Diana smiled in relief when the doorbell rang. Rescued. "I'll get it," she said, scurrying up from her place on the floor.

"No, no, let me." Nick rushed after her. "I insist."

"She's your niece."

"Only by blood."

They raced to the front door and opened it together, breathless and determined.

Sheila and her father stood there. Harry pushed his way in. "What are you doing, Diana? You're a mess."

"She must have blown up the oven," Sheila sneered.

Nick put his arm around Diana. She'd never appreciated the strength of a man as much as she did right now. She needed support, and he was there. "Nice to see you, too, Dad. What a surprise," she added.

"You invited us over."

"Tomorrow night."

"What difference does it make?" Harry moved into the hallway. "I wasn't coming when Logan was coming."

"Come on with us into the kitchen," Diana invited.

Nick said, "But, Diana—"

She turned to him and winked. "Sheila," she gushed. "I love your white dress. Is that new?"

Sheila and Diana walked in front of Harry, who walked in front of Nick.

Her stepmother-in-training, who, as far as Diana was concerned, was flunking the course big time, sniffed through the narrow passages of her rhinoplasty nose. "I went to Neiman's and it was only five hundred dollars. Such a bargain. It's hard to find white clothes in my size. Even the petites are too big."

"Isn't that something." Diana looked down at the woman, wondering how her father could have made such an awful mistake.

But there wasn't anything she could do about it. Jessica, on the other hand, could do quite a bit. And when she took aim, sending those green peas right in the center of Sheila's dress, she had.

Diana made the appropriate tsking noises. "Now, now, Jessica, you must stop sharing your food with the rest of us."

"That awful child," Sheila screeched. "Do you know what she's done?"

Nick cut in. "Please, ma'am, I would appreciate it if you would control yourself in front of my little niece here."

Diana couldn't help smirking. "I told you to come tomorrow, Dad."

"Peas will wash out," Harry said. "Besides, I can't stand being around a Logan."

"I'm a Logan," Nick reminded him.

"Diana, was someone else talking to me? I thought I heard a voice, but I know there's no one else in the room."

Diana's neck itched. The doorbell rang again. Both she and Nick headed back out.

"They're your relatives," he said.

She rolled her eyes. "Only one, and only by blood."

Diana went back to the kitchen, just in time to see Jessica shove more food on her face, her hair, ears and clothes. Even her feet were now covered. The floor, thick with food, had become slippery. Diana thought it was very unfortunate when Sheila lost her balance and landed on her bottom, screaming at everyone.

Never one to be ignored, Jessica threw the second spoon, and yelled, "Noooo." It landed on Sheila's head.

Diana was desperately attempting to keep a straight face, when Nick walked back into the kitchen with two more people. The man looked like an older version of Nick. The woman's lips were pursed.

"Diana, this is my dad, Charlie Logan. My mother, Patricia."

"You're a day early, Mr. and Mrs. Logan." She wiped her hands on the paper towel and held out her hand. "I'm sure I look a mess."

Charlie ignored her gesture. "Yes, you do. I can't imagine why my son wants to marry you."

Harry, who had been out of view, stormed over. "My daughter's too good for your son." He turned to Diana. "Do you understand, Diana? You will be married. But not to a Logan."

"Nick's not marrying any Smith. Look at your daughter. She's a slob."

"Now, Mr. Logan, that's not true." Diana's ego was taking a beating here.

"You know how many Smiths there are in this world?" Charlie sneered. "You guys reproduce like rabbits."

"Mr. Logan! That is so rude." Diana was shocked. She paused, calmed herself, then, pointing down to the floor, said sweetly, "Have you met Sheila?"

Jessica laughed, then stuck the carnation in her mouth. "No, Jessica," Diana cried out. She stuck her finger in the baby's mouth and pulled out petals. "Nick, call poison control. Hurry!"

"No-no-noooo." Jessica stuck out her tongue. Diana wiped the rest of the petals out of her mouth as the baby banged on the tray, sending more food flying.

"Harry!" Sheila, sitting in a direct line of vision for Jessica's throwing arm, screamed, "Get me up from here."

Diana's dad's lips were set in a distasteful grimace when he looked down at his wife. The normally perfectly coiffed Sheila now had a dress hiked mid-thigh, and her hair, shoulders and clothes were speckled with an array of Jessica's rain of food. Sheila looked so pitiful even Diana would have felt sorry for her if she had been someone other than Sheila.

"Harry, help me now," the stepmother-in-definite-failing shrieked.

"It's too late to help you. For that, I'm sorry." Harry turned his back on Sheila, focusing on the wall in front of him.

Diana followed her father's gaze. A layer of golden cheese and macaroni now speckled the beige wall. The tile floors had been wall-to-wall carpeted in strawberries, peaches and whipped cream. Food juices had mixed together, covering the tile with a slick, dangerous film.

"I want to help you, Diana." Her father squeezed her

arm gently, assuredly. "It's the least I can do. Go find me the mop."

"Do you mean that? Really and truly?"

"Have you ever known me to say something I don't mean?"

She shook her head.

Nick opened the door to the broom closet and pulled out the necessary equipment. "Thanks, Mr. Smith."

"Diana." Harry grabbed the supplies out of Nick's hand. "Tell that Logan boy I'll help you, but I'm not talking to him."

"I'm sure he heard you just fine. As did all the neighbors for miles." She closed her eyes wanting to shut them all out. This war had to end.

Charlie charged over to Harry, slipping the last few feet across the floor, but quickly regaining his balance. He grabbed the mop and bucket away. "Nick," he shouted. "You tell that idiot if anyone's going to clean up after my grandchild, it'll be me." Charlie shoved the mop toward Patricia. "Here. Clean."

"You've *got* to be kidding." Patricia swept past her husband, leaving the mop, pail and giant size bottle of Lysol behind her. Stopping by the fallen Sheila, she tapped her finger against her chin. "Didn't I see you at the Institut Maurice Paris yesterday?"

Sheila patted her hair, coming away with pieces of strawberries and clumps of whipped cream. "I don't know how you could possibly recognize me when I look like this."

Patricia held out her hand and Sheila grabbed hold, struggling to get herself to a standing position. "I was having the Facial Peel, and if I remember correctly, you were on the other side of the salon having the Firming Treatment. How did you like it?"

"Wonderful."

"Let's go get cleaned up." Patricia grabbed her newfound best friend's arm, leading her out of the kitchen. "Do you know Mrs. Leah Sargent?"

Sheila nodded.

"She had a face-lift, you know," Patricia said smugly.

"You don't say."

"Nick," Diana said when the older women were gone. "You need to tell your mom about Sheila."

"My mother can take of herself."

"Okay, but don't say I didn't warn you." Diana smiled at Charlie. "Have you eaten dinner yet Mr. Logan?"

Charlie didn't answer. He stood in front of the high chair, mop and bucket glued to his fingers, and stared at Jessica.

"Dad?" Nick called. "Dad, are you all right?"

Charlie said reverently, "You know, I still can't believe this is Cathy's."

"Jessica isn't a 'this,' she's a girl."

"I've never seen her. I've driven past her house, hoping they'd be outside, and I could get a look, but she was never there."

"You're a sorry-ass grandfather," Nick told him, all the anger he held in check coming through in each word.

"I know. I know. If I could start over and do things differently, I would."

No one spoke for several long minutes. Finally Charlie, his words catching, said, "She looks just like Cathy. She's beautiful. The most beautiful child in the world."

Harry snorted. "Not likely."

Charlie whirled around. Holding up a fist, he snarled, "Would you like to repeat that, moron?"

Harry pointed a finger in Charlie's face. "The most beautiful baby in the world is Diana's baby."

Diana cut in, "I don't have a baby."

"Someday you will. I'm letting him know right now that when that happens, yours will be the most beautiful."

"You want to say that outside, jerk-face?"

Nick came between both men, put a hand on each one's

chest and pulled them apart. "You two are acting like children. Spoiled children. I'm disappointed in both of you." Not that he expected anything different.

The doorbell rang for a third time. "Now what?" Nick lost all patience with this whole bunch and he didn't need another group of relatives descending on them. Diana's plan was crazy, it would never work. He hated that she'd be disappointed and he wished it could be different. Somehow, some way, he'd make it up to her.

The doorbell rang again and both he and Diana headed out of the kitchen at the same time. "You're blood," he said.

"No, you've got two more blood relatives in there than I do. I'll get the door."

Nick placed a hand on Diana's shoulder keeping her from going any further. "I'll get it."

"I'll come with you."

"Stay here."

There was something about the way he said it. Something about the way his mouth formed the smile, the way his jaw, so strong and determined, tilted at such an angle that she had to reach up and touch him, running her thumb over his bottom lip, feeling the slight raspiness of the afternoon stubble on his chin against the edge of her finger. "I'll stay here."

"Good idea." He took hold of her hand, and placed a kiss on her fingers and Diana knew she wasn't going anywhere. She would do anything he asked her to do, because she trusted him.

"Now gimme back the mop." Harry grabbed it out of Charlie's hand. He took the bucket, too, and went to the sink to fill it with water. "No one's going to help Diana but me. I'm her dad. I'm the future grandfather of the most beautiful children in the world."

Charlie had turned back to Jessica and didn't even rise to the bait this time. His granddaughter, covered from the top of her head to the tips of her shoes in food, stared right back at her grandfather—her up-until-this-moment, absentee grandfather.

Time was running out, Diana thought and she had made a commitment to Nick, herself, and their fathers, even if they didn't know about it, that they would end this feud. No matter what, she had to give it everything she had. "I'm going to heat up the leftovers from ¡Otra, Otra!," she told her father. Maybe, she could get them all to actually sit at the table together.

"I'll stay for dinner." Her father finished washing the floor, then he put the mop and bucket away. He took over chopping onions, tomatoes and jalapeño peppers.

"Thanks, Dad." From the corner of her eye she saw Charlie pull one of the chairs away from the table. He placed it right in front of Jessica's high chair and sat down. Wiggling a finger in her belly, he crooned, "Cootchie-cootchie-coo."

Jessica laughed at him, swatting at the finger, kicking up her legs, and then laughed more.

"Isn't she the smartest baby you've ever known?" Charlie asked, although as far as he was concerned, the answer was obvious.

"Nooo," laughed Jessica.

Diana sent her father a warning look.

"She's the smartest girl baby, I suppose," Harry begrudgingly replied. "But Diana here is going to have the smartest boy baby."

"That seems fair," Charlie said. "Until Nick has a boy baby."

Her father's face turned a bright shade of red and he made a move, but Diana rushed over to him and shook her head. "Don't you dare."

Harry's fists flexed at his side. Diana gave her father a big hug, and then a more tentative one to Charlie. "It's beautiful to see you two men getting along at last." They hadn't killed each other, and they were still in the same room. As far as she was concerned, that was positive.

"We're not getting along," Charlie grumbled.

"Not in this lifetime," Harry said.

"I'll be dead before that happens."

"I'll be dead first," Harry told him.

"There you guys go. Finally agreeing," Nick said, as he came back into the room and stood beside Diana. "Things are looking up."

Nick's arm went around her waist. The more he touched her, even casually like he was doing now, the more hopeful she became that maybe those fantasies she'd had might come true. He unconsciously massaged between the indentation of her waist and the flair of her hips. She practically melted into him. "Isn't it wonderful, Nick? They're having a discussion."

Diana smiled at Nick, then noticed the two men standing in the doorway. One carried two child-size chairs made out of a light-colored wood, and the other carried a matching little table. The back and front of the chairs were stenciled with little white bunnies jumping over carrots.

"Oh, my God." Diana covered her mouth with her hand and her eyes widened. "How did you—"

"Where did you—" Stunned, Harry moved closer.

Nick held out his hand and Diana grabbed on. "Diana, I have something for you." The men placed the small furniture against the north wall in the kitchen. "Remember when you told me about your table and chairs? No one should have to go without their memories."

"Oh, Nick. When? Why?"

"The 'why' is easy. Why? Because I like you." His self-deprecating smile melted her heart. Only Nick would think that recreating her lost table and chairs wasn't a big deal. When in fact, it was the nicest, most wonderful biggest deal anyone had ever done for her.

He said, "The 'when' question. I started last night. I

thought it would take a few days, but it turned out that some of my men came in, and we worked on it together, got it all done. Pretty nice, I think. I don't know what the one your father made looked like. I know these can't take their place, but maybe they'll give you some new memories.''

"Nick." Diana brushed her hand over the wood. The furniture was smooth and sturdy—perfect for kids to play on. "I don't know what to say."

"Don't say anything. Not yet. Let me show you one more thing." He turned the table upside down. On the underside he had carved out the words,

In memory of Elizabeth Smith
Mom and Diana forever together

"Oh, Nick." Diana covered her mouth with her hand. Her head shook slowly back and forth in disbelief. She didn't care if her love for him showed through her smile, her face, her eyes, or her body. He was hers, he'd always be hers, whether they had children or not. The table and chairs proved it. Now all she had to do was convince him of what he must already know deep in his heart.

Her dad seemed almost as stunned. "Well, I'll be. Would you look at that. Looks just like the set I made for Diana. The one Sheila threw out. How did you know?"

"Diana mentioned the table and chairs, and the rabbits. I used my imagination."

"Diana," Harry said, pointing a finger in her direction. "How many times do I have to tell you that when you find a boy whom *I* approve of, keep him."

"Daddy!"

"Now don't argue with me." Harry placed his hand across the table top and lovingly rubbed the finish. "He's a good man," he said quietly. "Don't throw him out." He paused, then winked at her. "Speaking of throwing out, you'll need a place to put these. I wouldn't bring them upstairs if I were you. I wouldn't trust Sheila.''

"I won't." Her gaze darted between the table and chairs and Nick. She could look at them forever.

Finally, Nick took her arm. ''Come on, let me help get dinner ready. I'm starved.''

With one more glance at her new little table and chairs, Diana went back to the kitchen and set herself to work. She set the large, round kitchen table for six. She breathed in the aroma of the fajita beef and chicken, which soon filled the kitchen. She poured salsa into a round ceramic bowl, and guacamole into another. Nick helped with the food, filling two big baskets with ¡Otra, Otra!'s famous home-made tortilla chips. Her father took over chopping onions, tomatoes and jalapeño peppers.

"Thank you again," Diana said softly. ''You've made me the happiest person in the world.''

Nick walked over and cupped her chin, then lowered his mouth and kissed her. ''Don't mention it.'' He brushed tendrils off her face. ''I plan on finishing what we started earlier,'' he said before moving away from her.

She could only hope he meant making love, and not that the table and chairs needed another coat of varnish.

12

DIANA WAS GLAD to see that Charlie had taken over the care of Jessica. He brought her to the sink and sat her on the counter, then gently washed her face and hands. Nick brought over a new diaper, handing it to his father.

Jessica's big, gruff grandfather laid his granddaughter down on the counter and changed her diaper.

Harry, who was by no means a baby expert by any stretch of the imagination, didn't let that small detail stop him from giving Charlie advice. "You've got the tabs on the diaper all wrong."

Charlie looked at the little girl. "No I don't."

"Yes you do. The tabs go facing back. If they face front, the kid can pull them off. She can't pull them off if they're backwards."

"You're crazy."

"Let me tell you something. When Diana has kids, they'll have their diapers on right. Backwards."

"You know what, Harry? The years haven't changed you a bit. You're still a damn fruitcake."

Harry yelled. "Take that back."

The two men came nose to nose in the middle of the kitchen. Nick grabbed an unsupervised Jessica, and sandwiched both of them between the two men. "Dad," he coaxed. "Mr. Smith. Come on, you guys. Let's be nice for one night, okay? Is that asking too much?"

Jessica looked at Nick and started screaming again. He looked at Diana. "See," he said. "Kids hate me. That's why I'm not getting married."

"Don't be silly." Diana rescued Jessica, strapping her into the high chair again. "Sit down here, Mr. Logan. You can feed Jessica for me, okay? I don't think she ate much at lunch. Most of it ended up decorating the kitchen."

Patricia and Sheila came into the room, arm in arm, laughing together. They walked right past the small table and chairs that Nick had made, and didn't even notice. Diana had never met two such self-centered women on earth before. Well, at least they'd managed to find each other. "Sit down." Diana pointed to the big table that was now laden with food. "Dinner's ready."

Patricia had managed to ignore Jessica earlier. But now she couldn't play the same, disinterested game. She dropped Sheila's arm, and as if in a trance, inched toward her granddaughter. She gazed at Jessica with such longing, that it almost hurt Diana to watch.

Little Jessica, unaware of the plethora of feelings she had unleashed, continued to play kick-the-grandpa's-leg with Charlie, the same game she had played with her Uncle Nick when he had tried to put her car seat in the Bronco earlier.

The hum of conversation in the room had gradually quieted as each adult focused on the baby and the grandparents who had, up until this day, denied her existence. Diana watched as Nick's father gazed at his wife. She felt as if she were seeing twenty years into her own future. Nick looked so much like Charlie, and whether Patricia realized it or not, Charlie's love for her was written all over his face.

Charlie stood up from his chair and went to his wife. Taking her arm, he led her closer to Jessica's high chair. "She won't bite."

"I know that," Patricia whispered.

"Sit down, Patty."

"She's lovely."

"Yes, she is." He gently guided her to the chair he'd been sitting in only moments before. "Just like you." He stood behind her, placing his hand on her shoulder.

"She's the most beautiful baby in the world," Patricia said again, resting her cheek on Charlie's hand.

Harry stared at the scene in front of him, completely transfixed. Diana saw a myriad of expressions cross his face. Sadness, melancholy and even something that she could only describe as longing. Longing for what, she couldn't imagine. She wished so much that she could pull him aside and ask him what he was thinking about right now. Did he wish that all those years of anger, and even jealousy had never taken place? Did he wish that he and Charlie could be friends again?

More than anything else, that's what she wanted to know. Needed to know. She did know one thing though. For as close as she and her dad were, she doubted he'd tell her.

"Sit down everyone," Nick said, breaking the silence.

Charlie shook himself as if coming out of a trance. He sat in the chair on the other side of Jessica. Nick pulled a chair out for Diana, and then sat next to her. Harry sat next to Sheila completing the circle.

"Dinner is served," Diana said, trying to sound cheerful. No matter what happened later, the truth of the matter was, her father and Charlie were sitting at the same table. And Nick had made her a little table and chairs that looked exactly like the furniture her father had made her twenty years before. This new set would bring her more sweet memories. In fact, she thought as she gazed at Nick, they already had.

No one made any move to start. "Help yourselves," Diana said, picking up the plate of steaming fajita chicken and passing it on to Nick. She gave the bowl of guacamole to her father, who put some on his plate and passed it to Patricia. She sniffed the guacamole, looked at Diana, made a face that bordered on disgust, then passed it to Charlie without taking any.

Diana counted slowly to ten. She didn't want to say anything she'd later regret to Nick's mother. Finally, in her very kindest, most understanding tone, she said, "I know it looks green, Patricia, I can call you Patricia, yes?'' Without waiting for permission she went on, "But I promise that's avocado, and not mold. We bought it from ¡Otra, Otra!. You should have seen Jessica yesterday. She plastered the guacamole all over her face, giving herself the first ever avocado facial.''

Patricia's eyes started to water, and she dabbed the tears away with her.

Diana looked at Nick, feeling helpless. "What did I say?"

Nick shrugged. "I don't know."

"It's nothing you said," Patricia assured her. "I'm sure it's wonderful. I have a reaction to jalapeño peppers. Not a bad reaction, just a little sensitivity. I grew out of the bad, bad reaction when I was a teenager."

Nick helped himself to a generous portion of salsa. "When we were growing up, we never ate Mexican food. My mom's 'sensitivity' is a little more than that. Try a raging allergy. When she gets around jalapeño peppers, her eyes water, and her nose runs. One time she ate something that had jalapeño peppers in it, by mistake. She ended up in the hospital because her throat started to close up."

"I didn't know about your allergies, Patricia. If I had, I wouldn't be serving this meal. But the truth is, you all were supposed to come tomorrow night. This is all I had in the house."

"Don't worry about me. I'm used to it. But how did Jessica react when she plastered the guacamole on her face?" Most places put some jalapeño peppers in it.

"The same as always, screaming, crying, carrying on. Just like she does when I get near her. Why?" Nick asked.

"Because in my family, this jalapeño pepper allergy skips a generation. None of my children had the allergy, but I bet Jessica has it."

Nick swore, then pounded his hand so hard on the table a glass tipped over spilling ice and water, and chips bounced out of the baskets and scattered. "Are you telling us there's a chance Jessica may have this allergy to jala-peños, too?" His blue eyes turned to thundercloud gray.

"That's what I just told you." Patricia acted all self-righteous.

"Damn. I don't believe this. Did Cathy know about this?"

"She knew I was allergic."

"Mom, all of us kids knew that. But did she know that the allergy skipped generations?"

Patricia shrugged. "I doubt it."

"Why didn't you tell us while we were growing up?"

"It's not something I thought was really important at the time. What was I going to say? 'Pick up your dirty socks,' and then add, 'Oh, and by the way, any children you may have will be allergic to jalapeño peppers.' Do you really think you would have cared?"

"We might have," Nick said.

"Nicholas," Patricia said in a condescending mother-like tone. "The last thing children will ever want to think about is that at some time in their future, their kids will be allergic to jalapeño peppers. Kids can't think past today, let alone tomorrow."

Nick leaned his chair against the wall, balancing on the two back legs. He ran his fingers through his hair in a jerky motion. "I can't believe this. Wait until Cathy hears about this."

"Why? It's certainly not a big deal."

"Oh, it's a big deal all right. You know, my sister has a wicked sense of humor. She was getting back at you, Mom. I know she was."

"For what?" Patricia asked. "I never did anything to her."

"Not much you didn't. Throwing her out of the house, and your lives when she needed you most. Shunning her. Pretending she and Jessica didn't exist. No wonder she did what she did."

"And what did she do?" Patricia asked.

Nick laughed disparagingly. "Cathy is one smart kid. I always knew that, I just never knew how smart. Or how devious." When he told his sister about this, he knew she would probably have a breakdown. She had without even knowing it, put Jessica in danger. If it hadn't been for Diana insisting on inviting their parents to dinner, they might not have found out either, until it was too late.

He looked across the table at his mother. "Are you going to see Cathy when she gets back?"

She nodded ever so slightly, but it was a nod. "I think what she did was wrong. Terribly wrong. Those are my morals and I'll stick to them until I die." Patricia brushed her finger across Jessica's cheek. "But I want to see the baby."

Nick rubbed his hand on his neck, then sniffed his palm. The *Nicholas X* aftershave and cologne were still there, still strong. He stood, went to the other side of the table and held open his arms. "Mom," he said. "Come here." His mother walked right into them. She hugged him and kissed him, and came away from the embrace with watery eyes and a runny nose.

"Don't cry, Patricia," Diana said. "This is a happy time."

"I'm not crying. I don't know what's wrong."

"I know exactly what's wrong," Nick said. "You, mother, have just been subjected to Cathy's revenge."

"By hugging you? Don't be silly."

"By hugging me when I'm wearing *Nicholas X*."

"I don't understand. What's *Nicholas X*?"

Nick told his parents about the cologne, soap, shaving cream and aftershave Cathy had created for him. "She told me the base ingredient is jalapeño oil. It smells good."

"It sure does," Diana seconded. "It makes me want to smell his neck and lick—oops. Sorry."

Patricia straightened her shoulders. "What are you saying, Nick? That she purposely made the toiletries with ja-

peño oil so that you would wear it, and then my eyes
ould water? But what about Jessica?''

''She didn't know about skipping generations, did she?
ou never told her that it went from grandparents to grand-
ildren, so she had no idea that when she was trying to
et revenge on you, she was putting her own daughter in
anger.'' The knowledge that all this time Jessica had been
iffing him, and getting sick made him feel like the worst
nd of uncle. And he wasn't even to blame for any of this.
till, he should have figured it all out. Damn.

Diana reached out for him. ''It's not your fault, Nick.
eally it's not.''

''It could have been a bad situation.''

''There's one good thing though,'' Diana said quietly.
She doesn't hate you. She never hated you. She was hurt-
g.''

''What I don't understand is this,'' Patricia said. ''I've
en you many times since Jessica was born, and I've
ugged you. How come my eyes never teared up before
day?''

''What you and Dad did to Cathy and Jessica is uncon-
cionable. You'll have to live with that for the rest of your
ves. Cathy had her fun when she created the stuff she did
or me. It smells good, and I like it. But when I came to
e you, I didn't wear it. I wasn't going to punish you for
hat you did to them, Mom. That's between you, Cathy,
essica and your conscience.''

Nick saw Jessica's shiny green face, with tears running
own her cheeks. ''Dad, take the guacamole away from
essica, please. She's giving herself another avocado bath.''

Diana ran over to Jessica and untied her from the high
hair. ''That's okay, Mr. Logan. I'll take care of her.''

Both his parents looked stricken, as they should have.
Ie felt like dog meat himself.

''I'm going to take a shower and wash this stuff off.
'ome on, Diana. Bring Jessica. While I'm in the shower,
ou can use the bathtub and give her a bath.'' At her ques-

tioning look, he added "It's a big bathroom. The shov
is in a separate room. You'll have privacy and so will I
Nick winked at Diana. "No wandering eyes."

"Why I never! What kind of woman do you think
am?" she asked in righteous indignation. Then in a sof
voice, she added, "Can you leave the shower door open

"Your wish is my command. Come on." Nick waved
the stunned guests, who were also covered with fo
thrown at them by Jessica and could use a shower ther
selves.

When they were alone, Nick had offered to share I
shower with Diana, and although she seemed tempted, s
had opted to dunk Jessica in the whirlpool bath where t
currents could do the dirty work.

Nick's world had about tilted upside down with the r
alization that Jessica had probably been having an allerg
reaction to him since she'd been born.

As the hot water from the dual showerheads sprayed ov
his body and the heat of the water warmed him, all though
went back to Diana and a total reevaluation of what I
future might now be.

Diana. The way she tossed back her dark hair. The wa
she looked at him with a mixture of shyness and desi
streaming together in her big brown eyes. Her sweetnes
her goodness and her generosity.

She had saved his family. She may have even saved Je
sica's life. He'd explain that to her, too. He knew how kee
she was on discovering something that would save th
world. As far as he was concerned, saving a life, Jessica
life, was like saving the world.

Diana. Everything about her bewitched him, captivat
him, allured him to her. He wanted to hurry and finish th
shower so he could be with her. He had never felt so goo
so complete as he did when he was with her.

Nick also knew there was one more person he wanted
get to know. Jessica. Now that she wouldn't be constant
screaming at him, they had a lot of catching up to do.

Nick scrubbed himself twice, and washed his hair twice, too, using the unscented soap and shampoo Diana had given him. If Jessica could smell anything on him after this, that nose of hers would put a bloodhound to shame.

Nick turned off the shower, and dried off, wrapping the towel around his waist. While he had hoped Diana would be in his bedroom waiting for him, he knew it probably wouldn't happen. Not while their parents were in the house. What he hadn't expected to see in his bedroom were his parents, Harry and Sheila, and Diana, sitting on every available surface, facing the bathroom door, waiting for him to come out.

"Are you all having a slumber party?" Nick asked, tightening the burgundy towel around his waist.

"Is that any way to dress in front of girls?" Harry bellowed.

"I didn't know I was going to have girls, or any company in my own bedroom." He turned to Diana. "A guy could hope though."

"They all came after me." Diana shrugged. "Protecting me from climbing into the shower with you."

"I'm sorry they succeeded." Nick crossed his arms and glared at the rest of his audience. "Sorry to have kept you all waiting. You can leave now."

"No," came a chorus of voices. "We'll stay."

Nick heard the familiar ripping sound. The same sound he had heard yesterday when he had discovered his shredded *Sports Illustrated* magazines. "Where's Jessica?"

"She's over there on the other side of the bed reading your copies of *Architectural Digest*."

Nick rushed over to rescue his magazines. Jessica sat in front of the nightstand. The top drawer was pulled open. Two boxes of condoms, forty-eight in each box, had been ripped apart and the contents lay scattered around her. Some packages were opened and flesh colored condoms were spread out across the floor in various lengths of unwinding. Others were still sealed in their foil packages. Jes-

sica had pulled one condom over her little foot, up to he
ankle. The rest was left dangling. The cardboard boxes the
had come in were torn into tiny pieces and that, too, ha
been scattered.

Diana followed behind Nick. "My, my," she said. "E:
pecting company, are you?"

Sheila followed behind Diana. "Diana, dear. I have
whole new respect for you." She picked a sealed packag
off the floor and looked at it. "Extra large." She slid he
glance sideways and downward toward Nick in awe.

"I know. That's still a little tight." Nick shrugged. Th
smile on his face not at all humble.

"Diana's a lucky girl," Sheila said. Then she walked b
Harry and slapped him on the back. "Peanut."

"What?" he bellowed. "What did I do?"

"Nothing," Sheila cursed. "Absolutely nothing."

Harry and Charlie went over to where Jessica sat sur
rounded by the condoms. Charlie, like a proud fathe
puffed out his chest.

Harry, like a deranged father, began to yell, "I do nd
care how many tables and chairs he makes you, I'v
changed my mind. I will not have my daughter living i
sin, do you hear me? I will not. Diana, pack your bags, and
get home. You're leaving for Duke in the morning."

"Nick," Charlie used a cajoling tone. "You make sur
you don't marry that girl. Anyone who needs that mucl
sex will wear you out before your time. Do you want t
look old like me?"

Nick's mother raised her eyebrow. "Wishful thinking o
his part," she said. "The old peacock."

Diana pulled one condom out of Jessica's grasp, and
peeled another off her arm where Jessica had rolled it up
like a rubber glove. Jessica gnawed a third foil package
and Diana pulled that one out of her mouth. "Yuck."

Jessica started to screech, missing her newfound toys.

"I'm sorry Nick," Diana said, sounding like she was a
the end of her rope. "I came out from bathing Jessica and

ney were all in here waiting for me. They insisted I ouldn't be here alone. I sat Jessica down in the corner, hinking she'd be safe there.''

"It's all right, Diana. No harm's done. I'm going to hrow some clothes on.''

"Nick,'' Diana softly called.

He turned to look at her.

"What were you going to do with all of these?'' She vaved her hand over the condom-strewn floor.

He gave her a lascivious grin. "When we're living in in, and actually *living* the sin, you won't have to ask.''

The smile on her face encouraged him. He bolted from he room, heading back to his dressing area, where he could hrow on some jeans. He was only sorry he couldn't pull Diana, and a handful of condoms in with him.

13

NICK CARRIED Jessica from his bedroom to the kitchen. For the first time since she'd been born, Jessica sat quietly in his arms. The little girl he held now was the sweet, docile baby, full of smiles and charm that he had always wished she'd been with him. This was the kind of baby that made a man want to have children of his own.

Diana walked next to him, smiling at him and talking little nonsense sentences to Jessica. Diana was the one person responsible for Jessica's future well-being. He only hoped he could find a way to thank her.

"She looks great in your arms," Diana said.

"Who? Jessica?" Nick knew she looked stupendous.

"Of course Jessica. She adores you."

"Nah. She doesn't." She loved him to pieces that's what she did. "You're just saying that."

"Sure she does."

"Yeah," he said, and he knew there was a sappy grin plastered on his face. "I have you to thank."

"Actually, I think it was more teamwork."

It would be like Diana to share the glory. Only he knew if there were a trophy to be given, it would be hers.

"Can I hold her?" his mother asked when they were gathered in the kitchen again.

He gave Jessica to her grandma, and found himself pretty reluctant to do so. For the first time, he understood what a nesting instinct felt like. He glanced over at Diana as she gathered up ingredients for some dessert she was going to make. When he thought of babies, the only one he thought

f having them with was her. The woman made him feel
,ood, he liked being around her.

More than that, there were things about her that he loved,
f love were a possibility. He loved the way she looked,
hat was a given. He loved the way her heart and spirit
vere generous. The way she thought about everyone else,
nd wanted to help them. Diana was a special woman, and
 e didn't want to lose her.

Was is possible that he loved her?

Nick watched her smile at Harry, then give Jessica a kiss
 n her cheek. She tossed her ponytail back over her shoulder, and said something to his father that made Charlie
 augh. Then she looked at him, and this time the smile was
 lifferent, warmer, more special.

Yes, he knew without a doubt, what he felt for Diana
 vas love.

Diana had everyone gather around the kitchen stove. "I
 was going to fix this tomorrow night when you were all
 here, but since you're here now, we might as well enjoy
 it."

She collected the ingredients for her soon-to-be-famous
 flaming dessert. "Now bear with me. I'm making most of
 this up, since I don't actually have a recipe."

They all agreed they wouldn't hold her to any failures.

"What I have here are bananas which I am going to slice
 up. Then in this skillet I'll heat butter, brown sugar and
 cinnamon."

"Smells delightful, dear," Patricia said.

"Thanks." Diana grinned at her while handing Jessica a
 piece of sliced banana to eat. "Now, I'll put the bananas
 inside this mixture, and heat them up, too." When the butter and sugar started to splatter, she said, "Rum time." She
 poured the rum into the mixture, too. "Where are the
 matches? I thought they were right here."

"Oh-oh," Harry squawked, "Get the extinguisher.
 Hurry, she's looking for a match."

"You are not funny," Diana said, a sharpness in her

voice, Nick hadn't heard before. She put a hand on her hi
and glared at her father. "How much more are you goin
to humiliate me?"

"Who, me?" Harry asked innocently. "Are you talkin
to me?"

"Just give me a match."

"What do you call that dessert you're making?" Patrici
asked.

"Bananas Foster Flambé. Now, don't say anything neg
ative, because everyone has a right to experiment. I'v
eaten this at Brennans, and I know it's wonderful. I'n
pretty sure of the ingredients."

"Whether you've got it the same way or not, it look
and smells fabulous. Jessica and I will love to have some.'

"I don't think it's a good idea for Jessica. There'
rum..." Diana hedged.

"You're right. I'm new at being a grandma."

"Here's a match, Diana," Nick said, handing her the
kind of matches he'd use to light a fireplace. The ones with
the very long, twelve-inch wooden handles. "I have faith
in you."

"Thanks, Nick," she said gratefully.

The way she looked at him made him feel as if he coulc
walk on water.

Nick watched everyone in the kitchen as Diana startec
to light the match. His mother and Jessica were standing
near the doorway leading out into the hall. Another glance
in their direction, and he saw they were no longer in the
kitchen, but safely out in the hall. Everyone else slowly
started walking backwards. Except for Sheila. She was sc
busy doing a touch up on her fingernail polish, she didn't
move at all. In fact, Nick doubted she even knew what was
going on.

Diana sniffed the ingredients in the skillet, and said.
"Um, this does smell wonderful." She lit the match,
touched it to the liquid in the skillet, and...it exploded!

Nick reached under the sink and grabbed the extinguisher. The fire was out in a matter of seconds.

"Diana, are you all right?" He wrapped her in his arms and held her tight.

"I jumped back just in time."

Nick kissed her lips, her cheeks, her neck, her head. Everywhere he could find, he kissed. "You scared the hell out of me. I don't know what I would have done if anything happened to you."

"Don't you see, this is a sign?"

"What sign?" he asked.

Diana gazed into Nick's eyes. She put both her hands on his head and brought his face down to hers and kissed him on his lips, over and over, and didn't stop. The kiss soon turned deep, and he pulled her close, knowing that life was precious, and he needed her in his.

Finally Diana pulled back and took a deep breath. "Oh, Nick. Whenever I'm near you, there's fireworks."

"That's the best news I've heard this hour."

"It's been a good day for you, hasn't it?"

"A great day."

"Is it safe to come back in the kitchen now?" Patricia asked, peeking around the doorway with Jessica, and grimacing at Sheila's now slightly-scorched appearance.

"Come on back, Mom," Nick said. "Everyone sit back at the table, I have something I want to say."

It took a few minutes for the families to find their way back to the kitchen table.

"I guess we won't be getting dessert here," Harry grumbled.

"You're too fat anyway," Charlie told him.

Harry started to get up. "You want to meet me outside?"

"Stop it," Nick said, his voice broaching no argument. "Diana has put together this elaborate plan so everyone would get together and actually talk to one another. Why don't you two men, and I use the term 'men' loosely since you're acting more like two year olds, grow up."

Harry pointed. "He should grow up. Never even seen his own granddaughter."

"I'm not going to argue with you, Mr. Smith—Harry."

"Call him Dad," Diana said.

Harry glared. "I don't think so."

Diana had to hide her smile behind her hand. Nick was discovering all kinds of things about her tonight. He particularly liked her wicked sense of humor.

"Not talking to Cathy was Patty's idea. Not mine," Charlie said.

"You're your own man. You should have done what's right," Nick told him.

"Where Cathy's concerned your mom and I are both sorry. We forgive her for what she did and we want to make it up to her."

"Charlie," Diana said. "Why would you have to forgive Cathy? She didn't do anything wrong. She fell in love and the product of that love is Jessica. It was the baby's father who did wrong, not Cathy."

"That's not the way I see it."

"The way I see it, Cathy is going to have to forgive you. Poor Jessica's had to suffer because of your misplaced pride."

Diana turned to her father. "We're all going to suffer because of your stupid pride. Nick and I have decided to live in sin. I know that if I tell you that, it will drive you crazy, since no father wants to know his daughter is shacking up with a man without the benefit of a marriage license." Then she turned to Charlie. "And you, Mr. Logan, I'll tell you that Nick and I are going to be married, because I know that if you think we're getting married, it will drive you insane, since the idea of Nick being married to a Smith is about the worst thing that could possibly happen to you."

Diana took a deep breath. Nick thought she was magnificent. She had everyone in the room hanging on to her every word.

"So," she finished. "You can all go home and be miserable."

Nick put his arm around Diana's waist and said to the men. "Our children will lose out since they'll never see their grandparents at their birthday parties, or Christmas or Thanksgiving. Because whose house would we go to? How would we choose? Is that what you want?"

"Absolutely not. I can forgive him." Harry stood up and pointed to Charlie. "After all, I'm a big man."

Charlie stood, too, and towered over Harry by barely half an inch. "I'm a bigger man."

Harry snorted. "Not where it counts."

"That's not what your wife just said," Charlie sneered.

"Why you friggin' twerp."

"You're a bas—"

"Dad. Stop it right now. Please. This isn't why we're here." Diana put her elbow on the table and rested her forehead in her hand. "If you two had been talking from the beginning, I may have graduated college by now."

"Diana," Harry said. "I didn't mind you going to all those schools. Really I didn't. Except I missed you a lot."

She looked at him. "I missed you, too."

"Why don't we take Jessica home with us tonight, and we'll pick Cathy up from the airport when she comes in. We can start over. If she forgives us."

"If you hurt her again you'll have to answer to me," Nick said. "She's not the same little girl who left your home two years ago. She's a woman now, and she's been on her own, and doing very well."

"I know," Charlie said. "We've been keeping track of how she's been doing."

"We love her, Nicky," Patricia added. "Both of them." She gave Jessica a big hug.

"Nick," Diana said as she went to the refrigerator and pulled off the instruction sheet. "You'll have to help them with the car seat, and make sure your dad reads all these instructions. I don't want anything to happen to that child."

She reached back to the refrigerator and took off the poison control number, too.

"I don't either," Charlie said softly.

"You know what, Nick. When everyone goes home tonight, I'm going to feel like celebrating," Diana said, giving Nick a hug.

Her father looked at her suspiciously. "When you say celebrate, are you talking drinking champagne, going to a movie, or using those condoms?"

"Why, Daddy, how nosy of you to ask." She reached inside her back pocket and pulled out a handful of the foil packages Jessica had thrown around earlier.

Harry started to choke. Sheila, her face flushed, said "Come on home, Harry. I'm feeling inspired." She picked a condom out of Diana's hand. Then she went back for another.

After her father and Sheila left, Diana went to the bedroom and packed a suitcase for Jessica. Nick grabbed a box of diapers, and threw bottles and some of the baby books Diana had bought into his backpack.

They met in the hallway. Diana held Jessica one more time. "I'll miss you so much, sweet thing," she said. "And remember, I owe you big time. You name your prize and it's yours."

"Nooo-nooo, bye-bye."

"Bye-bye."

Nick kissed Diana briefly on the lips and said, "I'll help them load the car, and then I'll be right back. We need to talk."

"Okay," she agreed. "We can talk."

Nick hadn't been gone more than thirty minutes, but when he came back to the apartment, he was struck by the silence. His first thought was that Diana had left him.

Then he saw the condom on the floor by his feet. There was another next to it, and another and another. A trail of condom packages, like the bread crumbs left by Hansel and Gretel.

"Diana?" he called out. She didn't answer.

He picked a few foil packages up off the marble, then followed the trail through his bedroom, the dressing area, and into the whirlpool bath area.

"Why are you just standing there staring?" Diana asked him.

Staring, is that what he was doing? Wasn't it normal to follow a trail of condoms to a room where a woman lay naked in the tub. Not naked exactly, she was definitely covered up. With whipped cream.

She reached for the can on the ledge and shook it. "If you get rid of your pants, I can make you good enough to eat, too." She squirted some of the whipped cream in her hand, then licked it off. "Yum." She smacked her lips and smiled at him. "Come on, Nick. I'm waiting."

He couldn't speak. He couldn't move. She put the can back on the ledge then dipped her finger into some of the whipped cream covering her breast, and held the finger up for his inspection. He inched closer to her, hardly breathing, his erection so tight against his zipper he hurt. Then she put her finger in her mouth and slowly, lavishly, licked the cream off, and he knew what she really said was that if he hurried, it could be him.

"How many calories are you?" he asked, his voice heavy with desire and need.

"It depends," she teased. "Do you plan to swallow?"

He gulped. "Diana," he breathed out her name, hardly able to concentrate on anything except what waited for him in the tub.

"Diana Foster Flambé," she corrected. She held the rum bottle up and slowly dripped the liquid over the whipped cream. The rivers of rum that intersected the white cream tantalized him, teased him, but still didn't uncover the Diana underneath. Only he could do that.

"Don't light a match," he said.

"There's already a fire burning inside me, and only you can put it out."

He didn't need a second invitation. Within seconds he joined her in the tub. He covered her body with his own, kissing her, licking her, tasting rum and whipped cream and the familiar, wonderful exotic taste of Diana.

He started at her neck and slowly worked his way down, hungry for dessert, eager to expose what lay under the creamy white topping. Her breasts were delicious, her belly button fine, but what came next, was exquisite, and special and his to lay claim to forever. He held her by her hips and drank of Diana, not able to get enough of the taste of her, the scent of her. When he felt her shudder, and he knew he was close to his own release, he protected himself and her, then entered her swiftly.

He thought it would end right there, only she held him by the hips and stopped him from moving. "Slow," she whispered. "I want this to last forever."

"I'll do my best. We've got all night, and at least sixty condoms left."

She smiled, reached for the can of whipped cream and sprayed him. Before he could move she began her own game of torture, licking the cream off his shoulders, and arms and chest. He couldn't take it anymore. His self-control was gone. He put his hands under her bottom and lifted her to meet him, needing to go deep inside her, to stake his claim on her forever. He didn't know how he held himself back until he heard her soft whimpers and felt her shudder beneath him. But he did, and when he reached his own peak, he thought he had died and been reborn.

"Nick," Diana called his name softly.

"Hum?" His eyes were closed, and he couldn't move. He could fall asleep right here with her under him. He wondered if they could stay this way for a few weeks.

"Let's take a bath and start this all over."

"That's a great idea. I'll be right back."

He got out of the tub, and headed for the dressing area, needing to take care of the used condom, and clean himself up. He came back with a warm washcloth, and slowly, languishingly, wiped the remaining whipped cream off Diana, down her neck, her shoulders, her creamy white breasts, the pink tips. He reached her ribs, the indentation of her waist, and paid special attention to her core.

Before he could finish Diana's sponge bath, Diana reached for him, stroked him, kissed him. "Is this how you are all the time?"

"Only with you, Diana. Only with you."

"I know you don't want commitment," she said, moving her hand down his shaft, cupping him below, making him groan with desire like he had never desired a woman before. "But we can date, if you want, and we agree on a time and place mutually convenient to both of us."

"Diana, we aren't going to date."

"Maybe we should for a while. I have so many fantasies. I could act them all out."

He groaned. A life with Diana meant more whipped cream. He could die right now a happy man. But he wasn't ready to go yet. He wanted her, and he wanted her permanently. "We aren't going to live in sin, either. We will live in marriage, but we'll do sinful things, like this. Making love to you feels so good it must be sinful. You got that?"

"Marriage?"

"You and me, we're getting married and I won't take no for an answer. It's commitment or nothing."

"Children?"

"They like me. I'll make a great dad." He smiled at her. They were meant to be together. "I'll make you the best husband. I love you. I think I have since the first time I met you at the awards dinner for our fathers. That was a long time ago."

"Really?"

"Do you remember the dance?"

"I'll never forget that dance," she said softly, brushing his hair off his forehead, outlining the lines of his face with her hand. "Nick, I love you, too." She kissed his lips tenderly, and the gentleness of her kiss had as much power to move him as the whipped cream did before.

"Diana, I feel that when we're together I'm the one who explodes."

She nodded. "That's the way with me, I'm afraid. Whenever I think of you, something eventually does blow up. But you know, when it's you, inside me, then I know all is right with the world."

HARLEQUIN ◆ PRESENTS®

Wedded Bliss

Penny Jordan   Carole Mortimer

Two brand-new stories—for the price of one!—
in one easy-to-read volume.
Especially written by your favorite authors!

Wedded Bliss
Harlequin Presents #2031, June 1999
THEY'RE WED AGAIN!
by Penny Jordan
and
THE MAN SHE'LL MARRY
by Carole Mortimer

There's nothing more exciting than a wedding!
Share the excitement as two couples make their very
different journeys which will take them up the aisle to
embark upon a life of happiness!

Available **next month** wherever Harlequin books
are sold.

HARLEQUIN®
Makes any time special ™

Harlequin is proud to introduce:

HEART OF THE WEST

...Where Every Man Has His Price!

Lost Springs Ranch was famous for turning young mavericks into good men. Word that the ranch was in financial trouble sent a herd of loyal bachelors stampeding back to Wyoming to put themselves on the auction block.

This is a brand-new 12-book continuity, which includes some of Harlequin's most talented authors.

Don't miss the first book,
Husband for Hire by Susan Wiggs.
It will be at your favorite retail outlet in July 1999.

HARLEQUIN®
Makes any time special ™

Look us up on-line at: http://www.romance.net   PHHOW

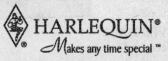

COMING NEXT MONTH

HARLEQUIN

Duets™

#3

THE COWBOY NEXT DOOR by Laurie Paige

Cybil Mathews bought her ranch knowing exactly what she wanted out of life: serenity and a world free from men! Just her luck to land sexy Mason Faraday as a neighbor. The rancher has an ego the size of Nevada—and a body born to wear tight-fitting jeans. Cybil is determined to stay footloose and fancy-free, but Mason's kisses are branding her heart as his own!

MEANT FOR YOU by Patricia Knoll

Caitlin Beck and Jed Bishop don't see eye to eye on anything— except their inability to keep their hands off each other. He thinks she's too uptight. She thinks he's too laid-back. All the pair has to do is finish renovating the Victorian house they bought together, sell it and they'll never see each other again. Meanwhile, she'll stick to her side of the house, and he'll stick to his. So why do they keep meeting in the hallway?

#4

ONE IN A MILLION by Ruth Jean Dale

Sophie Brannigan—a four-year-old penny-pincher—is the prime suspect in the theft of a one-cent coin. Quint Sterling is hot on her trail, and that of her mother, Amber—because both penny and woman are one in a million. He soon discovers he's no match for the little girl, but Amber is another story...

LOVE, TEXAS STYLE by Kimberly Raye

New York lawyer Suzanne Hillsbury is looking for love in all the wrong places. What she needs is an honest to goodness cowboy, one who believes in hard work, old-fashioned values...and looks good in a pair of jeans. Sexy Brett Maxwell seems to be just the man she's been seeking. Little does she guess that under Brett's Western bravado, he's more of a city slicker than she is...